ASKING FOR IT

By the same author

A TIME FOR JUSTICE

ASKING FOR IT

ANONYMOUS

CORONET BOOKS
Hodder & Stoughton

Copyright © 1999 James Hale

First published in 1999 by Hodder and Stoughton
First published in paperback in 2000
A Coronet paperback
A division of Hodder Headline

10 9 8 7 6 5 4 3 2 1

This novel is about crime, the victims of crime – and our
prevailing criminal justice system. But no character in
Asking For It is modelled on any real person, and no
character who fills a real job-description or who occupies
a real position in public life is in any way a portrait of any
actual holder of such office or position, past or present.
The motivations, relationships and conduct of all characters
in this book are entirely fictitious.

A CIP catalogue record for this title
is available from the British Library

ISBN 0 340 69296 0

Typeset by Palimpsest Book Production Limited,
Polmont, Stirlingshire
Printed and bound in France by
Brodard & Taupin

Hodder and Stoughton
A division of Hodder Headline
338 Euston Road
London NW1 3BH

MAIN CHARACTERS

PROFESSOR SIEGFRIED ALEXANDER, a criminologist
DELIA ATKINSON, a transsexual
THE BOY, Prime Minister
WILLY BRAITHWAITE MP, Chairman of House Select Committee
MARCUS BYRON, Crown Court judge
LUCY BYRON, his daughter
MISS AGATHA COWDREY, a prisoner
JEREMY DARLING MP, Shadow Home Secretary
BEN DIAMOND MP, Home Secretary
DICK DODGETT, a solicitor
GASTON DUBOIS, Hotel receptionist
DETECTIVE INSPECTOR PAUL GIBBS, CID
PAUL GLASS, criminal law adviser to the Home Secretary
DAVID GLASS, his son
JENNY GLENDOWER, a teacher
PHIL GLENDOWER, a teacher
SANDRA GOLDING QC, former mistress of Marcus Byron
HUBERT HARE, a social worker, Youth Justice Team
LIZ HEATH, a colleague of Auriol Johnson
MARY HEATHERINGTON, Prison Governor
SIMON HOARE, a solicitor
AURIOL JOHNSON, a journalist
EDMUND JOINER, junior political adviser to the Home Secretary
BOB JOLLY QC, a barrister
BRIGID KYLE, a journalist
ANTONY LAUGHTON QC, a barrister
AMOS LEWIN, an American journalist
DETECTIVE SERGEANT DOUG MCINTYRE, CID

KEITH MARINER, a social worker, Ruskin House
LOUISE POINTER QC, Marcus Byron's estranged wife
OLIVER RAWL, a solicitor
JUDGE SAWYER, of the Crown Court
FIONA SHEEHY (Helen Winter), an undercover police-woman
TOMMY, Lord Chancellor
SARAH WOODS, a solicitor
JUDGE WORPLE, of the Crown Court
PC CHARLIE WRIGHT

MIGUEL GARCIA, 17
LUKE GRANT, 14
ALLY LEAGUM, 14
PETE MCGRAW, 16
JASON MCGRAW, 15
TONY MARQUEZ, 17
CHARCO RIOS, 17

One

One street lamp in three flickers or fails on the streets of Great North after dark. They say that the moon and the stars themselves refuse to show themselves in the skies above this run-down quarter of London. Prostitutes gather round the big railway station, hurrying lonely travellers away to seedy rooms in ancient tenements owned by pimps, racketeers and drug pushers. Police sirens punctuate the troubled sleep of travellers too tired or too poor to find hotel accommodation further afield.

By local standards, the modest Winfield Hotel is upmarket. It's clean, it's secure, every room has its own shower, and prostitutes are rigorously excluded. Mrs Jenny Glendower has checked in at 3 p.m. on a Friday in August 1997. She is alone.

Shortly after midnight the night receptionist is surprised when she steps out of the lift, her room key (No. 36) suspended from the fingers of her left hand. The night receptionist is a young Frenchman in London to improve his English. As she approaches his desk, offering her key, Gaston Dubois notices a wedding ring and (probably) an engagement ring. She reminds him of the President's

1

wife, Mrs Hillary Clinton – though younger. Petite and blonde, she conveys the same sparkle and vivacity.

'Yes, madam?' Gaston discovers that he would like to detain her in conversation.

'My key,' she says.

'You're going out, madam?' He's proud of his abbreviated 'madam', of having learned to suppress the more extended vowels of the French 'madame'. He has read that you address England's Queen as 'ma'am'. As yet the opportunity to do so has not come his way.

'Yes,' she says. Is her fleeting smile offered to him or to some hidden, private corner of her life?

'Shall I call you a taxi, madam?'

'No need.'

That's all. A little black handbag with a gilt chain swings gaily from her wrist, beside a comfortably glinting Rolex ladies' watch. Gaston recognises a Rolex at five yards. He guesses that she has passed thirty; her cheeks have begun to hollow out, and there is an observable thickening of the waist and thighs that could suggest motherhood. She could be a foreigner, Swedish, Dutch or German, there are many in transit in the Winfield, but her accent, the few words she has spoken, belong to a native Englishwoman.

Gaston would like to engage her in conversation. It's a good way to learn colloquial English, better than any grammar or dictionary, and sometimes café talk or a chat in St James's Park can develop into pillow talk. But he has to acknowledge that this lady, with her bobbed blonde hair bouncing off her shoulders, dressed in a two-piece costume in flaming pink, her skirt fashionably parted at the back and riding well above the knee – well, he has to grant that he has yet to capture the heart of a lady clearly ten years older than himself.

She has reached the hotel door which will not open until Gaston presses the release button under the reception desk. The manager insisted that the door must remain locked from 11 p.m. The reinforced glass is plastered in familiar credit card stickers, Visa, Delta, American Express and the rest. She turns back to him with an inquiring look which gives him a moment of almost sexual pleasure.

He wants to tell her not to go out on to those streets alone, not at this hour. Why is she alone? A divorce, perhaps? Is she waiting for life to come and serve itself up to her on a dish? Is she making a break for it? If so, she should be warned that Great North, whose streets are plagued by drug addicts, pimps, pushers, prostitutes, is no place for a nice lady who looks like Mrs Clinton to make a break. Is she utterly innocent of the reputation of these dilapidated, dimly lit streets, where predatory eyes watch from doorways, parked cars and filthy alleyways? Was she born yesterday? Or has some painful personal tragedy rendered her impervious to a woman's normal instinct for danger? Perhaps she no longer cares. Perhaps she wants the worst for herself.

Perhaps she's asking for it.

Gaston Dubois releases the lock on the glass door. He's merely the night receptionist, it isn't his job to ask guests where they are going or why. She steps out on to the street, blonde hair swivelling as she scans to right and to left, then vanishes in the direction of the railway station.

Gaston takes note of the time registered on the digital clock above the reception desk: zero zero two five. It's as if he is instinctively preparing himself for the role of witness when the police come to question him about the crime.

She walks on small, neat feet, wearing her best Italian shoes, heels nicely elevated, and crosses the main thoroughfare opposite the great railway station, a complex intersection of streets arriving from all directions, each loudly demanding priority, car horns blaring. At the lights little green men timidly beckon pedestrians to cross if they dare. She dares.

Jenny Glendower has come to London from Yeominster to attend a teachers' training course on 'Domestic Violence and the Delinquent Child'. Very interesting, no doubt, but her mind had frequently wandered during the conference sessions, and she rebuked herself, as she often chided her pupils, her girls, for 'poor concentration'. Getting away from home for a short break had been her main motive in enrolling for the conference. A wife and mother of two needs a valid pretext: you can't just go. She had been accommodated free in a Russell Square hotel for three nights, but now she felt entitled to enjoy a few days to herself. She had found a hotel in Great North, the Winfield, which she could afford – though she felt guilty about spending £45 a night on a room with shower.

The Winfield is within easy reach of London's famous Theatreland, Oxford Street's exciting shops, Piccadilly, Leicester Square, Trafalgar Square and Covent Garden. All rooms are en suite, shower/bath, and are equipped with direct dial telephones, colour TV, and tea/coffee-making facilities. Hairdryers and irons are available on request. Included in the tariff is Full English or Continental Breakfast.

The area looked all right by daylight. She doesn't know London well. It's a big, distracting place to come to when your marriage has become stifling and insupportable. London is the place where something might happen to you, something happy and delivering.

Jenny Glendower stops to examine the window of a tatty shop calling itself VIDEOS BOOKS MAGAZINES. She sees *The Triumph of Vice*, a novel by G.W. Target; *A Baroque Novel*, by Brigid Brophy, and *Bring on the Virgins* by Porsche Lynn.

The painted women on the street, hustling away new customers off the trains, are not virgins.

She passes Eurowines and two big posters, one of them advertising 'Villains. A Masterclass in Evil', the other promoting 'Metalhead 2. Limited Edition'.

Now, strolling these alien streets by night, she becomes aware that she is losing her sense of direction. She is no longer sure where she is or how to get back to the hotel. She walks past Debbie's Hair and Beauty Salon – then a restaurant advertising itself as 'all night': it's called

Jenny's, but glancing inside she realises that it isn't for her. She pauses at the iron-grilled window of a shop called Call Saver, laden with images of mobile phones: cellnet vodafone oneZone. As a schoolteacher she wonders why these brand names come without capitals; she examines the lonely Z.

Passing a street light (few of them are in working order), she becomes aware of a shadow stretching along the pavement from behind her. Her own is smaller.

Several shadows.

The youths trailing behind her have emerged from a neon-lit, all-night corner establishment where they often play the machines and pool. It's called Game Zone and advertises itself on the street as 'Leisure Centre. Play Pool Here'. Charco Rios likes pool, a game played on a billiard table in which each player has a ball of a different colour with which he tries to pocket the others in fixed order, the winner taking all of the stakes.

Charco Rios is a 'take all' person. He likes to boast that half the police of London are looking for him.

Jenny isn't conscious of the video security cameras installed high above the shops which, at this hour, are shuttered and barred. The shadows stretching along the pavement from behind her seem to be lengthening – as if laying hold of her. She remembers a feminist campaign, one among the many she had half supported at a distance, called 'Reclaim the Night'. It meant 'make the streets safe for women after dark': women returning from work, women heading for theatres, cinemas and bars, women exercising their human right to be female without being attacked.

She has never been much of a radical. She's not a joiner or marcher. Born and bred in the West Country, you don't do that. You don't approve of the radicals who get themselves elected to the annual conferences of the National Teachers Union, either. People like her husband Phil. When they threaten strike action in the schools, you rouse yourself to vote No in the union ballot.

Or you forget to.

She can hear Phil's derisive voice mocking her timidity and conservatism. Phil is a rare thing in Yeominster, a Labour Party activist. He never forgets to fill in a postal ballot for the National Executive Committee or whatever it's called. He teaches the social sciences in the city's comprehensive, works evenings as a city councillor, and lives for politics. She had married him in the teeth of her parents' warnings: he's not for you, Jenny. But she and Phil had imagined themselves to be in love; when she got pregnant her parents had to make the best of it.

Now she has got away, just for a few days, from a disintegrating marriage, with Phil's consent – he's a good father, she has no worries for her two young children. They will be well fed, bathed, hugged and told progressive bedtime stories in which the big bad wolf somehow emerges as the exploited hero. Why is she in flight from such a good man, an exemplary father, a 'happy home'?

Happy?

Tomorrow – she glances at her Rolex and sees that

'tomorrow' is already 'today' – she will have lunch with a man she has not seen for many years. She may be falling in love with Oliver all over again, just by thinking about him so much. Finding an excuse for a meeting after all this time hasn't been easy and she fears that Oliver may not turn up; he has warned her that he's on night duty this week and may be 'collapso'. Something to do with a solicitors' rota. She carries his fax and the name of the restaurant in her little black handbag, but she has also taken the precaution of copying down this precious knowledge and leaving the details in the bedside drawer of her hotel bedroom.

She wishes one of the shadows stretched across the pavement behind her belonged to Oliver. She doesn't know that she will never return to bedroom No. 36 in the Winfield Hotel.

Yet Jenny still cannot believe that anything here, on these streets, is the main problem in her life. She understands young men, youths: they will follow you out of some adolescent compulsion, but they don't mean any harm. That has been pointed out during the teachers' conference by a very impressive speaker, Professor Siegfried Alexander, who convinced her that prison is the wrong solution for youngsters – perhaps for anybody – in nine cases out of ten.

For some reason she thinks of the young night receptionist in the hotel. By his accent she took him to be French. Quite good looking. Such a wistful look in his expression as he looked up from his newspaper to receive her room key. She could tell that he wanted to engage her in conversation. Now she wishes she had let him.

Shadows on the pavement engulf her. She experiences the first twinges of panic, of real fear. Jenny, you have gone clean out of your mind. I need a doctor. I need Valium, Prozac, a taxi or police car.

She wants to turn back, retrace her steps, though she has long since lost the trail, but she dare not because the hot breath of the youths is on her neck. Why not stop and ask them the way? Why not appeal to their gallantry? Hadn't Professor Alexander very wisely pointed out that young people will behave in accordance with our view of them? These lads who appear to be pursuing her are merely drifting in search of what Professor Alexander had called 'the excitement of the unplanned happening'. They are not beasts of the jungle, beyond morality, preying on:

This cunt in a short pink skirt, with swaying buttocks and asking for it.

The long shadows on the pavement are no longer silent shadows. They seem to be proliferating, emerging from cellars, passageways, wharves, warehouses, man-holes. These increasingly assertive, cocksure voices are not quite the adolescent voices she had 'heard' in her imagination when the impressive old professor with the faintly foreign accent – could it be German? – was deliver-ing his lecture.

She has become aware of herself as a prize.

Prize? Finally she stops and turns. She has to. Must confront them. She remembers that eye-contact saves you, a face and voice, something they can identify as human.

They stop when she stops. She sees them for the first time. Prize, did you say? These cocky, big-shouldered youths are not to be found receiving prizes in school at the end of the summer term. They are not to be found in school during any term. They do not recognise her rules or any rules.

Gaston Dubois imagines the detectives scrutinising the hotel register. They will examine the lady's signature: 'Jenny Glendower'. They will note that she occupied room 36, on the third floor, and had checked in shortly after three in the afternoon. They will demand the key to her room. They will search it. They will scatter white powders with expert professionalism. They will 'lift' fingerprints, footprints and heartprints.

They will descend the stairs with grim expressions and sealed plastic bags. They will start to question Gaston, casually at first, then with mounting insistence. Yes, the lady was unaccompanied. Yes, he could remember the exact time she stepped out of the hotel: 0025. Why had he noticed the exact time? Had she spoken to him as she left the hotel? Well, yes and no, not exactly. What kind of an answer is that, Mr Dubois? What are you hiding from us? And why do you have this small quantity of cannabis in your pocket, Mr Dubois? And why are you carrying this map of the Tower of London where the Crown Jewels are kept, eh? Hm?

Come with us, monsieur, you are the prime suspect in this case.

The front door buzzer sounds and he shakes himself awake. Someone is standing outside, demanding entry. Gaston leaves his desk and cautiously appraises the figure on the street: a swaying, derelict drunk in rags. Gaston shakes his head. The man begins to batter angrily on the glass door with a beer can, swearing.

Presently he shambles away. The old drunks are no problem compared to the young ones. Gaston had recently endured nine stops on the Piccadilly line next to a drunken soldier from the Parachute Regiment, known in France as *les paras*, who insisted on holding a photograph of Princess Di close to his groin to indicate that she had, or would have, given him a you-know-what.

It had been Gaston's duty to agree with *le para*, again and again, on pain of saying goodbye to his good looks.

He glances up at the digital clock: 0053. The lady has been gone half an hour. Leaning on the reception desk, he immerses himself in the English newspaper he likes best, the *Sentinel*. He particularly admires the columnist Brigid Kyle. She always makes sense and forces Gaston to study his dictionary. There is a regular small photo of the smiling Brigid Kyle at the head of her daily column: very attractive! In fact not totally unlike the lady from room 36 who has not returned.

Two

Shortly after one forty, the same night, some four miles away, a young lawyer awakes abruptly from a grim dream, groans and reaches for the yelling telephone beside his bed.

'Oliver Rawl here.'

'Eden Manor police station, Mr Rawl. Custody Officer Wright speaking. We have a client for you.'

'Do I know him?'

'No. He needs the duty solicitor. Your name is on the night rota.'

Oliver groans again. He's thirty-two but feels ninety. He studies the illuminated dial on his alarm clock. One forty-five – he has probably been asleep for an hour, long enough to sink into a dream about his nightmare client, Delia Atkinson, alias Derek Foster, alias . . . Oliver does not mind the many aliases so much as Delia's furious insistence that she never had been Derek Foster or any other male person. Men are the enemy. In creating them, Satan played a dirty trick on women. At the moment Oliver's telephone awoke him, Delia was about to strangle him on Blackfriars Bridge and dump his body in the Thames.

Not for the first time, either.

Oliver struggles out of bed after two botched attempts. Every fourth week his turn comes up on the rota as duty solicitor for Eden Manor Police Station. Every fourth week he goes virtually without sleep. The rota is entirely voluntary but any junior solicitor who declined service would rapidly be reminded of the facts of life, otherwise known as legal aid, the vast udder of public money feeding the criminal justice system.

So this will be a new client. But for how long? They tend to slip out of your grasp the next day.

He switches on the light without risk of disturbing Sarah; whenever either of them is on rota-duty, the other sleeps in the spare room. Earning a comfortable £50,000 a year between them, they can afford a spare room. If Sarah became pregnant, of course, that might be different. So might a good deal else.

Oliver first met Sarah Woods in a court waiting room, when he came to her defence after she was assaulted by two members of a girl gang she had failed to keep off a supervision order. 'Cunt!' they yelled, dragging her to the floor by her hair, then kicking her twice, before Oliver and Burns security guards intervened.

Actually, the Burns men did most of the intervening. Oliver reckoned his own role was largely moral. Her glasses were smashed in the fracas but she owned spare pairs. Sarah was keen on outsized oval glasses which made her pretty face look smaller and (Oliver claimed) more intimidating. 'A few minutes later I found myself living with Sarah,' he told friends.

Sarah Woods was the most attractive female to have invaded his sightline since Jenny Glendower, but Jenny was long ago, at university, and didn't really count. He described Sarah's normal expression as 'half-way between a Dutch scowl and a Bellini smile – but which Bellini?' Hers was a reluctant smile.

He switches on the kettle and bravely climbs into yesterday's clothes. He notices that his grey suit is dry, which seems to confirm that he is not a corpse floating in the Thames with one of Delia's black stockings wrapped round his neck. A keen motorcyclist, she claims to be an 'outrider' for what she calls 'The Forces of Progress'.

Oliver swallows half a cup of scalding instant coffee, black, with one lump of sugar, then closes the front door quietly behind him and double-locks it.

His N-registration VW Golf, the product of a small salary increase, hasn't been vandalised or stolen – TDA'd in the language of the courts – tonight. He heads north from Putney, crosses the river (in which his body may be floating) and finds Fulham Palace Road almost deserted. He and Sarah had drunk a bottle of chianti between them over supper in Pasta & Basta; he wonders how much of the 'between' is inside the fast-asleep Sarah and how much inside him. It must fall safely below 80 milligrams of alcohol in 100 millilitres of blood. Losing your licence is serious for anyone; for a solicitor, more than serious. Someone must have spiked my lemonade, officer!

One of Oliver's clients had been asked by the police why, if he knew he was way over the limit, he hadn't walked home. 'I was too drunk to walk,' he explained.

Oliver had declined to carry this 'mitigation' before the court. The laughter of magistrates, rare as it is, can disturb your sleep for a week.

Jenny Glendower cannot guess the names of the youths who have taken her captive without – as yet – laying a hand on her.

Extending for hundreds of yards down one side of the long street is the vast, bleak, faceless all-brick flank of the Great North railway station. On the other side, her side, are shops fashioned out of other old warehouses, with numerous locked gates and doors plastered in posters, leading to inner courtyards she will never glimpse.

Duke of York pub.

Courtyard Theatre (August only).

Big silent gates without eyes, ears or human heart.

Caledonian Fish and Chips.

Yum Yum Chinese and Peking Cuisine.

So many winos and addicts are stumbling on street corners that she could almost regard her own youth-guard as protectors. But where are they carrying her? They pass Clothes Bank, Thanks, Scope for People with Cerebral Palsy – a huge iron container set down beside the bottle bank (clear glass containers only) and the paper bank.

She asks the boys whether they know the district and whether they can help her find her way back to the Winfield hotel. Either they don't know or they don't wish to tell her. Their shadows are all around her and their unpleasant breath. Most of them carry cans of beer or alcopops: Hooper's Hooch, Whitbread's Two Dogs and Cola Lips. Still this side of panic, she tries to be friendly by examining the labels.

The largest of them, a black boy with the broad, muscular body of a fully developed man, has recently emerged out of the shadows. Now he lopes along beside her, quite possessive, his big hand occasionally prodding her to keep walking in the direction they want her to go. She would not guess, under the erratic street lighting, that Luke Grant is only fourteen years old.

Charco Rios is seventeen.

Pete McGraw is sixteen.

Little Ally Leagum is fourteen.

Charco and Pete are both clients of the solicitor Oliver Rawl. Luke and Ally belong to Sarah Woods. Never mind the others. Charco, Luke, Pete and Ally are enough for one woman alone by night.

Jenny Glendower may never discover who they are. That's the way they want it.

The question 'is anything known?' has been asked by Youth Court benches on no fewer than sixty-one occasions with regard to one or other of the eight boys now surrounding Jenny Glendower outside a Chinese takeaway under the steady scrutiny of a video-camera sited high above a shuttered off-licence fifteen yards up the street. The Chinese takeaway is called 'Peking, Cantonese and Vietnamese Cuisine'. Between it and the off-licence is a darkened dental surgery, with the bottom half of its window permanently screened out, advertising the services of N.Y.D. Chen, B.D.Sc (New South Wales).

The video camera never sleeps. Inscribed on it, beyond Jenny's gaze, is 'Delta Fire & Security' and an 01753 emergency number.

Is anything known? Virtually every day of his working life Oliver Rawl hears this simple phrase uttered coolly by a presiding magistrate. It's a question that may be directed to the social services staff at the back of the court, or to the Probation officer, or to the Prosecutor. 'Is anything known?'

Sometimes the magistrate asks, 'Anything previous?'

A list of previous cautions and convictions is then laid before the bench, after being shown to the defence solicitor for comment and correction. The solicitor may then lean across the table to show it to the boy himself. Luke Grant or Pete McGraw stare at the proliferating pages with dumb helplessness. Different charges before different courts become hopelessly tangled in their heads.

'Is anything known?' The question may be put when bail is the issue, or before passing sentence – but never before a trial. Bias must be avoided before a trial. Yet not everyone is agreed about that. In a famous, or notorious, article denounced by the Bar and every civil liberties group, the *Sentinel*'s columnist Brigid Kyle had called for a reform of the law. Juries, she insisted, should be informed of previous convictions before retiring to consider their verdict.

Everyone assumed that this must be Judge Marcus Byron's view, too. Gossips and chauvinists whispered that a typical Brigid Kyle column was dictated to her across the pillow by the man known in the tabloids as the People's Judge.

'Another outbreak of mad judge disease,' Oliver commented to Sarah. 'I hear it can spread to humans.'

Defence lawyers are not fond of Marcus Byron.

Jenny Glendower and Oliver Rawl are this moment several miles apart, he to the west of the city, she to the east, he safely inside his N-registration Golf, she alone and frightened on the grim streets of Great North. If Oliver could see them, he would know at once that all the youths surrounding Jenny are on bail. In each case one condition of that bail is to observe a night curfew, which means that they should not be out on this street, or any street, after nine p.m. If police patrols recognise them, they can be slammed into the cells overnight and brought back to court the following day, where they are colloquially known by magistrates and court clerks as 'overnights'. List-callers are expected to bring 'overnights' into court as soon as possible after ten a.m., but in practice every kind of complication arises.

All these youths have broken their curfews many times. Again and again. They know that magistrates will remain powerless to do much about it, except deliver pompous speeches and warnings about 'next time', while the youth slouches, hands in pockets, his jaw lazily masticating on gum. As Brigid Kyle has observed, 'next time' is the operatic chorus of the criminal justice system.

*   *   *

Sarah, too, is awake. Oliver's phone had rung long enough to penetrate the spare room. Had they drunk too much chianti at Pasta & Basta, was he over the limit? You should never touch a drop when duty solicitor. But your week as duty solicitor is the one when you most need a drink. Several.

The problem with driving at night is not that you are going to hit something, but that something is going to hit you. It doesn't matter who was responsible for the accident, both drivers are invited to blow and pee.

Sarah knows Oliver's route to Eden Manor police station every yard of the way. She imagines him traversing an eerily empty Broadway and heading up the High Street. Has he checked that his car doors are locked as he approaches a set of traffic lights notorious for car robbery and its close cousin, 'aggravated burglary'?

Sarah can read Oliver's thoughts at any distance. It's too much to ask, he's telling himself, that the client awaiting him in the cells has done something really bad. Murder and rape are the prime cuts, bringing loads of ongoing legal aid money to Oliver's employers, Hawthorne & Moss. Like a popular play, murder, attempted murder or rape runs and runs, except that it ends up in the Old Bailey rather than on the stage of the Lyric, Shaftesbury Avenue. But much depends on whether the overnight client already knows you. If he doesn't, he may drop you the next day.

Hearing the front door close, Sarah had climbed out of bed and made herself a cup of Horlicks while turning a blind eye to the unwashed dishes piling up in and around the kitchen sink. If she wasn't going to sleep she might as well catch up with yesterday's *Times* report – every salacious detail – about the female naval officer who is accusing the male army colonel of the most incredible sexual vendetta after she broke off their affair. Sarah would dearly love to get involved in a case of that stripe, instead of spending her prime years defending the indefensible, the young robbers and rapists of Eden Manor. No matter if she was representing the chauvinist colonel rather than the woman – but this thought immediately reversed itself. Could she do it?

Oliver could do it. He could do anything. He's shameless. He's overdue for a haircut. When she first met him, his unruly locks were spilling over his ears; as he helped her to her feet in the court corridor, after the blue-shirted Burns men had hauled her two young female clients off her, Sarah's first thought had been, 'I've seen this thin bloke around, trying to look on top of everything.' Oliver's first words to her had been stunningly impressive: 'Are you all right?' She'd said yes but she wasn't. He'd insisted on driving her to hospital for a check. Later he'd cut his hair manically short, but now it was half-way back to a mess. When she chided him about it, he said no, he looked the part.

'What part, Oliver?'

'That's what I'm trying to find out.'

On these comfortable thoughts Sarah takes her Horlicks back to bed, but sleep continues to elude her.

*　　*　　*

21

Pete McGraw, sixteen years old, has now moved in closer to Jenny Glendower to ask for a kiss. Each of the boys has been trying this on in turn – their first try with a grown-up woman – guffawing, larking, but they don't seem insistent on the kiss.

Pete is grinning at Jenny rather charmingly beneath the deep peak of his baseball cap. His wiry hair is dyed bright yellow but the dye stops well short of the scalp. She would not guess that Pete is already a father – and Pete himself has let it slip from his mind. He had been one of the younger fathers in Downton Juvenile Offenders Institution. He even knew his child's name (also Pete) – though he hasn't seen his girlfriend or the baby recently. Can't remember when. Pete carries a can of Foster's in his left hand. It's empty and he wants another.

She couldn't guess, either, that this youth is Oliver Rawl's client. Even now, alone and afraid, her mind keeps turning speculatively to what Oliver will be like when she sees him again tomorrow, after a gap of eight years, three months and nine days. (She has kept her old diaries.) You cannot confide to anyone in Yeominster. It would get straight back to Phil. She'd read a feature article about young lawyers and there Oliver was, looking a bit severe or shy, with most of his friendly locks chopped off – photographed alongside his partner, whose name Jenny took care to forget. The article said they lived in Putney. Jenny had gone to the library and found his name in the telephone directory. Before leaving for the teachers' conference, she'd plucked up the courage to phone him at home. A rather dry voice, undoubtedly

Oliver's but rather grudging, as if he wanted to be left in peace, greeted her on the answerphone. She couldn't quite bring herself to leave a message. His partner might hear it.

Well, why not? Why shouldn't she hear it?

Like Luke Grant, Pete McGraw is black, though not so fiercely so as Luke, who is the same colour as the famous Judge Marcus Byron. The only white adult Pete trusts is his solicitor, Oliver Rawl, which Pete pronounces 'Rolls' and spells that way if he ever has to. Born in Guyana, Pete had been brought to London when a toddler. Now he 'lives with' his single-parent mother (when the Youth Courts inquire), though that's scarcely a regular piece of truth. His mother had proudly shown 'Mr Rolls' a snapshot taken when Pete was only four. Oliver saw a rapist's eyes glaring from the small face.

Pete again has his arm round Jenny, asking for a kiss. He smells of something, maybe it's the drugs she has read about – they all smell of it.

She knows she should cry out for help but can't. They have already bonded her into a kind of intimacy which holds her captive.

Yes, she and Oliver had been sweethearts at the University of Warwick. Towards the end of the affair – though she had expected it to be the end of the beginning – they had gone on impulse to Nice together, taken a charter flight in mid-July and been naïvely surprised to find every hotel '*complet*'. Finally a taxi carried them up into the hills, to a beautiful hotel near Saint Paul de

Vence, far too expensive but only for one night, and in the morning, when they were having breakfast on the veranda, a maid came out clutching the bloody sheets from their bed and strode indignantly towards what they supposed was the hotel laundry. Jenny had been having a bad period but you couldn't come all that way, with the scented trees whispering in the warm breeze off the Mediterranean, and say No.

'No,' she says gently to Pete. 'I am a married woman. Please help me find a taxi.'

Pete McGraw passes briefly across Oliver's mind as the night-duty solicitor drives through virtually empty streets towards the Broadway. In a valiant attempt to harvest some favourable opinions about his client Pete, Oliver had sought a written report from the school from which Pete had long since absconded, Eden Manor Comprehensive. But none arrived.

Finally Oliver had insisted on visiting the Headmaster, Mr Richards. He arrived on time but was kept waiting half an hour. When he was finally shown in, Mr Richards neither stood up nor offered his hand.

'Anything positive you can say about Pete McGraw and his prospects would be of help,' Oliver explained.

'Of help to Pete or to the general public?'

Clearly the Headmaster did not welcome the interview. Oliver was less than astonished. One of Pete's earliest and most trivial offences had been to assault the Headmistress of Eden Manor Primary School.

24

'We have seen little or nothing of Pete for the better part of three years,' Mr Richards told him. 'Pete concluded at the age of twelve that school was not a place compatible with burgeoning manhood. He is simply another disaster. One of our constant headaches is delinquent dropouts like Pete turning up in the school to pay off old scores or exact vengeance. You know what happened at the primary school?'

'Yes.'

Mr Richards smiled sourly. 'No doubt you represented him on that occasion as well?'

'Yes.'

'No doubt you are only doing your job.'

The alleged assault had been on the Headmistress of Eden Manor Primary School, Mrs Jameson, and had been witnessed by the school secretary, Deborah Rich. Pete had pleaded NG (as usual) and gone to trial before the Benson Street Youth Court. He had taken umbrage because Mrs Jameson was constantly hauling in his mother to dress her down for the disruptive behaviour and absenteeism of his younger brother, Jason. After one such session, which Pete had taken upon himself to attend, he had burst back into the school office, with Jason following and apparently attempting to restrain his big brother from striking Mrs Jameson.

According to the prosecution, Mrs Jameson had backed away as Pete advanced on her, shouting and brandishing a fist. Having asked Deborah Rich to call the police, the Headmistress finally slipped out to her own office, receiving a flat-handed blow on the back of her head as she passed through the door. She did not see Pete hit her. Her head jerked under the impact and she suffered neck pains for some days.

So she said. So she told the police.

Jason had made a section 9 statement denying that his brother had struck the Headmistress, but the Crown predictably refused to accept it and insisted that he appear in court as a witness for cross-examination. Mrs Jameson and Deborah Rich turned up on the trial date but Jason didn't and they had to be sent home. After five adjournments, Jason finally showed up.

Obviously Oliver could not challenge the probity and good faith of a Headmistress and School Secretary but, cross-examining Mrs Jameson, he wondered whether Pete had not merely been gesturing angrily, rather than attempting to hit her. As for the blow that did land, she didn't see who delivered it – might she not have struck her head on her office door in her haste and confusion?

'A perfectly understandable mistake,' Oliver added.

'No, it was a glancing blow with the back of the hand.'

'Did you turn to see who had hit you?'

'No. I went straight into my office.'

Called to give evidence, Deborah Rich was sure that Pete had been attempting to hit the Headmistress. She replicated his stance and hands for the benefit of the court. Jason had been hanging on to Pete's arm in an effort to restrain him. She had seen Pete strike a glancing blow with the flat of his hand on the back of Mrs Jameson's head as she hurried out.

'You phoned the police while the two boys were still in your office?' Oliver asked Deborah Rich.

'Yes.'

'What number did you dial?'

'999.'

'So your eyes were on the phone?'

'Yes, but I swivelled my chair around to watch as far as the phone cord would allow.'

'But your attention was distracted because you were still on the phone?'

'I saw him hit her.'

'You claim that Jason was saying, "Pete, don't hit her, don't hurt her"?'

'Yes.'

'You didn't say that in your written statement.'

This was a routine ploy which invariably confused the witness. Deborah Rich was shown her original statement.

'In your statement,' Oliver continued, 'you said that Jason was saying "Stop" to Pete.'

'Yes.'

'It makes a difference, doesn't it?'

'Well, I – yes, but—'

'Your statement was made soon after the event when your memory was fresh. We are now almost seven months after the event.'

'I remember it very clearly.'

'What do you remember very clearly: what you said in your statement or the version you have given this court?'

The third prosecution witness was the police officer who had called at the McGraw household later that day. The constable testified that Pete had told him to 'Fuck off'.

'Had you cautioned him when he allegedly said that?' Oliver asked.

'No. I did then caution him and he walked out of the house.'

'Has Pete ever been interviewed?'

'He refused to come for interview.'

'He was never arrested?'

'No.'

'That's rather unusual, isn't it? I put it to you that you didn't take the charge seriously, you thought it would blow over.'

'I am not responsible for deciding whether charges are brought.'

Despite misgivings, Oliver decided he must put Pete himself in the witness box. If the defendant remained silent, the magistrates would draw their own conclusions – they always did. Reluctantly removing his baseball cap from his mop of gold-dyed hair, Pete told the court that he had been emotionally hurt by the way Mrs Jameson treated his mother.

'So you went back into the office after your mother had left?' Oliver asked his client.

'Yeah.'

'What did you intend to do?'

'I dunno. I was angry. I lost my temper.'

'Did Jason say anything?'

'Jason was saying to me, "Don't, don't, let's go home."'

'Don't what?'

Pete shrugged. ''E must o' meant, "Don't go back in there."'

'Could he have meant anything else?'

'Nah.'

'What were you doing with your hands when you went back into the office?'

'I was using my hands expressively. I was holding out my hands clenched sort of thing, I can't remember.'

'Did Mrs Jameson think you were trying to hit her?'

'Yeah, she was holding a book, a file or somethin', in front of 'er face.'

'Was Jason physically restraining you?'

'He was holding my left arm. I could have punched her if I'd wanted to.'

'Did you strike the back of her head as she went out?'

'Nah.'

'Please stay where you are,' Oliver concluded. 'My friend will have some questions to put to you.'

The prosecutor looked at Luke. 'You say you were not trying to hit the Headmistress?'

'Yeah. Nah.'

'Which?'

'I never.'

'You said you were merely waving your hands "express-ively"?'

Pete hesitated. 'Yeah.'

'When did you learn that word – "expressively"?'

Pete shrugged. The prosecutor's implication was clear:

when taking 'instructions' from Pete, Oliver had planted the word into his head.

Finally, young Jason entered the witness box, shy but sprightly. He remembered Pete complaining that Mrs Jameson was always giving their mum a hard time. According to Jason's version, when he'd tried to dissuade his big brother from returning to the office, Pete had said, 'I'm only going in to talk to her.'

'He was sort of jabbing his finger at 'er.' Jason demonstrated.

'Did Pete strike the back of her head as she went out?'

'Nah, never.'

Summing up, Oliver urged the magistrates to remember that the charge against Pete was common assault, and not using threatening words and behaviour. Therefore not too much emphasis should be attached to Pete's angry behaviour, or Mrs Jameson's fear of him.

'I put it to you that both ladies over-reacted. Mrs Jameson could have struck her head on the door. Being in fear of a blow, she imagined that she had been struck by a human hand. Regarding Miss Rich's evidence, I should remind the court that she is Mrs Jameson's subordinate and works with – and under – her every school day.'

He saw no reason to remind the court that Jason was Pete's younger, and much smaller, brother, who lived in and under him every day of the year, Pete's periods in Downton Juvenile Offenders Institution apart.

The magistrates retired for ten minutes and found Pete guilty.

'Is anything known?' the chairman asked.

Pete's list of previous was not then what it was later to become, and he got off with twenty-four hours in an Attendance Centre – twelve Saturday afternoons. Oliver reckoned he would have been a genius to have won that case.

'Or any case against Pete,' Sarah had remarked.

Now, many months later, with Pete's criminal record a yard longer, Oliver faced a hostile Mr Richards in the Head's office of Eden Manor Comprehensive.

'I hear they locked him away. For gang rape, wasn't it?'

'He's out now, on parole.'

'I'm sure you do a good job for your clients, Mr Rawl, but Pete McGraw is no longer *my* "client".'

Oliver had left the school empty-handed, having wasted a precious morning. The crime that had landed Pete in Downton remained as vivid in its detail to Oliver as if it had occurred yesterday.

A dozen boys had emerged from a bowling alley tanked-up and barging any pedestrian in their path. Crowding on to a bus without fares, they waylaid two girls travelling home from school, threatened them, insulted them, and dragged them off the bus. When the driver stopped the bus and tried to intervene, he was struck a blow or blows which left him prostrate on the pavement.

It was a story well worth cutting short, like so many that occurred on the Eden Manor estate. One girl, Sue, they raped a total of nineteen times in a filthy, urine-soaked basement littered with condoms. She was spread-eagled on stone stairs while her friend Zoe was done inside a large cupboard in the gang's rubbish-strewn den. Sue later told the police that there was even a bin especially for used condoms. She recalled how the gang queued up outside the basement door, waiting their turn.

'They seemed to be shy of watching each other.'

The leader of the gang, later identified as Jackson Saint, entered first: 'He came down the stairs, he shut the door, and got on top of me. He put his penis inside me. I could hear male voices outside the door. They were talking and shouting.' The third boy who had her took longer than the others. 'I could hear shouts of "Hurry up". He asked them to give him a few more minutes.'

The boy who needed more time on the job was later identified as Pete McGraw.

The attack lasted more than two hours.

The two girls were taken to the police by their parents. A few days later they were waylaid and led aside within full view of their homes and warned by Jackson Saint and Pete McGraw that they would be shot if they ever gave evidence.

'Yeah, bitch, shot dead.'

Jackson Saint had showed them a gun. Allegedly.

The girls were put under police guard round the clock. Special hotlines were installed for their families.

The case went to the Crown Court. It was good gravy for Oliver Rawl's firm, Hawthorne & Moss (no connection with the two famous motor racing drivers), who represented three of the 'alleged offenders'. So serious a case, with so many defendants, runs through endless court appearances, including 'non-effective' dates, and soaks up the legal aid. The 'bundles' containing the 'disclosures' passed back and forth between the Crown Prosecution Service and the defence lawyers.

The *Sentinel*'s feared columnist, Brigid Kyle, had published a polemic about that, too, bringing a stern rebuke from the Law Society. 'Justice on the cheap is no justice', the Society's press release reminded the nation.

Immediately after his arrest, Pete had told Oliver flat – eye to eye – that he knew nothing about the gang rape of the two schoolgirls and had been nowhere near the scene of the crime. When the Crown came up with identification evidence from the bowling alley staff, Pete changed his story: yes, he'd been with the lads until the trouble on the bus, then he'd 'peeled off', not wanting 'to get into anything'.

'You'll need an alibi witness to confirm this,' Oliver warned him.

Pete had shrugged. 'Dunno.' He'd just 'wandered about', not meeting anyone in particular. 'Dunno.'

Then the battered bus driver also identified Pete.

And the girl he had allegedly raped, Sue, remembered him well – after all, he was the one who had needed more time on the job than the others. The others had yelled his name through the door.

The Crown disclosed this in its 'advance information'. The prosecution is not allowed to 'ambush' a defendant in court by withholding vital evidence until the trial.

Oliver had visited his client on remand in Downton and made it clear to Pete that he was advising him to admit the facts but plead Not Guilty on the technical grounds of duress. You might think you needed to explain such a legal distinction to an uneducated lad of fifteen, but there was no need: these streetwise boys were all keen students of law. Even Pete could spell duress.

'It's up to you, Pete, but I advise you to abandon your alibi.'

'I told ya! I was never there. You're supposed to believe me. That's your job.'

'I'm advising you that the court is unlikely to believe you.'

Would a 'timely' change of direction make much difference? Was it too late to be 'timely'? Admittedly Pete, like all the other boys involved, had refused to make any statement to the police, and had then dragged the system through all the protracted preliminaries of a contested trial – but it was never too late to fish up duress.

'Were you intimidated, Pete?'

Oliver would not have wanted to be overheard by Sarah asking this question, just as she could do without his ears when she resorted to the same desperate tactic of 'leading' a client.

Pete thought about this then nodded. 'Definitely.'

'You didn't want to rape those girls?'

'Nah. I tried to get away but Jackson, he grabbed me, and some of the others, they dragged me back in and called me a cunt. Jackson, he said, "We're all in this together, it's a gang-bang, got it?"'

'You're afraid of Jackson?'

'Everyone is. He'd cut you as soon as look at you.'

Oliver noted that Pete had never shown a flicker of

remorse about what they had done – but that of course could be explained by the fact that he hadn't done it. Now he had done it, and remorse was very much part of the mitigation agenda.

'Any regrets, Pete?'

'Yeah, who wants to be banged up inside this place?'

'I meant – any regrets for the victim, for the girl?'

'Yeah.'

Neither before, during or after their trial in the Crown Court did any of the boys show a trace of genuine regret. They were too busy blaming each other, or basing their defences on pleas of intimidation, to spare a thought for the two victims.

All the boys were black and so was His Honour Judge Marcus Byron, a sentencer much feared among criminals and much denigrated by progressive pundits.

The trial took place a month before Marcus Byron's highly publicised downfall.

Pete McGraw, Charco Rios, Luke Grant, Ally Leagum and the other youths surrounding Jenny Glendower have been lingering outside 'Peking, Cantonese and Vietnamese Cuisine'. The Chinese take-away remains open – the Peking night knows no closing time. In the modern economy, the supply-side economy, there is no shortage of casual workers, burger-house and ethnic food staff prepared to work at any hour.

Perhaps the boys, the youths, are discussing what to do with her, she isn't sure, and the fragmented snatches of conversation Jenny picks up seem to belong to a language, an argot, foreign to her. The small Filipino boy periodically bursts into high, excited speech, but no one is listening to him.

When the youth they call Charco speaks, everyone listens. But he doesn't say much. His is the most evil face she has ever seen. The young years seem to have been expelled from it by a corrosive acid of permanent rage.

Her stomach registers the odour of sweet and sour sauce mingling with pork, chicken, bean sprouts in black chilli sauce and egg fried rice – for a moment these kitchen smells had suggested comfort, safety, family life. A weary young Chinese woman is leaning on the counter watching television. The kitchen is out of sight, at the back, and the front of the shop is bare, bleak. Jenny catches her own reflection in the window – and an accompanying platoon of unwelcome reflections. Two wear baseball caps but the largest, a black youth, goes bareheaded. Her guard of honour. She remains unaware of the video camera above the closed, steel-shuttered off-licence up the street.

On desperate impulse she attempts to enter the Chinese take-away, it may be her last hope, but her path is blocked. They don't use their hands on her, not yet, no need, hands are for later, for serious business.

'Where you from?' the tiny Filipino boy asks cheekily – as if he, not she, were the native denizen here. She realises it's true; she is the stranger here, lost. It's their city and her Rolex watch is now theirs – though it remains on her wrist.

They hustle her on, keep walking, lady. They pass

All Saints Church. 'Jesus turns my darkness into light', it says outside. 'Jesus said, "I have come that you may have life; and have it to the full." John 10:10.' She remembers Oliver Rawl, long ago, when they were students and lovers, asking why the Protestant Jesus was so fond of semi-colons. Typical of Oliver. Had he changed?

She would find out tomorrow. Or would she?

The youths may have planned something – or not. Their unplanned actions are often their most violent. But it depends on the drink and drugs intake. When they plan to rob a particular store, or TDA a car which is asking for it, maybe a VW Polo or a Fiat Punto or the flash new Ford Fiesta, nobody may get hurt. Unlike their elder relatives, they don't steal whole cars for the market, for profit, merely for the ride: what gets taken is the stereo system and any other nice thing found to be asking for it. Flashing red lights on the dashboard and engine immobilizers merely cause extra damage.

Yeah, nobody may get hurt. But different outcomes apply when the target is the first vulnerable pensioner to emerge from the Post Office clutching the week's sixty quid. You never know what may happen when they focus on you. When their gaze settles. It's as if you've insulted them, challenged them, just by daring to show your tired, old face or your war veteran's limp. At night their thoughts may turn from robbery to sex, from free-ride Fiestas to cunt, particularly if the cunt shows signs of drifting, or 'cruising' (the word they favour), or trying (like Jenny Glendower) to keep track of her own footprints, the invisible string leading back to her phantom hotel in its nowhere street.

Of course they know her hotel. They had begun to shadow her almost from the moment she stepped out of it, all alone, little handbag on her wrist, blonde hair swinging, tripping along on high heels.

Too good to be true – and asking for it.

Jenny can no longer fend off fear and panic. She sees a rare taxi with its orange roof light illuminated and runs a few steps towards it, hand uplifted. Her cry chokes in her throat. Not a sound comes out. The taxi slows, as if thinking. Maybe the driver sees her, but he also sees the gang of youths. His diesel engine throttles away.

'No taxis tonight,' says little Ally Leagum. 'You enjoying yourself with us. We going to have a party.'

Ally is only four foot eleven but claims five foot for his cock. The others know him as the fastest tongue on the street. His speciality is winding up adults. Sentenced to Saturday afternoons at Wesley Chapel, a north London Attendance Centre, he had been chewing gum during a First-Aid class when the instructor asked him the first thing you should do if someone is knocked down by a car.

'Go through his pockets,' Ally replied.

'And you, son, had better take your hands out of yours.'

Ally has been breached five times for turning Wesley Chapel into a Non-Attendance Centre. The magistrates pretend to run out of patience but where can they run to? At fourteen Ally was out of bounds for custody and he knew it. The Multi-Agency Cautioning Panel had urged the police to grant Ally caution after caution, month after month. Ally had twice been granted the Met's Super Caution, a group session to which parents were invited but never came. Films were shown to ram home the 'last chance' lessons to rows of empty chairs. For Ally's social worker in the Youth Justice team, Hubert Hare, it was never quite the last chance saloon. Even after Ally had breached conditional discharges three times, Hubert's pre-sentence reports recommended a fourth, a fifth. Whatever had been proven or admitted in the course of Ally's trial before a different bench of magistrates, vanished, or became clouded, after Hubert interviewed Ally for the PSR.

He stuck out his foot to prevent the door hitting him and the glass smashed. Ally's problematical relationship with his own self-esteem is the result of family circumstances for which he cannot be held responsible. A conditional discharge would place the responsibility on Ally to stay out of trouble and make clear to him that this type of behaviour will not be tolerated.

The video camera above the off-licence observes the group move on and away. It registers the woman's pink suit among the boys' darker clothes in the language of black and white.

Two minutes later a sudden loud chatter in Cantonese can be heard from within the take-away. They had feared that the woman would succeed in running inside the shop, seeking refuge, begging them to call the police, and that the gang would come in with her and demand free food, spare ribs and pork chop suey, before robbing the cash till. But now they have all gone away, those big black boys, very good news.

Jenny wishes she could call out to Phil, or to her late, beloved father, who had never fully come to terms with Phil's politics. Or to Oliver. She wishes this awful night would vanish into a dream and it could be tomorrow, having lunch with Oliver.

The small Filipino boy is tugging at her arm, grinning.

'Nice time,' Ally Leagum keeps saying, winking. 'You looking for nice time.'

She had tried Oliver's number again but it was the woman who answered – Jenny remembered her pretty face, the big oval glasses, her sleek, super-competent hair style, from the newspaper article. But Jenny had buried her name.

'Are you a client?' the woman asked her. Her voice was faintly 'London' – or was it 'Thames'?

'Oh no, just a friend from . . . long ago.'

She'd almost said 'from the past' but that sounded too dramatic, somehow. If you shared a 'past' then something had happened. The 'past' sounded like a relationship, not merely a distant time zone.

'I'm coming to London . . . for a conference . . . and I thought we might meet up for a coffee,' Jenny explained.

'Oliver should be back about seven-thirty,' the

woman answered brusquely. 'I can give you his office number.'

'Oh, I wouldn't want to . . . he must be very busy.'

The woman gave her the number of Hawthorne & Moss with a speed that seemed to suggest, 'I'm busy, too, though you might not guess.' She did not offer her own name.

Gaston Dubois wearily glances up at the digital clock above the reception desk of the Winfield Hotel. It must have stopped: only two o'clock. Four hours to go, *merde*. What kind of a life for a brilliant student, a *terminale*, from Bordeaux? The blonde lady in pink has not returned. Why worry? Why had she not allowed him to call a taxi? Who knows about women?

He begins to worry for her again. In Gaston's considered opinion, the young blacks and Asians are the big problem in this area of London. Very aggressive people, very hyped-up and physical, always shouting in London-speak. Youngsters who cannot bear to stand still for a moment in their trainers and Reeboks. They see a lamppost and they have to dance with it or pull it down. They see a watch on your wrist and they must have it. Show them a crowded pavement and they have to scythe through the pedestrians at great speed on their bikes.

His sleepy brain is moving backwards. Now he wishes all over again that he'd warned the pretty blonde lady before she left the hotel, alone, at 0025 hours. He is 'kicking himself' – another of the English phrases he'd recently picked up. That was why one spent a year in London, working in burger bars and hotels, to learn to 'kick oneself' and to say 'Cheers' instead of 'Thank you'. His professors in Bordeaux knew nothing of the real English vernacular: they were the sort of bourgeois 'potheads' (new word) who said '*oui*' (yes) instead of '*weh*' (yeah).

Where is she now? What has become of her?

Three

Approaching Eden Manor police station, Oliver's head is slowly clearing of sleep and the chianti consumed at Pasta & Basta.

Yes, much depends on whether the client you find in the police cell already knows you. A duty solicitor is there to advise the arrested person in the first instance: to listen, advise, and take instructions. But unless the offender (alleged) already knows you, he's likely to change his solicitor the next day or week. The very fact that you were available in the middle of the night, unshaven and blinking in the harsh light of a police station, may convince him that you're not the top-notch super-lawyer he deserves. So you lose him and Hawthorne & Moss loses the long gravy trail.

Quite often your middle-of-the-night client already has his own solicitor but cannot contact him because the bastard has wisely switched off all his phones. Very few people in serious trouble have not been in trouble before. The exceptions tend to be domestic cases, sexual rage, mayhem at home, usually fired up by drink and drugs. These are the ones who weep all night in the cell while studying the blood on their hands.

A month ago he had been called by the Custody Officer at three-thirty in the morning, half an hour after he had fallen asleep. Since midnight he had been kept awake, entertained by yobs yelling, cursing and scuffling in the street. On arrival at Eden Manor he had been led to a cell where he found a shattered man of his own age, fresh from killing his girlfriend in a drunken stupor, first attacking her with a knife and finally strangling her.

Then he'd called the police. When they came, he sobbed and confessed and had to be restrained from drunken attempts to 'revive' the dead woman.

Despite the initial confession, which had not been made under caution and would be inadmissible evidence, Oliver advised him to answer no questions when formally interviewed, beyond giving his name, date of birth and address. The man had followed this advice twenty-four hours later, after the police doctor finally ruled that he was in a fit condition to give an interview.

'Why did you call the police?'

'Nothing to say.'

'Why did you confess, at the scene of the killing, that—'

Oliver intervened. 'No caution had been administered.'

Is this what Oliver wants to do with his life? On the whole, it is – but increasingly he wonders. Sarah is less prey to self-doubt, or she is better at masking it.

She hadn't mentioned Jenny Glendower's call either. What time had he suggested for lunch tomorrow with

Jenny? How would he get out of bed? Ten to one, he'd have to spend most of Saturday at the police station. Do I want to see her after all these years? I expect she's had babies and put on weight. Those West Country girls and their cream teas. She'd once taken him home to Yeominster to meet her family. Nice people, salt of the earth. The food came and came until he was embarrassed. So much to eat, you must be expected to propose marriage.

Had Jenny wanted to marry him? He can't remember. He tells himself that they had somehow drifted apart, after the trip to Nice, and the bloodstained sheets, but suspects that he may be reorganising history to cushion his conscience.

'Oliver is very much the hero of his own narratives,' Sarah had told his boss, Dick Dodgett, when they invited him to dinner. 'Even his defeats in court are incredible victories.'

'Really?' Dodgett lifted his famously engaging bushy eyebrows, affecting surprise. 'You mean this modest young man I know is not the real Oliver?'

Oliver had hastily asked Dodgett whether he knew the story of the two Irishmen who attended the millennium celebrations but were disappointed by flop fireworks, failing lights and under-baked potatoes.

Dodgett shook his head. 'Tell me.'

'Paddy finally announces his verdict to Seamus: "This is the last millennium I'm attending."'

Dodgett laughed. 'I expect you've heard it before,' he said to Sarah.

'It's possible. Stand by for the one about the old Irishman who loved golf.'

Dodgett turned expectantly to Oliver. He regularly repeated Oliver's jokes as his own.

'We'd better wait until Sarah is washing the dishes,' Oliver said, 'and ironing my shirts.'

Now, tonight, he wonders whether he will find either of his two favourite young clients in the cells at Eden Manor. If he had to choose between a dialogue with a blood-splattered Charco Rios or a sleepy chat with a bemused Pete McGraw, he'd settle for Pete any night.

His mind swings back to Pete's trial for the gang rape of the two schoolgirls. Judge Marcus Byron had presided shortly before his sudden and catastrophic downfall – though Sarah claimed to have seen it coming. A lot of women – and in particular lawyers – evidently shared her intense hostility towards England's most famous black judge. Probation officers, male or female, loathed him.

Certainly Marcus Byron was a judge much feared by criminals. Oliver knew him not only by reputation but also from his frequent utterances in the press and on television. He enjoyed an astonishing popularity with the public but rather the opposite within the legal profession, where he was dismissed as an ambitious demagogue, a politician *manqué*. Oliver had once shared these views, but now he was less sure, and had to concede that Byron conducted the gang-rape trial efficiently and fairly. He neither bullied nor hectored.

There was one exchange between Judge Byron and Pete's counsel, the smooth Antony Laughton QC, which even Oliver had secretly enjoyed – although Oliver was supposed to service the vanities of the silk (who belonged to the same club as Oliver's boss, Dick Dodgett) and his junior barrister. The judge had leaned forward:

'You say the boy Pete McGraw was intimidated into raping the victim?'

'I do, your Honour.'

'By others in the gang?'

'He was afraid of Jackson Saint in particular.'

'Afraid of what? Of violence to his person? Or of shame and ostracism if he did not conform?'

Antony Laughton hesitated: the trap had been laid. If he chose 'shame and ostracism', Pete would be found guilty and the judge might knock a few days off the sentence; if he chose fear of violence, as he had to, Marcus Byron would be waiting for him. There was no way out for Laughton.

'He was afraid of being beaten up,' the QC answered. 'Or worse.'

'And was any such threat made against him before he committed the rape?'

Marcus Byron was the wrong judge to try anything on – apart from wig and gown – but the pre-sentence reports had not yet been written when the Lord Chancellor announced Byron's suspension from the Crown Court circuit – a decision that divided the nation. To celebrate, Antony Laughton threw a champagne party attended by many of the Bar's leading lights. Dodgett was invited but not Oliver, for whom Laughton displayed a palpable lack of affection.

'Antony has his likes and dislikes,' Dodgett consoled Oliver, who needed no consolation.

Six weeks later, passing sentence, Byron's successor on the case, Judge Worple, had incensed the prosecution and astonished defence lawyers, Laughton included. Convicted of raping both girls, Jackson Saint, the leader of the gang, got four-and-a-half years' custody on each count – to be served concurrently.

Concurrently rather than consecutively! Four-and-a-half years rather than the nine expected! Oliver glanced towards Antony Laughton, whose mouth had curled enigmatically into some kind of arabesque. Had Worple gone soft in the head? Was he anxious to put clear water between himself and the disgraced Marcus Byron, the 'hanging judge'?

Oliver's client, Pete McGraw, got off even more lightly. His professed fear of Jackson Saint, and the fact that by his victim's account he was inhibited and 'slow' in the act of rape, got him down to eighteen months, almost a year of which he had already served on remand.

Judge Worple ruled that the identities of all the defendants, normally protected by their age, could be revealed as a deterrent to others. Hence the waspish comments later made to Oliver by Mr Richards, Headmaster of Eden Manor Comprehensive.

Of considerable interest to Oliver and Sarah – and everyone else – was Brigid Kyle's column in the *Sentinel*. It was a family scandal that had brought down Marcus Byron; the Lord Chancellor and the Lord Chief Justice had been incensed by his failure to curb his daughter

Lucy's delinquencies. It had also become clear that Byron, although married to a leading QC, Louise Pointer, was having an affair with Brigid Kyle, his loud champion in print. Therefore journalists, lawyers and politicians read her comments on Judge Worple's gang-rape sentences as if they were Byron's own.

Sarah Woods said as much over her breakfast *Sentinel*.

Oliver almost smiled. 'You have reminded us all more than once that a strong-willed woman like Brigid Kyle speaks for herself.'

Sarah's marmalade spoon remained poised in mid-air.

'What do you mean by "us all"?'

'Hm. Merely that your view about that has been quite extensively telegraphed.'

The marmalade hit the toast. 'You can have the last word.'

It was a joke between them, a not unsubtle one: in court the last word spoken is not always the winning word – because it belongs by right to the defence.

Brigid Kyle (or Marcus Byron) criticised as 'slippery' some of the arguments put before the court by the gang's highly paid barristers, all of them 'instructed' at the taxpayers' expense. For example, Jackson Saint had changed his plea to Guilty ten minutes before he was due to go into the witness box, after the two girls, the victims he had threatened for the best part of a year, bravely went through with their evidence (given from a separate room over a video link). Jackson Saint's counsel invited the court to take into account

Jackson's 'timely plea of guilt and the contrition it represented'.

Ha ha ha (wrote Kyle). By maintaining his innocence until the eleventh hour, the street-wise and recidivist young thug Jackson Saint, who fancied himself as the boss of all teenage Yardies, had not spared the taxpayer the £60,000 it cost to stage a trial, nor had he spared his victims months of anxiety and fear. Did not barristers and legal-aided solicitors in the lower courts encourage clients to take it all the way? Did not unholy prolongation fatten their fees?

'This is now happening all too often', Kyle warned. She did not believe that soft sentences would deter other teenage 'Yardies' or 'Triads' or 'Space Invaders', who roamed the streets under gang names like Younger Younger, dragging schoolgirls off buses, shutting them up in stinking hovels, then raping them one by one, at leisure, no hurry.

Kyle's article caused an uproar. Had she been lying in bed beside Judge Marcus Byron, as she wrote it? Had he virtually dictated it to her?

The Chairman of the Bar wrote an indignant letter to *The Times*. Of course he could not hint even by innuendo that Ms Kyle had written her article while experiencing an orgasm brought on by Judge Byron. (Which was the way that Oliver put it to Sarah over a late Saturday breakfast of egg, bacon and, most naughtily, sausages.) The Chairman of the Bar explained that while it would obviously be improper for him to comment on this or any other particular case, he deeply regretted Brigid

Kyle's unjustified slurs on the legal profession, this new display of the hostility for which she had become, alas, notorious.

'The guilty, after all, are as much entitled to first-rate legal representation as the innocent.'

The popular press also expressed outrage about the sentences. 'Is Our Justice System Going Soft?' screamed the *World*'s vivacious Auriol Johnson, once an assistant to Brigid Kyle but now her bitter rival.

What Judge Worple's scandalous concurrent sentences mean [blazed Auriol] is that two rapes incur no greater penalty than one. It's no wonder that vile gangs can roam our streets raping with impunity. They've got nothing to fear from the kind of sentences handed out yesterday. Our courts just don't seem to have any balls when it comes to dealing with evil slime like this sick six. Say this for the disgraced Marcus Byron – at least he has balls. You can hear them bouncing in the *Sentinel* columns of his randy 'friend', Brigid Kyle.

Hugging this moralistic polemic were some useful telephone numbers: RANDY TART WHO WANTS TO MAKE YOU SPURT! 07000 780 274. A large spread advertised FREE PORN MAG WITH THIS ISSUE. TWO FOR THE PRICE OF ONE!

Auriol Johnson had once worked for Brigid Kyle. They had quarrelled fiercely – according to rumour blows had been exchanged in Groucho's. Since breaking away into the tabloid press, Auriol had hounded Brigid in print without respite.

'A few more years for these callous young brutes wouldn't cause many tears. *Just cheers*', she concluded.

But – as Oliver commented to Sarah – the fire-eating Johnson, whose blonde head topped her columns, did not venture to propose how many more years.

'Four-and-a-half more years for Jackson Saint,' Sarah said dryly. 'As for your slow-coming Pete, I'd bang him up for at least three.'

'Am I hearing a paid-up member of Liberty? Am I listening to the woman who sees no virtue in prisons? Did I ever expect to hear Sarah Woods damning Marcus Byron as a softie?'

'In rape trials the judge should always be a woman, period. I expect Byron secretly thought the two girls were asking for it just by being on a bus.'

Pete McGraw came out of Downton almost immediately after sentence, having already served the best part of a year on remand. He was supposed to report twice a week to the local Youth Justice Team (to learn more about 'anger management' and the effect of rape on the victim) but failed to show up. Oliver's warnings had no effect – the 'lawyer' in Pete knew that the Youth Justice Team was reluctant to bring him back to court, and the court could do little about it anyway.

The 'dozy' Pete, forgetful father of baby Pete, had since that time been arrested three times, charged with robberies in the Camden area and the Great North area . . .

* * *

Which is precisely where Pete is tonight, despite a night-hour curfew as one condition of his bail, and a ban on entering the Great North postal code as another.

'You'll keep out of N1, is that understood, Pete?' the stipendiary magistrate had warned him.

'Yeah.'

The gang are marching Jenny Glendower along Great North Way, where the vast, bleak, dirty-brick hulk of the railway station extends for hundreds of yards, on and on.

VIDEOS BOOKS MAGAZINES

Hadn't she passed that earlier? Or is this a different one? Are they walking her in circles?

Yes, they are! *The Triumph of Vice*, a novel by G.W. Target. *A Baroque Novel*, by Brigid Brophy. *Bring on the Virgins*, by Porsche Lynn.

Yes! Once again she is walking past Call Saver, with its uncapitalised brand names, cellnet, vodafone and oneZone.

The little Filipino keeps grinning 'Nice time' at her. Pete takes her wrist again, displaying an intense interest in her Rolex watch.

But so are they all, not least the huge fourteen-year-old black boy, Luke Grant. Luke shows Jenny his left hand with a grin, as if flashing his private parts, and she sees the cigarette burn between thumb and forefinger. He carries the deep scorch mark, which has turned into a scar, at the point where the charcoal skin on the back of his left hand merges with the pink-grained palm.

All the lads are showing her their burns now, as if keen for her admiration, all except Charco Rios who disdains such antics. Charco is a leader, a *caudillo*, a chieftain. He lights a cannabis spliff with a big gas lighter whose whooshing flame throws his evil face and cat's eyes into stark relief.

Charco Rios is seventeen and looks older when he hasn't shaved. He was nine when his mother brought her three sons to Britain from Colombia. His father is a Mafia mobster currently in jail and known as Acid Man after his favourite method of attack. His mother has been in domestic service, cleaning the houses of foreign businessmen, but nowadays she lives mainly off state benefits and complains she can't cope.

He is semi-literate after years of truancy; an intelligence test had placed him in the bottom nine per cent of the school population. But the test was conducted in a classroom, with numbers, words and diagrams – nothing to do with the practical intelligence of the streets and housing estates. In those terms Charco regards himself as a genius.

Leading Jenny Glendower's gallant escort across the dimly lit streets of Great North, he is kingpin. Members of other youth gangs and even adult pimps will move into the shadows, surrender territory, at his approach. He is the 'mad Aztec' whose gang models itself on the Triads, meeting up in amusement arcades and pool halls, resorting to violent mugging to feed and fund their drug habits – and for pleasure.

Unknown to Jenny, Charco Rios presently carries a

knife of different design to – but no less lethal than – the one that he had thrust into the Headmaster, Edward Carr – a notorious murder still unsolved. Such had been his swaggering confidence that no kid who'd observed the crime would dare 'gas' to the pigs, that Charco had for some weeks afterwards disdained the simple precaution of disposing of the fatal weapon. But now the police are looking for him and he walks abroad equipped with a different blade. Charco's dad had taught him how to use every kind of knife before being locked away for fifteen years.

The murder of Edward Carr, on the street outside St James's School, where he was Headmaster, had dominated newspapers and television for weeks. It seized the nation's imagination. Only forty-one years old, Edward Carr was the father of four young children; his widow Emma, herself an ex-schoolteacher, proved herself to be an attractively feisty woman, angry but not vengeful. Everyone, from the Queen down, sent messages of condolence to Mrs Carr and her family. The Home Secretary declared himself 'shocked and appalled'. MPs delivered 'enough is enough' speeches up and down the country. Moralists moralised, pulpits thundered. Lessons had to be learned, whatever those lessons might be. Something or other was 'perfectly clear'. The general secretaries of the teaching unions issued dire warnings: while applauding the dead man's gallantry, they insisted that teachers could not be expected to stand in as policemen or security guards. If violence erupted inside a classroom, the teacher should leave. What happened outside the school gates, as in the Carr case, was cause for a phone call to the police, not personal intervention. Don't 'have a go'. Heroism was strictly for those paid to be heroes. Heroism was a job description. What had been called 'citizen's arrests' were out of fashion. The Battle of Britain was now strictly for the men and women in blue.

As a teacher, Jenny Glendower listened to this storm of sentiments with intense interest. It so happened that Edward Carr had been a respected and popular teacher at her school in Yeominster before his promotion as Head of St James's in London. Jenny had known him and Emma Carr quite well – and their children. Many times she had been tempted to write to Emma Carr, or even telephone her, to express her sympathy and anger, but Jenny had shrunk from the intrusion, from finding words that could possibly measure up to the tragedy.

Perhaps she hadn't known the Carrs all that well, after all.

The police drafted in a hundred extra detectives and constantly predicted an 'imminent arrest' – yet Charco Rios has never been apprehended. No one has gassed or grassed despite intensive questioning of ever-widening circles of teenagers in police stations and around the grimy, urine-stained, tin-can-littered, graffiti-defaced council estates.

Some facts were clear. Edward Carr had died after he ran out of the school yard to help one of his pupils who was being attacked by a gang outside the gates. Other kids who had witnessed the event, and seen their Head stagger back into the yard before collapsing, confirmed the general physical description of the gang – there had been three of them, all wearing brightly coloured 'Triad' bandannas round their heads, none 'English' in appearance.

Children on the streets around St James's School, Great North, seemed to know from the outset what gang had been responsible, though their 'knowledge' differed, some naming the Wo Sing Wo and others the 14K group. It was general knowledge among the young that Mr Carr had died while intervening in a vendetta: the gang, whoever they were, had come to settle scores with a pupil at the school. According to unconfirmed rumour, the boy was Sudanese.

Father Bernard O'Brian, director of the local Marian Community Centre, told reporters: 'Kids in their mid-teens are running the streets around here. This is not just a school problem, it's a community-wide problem.'

Detective inspectors, detective sergeants and detective constables visited house after house occupied by Filipinos, by immigrant families from Hong Kong, and by 'illegal' Chilean families living without proper Home Office residence permits. More than 200 statements were taken down. The police held frequent press conferences promising 'due protection' for any witness who assisted with their inquiries.

A computer millionaire specialising in virtual reality games offered a reward of £100,000.

This generated a rush of useless 'information' and

hoax calls. Among those claiming the reward, a youth with a long criminal record, Ally Leagum, told the police that he had been approached by 14K at an amusement arcade in Piccadilly. He further confided that the gang wore bandannas, baggy trousers and loose shirts, to accommodate weapons. 'They reckoned I looked healthy on the street,' Ally explained, describing how, working with a lookout, he had at one time (but no longer) made a habit of lifting quantities of Yves Saint Laurent shirts and designer jeans from targeted shops. Ally boasted about his own progression from 'jackings' (street robberies) to extortion – which involved collecting protection money from restaurants and shops.

But who had stabbed Edward Carr? About that little Ally Leagum was a whole lot vaguer. Though a wordsmith of some artistry, with ambitions in the field of what he called 'scripting', he was definitely short of names.

The computer millionaire sat on his money.

Is it water that Jenny can smell now? She has heard of a famous canal which traverses Great North. But where exactly? And where are they taking her? She is led over a temporary raised platform flanked by high wire traversing major road works in progress, though not at this hour – it's now 0215 on her Rolex. Beyond her own means, the gold watch had been an extravagant wedding present from her parents – as if they were reminding her (and Phil) that she was marrying beneath her. She notices that not everything is dereliction here: smart enclaves are emerging, post-modernist conversions. They pass a huge plateglass door and window, with black wooden frames:

DEGW
online magic
an agency.com company

Jenny wonders what agency.com means.

The youths who have taken her prisoner do not wonder and do not see. The big black one who most frightens Jenny sees only what he wants to see, which is not much.

Only fourteen years out of Maisie Grant's overworked womb, Luke Grant has committed many sins, too many to count. He has been out of school and at large since he was eleven, when he was expelled for bullying and disruption. His active sex life had begun at the age of nine; by any standard he is over-sexed, and for Luke mutual consent has never entered into it. For Luke sex is force, sex is taking. But his victims are invariably 'asking for it', he's always quite clear about that; Jenny Glendower is already asking for it, has been asking for it ever since he set eyes on her and his cock began swelling in anticipation. These cunts, he knows them better than they do, they only pretend not to want it, and the only reason they don't say yes is spite, to make him feel bad about himself. He's doing them a favour.

He has a deep laugh beyond his years: 'I done 'er a favour.'

*   *   *

Visions of Luke Grant roaming the streets like some huge, baffled animal haunt his solicitor, Sarah Woods. She is still awake, more than an hour after Oliver departed into the night. You lie awake and everything crowds in on you, a gallery of the damned.

She wonders about the woman who telephoned a week ago, asking for Oliver. Not a client. Sounded like a voice from the past, shy, diffident – guilty. Sarah had given her Oliver's office number, then waited for him to say something about the woman, but he hadn't. Damned if I'll ask. He's attractive and knows it.

Sarah has been representing Luke Grant since he was put in care. He has always treated her with the utmost respect, grave and gentlemanly in her presence – he even opens a courtroom door for her and steps aside to let her pass! You don't see *that* often! He is due back at Benson Street Youth Court on Friday, but will he turn up? He lives in a local authority hostel in the borough of Sedge Hill under a civil care order, not under a criminal court order, and therefore the hostel staff are under no obligation to make sure he gets to court.

They couldn't if they were.

Such technicalities are the bones and flesh of a solicitor's life. The law is a mesh of rules and Luke breaks most of them.

His mother Maisie always says to Sarah, 'What could I do? He was out of control.' Not that you see much of Mum. Long ago she gave up accompanying him to court.

Of course there is no father. Luke is one of five children by three different fathers. He had been put in care after he'd been found assaulting a younger male cousin. He had his erection six inches up the screaming boy's anus when uncles and neighbours came running. It then emerged that he had sexually abused all of his siblings, male and female, threatening to 'hurt' them if they said anything to anyone.

Luke could say 'hurt' quite softly. 'I wouldn't never hurt nobody,' he told her.

He is saying it to Jenny Glendower now, pulling her past the boarded-up Red Lion pub, heading for the darker bank of the canal, his hand on her wrist.

'Wouldn't want to hurt you, eh?'

Sometimes he brings himself to court, without escort. Sarah is never sure why, bored perhaps, this huge boy with a prominent burn mark on one of his restless hands. Attempts by magistrates to summons the mother or bind her over are futile because Luke is in care, so how can she control him? Besides, how can a court deliver a summons to her? She is 'never' living at the address in the files, and she 'never' receives the letter even if she is living there. As Sarah commented to Oliver, magistrates and court clerks have a touching faith in the post, in the Royal Mail – comfortable, middle-class people whose morning mail is delivered through large brass apertures, falling softly on to good carpet, where it lies, like an obedient dog, to be claimed by the addressee.

Nobody in their family trashes it.

Luke Grant has never said an angry word to Sarah. He nods obediently when she tells him what he must and must not do – but as soon as the streets separate them he wanders off into his own head, his own rampant penis, his incontinence, his crimes, spilling his sperm over the city. He's too young for prison, though he's powerful enough to King Kong most of the senior bullies in Downton. To put a boy of fourteen inside on remand you need secure accommodation, but a court is close to powerless if Luke's local authority, Sedge Hill, claims there isn't any secure accommodation available.

If it so claims? It always does. Secure accommodation would cost the local authority close to £3,000 a week. No way.

Sarah's duty, of course, is to keep Luke free of any form of confinement, even though confinement is what he needs for his own good and protection.

This summer night smells bad to Oliver Rawl. Driving past Eden Manor estate, forcing himself to keep the speedometer down to 35 mph, he notices groups of youths loitering around the more likely parked cars. He knows the system: the boy at the corner is the lookout. We must be tough on crime, the new leader of the nation has declared, and tough on the causes of crime.

That's the bit the new government seems to have forgotten almost before it took office. The Home Secretary, Ben Diamond, promises to outdo his Tory predecessor with a manic programme of Action Plans and Clamp Downs. Even his political friends call him Rough Diamond and *Private Eye* now has a regular column devoted to the violent crimes of Ben Roughneck.

Even granted the will, and the investment, decades of neglect have to be undone. Give the boys jobs, yes, give them skills, certainly, but what about the virus that runs in the bloodstream of families who by now have lacked fathers for several generations back?

Parking outside Eden Manor Police Station, Oliver realises he is reluctant to have arrived. Removing the coded security disc from the car's transistor, and his briefcase – by day solicitors now carry denim haversacks purchased from camping shops to accommodate the sheer bulk of files – he hears the click of central locking, which, he knows too well, will only mean that a skilled and determined thief will inflict greater damage in the five or six minutes it takes.

Outside a police station? Yeah, anywhere.

Something in his head is warning him – of what? It's as if Sarah is screaming across the five miles now separating them, 'Don't go in there, Oliver! Turn round and come straight home! Please!'

Well, he's tired, that's all. Fatigue makes you jumpy.

The first thing he notices is that there are more police on hand, far more, than you'd expect at this time of night. Half the Met seems to have congregated at Eden Manor. It has to be murder and no ordinary murder, either. Not only Custody Officer Charlie Wright is there, but also Detective Sergeant Doug McIntyre, for whom Oliver has more respect than affection. He likes Charlie Wright, though.

'Cup of tea, Oliver?'

'Thanks, Charlie.'

'The usual? Milk and one sugar?'

As a very young apprentice solicitor, wet behind the ears and a keen member of Liberty, Oliver had been shocked, appalled, by the way he was treated in police stations, but now, looking back, he recognises that he had been naïve and too stiff, too pompous, in his dealings with the Met. Four years ago he would have refused the tea: he was not to be bribed, compromised! But he had gradually slid off his high horse. Cops are people, many of them deeply attached to the local community and what they suffer from kids and young hooligans. And what do they hear from residents, from the public?

'Fat lot of good it does to call you lot. All I get for my pains is a brick through the window and they're back at it, the next night.'

Every resident of Eden Manor knows the courts are a load of rubbish. Everyone knows that when the vandals step out of Benson Street Youth Court with another conditional discharge, they give them each a free pair of trainers and a cheeseburger. Everyone knows that magistrates like Lady Harsent would give King Kong a conditional discharge after he'd eaten an inter-city express. It's a fact.

'Now remember, Darren, that you haven't been let off, quite the contrary, this conditional discharge will be hanging over you for a year and if you are ever, ever again, so foolish as to . . .'

Yeah. They even send the little bastards on free safari holidays in Africa, taxpayers' expense. And it's clever dicks like Oliver Rawl who stitch up the system.

Grow Rich On Crime. It's pinned up over every legal aid lawyer's desk. That's another fact.

'The charge is murder,' Doug McIntyre tells Oliver. 'Of Edward Carr. The boy claims to be someone else but we know who he is.'

'Who does he say he is and who do you claim he is?' Oliver asks McIntyre.

'He calls himself Cesar Alvarez. From fingerprint evidence we believe him to be Miguel Garcia, suspected of aiding and abetting Charco Rios in the murder of Edward Carr.'

'He's violent,' Custody Officer Wright warns Oliver, 'and still high.'

'Hm.'

McIntyre shows him a long blade, now wrapped in a Cellophane bag and neatly labelled. They had taken it off the prisoner after a violent struggle on the Eden Manor estate. Two police officers had suffered cuts.

'Though nothing serious by most of your client's standards,' McIntyre tells Oliver sardonically.

Oliver nods, declines to be provoked. Say nothing, just listen. There are no facts, merely alleged facts. 'If we ever have children,' Oliver recently remarked to Sarah, 'we'll teach them the alleged facts of life.'

'OK, I'll talk to him now,' Oliver tells Custody Officer Wright.

'I'd just as soon send a constable into the cell with

you,' Charlie Wright proposes – though he knows in advance that Oliver won't consent, indeed he might not fully respect Oliver if he did. 'If only for Sarah's sake,' Charlie adds.

That's touching. They like Sarah here; she even brings them, particularly the female officers, amusing Beryl Cook birthday cards. Charlie Wright respects Sarah, but warily. 'Your missus,' he says when he's had a pint or two, 'is a hard lady. You don't try anything on with her, do you?'

'You don't,' Oliver agrees, aware that Charlie is really asking how you get Miss Sarah Woods into bed and what happens when you do. Oliver knows the answer, but is disinclined to quench Charlie's curiosity. Nor need he add that Sarah cannot be persuaded that Charlie Wright is anything more interesting than an overgrown, over-age, football-addicted boy.

'For which,' she adds, 'the Latin word is *puer* and the adjective "puerile".' (This probably covers the sports-addicted Oliver as well.)

He and Wright have reached the cell door. Wright takes a long look through the spyhole.

'Shout sooner rather than later, Oliver.'

Oliver has enjoyed more than a few off-duty pints with Charlie Wright. Charlie leads two lives, or perhaps (Oliver speculates) nine. At certain hours and times of the week, this steady, kindly PC Dixon of Dock Green assumes a shadowy identity as a 'football intelligence officer' for a swathe of London. He does what he does in dark glasses, leather jackets and tattoos. Charlie's passion is football hooligans: who they are, where they are, what they are planning for next Saturday or weeks ahead.

Lovingly he monitors their 'week' and intercepts their mobile phone calls. 'I know what they have for breakfast every day of the week.' Chief Constables with university degrees and years of staff courses at Hendon Police College hang on Charlie's 'intelligence-led knowledge', deploying at his wink and nod tout squads, gates squads, dog squads and large numbers of policemen, some disguised as hooligans, others in blue, at vast expense, which is recouped from the clubs.

'A big match can cost a major club £30,000 in police expenses. Of course it's the TV franchises that should pay but the law doesn't allow it.'

To make up for it, Sky TV is now contributing to police benevolent funds. But Sky rules the roost; they can alter the times of matches at the last minute, to avoid clashes with other televised sport, giving the police a choice of 11 a.m. or 5 p.m. The police never fail to opt for the former, even on a Sunday.

'Alcohol is the enemy. By five you have a nightmare.'

For Charlie the entire point of football is football hooligans. He will tell you, 'Fifty-two matches at two grounds, 263 arrests, 208 charges,' even before you ask him for last year's statistics. Charlie loves knowing what the public do not know, namely that the hooligan leaders of Chelsea, Spurs and Arsenal are in touch with each other long before the fights, arranging battle venues and altering them at short notice, again by phone, if Charlie shows signs of sniffing them out.

'They'll set it up a mile from the ground, in some residential road. The locals are terrified, cars are damaged, windows smashed. We have to be there first. But to be there first you have to have the knowledge.'

The knowledge: he uses the word lovingly, possessively, like a London taxi driver. 'And I'm not talking about the mini-cabs, which are mainly owned by "them".'

Charlie is fond of his own racism. 'But don't quote me, Oliver.'

He loves telling stories, always preferring the present tense: 'Kick-off is at three. By two forty-five only a quarter of the crowd is in the ground. They're in the pubs to the last minute. Then they demand that the match be delayed because three thousand are jammed in a queue at the gates.'

Basically, according to Charlie, the police spotters in the crowd must get to the hooligan leaders before they lead the mass of drunken fans into vast confrontations from which they themselves – as the video cameras show – slip away out of the fray.

And your typical hooligan leader? He is aged between twenty-seven and forty, older than you might expect. He operates a military-style hierarchy, with one absolute leader and several officers. Typically they are into drugs and drug dealing, do no regular work, and love mobile phones. 'It's all about power and a game of wits with us,' Charlie says. 'Power. To avoid police intervention they'll take elaborate routes to away grounds, they'll get off a hired coach and walk the last mile.'

Charlie (and his Chief Constables) regularly complain that too few of those arrested and charged inside the grounds are subjected to Exclusion Orders by the courts. But – 'No offence, Oliver' – some clever lawyer is always on hand to cast doubt on the identification evidence. Gloomily Charlie admits that most of those brought before the courts are cannon-fodder, not 'the makers and shakers'.

Oliver is wondering about cancelling his lunch date the following day. He can hardly call Jenny at this time of night. He was surprised she had settled for a hotel in Great North; she must be hard up, too many children probably. He remembers having looked away – how many years ago? – when the French hotel maid had appeared carrying those bloodied sheets.

Now the cell door closes behind Oliver and the key is turned from outside. Oliver Rawl has entered a cell with an invisible inscription over the door: Hell Starts Here.

Even legal-aid solicitors may die before their time.

Pete McGraw is now pressing up close to Jenny Glendower. Her body is no longer her own. She is forced to walk in step with her captors, otherwise she would be dragged. They are leading her into ever darker streets and alleys; those lamps still functioning fall further apart, frail matches flickering in a darkened cellar – and always the smell of water, of the canal.

The most dangerous of these youths is Charco Rios. Charco has beaten up old grannies, he has set their hair on fire and used their pension books for toilet paper. His mission tonight is to lead his gang to the new home of a pool hall attendant called Tony Marquez, a stupid fuckhead who thinks he can give evidence in the Edward Carr case and hopes to collect the big money reward. Ideally Charco would like to take with him the two boys he can trust, Miguel and Gregory, but he has good reason to believe that the police are tailing them night and day. He has picked up tonight's rabble from the Game Zone pool hall, with others tagging along, shitheads like Luke and Pete who can think about nothing but cunt, and this cocky squirt Ally, a midget hanging on the end of a shouting prick.

This woman they've picked up is just a diversion from the night's serious business, yet even Charco has found her diverting. Girls are generally beneath his attention-line, and he is yet to look one straight in the eye. Yet this mature woman with the blonde hair, who has fallen into his hand like a ripe pink fruit – she's something else. She's asking for it. She's had sex a thousand times, you can tell from the way she walks and smiles, the mascara round her eyes, the powder on her skin, the reek of perfume. Charco is convinced this smart bitch knows it all, blow jobs, hand jobs, look at that Rolex on her wrist – someone must have been getting something for his money.

Jenny Glendower loses her gold-chain handbag seconds after she surrenders her Rolex. After Pete removes the watch from her wrist, Charco takes it from Pete. Charco's alert gaze flickers into the darkness ahead and behind, seeking out the darkened police car that will betray that this woman is Plain Clothes, a bait, a trap. The bitch is too good to be true.

Charco distributes the money and credit cards before tossing away the empty bag. She attempts to go back for it but they intercept her little, high-heeled scamper with their big bodies.

'It's of sentimental value,' she pleads. 'My husband gave it to me.'

She hears someone mocking her accent, as if she sounded like the Queen. Perhaps she does. 'My husband and I.' They don't speak the language she hears and uses in her own school, close to the precincts of Yeominster Abbey, a place of dedicated education, academic ambition and parent-driven endeavour, lying under the validating gaze of a fine, neo-Gothic abbey spire. The boys now driving her through filthy streets like a captured sheep do not sing in choirs or wear white cassocks. God for them is not even a swear word.

Jenny is very tired now and there are tears – tears of rage as well as fear, a rage directed not only at the oafish grins and bad breath pressing against her but also at the heartless city that refuses to know about a kidnapped woman, offers no help, doesn't heed, doesn't listen.

'What would your mother think of you?' she chides Luke Grant.

They don't have fathers but surely they have mothers. There is no reaction: to mention a mother is like quoting from the Bible – it belongs to another part of life, not here. Here is the adventure playground without frontiers.

'How about a party?' little Ally leers.

This comes – again, again, again, like a needle stuck in an old gramophone record – from a boy less than five feet tall with an impish smile fixed across his Filipino features: as if he's challenging her to wipe it away. He shows her what he claims are Ecstasy tablets and keeps jabbering about a 'rave'. He offers to sell her one for 'ten smackers' – even though they have taken all her money.

Perhaps he has a sense of humour?

'Ten quid, you mean?' She tries to sound colloquial but her vocabulary is of the wrong time and place. 'Your friends took all my money,' she adds in a voice that no longer belongs to her – she hears it like a playback in an echo chamber.

'On credit,' he grins. 'Pay in cunt.'

Ally Leagum will some months later win notoriety by giving the V-sign to photographers gathered outside the Old Bailey during his trial. Ally had come to England at the age of ten with his two brothers, two sisters, mother and English stepfather, a heavy drinker and wife-beater from whom Ally's mother has since split. The family is now living in Housing Association accommodation in Hackney.

The local police know the address by heart. So does Ally's solicitor, Sarah Woods. It's where you never find Ally. Whenever Sarah meets him, in her office or a court waiting room, he makes a routine cheeky pass at her or, as Oliver quips, 'what passes for a pass'. Ally attends Cardinal Manning comprehensive school – or he once did. School doesn't suit his temperament. He's currently on bail for robbery and possession of an offensive weapon. Ally is never short of knives. Every member of Jenny's gallant escort is carrying one.

'There's no stopping them,' Hubert has more than once sighed to Sarah when they confer in the corridors of Benson Street Youth Court.

'Hubert' is Hubert Hare, a trained social worker and a member of the Borough's Youth Justice Team.

Sarah and Oliver do not need to remind each other that those of their young clients who join Hubert Hare's case load are fortunate indeed. Faced with multiple burglaries, every driving offence in the book, demanding money with menaces, possessing a bladed weapon, Hubert never flinches, never recommends custody. Never this time.

What Hubert most cherishes is the Youth Justice Service's Offending Behaviour Group, an eight-week course that Ally Leagum, Luke Grant and Pete McGraw had occasionally attended but more often skipped. 'It's the right environment for him,' Hubert invariably assured the magistrates. 'We can explore his reasons for offending, managing his anger, and we can discuss practical ways of turning him round. We also' (Hubert never forgets to add) 'consider crime as experienced by the victims.'

Sarah and Oliver know that the most 'serious' punishment administered by the Youth Justice teams, a supervision order, amounts to little more than an hour a week discussing personal issues such as benefit payments, getting into education and training, and relationships. This level of intervention is far lower than the 100 hours over six months which (research has indicated) is needed.

That's another of the bees in Marcus Byron's bonnet – what he calls 'supervision orders when you feel like it'.

It is no part of a solicitor's job to question this tender nurse-maiding of cynical little brutes like Ally; Sarah and Oliver are in business to achieve 'justice' regardless of whether it leaves society at the mercy of their clients. When a lad involved in a robbery has been chased and caught, their duty is to remind the court that 'the goods were recovered undamaged'. If a prosecutor applies at the last moment to run two charges together, attempted theft and going equipped for theft, on the ground that the facts are the same for both charges, they automatically object on technical grounds: inadmissible evidence. And the give-away shoe-print during an alleged burglary? Well, it measured only 3 on a 1–7 scale of forensic certainty – and it was found outside the broken street door, not inside.

Justice means forcing the prosecution to prove its case 'beyond reasonable doubt'.

Gaston Dubois prefers the night job as a hotel receptionist to working in the kitchens of Burger King, but it's 'nothing to write home about'. Gaston enjoys his own private joke, which he does not attempt to share with his parents, that if there is 'nothing to write home about', one does not write home.

In his imagination the cops of the Metropolitan Police have already arrived.

No, no, any moment now the blonde lady will reappear, wave cheerily at him through the glass doors, beyond the credit cards, awaiting his virile press of the button.

'Just needed a spot of fresh air.' She will smile. 'Needed to unwind a bit.'

Gaston yawns. Night work does not entirely suit him. He often finds himself nodding off during afternoon classes in the Holborn College of Languages. He has learned a variety of English words for 'sleep', including snooze, slumber, snog and kip. Early during his stay in London he had taken a girl student for a walk in Hyde Park, laid down on the grass under the sun, closed his eyes, and told her he would like a brief snog. He still cannot understand why she took such offence.

Gaston shudders for the lady. Great North is the worst place he has ever seen. Walking to work at night from the tube station, he regularly runs the gauntlet of prostitutes, their sullen black pimps watching from extravagant cars. He passes lurching drunkards, pale drug addicts with need-haunted eyes, gangs of idling youths waiting for a picking, a target. Gaston has to force himself not to run after dark.

To run is asking for it.

The smell of stagnant water is much closer now. Or it could be her own urine. For the first time since infancy, Jenny has wet herself.

'British Waterways', it says on the gate. 'This gate is

locked every night between dusk and — a.m.' No time has been filled in. And it isn't locked, anyway. Now foliage, branches of trees, press around her. She can smell the water. Fifty – or is it twenty? – yards across the canal she sees ultra-modern office buildings, a big wharf, orange buoys, moored boats. Small black birds drift on the surface; when she hears their chirp she recognises moorhens. There are plenty around Yeominster.

Jenny remembers that she can swim and swim well – she has even won prizes for the butterfly. She knows that she should dive in right now and strike out for the other side.

'Is this the area known as Little Venice?' she asks politely. 'I'm a stranger here, you see, but I've heard of Little Venice.'

No answer. They don't know where Big Venice is, either.

One of the smart new buildings across the canal is illuminated by a row of floodlights sited several feet above the ground. But this side of the canal, her side, is without a single lamp.

She catches one tantalising glimpse of the Post Office Tower, a bright-burning candle in the distant sky.

Mrs Jennifer Glendower, mother of two, is now kneeling beside the canal, weeping and begging. The old cliché keeps somersaulting in her aching head: rape is a fate better than death.

But what is worse than both?

'Please,' she whispers, 'please don't.'

Four

Time, now, to touch on the remarkable history of the preceding year, the immediate prologue to Jenny Glendower's dire night on the streets of Great North.

Though he could never remember when last he had his hair cut, Oliver Rawl could have scribbled the sequence of recent events on the back of his hand – were it not already occupied by Sarah's early morning reminders about loo paper and washing-up liquid running low. Thus:

- February 1996: Pete McGraw is involved in a gang rape of two schoolgirls led by Jackson Saint.
- October 1996: Murder of the Headmaster Edward Carr. Police investigations lead to hunt for three youths – identified many months later as Charco Rios and two accomplices, Miguel and Gregory.
- November 1996: Judge Byron presides at trial of Jackson Saint, Pete McGraw and others.
- December 1996: Marcus Byron's daughter Lucy convicted of street robbery.

- December 1996: Judge Marcus Byron suspended from the Crown Court bench.
- January 1997: Lucy Byron sentenced to eighteen months by Judge Sawyer.
- January 1997: Lenient sentences by Judge Worple on Jackson Saint, Pete McGraw and others for the gang rape. Press outcry.
- February 1997: Pete McGraw released from prison.
- May 1997: General election.
- June 1997: Marcus Byron reinstated on the Crown Court.
- August 1997: Jenny Glendower leaves message for Oliver that she will be in London. Oliver is called out on night duty rota to Eden Manor police station.

Of Lucy Byron, Oliver and Sarah knew little beyond what they read in the newspapers. Only later, when by a small twist of fate Sarah became Lucy's solicitor, did they learn the full story. It was a story that would draw Sarah Woods into the greatest crisis of her professional life.

Lucy Byron was proud of one thing: at seventeen she was the only girl in Britain who could claim to be the daughter of a judge and in prison. Other judges had other daughters, some of whom were doubtless no better than they should be; but only his Honour Judge Marcus Byron had been publicly humiliated by a daughter's calculated little rampage into crime.

Lucy's father owned a Rolls with a flash registration plate, MB1. He and his new wife, Louise Pointer

QC, occupied a smart flat in a *beau quartier* of South Kensington, very posh. Although Marcus insisted on sending Lucy to an expensive private school, it became an article of faith with her that he didn't love her and couldn't care less – even though her broad nose and wiry hair clearly belonged to His Honour. She would drift into school, invariably late, wearing the Sudanese nose ring banned by the Headmistress, and non-matching psychedelic socks (also banned) beneath carefully torn jeans. She weighed less than eight stone, yeah, and she wrote most of the school magazine, most of it censored by the Head – and she drifted into a kind of love with Dan, the youngest son of a violent criminal family who terrorised Eden Manor estate, the Richardsons.

After a flying visit to Eden Manor, that bitch Brigid Kyle, Dad's latest pussy, had bravely reported to readers of the *Sentinel*:

Hordes of youngsters swarm around on summer evenings, loud-mouthed and foul-tongued. A boy earns respect only by trashing everything within reach. They hunt in packs, snapping car aerials, smashing car windows, ripping out radios. Eden Manor is a factory for the manufacture of yobs.

From Lucy's involvement with Dan Richardson everything else was to follow:

A sixteen-year-old girl was arrested yesterday and

charged with possession of Class A drugs at Eden Manor police station. It is understood that Judge Marcus Byron telephoned the station to make inquiries later in the day.

Appearing before the Benson Street Youth Court, charged with possession of crack cocaine and Ecstasy tablets, Lucy emerged from this 'first appearance' with one bail condition: residence, every night, at home. Lucy lost no time in breaking bail. She took off. Just like her dad. Yeah, big, handsome muscular Marcus with his many ladies and his love of expensive mountain bikes, each new one a metal mistress between those powerful thighs in their tight black Lycra shorts – Dad off on a sponsored bike ride to the Pyrenees to raise money for Justice for Victims, another of his publicity stunts and ego-trips.

Lucy took to the road in her own fashion of loose-fitting denims, Indian cottons, and Sudanese nose-rings. She had made a habit of joining the New Age Travellers every August. On this occasion breaking her bail conditions was merely a bonus. She went without a word to her mother. When her dreaded GCSE results came through, no one would know where to find her in the threatened forest groves of Wiltshire.

The New Age Travellers were set on thwarting a new motorway that was due to cut a swathe through a hundred acres of open parkland and precious trees in west Wiltshire. The tree village was constantly harassed by bailiffs and private hirelings of the road contractors. The more athletic resisters were living in tree huts and growing dreadlocks – Lucy learned to climb a rope without spilling a mug of tea. In the evenings she sat cross-legged beside her new friend David, rolling spliffs while wood smoke drifted pleasantly up through the high trees, the silent sentinels of the camp. The unsilent sentinels were the mongrel dogs.

Lucy first got to know David Glass at the camp, although there had been occasional childhood encounters due to Marcus's long-standing friendship with David's father, the Cambridge criminologist Paul Glass. Lucy felt a certain affection for David, with his measured gaze and thoughtful tone. He was the first boy she had known who didn't seem to have anything to prove. He sat cross-legged by the camp fire, at ease with himself, taking short drags on his spliff, and talking about the heritage of the seventeenth-century Diggers.

When Lucy finally decided to return to London, she ruthlessly turned the heat on MB1, her dad. Although skinny and timid, with bad eyesight, Lucy learned to pretend to enjoy the physical aggro as a member of the girl-gang headed by Dan Richardson's sister, Trish. Linking arms in the High Street near Eden Manor, the shrieking girls filled the width of the pavement and everyone else had to jump for it. Following her arrest, along with Trish and another girl, for the street robbery of the actress Teresa Kent, Lucy was bailed to reside with her father and his wife Louise.

The Times reported that the Lord Chancellor was poised to invite Judge Marcus Byron to stand down 'in view of legal proceedings affecting a juvenile'. Yeah. Gotcha. The Lord Chief Justice, or was it the Lord Chancellor, or the Lord of the Rings, summoned Daddy for a brief 'interview':

'There have been too many scandals, Marcus. Too many. And too many angry ladies in the frame. A man who takes on the Government is hardy; a man who takes on the entire female sex is foolhardy; a man who takes on both is a fool. We don't need judges who so fascinate juries that they don't listen to the evidence.'

A week before her Crown Court trial, Lucy vanished without a trace, leaving behind her a one-word message daubed in shaving soap on the bathroom mirror: 'Bye!' She was again in breach of her bail.

Lucy's trial finally destroyed Marcus's marriage. Gallantly, and perhaps unwisely, his wife, Louise Pointer QC, had broken a code of practice by volunteering to represent Lucy. No one suffered more cruelly than Louise as one revelation after another spilled out during the trial. That appalling parade of witnesses – the women in Marcus's life. The parade had been orchestrated by Lucy herself; it was Lucy who had written the script all along. Marcus would always respect Louise's courage, her sheer professionalism, as the ground opened under her, but the damage was irreparable. Louise bitterly described herself as 'the laughing stock of London'. On any day she might open the *World* or the *Standard* to find a grim little photo of herself surrounded by pictures of Marcus's smiling mistresses, past and present. Their marriage was at an end. Marcus took refuge with the woman he loved, moving in to Brigid Kyle's Georgian home in Pimlico.

There was no segregated unit for teenagers in Holloway. Lucy was miserable and terrified from the moment of her arrival. Holloway is the only women's remand centre from the south coast to Norfolk, and many of the inmates find themselves far from family and friends. Lucy quickly learned how visitors keep you sane; without them, a woman can feel herself utterly forgotten and forsaken by the world outside.

David came. She refused to see her father. David brought her a telephone card charged to his BT account. It required a four-digit PIN number locked in her memory, and therefore could not be stolen from her unless the bully twisted her arm until she yielded up the number.

There was no shortage of bullies. Holloway was hell, overcrowded and understaffed, with 500 prisoners, mostly on remand or awaiting sentence – not a few of whom had been sent there by Lucy's father. Lucy found herself in a dormitory with two prostitutes and several Schedule 1 offenders, women convicted of sexual offences against young people, including abuse of their own children. Desperate to make phone calls, she quickly realised she was no match for the tougher prisoners in the jungle of the telephone queue: only one phone for every thirty-five prisoners and quite impossible to get to and everyone swearing and tearing hair and shouting about their children while the one on the phone went on and on until everyone was herded back into the cells. At every turn someone was demanding something of her, threatening, bullying. Exercise time and 'association' time were constantly reduced or cancelled. The clothing situation was ghastly; no shoes or underwear were available; the Women's Royal Voluntary Service had been forced to stop supplying clothing because its storeroom was shut down. A parcels office was shut for long periods.

Money disappeared from registered mail and from inmates' cash arriving on the wings. Lice infested hair and bed linen. Nothing was done.

The whole prison was screaming for drugs. The crack users were the most violent. Drugs came into the prison packed into a condom or the finger of a plastic surgical glove hidden in the vagina. Even the women who'd never gone beyond cannabis were turning to heroin and cocaine because they were detectable from random tests for only forty-eight hours, whereas cannabis residue could be spotted for up to thirty days.

But the worst thing was the long hours of confinement, up to twenty hours a day: the longest lock-up extended from the last main meal, at half past three in the afternoon, through to seven thirty in the morning. At weekends it was even worse: prisoners were allowed out of their cell for only an hour a day. The sound of screaming and sobbing was incessant, night and day.

The older women enjoyed filling a girl's mind with

fears and dark threats. They were always trying to sell you drugs. You heard about D1, a medical unit for detox and kicking the habit, where bullying and intimidation were rife. You heard about C1, notionally reserved for the mentally ill, the suicidal and compulsive arsonists, full of paranoid women whom no outside hospital would take. Some women called it 'the self-injury unit'.

Lucy had seen on late night television a black and white film called *Yield to the Night*, starring the young Diana Dors as Ruth Ellis, the last woman to be hanged in Britain. Now, incarcerated in Holloway, the prison in the film seemed totally unreal, so clean and orderly and hygienic. Yeah.

One of Lucy's ever changing cell-mates, Annette, was due to give birth. She asked Lucy to help her with writing letters and the spelling. Lucy did help, although she didn't believe in spelling, only in expressing what you felt, what you experienced, and in that respect Annette was just fine.

Dear Beverly,

I thank you for your letter and would off wrote sooner, only I have Just Received it 6th Dec, I would like to say that life in here has got easier. But since writing to you because off stress, I have been ill, as they are short staffed, I am locked up 22½ hours a day, I havent even had a Bath for 3 days, as it is meals and rooms. I was very down getting to a phone in here as there is only one for 35 prisoners and it is quite impossible to get to and I cannot and do not have the energy to stand there arguing. So I get worried about my daughter Louise who is at her nannys.

Soon after this letter was posted, Annette was taken from the prison to the maternity hospital in handcuffs. She spent hours in labour in the delivery room with a guard at her side and whenever she went outside to the toilet or to phone her mum her legs were shackled.

After Annette's return to Holloway with her new baby, a boy, Lucy helped her compose a letter to her solicitor:

I went into labour at 7 oclock and abulance was called. I was Handcuffed to an officer, with not the normal handcuffs But Big Black ones, which are used in Top Security Situations they were heavy and hurt I was devastated. I collapst crying Please dont I said, But they said they had to. I was taken to Whittington Labour ward, were I was in early Stages of labour, the two officers chained me to the Bed and Sat down next to me, I asked them to Please leave as I was in Pain imbarrest crying. I couldnt even cry, I hid under the sheet sobbing. My daughter came to see me at the hospital on the Sunday and my best friend Lilly, she collapsed crying and my daughter Bella, well the look on her face will live with me forever, but

she is a polite child and was not rude to the officers. I tried to explain it was their job, she is
nine.

Annette's solicitor kicked up a fuss. The episode was
raised in the House of Commons. A spokeswoman for the
prison service explained: 'If you are capable of getting up
and walking downstairs and making a telephone call, there
is a possibility you could escape.'

Under directives from the Home Secretary, every
woman prisoner in England and Wales was now handcuffed or chained to an officer during outside visits. All
2,500 female prisoners had to wear ratchet handcuffs on
their way to hospital, to the courts, and even when visiting
their children.

Annette's partner, who was serving four years in jail,
had not yet been allowed to see the baby nine days after
its birth. Annette refused to give the boy a name until she
could talk to the father.

Four weeks after her trial, Lucy was taken back to the
court and told to stand up when Judge Sawyer came in
and to stand up again when he sentenced her to eighteen
months.

They took her by Securicor van to Oak End in
Berkshire. She couldn't see out of the van; couldn't see
the tall firs, the heaths, the red-brick villages, the sturdy
clumps of rhododendrons that would yield a riot of colour
in summer, the posh stockbroker houses with gravel drives
set back behind white-painted fencing. She couldn't see
the grazing horses and cattle. She was a prisoner in

transit, her slender brown wrists cuffed together, her heart stretched by apprehension. Holloway was hell but better the hell you know . . .

She knew that most of the tougher prisoners were sent on to Oak End from Holloway, including the 'lifers', though she'd been told that female lifers have rarely committed more than one crime, usually something personal, private, just that once. Most of the really tough ones, the recidivists, the ones to fear, the 'she's back with us' types, were never in for more than two or three years.

Agatha Cowdrey – universally addressed as Miss Cowdrey by staff and inmates – was to prove the exception.

Marcus Byron had inspected Oak End some two years earlier, when the prison governor received a visiting party of Crown Court judges. At that time he had not yet sentenced the large-framed spinster Agatha Cowdrey to life imprisonment after the jury had found her guilty of murdering her elderly cousin.

He had driven MB1 slowly over the humps of the long driveway, passing GOVERNMENT PROPERTY NO UNAUTHORISED VISITORS signs, until he reached the smaller notices promising a commitment to racial equality and a caring regime. He parked outside the first gate, admiring the hanging gardens of geraniums which graced the prison itself. Above them coils of barbed wire decorated the flat roofline.

Locked inside, behind massive metal doors, were 140 female prisoners aged fifteen to sixty-eight.

The visiting judges were received by the Governor, Mary Heatherington, a woman in her fifties with a ruddy complexion and a brusque sense of humour.

'I have to warn you that you may encounter some of your "clients" within these walls. They may not feel you did them a good turn. My advice is to show no sign of recognition. And please keep together. Two prison officers will escort us – just in case.'

The Governor was asked what proportion of the staff were male.

'About one in five. They are particularly concentrated at the two main gates. When a prisoner has to be physically restrained, it is normally done by three female staff, one on each arm, one holding the head.'

Inside the lecture room they had found the words 'Caring, Compassion, Respect' written in large red letters on a white board.

'This is where we hold our anger management class,' Mary Heatherington explained. 'During the last class, devoted to the subject of tolerance, one prisoner punched another in the face and we had to sound the alarm to summon extra staff.'

The visiting judges smiled, then felt guilty about smiling.

Leading the party towards the hairdressing salon and the garment workshop, Mrs Heatherington was asked whether women prisoners were likely to be victimised for crimes of violence or sexual offences.

'Once a woman is in here,' she replied, 'it's largely irrelevant what they did outside. Most of them invent their own stories.'

Marcus didn't fully believe this and doubted whether the Governor did either.

'What's the worst punishment you can hand out to a prisoner brought before you for Adjudication?' he asked.

'To be locked in a bare cell, no furniture of any sort, for twenty-three hours.'

'How often do you do that?'

'On average once a week.'

Earlier in the day the Governor had placed four troublemakers in segregation, but she declined to take her visitors to the unit, though pressed to do so.

'It's a bad enough experience for them without being stared at by a group of men.'

The Governor was asked about random drug testing.

'Sixty-five per cent of our inmates are here on drug or drug-related charges. Yes, I favour random drug testing, though we don't yet have Home Office authorisation here. The downside of testing, of course, is that the prison staff have to face addicts short of their fix.'

The modern gymnasium drew from Marcus a comment about 'better facilities in here than they'd get outside'.

'It's a point of view,' Governor Heatherington said.

'Each of these darlings is costing the taxpayer £24,200 a year,' he persisted.

'Our budget here is £3.5 million, but seventy-six per cent of that goes on staff pay.'

'The more liberal the regime, the more staff.'

'Yes. But so long as part of our remit is rehab, you have to teach skills and self-respect – and that means facilities. I ask you all, as judges: is a woman likely to butcher an old lady just to get access to a first-class prison gym free of charge?'

Discreetly she drew their attention to a freckled red-head in a brightly coloured leotard, working hard on weights and a gleaming silver exercise machine under the supervision of a male instructor.

'She's in for life, that young woman, with a long tariff against which she's appealing. Frightful crime – butchered an old pensioner with a hammer. Looking at her, you wouldn't believe it, would you?'

'I'd believe it,' murmured Judge Worple.

'Ah, I see. Perhaps we'd better move on.'

Marcus now fell behind the group to admire two young black women playing volleyball. He felt sure he recognised them – while high on crack cocaine they, too, had robbed an old lady for her petty cash, given her a shove, seen her hit her head on the floor, then set the place on fire. The old lady had survived. Survival makes all the difference. But should it? Marcus and Paul Glass had often debated, during Marcus's weekend visits to the Glass family in Cambridge, sipping Pimms under their lime tree, whether murder should be punished more harshly than attempted murder.

Marcus had given these two black women ten and

eight years. Breaking into the old pensioner's home, which they believed to be empty, they had been surprised by her creeping, tremulous arrival from a back room. There she lay, stunned on the floor, and they set the place on fire – that should have been a life sentence! Clearly they had not intended her to survive. But she had survived. You cannot have 'murdered' a person who survives.

Did they recognise him? Of course they did, you don't forget Marcus Byron, and they were now according him closer attention than their volleyball.

Governor Heatherington had walked back from the main group to retrieve him. 'Please keep with the group, Judge Byron, that's an absolute rule for visitors – not least for visiting judges. I believe I explained that.'

'My apologies,' he murmured.

Everywhere they went, every corridor they traversed, it was keys keys keys. Huge bunches of keys swinging from the belt. Lock unlock lock.

As soon as they had entered the 'therapy wing', a pale, haggard woman approached the Governor.

'My dad's dying. You promised me you'd let me go and see him.'

'Elsa, I said I'd look into it.'

'He'll be dead while you're still looking.'

Governor Heatherington's normally relaxed features tightened. All the visiting judges understood the dilemma that she could not convey to the prisoner. Following a succession of highly publicised prison escapes, the Home Secretary, Jeremy Darling, had savagely clamped down on

security, which in practice meant restricting compassion-
ate leave and home visits. The press screamed every time
a prisoner went missing.

'I don't mind if they take me to see my dad in
handcuffs,' the woman sobbed.

Later, crossing the yard, the Governor sighed: 'Every
male prisoner who commits robbery or rape while on
home leave or parole makes life harder for our women.'

'But women prisoners are also known to take advantage and abscond,' Marcus commented.

'They abscond, they are retaken within days, usually
clinging to their children, the public is not endangered.'

The Governor was again asked how much the prisoners knew, or wanted to know, about the crimes the other
women had committed.

'Once they come in here, we don't really care what
they did outside,' she insisted.

'Yet you put lifers in a separate wing,' Marcus challenged her.

'They prefer to live within a shared experience. You
have to remember that many of our lifers are disturbed
and bewildered people. They did this one, terrible thing.
They try to hang themselves by their own bra straps.
Youngsters, who are far more street-hardened than they,
can taunt them cruelly.'

What most disturbed Marcus was to find teenage
girls, young offenders, mixed in the same wings as mature
women. He knew that this was not only wrong but
illegal. Although 'lifers' (about fifteen per cent) were still
confined to their own wing, even Schedule 1 prisoners

guilty of sexual offences against children were mixed in with the girls.

He pressed Governor Heatherington on this. She replied calmly but he did not cherish her calm.

'Well, of course you can't mix boys in with men. But as you know there are no separate institutions for girls under twenty-one. Often girls benefit from the mothering of older women. It gives them a keel.'

'But you are supposed to provide separate accommodation wings for the young offenders, Mrs Heatherington.'

'I have to refer you to the Director of Prisons on that, Judge Byron. We believe that we are entitled to mix selected women with girls – but I believe the issue is going to the High Court.'

'If you have put Schedule 1 women in with the girls, that's hardly selection,' Marcus said. 'It's a recipe for trouble.'

Governor Heatherington nodded. 'We don't want to. Pressure on space is the result of your courts putting rapidly increasing numbers of women into custody. Only ten per cent of our 140 are young offenders. If we could build a separate wing for the YOs, fine – but we are as we find ourselves and we can't leave cells empty.'

'But there must be lesbian pressures on those girls,' Marcus pressed her.

'Yes, sometimes in the exercise yard you observe a coupling and a pair of hands disappearing. In the shower room it happens but you rarely observe it. The other problem, of course, is lifestyle. The girls display noisy and often boisterous group energy, they throw water about, they play their radios very loud, it drives some of the older women round the bend.'

By the time Lucy arrived at Oak End, a major reform had taken place: under a court order the YOs now occupied two wings of their own. The number of under-21s had leapt to 69 out of 135 inmates. Lucy was glad to have a cell to herself but at first suffered loneliness and claustrophobia when locked up for twelve to fourteen hours a night. If you wanted to pay a visit you pressed a buzzer and the night duty officer would unlock your cell electronically when the toilet was free. Three visits a night were permitted, each at a maximum of six minutes. A big fuss ensued if you stayed longer. Wednesdays and weekends were the worst because you got locked up from 5.45 p.m. instead of eight.

Her first days in Oak End were mainly spent in the Education Department and in various assessments by governor-level staff.

'Religion?'

'Rasta,' she said. 'And I need a special Rasta diet.'

'Unfortunately that's not a religion recognised by the Prison Department. Are you a vegan – we do cater for that, though we discourage it.'

'I'll starve then.'

But she didn't. She was hungry and gulped down the breakfast served on the wing. When they were brought to the dining room for the mid-day dinner, one wing at a time, by prison officers communicating with each other by radio, she found a menu offering cheese 'n' onion quiche, baked fish, chicken 'n' mushroom slice, jacket potatoes, chips, boiled potatoes, rice, beans and fresh fruit.

The four wings were brought to the modern dining hall on a rotational basis. In time she learned that if you were the last wing down, the chicken, baked fish and chips had invariably gone. Even the women who liked to moan about being overweight went straight for the chips.

She was interviewed in the Health Centre by one of three visiting psychiatrists and examined by a venereologist. The psychiatrist was an Indian, a Sikh, a Mr Singh. He wore a turban and looked rather solemn as he flipped through her personal file, sighing frequently.

'Are you pregnant, Lucy?'

'Should I be?'

'Lucy, tell me, did you deliberately send yourself to prison?'

'Yeah.'

'And do you regret it now?'

'I regretted it during "association" yesterday evening. There's a girl several cells down from me, she's a psycho and she dragged me into her room, her cell, and she began boasting to me what she'd done, and how she'd love to do it again, but they'd never pin it on her, she's in here for something else.'

Mr Singh looked even graver. 'Who is this girl?'

'No idea. Wouldn't tell you if I knew.'

'What did she claim she had done, Lucy?'

'She says it was years ago, when she was only twelve.

She was in a car with some blokes. They picked up a young woman in the early hours after she'd left a club. She says she stabbed her thirty-two times with a six-inch knife, through the ribs, in the heart, in the vagina and the anus. When it began to get light they left her body slumped against a cemetery wall. Four years later they haven't been able to pin it on anyone.'

'Hm.' Mr Singh was taking notes. 'There's a girl in your wing who has told that story to many inmates, usually newcomers. She enjoys threatening to kill them if they say a word. Correct?'

'Yeah.'

'She is a deeply disturbed person. Frankly, she should be in secure medical accommodation. The Governor has written many letters – but there are no beds. In our view, there is no evidence that she committed that crime, although the police confirm that such a terrible crime did take place. We believe she read about it in a newspaper and then fantasised her own involvement. Do you understand the word "fantasised"?'

'She says she can still hear the terrified screams of the woman she butchered. It turns her on. She'd love to do it again.'

'Yes, she always says that.'

Mr Singh then gently asked Lucy whether she regarded herself as someone likely to hurt herself. 'Are you at risk from yourself?'

'All the time. Story of my life.'

'What kind of injuries did you inflict on yourself?'

'Drugs. That's an injury, isn't it?'

'Yes.'

'Crime. That's another injury, isn't it?'

'Do you mean your motive was to hurt yourself, or do you mean that when you think about the victim—'

'No!' Lucy bit her nail. 'Do you have a detox unit here?'

'We'd have to send you back to Holloway. I advise you to kick your habit and to get out of prison as soon as you can. The worst thing about prison, in my considered experience, is not the confinement but the other prisoners. Many of the older ones are deeply disturbed people. But in general you will encounter too many cynical people for whom bullying, deceit and manipulation are the only way of life they know.'

'Or the only way of survival.'

'You are obviously an observant person gifted with intelligence and education.'

'I failed most of my GCSEs.'

'But deliberately. Try to apply your intelligence to yourself as well as about others.'

For a girl of seventeen, education classes were optional, but Lucy drifted in out of boredom. A very posh lady who – you couldn't believe it – turned out to be a prisoner and – out of this world – a 'lifer' as well, was offering a weekly class in clay modelling. This was Miss Agatha Cowdrey. She had exceptionally large yet delicate hands which enjoyed a magical interaction with clay. One minute it was just a soft, formless lump, and the next minute your face appeared in it. Then she taught you how to glaze and bake in the kiln which had been presented to Oak End by the charity Art Inside.

Lucy liked Miss Cowdrey at once. Miss Cowdrey was rather famous throughout the prison because she was so posh and addressed everyone as 'deah' – even some of the younger prison officers: though if she was cross with them, she addressed them as 'Miss Sharp' or 'Miss Simmonds', rarely getting the name right.

Miss Cowdrey was also famous because she had murdered her elderly cousin for her money. Miss Cowdrey said nothing about this when a prison officer was within earshot but, no sooner alone with Lucy, she fixed a steely gaze on her:

'You don't imagine I could do such a thing, do you, deah?'

'Oh . . . no.'

'I could never teach the fine arts to someone who doubted my complete innocence.'

David came to see Lucy; he never missed a visit, two a month. The prisoners and their visitors sat at separate tables in a large, airy room, leaning forward and lowering their voices, while a prison officer stood discreetly in a corner – watching. On the first occasion David turned up loaded with gifts, but Lucy had to explain what you could or couldn't bring to Oak End: almost anything to eat, chocolates, a cake, a fruit pie, would be torn to shreds or mangled to pulp by their fucking drug-search. Cigarettes, forget it! But books and money were OK, within the regulated limits, and phone cards were gold.

Brigid and Marcus had sent her curtains, pictures, a bedspread, cassette tapes.

David confided that his father was rumoured to be in line for a top legal job in the new government.

'We're moving from Cambridge to London.'

Lucy brought her small, chocolate-coloured features close to his and offered him a fierce scowl.

'Yeah? A big new job in the big new government, eh? Power! Money! Sir Paul, is it?'

'Dad calls it "translating principles into performance".'

'I know what I call it.'

'I can't blame him. It's his life. And I'm only my dad in transit.'

'Yeah? Meaning what?'

'They try to understand us, the aliens from their loins. We are programmed to be them, one day.'

'Not me, motherfucker!'

Since his suspension from the Crown Court, Marcus had spent most days alone. The hands of his beloved fob watch crept where previously they had cantered. He rarely went further than the corner shop to buy a newspaper or a packet of cigars. There were few visitors. He listened to messages for Brigid stacking up on her answerphone. His own mobile lay beside his work table, immobile. The friendships he had taken for granted withered on the dying vine of disgrace.

'Treason doth never prosper: what's the reason? For if it prosper, none dare call it treason.'

He read biographies of powerful men who had fallen from grace. He was now inhabiting his own St Helena. Disgraced and mothballed, Marcus Byron attempted to immerse himself in the doubtful pleasures of self-education: Beldam's *The Great Philosophers Made Easy* sat beside the biographies. A French philosopher called Descartes had come up with the brilliant (Beldam said) observation, 'I think therefore I am'. Sighing, and reaching for the whisky which had now infiltrated his day-time hours, Marcus arrived at his own version: I was therefore I am.

Would a change of government earn him a reprieve, a return to the Bench, to wig and gown? Brigid warned him that there was no such thing as gratitude in politics. 'If you steal a pound to give to a pauper, he will thank you, sir, but he will regard you as a thief and watch his own pockets when you are around.' She was right. A flamboyant, incautiously outspoken judge may have served the Opposition's purposes, but such a figure might appear too much of a good thing when the Opposition became the Government.

Though he fought against a corrosive lethargy, his mountain bike stood unused in the front hallway.

He brooded about his daughter Lucy. He cried. She had been refusing to see him. He enjoyed no parental right of access. A prisoner sees whom she chooses to see but only twice a month, until good conduct has doubled the entitlement. It was David she wanted to see.

Only Brigid Kyle's love consoled him. There wasn't a public figure in the land who didn't pray that the flame-haired journalist would overlook his stupidity, incompetence, hypocrisy or extramarital affairs. Composing her now-famous polemic, 'Asking for It', the *Sentinel*'s leading columnist took as her 'text' a recent event; a hospital doctor accused of raping a female colleague in a medical storeroom had argued in his defence that the young woman had consented to intercourse or, if he had misunderstood her signals, she was by her flirtatious demeanour 'asking for it'.

Brigid ran rapidly through a variety of cases in which men claimed that women had been 'asking for it'. She noted that women 'asked for it' even when it was admitted that they had not 'asked for it', indeed had explicitly asked for it not to happen, but evidently the very existence of an attractive female put a certain type of male beyond self-control, he just couldn't help himself, his free will evaporated as if under hypnosis, or drug chemistry – and the woman ought to know that. If her body, her legs, her breasts, her smile were unbearably provocative, arousing, to men, or some men, or to this one man now in the dock of the Old Bailey, then the woman ought to know that and do something about it.

Like what? asked Brigid Kyle sardonically.

Vanish? Vaporise herself? Wear a nun's habit?

Well, there she was in court, the victim, the woman

doctor with long raven hair, eyelashes to match, earrings, wearing a two-piece suit in black leather. So what did the defendant's counsel, Antony Laughton QC, say to the jury?

'Is it altogether fair that a young lady who clearly and obviously dresses to beguile the opposite sex, the queen bee attracting the drones, the young woman who is attractive in a definite sort of way, which sends a signal, should suddenly decide to cry foul because somebody finds her attractive?'

Brigid's fingers paused for a moment over the keyboard. Marcus was standing behind her, a paisley dressing gown hanging loose from his broad shoulders, and wearing nothing underneath. His hand had begun to caress her neck.

'Marcus, let me finish.'

'You have style, Kyle.'

'Style, Marcus?'

'Yeah, style as a writer, style as a cook, style in bed. And you're asking for it.'

A month after the general election Marcus Byron was reinstated as an active member of the Crown Court circuit, by the new Lord Chancellor. It had been widely predicted in the media.

Brigid hugged him and buried her misgivings. She feared that while Lucy remained in prison, Marcus would encounter painful inhibitions about sending women into custody, especially – though it was never for the judge to decide – if they might be sent to Oak End. But Brigid knew how he yearned to stride, once again, across the world's stage.

Marcus's return to the bench was reported by the press as a national event. Here was a judge who had outspokenly broken the 'rules', flouting the élitist codes, the conspiracy of silence, that left the suffering public helpless before the criminals. There was scarcely a household in the land, from the manor houses to Eden Manor, where his suspension from the Crown Court had not aroused heated debate.

Journalists and television cameras gathered on the street outside the handsome house in Pimlico he shared with Brigid Kyle.

'Do you feel that your suspension was justified?'

'I believe that the previous Lord Chancellor had no alternative, in the circumstances.'

'So why is it right to restore you to the bench now?'

'Time heals. Things have moved on.'

'Does that mean that this is a political decision?'

He smiled warily. 'You'd better ask the politicians.'

'Do you have political ambitions?'

'No.'

'What can you say about your marriage to Louise Pointer?'

'We are separated.'

'Do you intend a divorce?'

'That is a private matter between ourselves.'

'Your own daughter is in jail for robbery.'

'I see no connection.'

'The next woman you sentence to custody may end up alongside your daughter and looking for vengeance?'

This was the thrust he dreaded; the one that Brigid had warned him would come up. The new Lord Chancellor had made the same point to him, privately: 'Would you be inhibited?' Part of him had thought 'yes' but the whole of him had said 'no'.

Even Brigid had counselled him to stay off the bench until Lucy came out.

'Is it true,' asked Auriol Johnson, 'that your daughter has been refusing visits from you?'

'I think that is equally a private matter,' he snapped back, and strode towards his car, smarting.

His return to the Crown Court did not produce (as *Private Eye* had wittily predicted) 'a doubling of the prison population within the week – women excepted'. The new Judge Byron struck the lawyers in the well of the court as careful and reflective. 'It won't last,' a QC told Sarah Woods in the corridor. 'He loves to punish.'

For his Honour, meanwhile, the routine of Great North Crown Court is pleasantly familiar. There, beneath him, sits the faithful stenographer rattling away with her gaze calmly fixed on whoever is speaking, as if she is lipreading as well as listening. The wood panelling and the elaborate levels, his Honour up top like some black god in a ceiling fresco, the clerk directly beneath his Honour, anticipating every decision, whispering into a telephone to fix future hearings and trial dates.

At the lunch interval Marcus courteously conducts two lay justices, who are sitting with him on appeals from the magistrates courts, through the long, high corridors hung with solemn portraits of the good and great, to the judges' dining room, a magnificent period piece constructed in the heyday of Empire. The judges take their aperitifs standing before sitting down for lunch. Judges Worple and Sawyer greet him with casual affability, as if he has never been away. As if Sawyer had not sent Lucy to jail. Nothing is mentioned, not a murmur.

Marcus is a relaxed, affable host to his lay colleagues. 'The big difficulty here is getting out of the building after five o'clock,' he confides. 'You may find the court respectfully rising for you one moment, and the next you are scurrying around picking up phones on empty desks and begging to be let out. You may end up scrambling through the crowd of defendants and lawyers.' He chuckles. 'Not always a comfortable exit.'

By mid-afternoon he is frequently berating the Crown prosecutors for failing to produce documents from the filing system.

A short, thickset and very correct man from Birmingham appears. He has been ordered to pay £850 compensation to a woman whose jaw he allegedly broke. He admits the assault was unforgivable but he has not been able to obtain certified medical evidence that her jaw was actually broken. His letters to the CPS have gone unanswered and his phone calls met with a curt 'Call you back' which never happened.

Marcus growls at the prosecuting barrister and grants the man his travelling expenses.

'Adjourn. We agree that evidence will be served in this

court. Find a date in four weeks,' he tells his clerk, seated beneath him. As usual, the clerk has already anticipated his decision. Clerks in magistrates courts are qualified lawyers; here they are unqualified mind-readers who know a judge like a jockey knows a horse.

Standing before him now is a young Asian, very nervous, having pleaded guilty to domestic burglary. This case is not an appeal but for sentence, having been committed to the Crown Court. No need to require the young Asian to testify; no need for the usher to put a Koran in his hand and require him to read from a printed card: 'I promise before Allah that I will truthfully answer any question that I am asked.'

Marcus and his lay colleagues leaf through the pre-sentence report from the Probation Service while listening to a brief resumé of the facts by the prosecutor. An elderly woman of seventy-five had been terrified to hear her doorbell ringing in the middle of the night. Then she saw the handle of her locked bedroom door turning. She was able to dial 999. The young Asian was found in a garden shed along with her television set and radio. Nothing of great value stolen but nevertheless a domestic burglary and aggravated by two factors: done at night and with the occupant, an old lady, terrified in her own home.

A junior barrister from Antony Laughton's chambers is addressing them:

'I realise that your Honour and your colleagues may have difficulty in not imposing a custodial sentence but this is a first offence, a young man of good character, not very bright if I may say so, a moment of weakness after he lost his job as a car mechanic through, may I add, no fault of his own – the entire garage closed down. He has done nothing since.'

Marcus nods. 'We'll retire.'

'Court stand!' cries the usher.

Normally, sitting alone, Marcus wouldn't need more than a moment before settling a case like this, but he's conscious that he has tended throughout the day to take his two lay colleagues somewhat for granted, and now he is determined to give them their head in the retiring room. Which is his office.

Reaching it, he seats them and offers a courteous apology.

'After all, you justices give your time and your talents to society for no material reward.'

The male justice quickly demurs and declares himself to have been properly consulted, but the lady is prickly:

'Just a glance from you, Judge Byron, so that one could have caught your eye from time to time, would have been appreciated.'

'I plead guilty, Mrs Brown.'

'Lady Braun.'

'I apologise again. It's no excuse, but I sit nine days out of ten alone and—'

(She must know that during the past six months he hasn't been sitting at all.)

'Perhaps we should discuss the present case,' Lady Braun says. He can guess that she chairs the bench in her magistrates court; doesn't like playing second fiddle; and doesn't like what she has read about Marcus Byron.

'Of course. What is your view, Lady Braun?'

It turns out to be a somewhat lengthy view, quite correct, accurate, balanced and she's certainly not amateurish about the law – but it's all in Marcus's head, it's *understood*, does it need spelling out?

He turns to the male justice, whose grave expression conveys doubt.

'Mr Jackson?'

'I agree entirely with my colleague. But I do think we are dealing with a rather simple-minded young man of previously good character. And he did plead guilty.'

'At the eleventh hour,' Lady Braun objects, 'when all the witnesses were in place.'

Marcus's gaze remains fixed on Mr Jackson. 'What would you give him?'

Mr Jackson hesitates. Crown Court judges are notoriously more harsh than magistrates in sentencing. He doesn't want to appear soft because the Home Secretary and the press are constantly telling him not to be. On the other hand—

'In this case I would prefer a non-custodial sentence. Say one hundred hours of Community Service. Plus compensation.'

'Compensation?' Marcus asks him. 'All the stolen goods were recovered and restored to the old lady. You may have in mind some kind of compensation for the fright she suffered – it could have killed her. Weed her garden? We don't know whether she has one. Paint the front of her house? She's not likely to be the owner.'

'We have to stamp on domestic burglary,' Lady Braun says, 'particularly when aggravated.'

Marcus agrees. But somehow he doesn't want to agree with Lady Braun. He rather likes Mr Jackson's attitude. Would prison do this young Asian anything but harm?

Lady Braun almost reads his thoughts – perhaps they're in his big, handsome, too-famous black features.

'We're never dealing with a particular defendant alone,' she says. 'We have to send a clear message to potential burglars – and to society, the victims.'

Marcus sighs inwardly. Quite right. Doesn't like Lady Braun. Would rather go to bed with the young Asian burglar.

'How long inside?' he asks Lady Braun.

'Two years.'

'First offence,' Marcus reminds her. 'No previous.'

'That's why I didn't say three years.'

She's right! The bitch! Two years would have been his own sentence, straight away, off his starched cuff, if he'd been sitting alone. But he has respect for Mr Jackson – there are ways and ways of looking at things. Isn't that the problem with all these demagogic Home Secretaries, Jeremy Darling and now, since the election, Ben Diamond – they want to rob the judiciary of its independence of judgment.

They return to court.

'Court stand!'

The bench sits. The young Asian remains standing in the dock. It will be one year inside.

Later, after his lay colleagues had fought their way out of the vast building, Marcus was seated at his desk, signing warrants and sipping a very small whisky, when the telephone rang.

It was the Home Secretary, the Rt Hon Ben Diamond, on the line.

'I need to talk to you,' said Big Ben, 'as soon as possible.'

'Yeah?'

'Not a word about this to anyone. And I do mean anyone. Agreed?'

Charco's gang have dragged Jenny to the strip of deserted wasteland bordering the water. Kneeling and weeping in terror on the banks of Great North's stagnant canal, the old cliché keeps somersaulting in her aching head: rape is a fate better than death.

'Please,' she begs, 'please don't.'

In human beings there is always a space for decency, for sentiment – for mercy. These, surely, are just ordinary boys. They all, without exception, have mothers – somewhere. But where?

Five

Sarah Woods took an internal call from the reception desk at Chapman & Burnett. One of her clients had turned up, without an appointment, and 'very nervous'. Could he see her at once? For Sarah, this was par for the course – some made appointments from their stolen mobile phones but mostly they just came, insisting on an immediate audience. They were always in a hurry, often with good reason.

Tony Marquez entered her office wearing a baseball cap and a huge pair of dark glasses. Politely he removed the cap and then, after a moment's hesitation, the shades – a rare concession to courtesy among her boys. She'd always rather liked Tony. All his offences had been non-violent, he was never found carrying a weapon, and she felt that it was only through distant family links and antecedents that he had unfortunately fallen in with Charco Rios. But that, he had sworn on his mother's name, was in the past.

'Hullo, Tony. Sit down. I thought you were going straight.'

'I am, Miss Woods, God help me that's the truth.'

She took his file from a steel cabinet and quickly flipped through Tony's 'history', his 'previous'.

'No charges against you for almost a year. Last year you were given a six months' supervision order for handling stolen goods – second such offence. Your social worker, Hubert Hare, writes to say you have completed the order and made good progress in confronting the causes of your offending.' She sighed. 'So what's new, Tony?'

'I ain't done nothing, Miss Woods.'

'Hm? So what brings you here in such a hurry?'

'It's something I heard, like.'

'Overheard, you mean?'

'I've had this job in the pool hall for six months, right? General cleaning and tidying up, like.'

'And what are they accusing you of?'

'Like I said, Miss Woods, nothing. You remember I used to run around with Charco and his pals Miguel and Gregory?'

'They robbed and you handled?'

'Yeah, well . . . Anyway, Miguel and Gregory, they turned up in the pool hall and played some balls, then they came across to me and started bragging.'

'What about?'

'What they'd done.'

Tony stopped. His hands were shaking. He glanced towards the door of Sarah's office as if calculating his chances of making an escape. Sarah waited.

'It's the murder of that bloke,' Tony murmured.

'Which bloke, Tony?'

'That Headmaster.'

'Edward Carr?'

'Yeah. Outside the school. Miguel and Gregory were boasting how they'd gone with Charco to beat up a boy with a dumb-bell because he'd done Miguel over, and then this bloke had run out, they didn't know who he was, to try and break it up.'

Sarah was taking notes now, even though it added to Tony's nervousness.

'I don't want none of this written down, like, Miss Woods.'

'It's for my eyes only, Tony. Go on with your story.'

'It ain't no story, it's the truth, on my mum's name. Then Miguel, he started boasting to me how they were on TV news every night, and how the BBC, Carlton and Sky couldn't put a name to them, or a face, because the pigs were still running in circles eating their own tails.'

'Yes, I see. But there's one thing you haven't mentioned – did they say who killed Edward Carr?'

Tony Marquez swallowed hard. 'I hear there's a big money reward from that computer games tycoon.'

She smiled.

'It's not the money, Miss Woods, honest, I'm telling you on my mum's name, I was shocked by that killing like everyone else.'

'So why have you come to me?'

He twisted his cap in his lap, eyes down, adam's apple still pumping.

'Thought you might pass on what I've told you.'

'Tell the police, you mean?'

He nodded.

'You're afraid to do so yourself? And probably with good reason.'

He nodded again, his tongue sliding over dry lips.

'Thing is, Miss Woods, the pigs, I mean the police, they'd believe you, like, and no one need ever know it was me, and then you could make sure I got the reward, like.'

'Tony, your evidence is useless unless you allow yourself to be interviewed by the police. They'll need to cross-examine you. If they bring in Miguel and Gregory, they'll almost certainly insist you attend an identification parade.'

'Yeah.' Tony twirled his baseball cap. 'I'm not going to no police station.'

'That's not a problem. Plainclothes detectives could take a statement from you at home.' She glanced inside her Tony Marquez folder. 'Where are you living now? Still at 57 Emerson Court, Great North?'

'Yeah.'

'Still living with your mum and the two younger ones?'

'Yeah. I'm not having the pigs come to our place.'

'The pool hall where you work?'

'No way! Too many of Charco's lads around there. See, thing is, like, I'm thinking here.'

For a moment she didn't catch his syntax.

'Here, Tony? You want me to bring the police to interview you here?'

'Yeah, you could represent me, like.'

'Tony, you'd be a witness not a defendant. Witnesses are not "represented".'

But even as she spoke she wondered. Supposing Tony had in fact been involved in the murder of Edward Carr and was now trying to shop his friends because he couldn't resist the lure of the £100,000? Or the police might take that view and arrest Tony, bring a charge even, to increase the pressure on him. Tony, after all, was not the ideal citizen stepping forward bravely in the interests of justice: Tony had a record, and every item on that record linked him to Charco, Miguel and Gregory.

So maybe he did need to be 'represented'. But invite the police here, to the offices of Chapman & Burnett? Sarah and her colleagues were defence solicitors and their livelihood depended on the clients' absolute trust.

Oliver, too, kept crossing her mind, though hazily. Charco Rios was Oliver's client. If Sarah took Tony to the police, Charco would find out sooner or later. Charco was well aware of her relationship to Oliver – all these street-wise kids were fast on to things like that. Her imagination saw the unrecovered knife penetrating Oliver where it had pierced Edward Carr – through the heart.

But Edward Carr had been murdered – a crime that had shocked and shook the nation. As a decent citizen she had no right to withhold information. She might, later, even be charged with something threatening to her professional standing.

No, not really: Tony was her client and all conversations with clients are privileged.

'Tony,' she said, 'I'd like to help you if I could but my hands are tied by my code of practice.'

He stood up, crestfallen. 'So what do I do, Miss Woods?'

'If you want to call in the police, they'll insist on visiting the pool hall where your conversation with Miguel and Gregory took place. I think you would have to leave your employment there immediately, and I also think that you would have to request police protection for yourself and your family.'

His baseball cap was back on his head. 'Yeah. Can you help me out on that, Miss Woods? I mean, like, you know the right ones to talk to.'

'Definitely not.'

'So I'm on my own?'

'I'm sorry. You can always avoid all risk to yourself by doing nothing and keeping your mouth shut.'

'That's what you're advising, is it?'

'I'm not advising anything, Tony.'

Sarah took her lunch break a couple of hours after Tony had followed his baseball cap out of her office into his own painfully lonely dilemma: fear and greed. Yes, she quite liked this youth, but by the lunch hour she had discovered where her moral obligations lay – and she had also decided to consult none of her seniors or colleagues. If Tony Marquez's evidence could assist the police in bringing Edward Carr's killer to justice, then her duty as a citizen must prevail.

She alighted from the bus a good mile from the premises of Chapman & Burnett, in an area with a different telephone dialling code, at a busy intersection which now paraded four modern booths.

She dialled 999, asked for police, then the special hotline number allocated to the Edward Carr case. She was put through immediately.

'Edward Carr hotline, can I help you?'

'Yes, I have information on a potential witness.'

But the response to this was profoundly disconcerting.

'Your name and current address, please, madam.'

'This is an anonymous call,' she insisted.

'I'm sorry, madam, we need a reference.'

'But the police have given press conferences inviting anonymous calls from the public.'

'Madam, we simply guarantee anonymity to the caller. There's no shortage of hoax calls on a case like this. We also receive deliberately misleading information.'

Panic seized her. They could trace her booth in seconds and send a patrol car and—

But what she then overheard was fragments of a rather bored, obtuse conversation in the police inquiry room. 'There's this woman who doesn't want . . . her name . . . She says . . . Sounds educated.'

A male voice came on line. 'Madam?'

'Yes, I'm still here, though it's a miracle.'

'I understand you have information you can give us.'

'Yes, I do. It's about a potential witness in the Edward Carr case, a pool hall employee called Tony Marquez.'

'How do you spell that?'

'M-A-R-Q-U-E-Z.'

119

'And your information, madam?'

'I have reason to believe he may be able to assist you with your inquiries.'

'Can you explain the source of your information, madam?'

'No.'

'Do you have an address for this Marquez?'

'No, but I believe he works in a pool hall in Great North.'

'Name?'

'That I don't know.'

'If you have reason to assist us further, can you please quote the reference number now logged against the present call?'

She took it down in her diary and rang off. Then she committed it to memory – she had a knack with numbers.

She had barely stood herself at the bus stop for the return journey, some fifty yards from the telephone booth, when a patrol car glided round the corner and parked. A female officer emerged from the front passenger seat and went inside the booth to check the number.

No bus in view, Sarah decided that she needed more black tights and disappeared into a department store.

Working late that evening, she wrote an unsigned letter on un-letterheaded paper to the Commissioner of the Metropolitan Police. Finding a pair of plastic washing-up gloves in the firm's kitchenette, she put them on before handling paper and envelope. Writing fast – no revisions needed – Sarah Woods described the police's behaviour in sending a patrol car to the telephone booth as 'an absolute betrayal of promises made to the public', 'an infringement of civil rights', and an 'absolute disgrace'. She copied the text on to a 3.5 inch floppy disk but took care not to register it on the main-frame hard disk. The floppy went into her handbag. Even the postage stamp she attached to the envelope was held in gloved hands, using water to lubricate the sticky side rather than saliva. She broke her journey home at a post box far from the office.

The new Home Secretary, Ben Diamond, had culti-vated a public image as hard as nails, among the biggest of the Boy's big hitters. Brigid had first studied Ben's campaigning style during the last Euro elections. Party headquarters had fastened its Cyclops eye on a number of edible constituencies. The candidates for the European Parliament were scarcely known to public or press, but the party perched them on the shoulders of the big barons – and no baron loved campaigning more than Big Ben. Heading for the open markets, he launched straight into his music hall act, heckling his audience, jabbing a finger at 'You, madam' and 'You, sir'.

'Isn't this Tory Government the worst since records began?' Next came his xenophobic anti-Brussels routine, mocking the bureaucrats of EuroDisneyland. 'They won't be content, madam, until they make us eat straight bananas and cucumbers.'

There followed a ritualistic tribute to the last Labour leader, taken by death, bringing to Brigid's mind a phrase she knew she couldn't use: 'Tactical voting is reinforced by tactical grieving.'

At this juncture an elderly bloke who might or might not have been drunk, but who knew the music halls as well as Ben, began heckling:

'I haven't voted Labour since I dropped a pound note and Harold Wilson pocketed it.'

'Try it on me, sir,' Ben shot back – meaning that pound notes had been abolished.

Later Brigid had followed Ben to a meeting of senior citizens – mainly women. A lady asked why the Labour Party had given away the empire and let in 'people we don't want'. The next lady hoped Ben was going to abolish the European Parliament. Then all the ladies were humming indignantly about the recent European Court of Justice ruling in favour of women who had been dismissed from the British army when they became pregnant.

Women, reflected Brigid, beware ladies. The temperature mounted (though genteelly) as French farmers burned alive our sheep, Germans banned our infected beef, and our livestock in transit suffered the old Continental cruelties. This led on to the Spanish habit of beating donkeys and – if Brigid grasped the point – of photographing apes whether they consented or not. Having taken away our national passports, the donkey-beaters would soon be off with our pounds.

Like Harold Wilson.

Ben laughed, he beamed assent, he couldn't agree more, with everyone about everything, but – he sternly warned, wagging a finger in admonishment, remembering that British electors admire a touch of steel – Europe was 'a mess we have to clean up, not turn our backs on. It won't go away'.

Ben was coming across as tough, efficient, strong-willed, a man for all seasons. The man to kick-start the Boy's new image campaign to get across the Big Picture.

The Boy let it be known that Ben Can Handle It.

Handle crime. Get it down.

And Ben wanted Marcus Byron on board his Master Action Plan.

Nothing aggravates the press like a story that has been kept from them. It is their version of aggravated burglary. Brigid knew the truth, of course, but was the soul of discretion. Ben Diamond wanted Marcus to chair a newly empowered Criminal Law Commission.

'You know the inevitable price of secrecy, my darling? When they catch on, they'll fasten their teeth in the "conspiracy" and shake it, day by day, playfully and malevolently, like a cat with a half-dead mouse clamped between its teeth.'

'Yeah.'

Marcus Byron's clandestine meetings with the Home Secretary and senior Home Office officials were carefully shielded from the media. Forbidden to travel in his own Rolls, MB1, Marcus was whisked out of London in a limousine whose smoke-tinted windows yielded no hint of the famous black judge within.

The first meeting took place in the private dining

room of one of Surrey's most charming riverside pubs. Marcus recognised the forecourt as soon as he stepped out of the car: this was Tyndale, where he had been led into a fatal trap by the Congress for Justice one summer afternoon, resulting in another deadly whirl of headlines. Marcus could guess that Ben Diamond remained ignorant of the connection; evidently there were officials within the Home Office at 50 Queen Anne's Gate who did not want Marcus to forget that their memories were long. They were back into the timeless civil service game of thwarting their new master by 'Yes, Minister, but—' To the Oxbridge-educated bureaucratic mind, Marcus Byron had become an Untouchable. Judges should not have daughters in prison. Even his recent reinstatement as a Crown Court circuit judge was deemed a mistake – but a relatively harmless one.

A crucial role in policy-making was another matter.

Marcus knew Ben Diamond less well than dear old Max Venables, the Shadow Home Secretary adroitly disposed of by the Boy the morning after the general election. Max was deemed too soft, he couldn't entirely shake off his liberal heritage, so he was ditched. His little goatee beard was now lost somewhere in the back benches of the House.

Brigid doubted whether Big Ben knew what he was up against, not only within the Home Office but throughout the criminal justice system.

'Don't say yes,' she had warned Marcus ahead of the first clandestine meeting at Tyndale.

He chuckled. 'Did I ever say yes to anyone but you?'

'Now, you listen to me, Marcus Byron. Normally they would opt for a very senior High Court judge, so why do they want you?'

What most encouraged Marcus was the appointment of his friend Paul Glass as Special Adviser to the Home Office's Criminal Policy Directorate. Both he and Paul had been devoted pupils of the brilliant and eccentric Oxford jurist, the late lamented Geoffrey Villiers. Plucked from his Cambridge fellowship in Criminology, Paul was strongly supporting Marcus's appointment.

'You and I will work in tandem,' Ben Diamond was explaining to Marcus, leaning across the table with beguiling sincerity, 'to break the vested interests and crack heads. English law is not only a thousand years old but several centuries back from modernity. There have been endless reforms but nothing has really changed.'

'Yeah,' Marcus agreed, 'the devil is always in the detail. The big hunting eye sweeps the horizon, looking for the heavy kill, and doesn't notice the termites.'

Ben Diamond nodded appreciatively. His own man, he esteemed men who were their own man. 'That's why, Marcus, we want you to head up a new Criminal Law Commission.'

'Yeah? What's the matter with the one we've got?'

'Everything. But that's strictly off the record.'

'Everything said here is strictly off the record,' added one of Ben's four Private Secretaries, pointing his thin nose at Marcus.

'It's not simply a matter of personnel,' Ben said. 'It's a question of powers. What the Government wants is less paper and more speed. The new Criminal Law Commission will propose and I will dispose – and fast.'

'Of course,' the Private Secretary interposed, 'the Secretary of State will still request the advice of the Home Office before he introduces legislation.'

Scrutinising the carefully reserved expressions of the senior officials sipping orange juice and mineral water around the table of the Tyndale Arms, Marcus shared Brigid's misgivings. Their heads nodded obediently whenever the Home Secretary beat out his 'points of policy', but their fathomless eyes did not nod.

He lit his pipe now, without asking permission, the only overt smoker round the table. Ben didn't smoke and didn't believe that smoking was part of tomorrow's Big Picture. As the rich aroma of Alfred Dunhill's Baby's Bottom tobacco filled the room, it became apparent that Marcus Byron was in no hurry to sign up for the job. Wasn't he perfectly content to be back on the Crown Court? Did his ambitions reach beyond that?

'Don't say yes,' Brigid had begged him. 'Think twice, my darling!'

He had sighed. 'Why did I fall in love with an Irish fire-eater with gorgeous red hair and a body out of the movies? Love is always a mistake.'

'You mean lust.'

'Did I ever lay a hand on you?'

She knew in her heart's knowledge that he would say yes to Ben Diamond, eventually – just as he would stare, like a small boy, at a beautiful mountain bike in a shop window, swearing not to buy it, until one day it was there, in the front hall.

'I want to work with Ben,' Marcus had admitted, 'even if we get only half of what we both believe in.'

'Half's a lot, Marcus.'

Paul Glass's son David and Marcus's daughter Lucy had discovered mutual love, slowly and diffidently, the previous summer while resisting Mammon in the Wiltshire Tree Camp.

Arrested for trespass in and around the camp, most of the New Age Travellers instructed a London firm of solicitors known for its expertise in this uncertain area of law. Chapman & Burnett sent Sarah Woods to represent batches of defendants passing through the local legal sausage machine.

David Glass had been charged with obstructing bail-iffs. In his case it was a first offence and the police would have settled for a caution if David had been prepared to co-operate. A caution requires the consent of both parties. David was fiercely loyal to Traveller doctrine: make them prosecute. Fill the courts.

'Every case similar to yours,' Sarah warned him, 'has resulted in a conviction – except on two occasions, when technical questions of identity prevailed.'

'Fine. Let them convict me.'

'Then you will have a criminal record to plague you.'

'It's no skin off my nose. Listen: a friend of mine did accept a police caution because he'd got himself into a mess over working for exams. He was hectored for ten minutes by an Inspector who reminded him of Adolf Hitler.'

Sarah was not to be swayed. Her steady brown eyes remained fixed on him through the large, oval lenses.

'The police have conducted several experiments in cautioning techniques. Some youngsters get the Hitler treatment, while others are treated to a softly-softly visit from a WPC, who knocks politely on the family door and gently explains the advantages of keeping out of trouble. "And if there's any help you need, do ring this number." Right?'

'So?'

'Six months later, another officer visits all the cautioned kids and their families. He asks what they can remember of what was said to them when they were cautioned. All of PC Hitler's victims recall every word, but none of WPC Softly-Softly's clients can remember very much.'

'I remember Dad mentioning it.'

'It was your father who wrote up the findings in the *English Law Review*.'

David smiled ruefully. 'He's a hard liner – just like my friend Lucy's dad.'

'But you won't accept a caution?'

'Lucy would despise me.'

'Ah.'

In the event, a minor trespass charge against David

Glass was dismissed by Wiltshire magistrates after Sarah had addressed them, eloquently stressing his excellent family background and unimpeachable character.

'Does this sincere, idealistic young man, with his fine prospects, who deeply regrets what he has done, deserve to be damned by a criminal record?'

Sarah hated to pander to the perverse logic of the rural courts, and sometimes even the more progressive Inner London ones, by which a young person of 'good' family was treated more leniently than one whose over-stretched mum was permanently on benefit and changed her partner every few months. But Sarah's only duty was to her client.

It was through David's influence that Sarah later came to be Lucy's solicitor as well. David recommended Sarah Woods to Lucy during his second visit to Oak End prison, by which time Lucy was feeling less truculent than when she had stood up in the Crown Court and incriminated herself.

'Sarah is definitely progressive,' David assured her, then hesitated. 'She doesn't much care for your dad, either.'

Sarah, too, had hesitated to take on Lucy as a client. 'Hot potato but interesting,' was Oliver's comment. 'After all, how many of our clients insist on going inside? Besides, Marcus Byron and Brigid Kyle will invite you to dinner. I hope you'll take your partner along – if you have one.'

Oliver was right: you couldn't resist getting involved with somebody as enigmatic as the self-wounding Lucy

Byron. Lucy wasn't Luke Grant, rapist. She wasn't that vicious little Filipino, Ally Leagum.

On arrival at Oak End, Sarah was subjected to the same humiliating search procedure that Home Secretary Jeremy Darling had imposed on all visitors. Two or three cases where solicitors were proven to have smuggled in illegal substances were enough. A female prison officer required her to sit down and remove her shoes. Not only were the insides examined but also the soles of her feet. The officer ran a finger inside Sarah's bra. Then a drug detection dog subjected her to a thorough sniffing. She began to laugh as the alternative to screaming.

Sarah's first meeting with Lucy took place in a Visit Centre monitored by closed circuit television on the alert for incoming drugs. Sarah had arrived at Oak End burdened by files on half a dozen cases, but a prisoner has time on her hands, and the garrulous Lucy took pleasure in grilling Sarah about her beliefs.

'What are your convictions, Ms Woods? Mine are drugs and robbery.'

'My convictions, Lucy? I believe in instant capital punishment for girls who rob actresses that their dad dived into bed with. After all, if he hadn't loved women, in one case your mother, you wouldn't be floating around, making a fool of yourself, and behaving like an arsehole, would you?'

Lucy was stunned. 'Fuck yourself,' she murmured.

'Here and now?'

Ten minutes later (time was up), Lucy said, 'You're on.'

'You mightn't be so lucky,' Sarah said.

'I'm the ideal client. I'll be in trouble the rest of my life. Guaranteed. So where's the spliff? Where's the joints? Don't look so shocked. What's the use of a solicitor if she doesn't bring the stuff?'

A few days later, Sarah received a phone call from Judge Byron. Oliver had predicted it: 'He'll be straight up your skirt.'

'Thank God,' Marcus had said, 'that at long last Lucy is out of the hands of dishonest lawyers dedicated to their own devious ends – and to my destruction.'

It was a powerful, intimidating baritone. Sarah had often bowed to it when leaving the Crown Court.

'I'll do my best for her, Judge Byron.'

'Please call me Marcus. She needs a young solicitor, and a woman. But gaining her confidence will be hard work. Uphill.'

He did not add that he remembered Sarah as an attractive woman appearing in the Crown Court, seated in front of counsel, leaning back to whisper information or to point out vital facts contained in the 'bundle' (the prosecution's advance information) which the bewigged QC or his junior has been too in haste to absorb. Marcus understood that a good solicitor gets to know her young clients, absorbs their chaotic lives, their lies and denials. The barrister, by contrast, is paid huge fees never to go near a client.

Sarah made a point of visiting Lucy in Oak End at least once a month. She encountered a temperament of violent mood swings, a dreamy smile one moment, a tight coil of barbed wire the next. Lucy would talk intelligently about an appeal, then deny that she'd ever considered it.

'Appeals are gravy for lawyers!' Lucy mocked.

'Well, you'd probably be out on probation by the time it was heard.'

Soon after the general election and Ben Diamond's journey to the Palace to be sworn in as a Privy Councillor, the automatic strip searches ended at Oak End and other prisons.

Lucy was now allowing her father the occasional visit. Sarah became deeply concerned about the effect on Lucy's relationship with other prisoners. The arrival of the famous black judge rapidly became news throughout the prison. Old resentments flared up among the women he had sentenced. On one occasion, after MB1 had glided away, Lucy was assaulted in the dining room by a woman from one of the adult wings. This was Mo Cripps, whom Judge Byron had sentenced to twenty years after a jury found her guilty of causing death by arson. Cripps was alleged to have poured petrol through the front door of a council house and set it alight, killing a young mother and her two infant children. This followed a feud over the young mother's common-law husband, with whom Cripps had been having an affair. Fire crews had found the burned body of the mother, her arms outstretched over the younger of her children; the other child lay only feet away, huddled below the bedroom window.

Now Mo Cripps came across from her table to Lucy's, picked up her full plate, and threw it in her face.

'Give that to the fucking judge, you bitch!'

Lucy had to be rushed to the Health Centre to have her burns treated.

Governor Mary Heatherington informed Sarah that under rule 43 she had twice been forced to place Lucy in the segregation unit as a prisoner 'at risk'. Lacking the separate 'at risk' units found in the larger male prisons, Oak End was forced to impose on the victim the same lonely regime as her tormentors.

'And I must advise you, Miss Woods, that every visit Judge Byron makes to Lucy only worsens her plight. A transfer to Bullwood Hall in Essex would merely replicate her predicament. Quite frankly, she would be better off in a Northern prison, like Style, outside Judge Byron's circuit.'

'Yes, but—'

'I understand all the "buts" of such a transfer: too far to travel for Lucy's friend David – and for you.'

'That may be why Lucy hasn't told me that she is being victimised,' Sarah said. 'Have you informed Judge Byron?'

'That's your job, Miss Woods.'

On one occasion Marcus persuaded Sarah to travel with him to Oak End in the Rolls. She preferred the train – you could work on a train. Even before they left the outer suburbs of West London behind them, Sarah discovered that Lucy was not the sole subject on Judge Byron's mind. His left hand frequently strayed from the wheel; nothing outrageous, nothing high on the thigh, but certainly enough for a sexual harassment complaint by a young female barrister if Marcus had been her pupil master or head of her chambers. But he wasn't, he was merely father to her client.

She didn't tell Oliver. He would have enjoyed every detail and she wasn't having him enjoying himself. Oliver had been annoying her again – about a large painting she'd bought. Sarah liked spending money on what Oliver called 'bad paintings by charlatans'. A reproduction Monet or Manet was good enough for him, though he grumbled at the framing fees, but Sarah had once been an art student at the Chelsea and she believed in 'living art'.

Which Oliver interpreted as 'artists you've rogered, most of them called Ivan'.

Oliver's working life had become unpleasantly dominated by his least favourite client, Charco Rios.

Following the murder of the Headmaster, Edward Carr, the police, acting on rumours among pupils of St James's School and wider circles of gangland kids, had turned the Rios council flat inside out, finding nothing. No knife, no leads. The family shrugged and gestured helplessly – they knew nothing and didn't understand much English anyway. Father in jail. Charco's self-assurance increased after he was brought in for questioning, interrogated for four hours, then released without charge. No witness had dared come forward to identify him as the killer – despite the huge reward offered by the computer games magnate.

Oliver had been present throughout the formal inter-rogation. Having been exposed to a large number of cynical youths, Oliver had no hesitation in rating Charco the least endearing he had ever met. Charco's criminal record, which included ABH with a knife, had little to do with Oliver's dislike of this arrogant, sneering youth. Advising Charco to say nothing during his formal inter-view was never an option. Charco Rios was too cocksure to remain silent. He knew nothing at all about the fatal stabbing of Edward Carr. So fuck you. He hadn't been there, had he? So fuck you. Nowhere near the scene of the crime. Miles away, in fact. So fuck off.

But where had he been? The police pressed him for an answer. He shrugged. Who can be expected to fucking remember what he fucking did, where he fucking went, on any day just like another? All he knew for certain was what he didn't do – and where he wasn't. So fuck you.

Oliver concluded that Charco was too shrewd to go in for investigatable alibis involving others. He pre-ferred the security of his own head, his own forget-fulness.

Months passed – no arrests. Then one morning Charco Rios appeared in Oliver's office, without appoint-ment or warning. He was followed in by the firm's flustered receptionist.

'Mr Rawl, this young man just barged straight past me. I tried to tell him. Do you want me to call the police, Mr Rawl?'

'No need, Lizzie.'

'You're sure?'

When she had closed the door behind her, still trembling with shock (though a receptionist at Hawthorne & Moss isn't exactly a stranger to rough types and irregular behaviour), Oliver asked Charco why he wanted to antagonise the people who were trying to help him.

'Gotta see you fast, so don't mess me about, got it?'

Without invitation he sat himself down. Despite the cockily crossed legs, the waggling trainers and the rapid mastication of gum, Charco Rios was obviously nervous. Very.

'Is that how your mother taught you to address people?' Oliver asked.

Charco leapt up. 'Leave my mum out of this, fucker!'

'What about your father then?' Oliver knew perfectly well that Charco's father was banged up in jail for a long spell.

'Fucker!'

'Is that your best word, Charco? Or your only word?'

'I'm not here for jokes!'

'Sit down and tell me why you're here. And show some respect if you want help. I'm busy.'

Charco's masticating jaw was working harder now and his narrow Aztec eyes darted distrustfully around Oliver's office, as if searching for hidden microphones.

'This is between you and me, right?'

'It always is.'

'Some fucker's been gassing.'

'Explain.'

'Some of the boys got high and started gassing.'

136

'They did?'

'Yeah. In a pool hall. To this fucker Tony Marquez I used to know.'

'About what?'

Charco's eyes narrowed as if Oliver was setting a trap, not to be trusted. 'They gassed a load of shit.'

'I repeat my question: what about?'

'What d'ya think, stupid!'

'Show respect, Charco.'

'And then this fucking fucker Tony Marquez thought he'd be a hero and run to the pigs.'

'How do you know?'

''Cos my friends went back couple o' days after to have a few words with that shithead.'

'To remind him he'd never heard what he'd heard?'

'Yeah. He'd gone, bunked. A few of the lads told my friends the plainclothes pigs had been there, sniffing around. Got it?'

Oliver wondered how many deadly knives this twitching, inflamed youth was carrying. It seemed possible, however, that Charco was genuinely seeking advice: whether to remain at the family home or 'take off'. Oliver knew that even the most violent youngsters find it harder to disappear, and stay disappeared, than adult criminals. This was especially true of 'ethnics' like Charco. They could only swim in ponds they knew and ruled. A lad like Charco could not be compared to the despairing beggar boys and druggies and girl prostitutes who vanished from northern cities into the vast sub-world of London. Charco expected his mum's dinner on the table. He wouldn't know how to live rough in a card-board box.

'Are we talking about the murder of the Headmaster, Edward Carr?' Oliver asked.

'Use your fucking loaf.'

'Respect, Charco. If you thought I was a fool you wouldn't be here, would you? Are you saying that your friends were boasting that they knew who killed the Headmaster?'

'The fuckers gassed. This fucking squealer Tony Marquez took himself straight to the pigs, hands out for the one hundred thousand smackers reward! He's dead, that one!'

Oliver could imagine the graffiti on the walls of the council estate where Tony Marquez was (presumably) now living: HOW MANY LIVES HAS TONY MARQUEZ? (or maybe 'LIFES').

'Your friends boasted that they had seen the murder take place?' Oliver asked.

'Who says it was fucking murder? The pigs! Could o' been self-defence or provocation.'

Oliver noticed that Charco wasn't as yet retracting his story of never having been near the scene of Edward Carr's murder – but the implication was clear.

'Did your friends mention your name to Tony Marquez?' Oliver asked his client.

'Might o'.'

'You're not sure?'

Charco hated not being sure about anything. Being sure was being a man, a chief, a leader.

'Are your friends in hiding?' Oliver pressed.

'Might be.'

'Charco, you want my advice, yes? You are not free to live anywhere you like because you are currently on bail for two other alleged offences, and a condition of your bail is that you reside and sleep at home every night without exception.'

'Fuck that. I gotta new place. You say a word to the pigs and you're dead. Got it?'

After Charco's departure, a somewhat shaken Oliver – he noticed that his hand was unsteady as he picked up the phone – put a call through to the senior partner of the firm, Dick Dodgett. He needed advice but he also needed the security of following the senior partner's judgment. A solicitor represents his client first and foremost, but he is also an officer of the court, any court, and has a duty to alert the police to a breach of bail or any future crime he believes may take place.

Easy to say.

Dodgett, it transpired, was in the Crown Court. Mobile phones are switched off in court – heaven may not help the lawyer who forgets. It would do no harm, in any case, to probe Sarah's reactions before calling Dodgett at home. If Tony Marquez had indeed talked to the police before hastily de-camping from his job at the pool hall, she ought to be told. As far as Oliver knew, she hadn't seen the reformed Tony for some months.

Perching on the edge of the bath, which had been liberally perfumed with one of the Body Shop oils that apparently eased away her tensions, Oliver delivered what he called 'a brief briefing'.

She listened abstractedly, clipped her toe nails, fiddled with the tap mixer. 'Soap my back,' she commanded. 'No, no, the lavender soap.'

Dutifully he did so. 'Have you heard from Tony Marquez?'

'No.'

'Do you think he went to the police or they to him?'

'I wouldn't know. Has Charco found out where Tony is now living?'

'He didn't say. He'll find out, anyway. Perhaps you should try to reach Tony Marquez. It's serious. Charco is dangerous and he's vindictive.'

'Probably bravado. Charco can't breathe without boasting and threatening. Pass me the towel.'

'Perhaps I should go to the police. I'm waiting to consult Dick Dodgett.'

'I don't think you should go to the police. Definitely not, Oliver.'

'I die if I do and I die if I don't. I can hardly wait for the next episode.'

'Oliver! Tony Marquez is not your client or your concern.'

'But he's yours.'

'No he's not. Not unless he comes to me. I'm not a protection agency.'

'You haven't seen him lately?'

'Not for months.'

'I just wondered.'

She was leaving the bathroom now. 'Why did you "just wonder"? I'd have told you, wouldn't I?'

Ten minutes later he got through to Dodgett at home. The advice he received from his senior partner was rarely spelled out. It was more a matter of hints and nudges.

'I'd say, Oliver, that each of us has a special, a unique "feel" for a particular client, and only each of us can arrive at the correct judgment.'

'What's your advice?'

'If you go to the police on this, Oliver, you might have to consider your own personal safety. Hm? You can't shop a client without telling him – or perhaps you can. Hm? And let's not forget that such a step would inevitably involve severing Charco from the firm's list of clients – and Charco is a very long loaf of bread. Hm? If he is ever charged – as he will be – the case is destined for the Central Criminal Court. The Old Bailey. Hm?'

Senior partners like Dodgett drove large, 2.8 litre cars on which the inscription 'Old Bailey' lay, invisible, beneath the Mercedes or BMW logo. Dodgett expected members of his firm to bring in three-and-a-half times the money they received as salary. You were given a monthly statement of the revenue ('charges') you had brought in. But then Dodgett might put you to work on one of his own cases for a week and your hours didn't show up on the financial ledger as yours. Fair?

You got paid. It evened out. Oliver was not a grumbler.

What Dodgett meant, between the lines, was, yes, give the police a log of any visits and calls you receive from

Charco, because the boy is in breach of bail, but disclose nothing about the substance.

'Whatever you decide carries my prior approval and authority,' Dodgett added. In other words, if any formal complaint were later made against Oliver to a court, Dodgett would be there, taking it on the chin. The senior partner was invariably as good as his word.

Two days later Detective Sergeant Doug McIntyre called at Oliver's office by appointment and formally asked him whether he knew where Charco Rios, who had broken his bail conditions and was wanted 'in connection with a murder inquiry', could be found.

'You will appreciate the seriousness of the situation, Mr Rawl?'

When Doug McIntyre called him 'Mr Rawl' the matter was grave; at Eden Manor police station they were normally on first-name terms, though warily – Doug wasn't the affable Charlie Wright, nemesis of football hooligans.

'Certainly. I don't know where Charco Rios is.'

'Has he called here at your office?'

'Once.' Oliver flipped his diary and gave McIntyre the date and time.

'Did he tell you he intended to take to the woods?'

'Obviously any discussion with a client remains privileged. I will tell you, however, that I felt good cause, as an officer of the court, to remind him of his bail conditions.'

'May I ask what constituted "good cause"?'

'No, that's privileged in my view.'

Oliver had felt himself balancing on a knife edge. On the one hand, nothing he told the police in his office could ever appear in the prosecution files or be quoted in court. On the other hand, you never know. The main thing he had to conceal was that Charco had done everything but admit complicity in the murder of Edward Carr. It was Charco who had killed Edward Carr with a single thrust of a knife through the heart. Oliver knew it in his bones.

And yet. And yet there is always this wonderful gap in the law between truth and proof. If Oliver could not be quoted, then what he told the police was not evidence.

'May I ask, Mr Rawl, whether since Charco Rios's last visit you have received any phone calls from him? I am not asking for the substance of such calls but simply whether you have received them.'

'Yes.'

HOW MANY LIVES HAD TONY MARQUEZ? HOW MANY LIVES HAS OLIVER RAWL?

The smell of the water is not a good smell, it reminds her of a kitchen rarely cleaned. A paved walkway runs beside the canal, and a few moored barges are floating at rest. Jenny wonders whether people are asleep in the barges; and whether they might wake up; and whether they might help her.

Six

She stumbles, moans. They are tossing her about, one to the other, laughing, as if she were a rag doll.

Most of the boys seem to have their hands on her now, exploring her breasts, and up her skirt, pulling at her clothes, jostling, jeering.

The little Filipino, Ally, has unzipped and is showing her his cock, grinning.

'You're gonna have nice time, white bitch, yeah?'

These words excite them further. Anything goes with a white bitch, she's asking for it.

Marcus arrived at his old Oxford college shortly before six. The porter led him across the front quadrangle, and then the new one to which Marcus had made a modest donation, where he was to lodge for the night. He showered, then fought his way into his black tie and dinner jacket. The invitation was for 6.45, drinks in the Senior Common Room before dinner. He was to be the guest of honour: tomorrow he would walk in procession to the Sheldonian to receive an honorary degree at Encaenia, the annual ceremony in memory of founders and benefactors.

Notification of the honour had reached him the previous year, and before his disgrace. During the months of brooding hibernation he had predicted to Brigid that he would receive a polite letter 'calling it off', but none came and now he was back on the bench, in the nick of time, relieving everyone of embarrassment.

Honorary degrees would be bestowed on poets, former political prisoners, explorers of the universe, actors, ballerinas and a few of the more literate retired politicians (if a politician ever retires). A procession of gravely flowing gowns with colourful hoods would proceed to the Sheldonian Theatre, a summer ceremony spiritually consonant with the Henley regatta, Wimbledon, cucumber sandwiches and a great deal of fizzy white wine.

He was of course used to walking in procession, splendiferous in whatever judicial robes, gaiters, wigs and sashes Central Casting had on offer at ceremonies to mark the start of the legal year and the opening of the Michaelmas sittings. Here in Oxford the Chancellor of the University would head the procession, with an abstracted air, as if looking for a good tea room.

But now, the evening before Encaenia, the Master of his college led his guest and the fellows into the great dining hall with its Elizabethan oak beams and its portraits of founders and worthies in ruff collars and the bleak, puritan expressions evidently expected of patrons and Masters. The present Master, Nash, placed Marcus at his right hand. Grace was said, and God was thanked in Latin by Dr Horace Smallbones, the college's senior classics tutor, who had already been a Fellow when Marcus was an undergraduate. The Master sat and they all sat. The fellows wore gowns over their dinner jackets but a guest was not expected to.

Marcus, who'd already had a few to drink in the Senior Common Room, and who by instinct adopted shock tactics when feeling a bit shy, asked Smallbones whether God was more at ease with petitions in Latin, Greek or Hebrew.

Smallbones affected to take the question seriously.

'And don't forget Arabic. The Archbishop announced only the other day that Muslims are now our brothers. It may be a pity that the Muslims haven't noticed.'

The Master congratulated Marcus on his restoration to the bench.

'Justice deferred,' he added, 'is better than nothing.'

Smallbones, however, was not happy with diplomacy.

'I hear speculation that you are to be the next Lord Chancellor after the present one has disgraced himself by extravagant expenditure.'

A spoonful of turtle soup hovered beneath Marcus's heavy lips.

'There haven't been many black bums on the wool-sack, Dr Smallbones. The blacks simply made the sacks.'

'When I was a boy,' the Master sighed, 'black was a rude word, almost a term of abuse.'

'I dare say our gays will soon insist on being called queers again,' quipped Smallbones, who had always been cheerily queer but never gay.

'Now we want all the gossip about our new Government,' the Master said. 'You have to sing for your supper, Marcus – I remember your baritone in the college choir.'

'I know nothing,' Marcus assured him.

Smallbones wagged his knife. 'Marcus, you cannot deny that you are close to the Boy and to Mrs the Boy.'

'The Mrs Boy is the correct term,' the Master corrected him. 'I read it in the *Official Gazette*.'

'It's Mrs the Boy,' Smallbones insisted. 'Is that not so, Marcus?'

Various views on this floated up the long high table, between the candelabra. Marcus did not contribute.

'About our young Prime Minister,' another fellow leaned in his direction. 'I'm told that the magazine *Vanity Fair* has already set him in its Portrait of World Power, alongside Clinton, Yeltsin, Kohl, the Pope, Bill Gates and that Hungarian speculator who robbed the Bank of England.'

'That chap,' Smallbones said, 'should have been knighted for getting the pound down. Now it's up again and I'm told that even Cunard can't afford me as cruise lecturer to Greece.'

'Do Cunard do Greece?' the Master asked sceptically. He went at Marcus again. 'I hear that the Boy and Big Ben have their eye on you.'

'Lots of noughts?' Smallbones asked Marcus.

'Noughts?'

'The things that are rather welcome on a salary cheque

– provided they surface at the end. Not being a mathematician, I've never understood why the more noughts you add, the bigger the sum.'

'It should get less?' someone asked. 'If six noughts follow a one, that should mean six denials of the one?'

'Marcus will think us frivolous.' The Master issued a general rebuke. 'So when were you last at Number Ten, Marcus? I hear they're recruiting Cambridge. Of course the Boy went to Cambridge. He'll probably close Oxford down. We will be airbrushed out of the Big Picture.'

Marcus smiled, remembering his visit to No. 10 at Ben Diamond's invitation, a chiaroscuro room, with light pouring through Georgian windows, lean furniture throwing down aggressively defined shadows. It was jackets off, bright white shirts. The Lord Chancellor and the Home Secretary were there, each supported by his inner retinue. They sat round the young king like so many barons of the realm behind their heraldic shields of ambivalent loyalty.

Marcus's brief report on No.10 was absorbed in admiring silence down the long table.

'Don't talk like that in public, Marcus,' Horace Smallbones chided, 'or you'll never get the job – whatever it is.'

On her next visit to Oak End, Sarah found Lucy in an unusually reflective mood.

'Shall I tell you something?'

'Yes?'

'I've been studying the women here.'

'What have you discovered, Lucy?'

'They all believe themselves to be the victims of a miscarriage of justice, a "scam", a "fix" by the pigs.'

'That's interesting.' (It wasn't news to Sarah but it would only have put Lucy down to say so.)

'But that's not the amazing thing,' Lucy went on. 'Everyone here assumes that everyone else is dead guilty and deserves more than they got. Of course you don't say it to someone's face but you say it behind her back. They all have an incredible faith in the integrity of British justice, even though they themselves were the victims of the filthiest prejudice, bribery and "set up".'

Sarah wore her most earnest expression. 'Amazing.'

Lucy scowled. 'That's not what you think. You think I'm in my cot.'

'Not at all!'

Lucy smiled slyly. 'Shall I tell you about Agatha Cowdrey?'

Sarah avoided glancing at her watch, rude in most circumstances but terrible to a prisoner.

'Yes, but we haven't got long and I'm here to discuss your parole, aren't I?'

Lucy ignored this.

'Miss Cowdrey is a tall posh spinster with large hands which are brilliant at clay modelling but which, on one peculiar day, were otherwise employed while disposing of a frail cousin.'

Sarah was taken aback by Lucy's lapse into stylish

English. Lucy had not told her about her days as editor of the school newspaper.

'Miss Cowdrey fervently denies she did it. It's odd how her expression never seems to change – like an animal's.'

'How long has she been inside?'

'That, *deah*, she does not divulge.' Here Lucy launched into an imitation of Miss Cowdrey. '"I could not possibly have known what was in Cousin Hettie's will, could I, deah? Cousin Hettie never told me. I never asked, of course – one doesn't. But after that terrible accident which I simply cannot explain everyone became convinced that I had known what was in Cousin Hettie's Will. People started crossing the street to avoid me."'

'What was the "terrible accident"?' Sarah asked.

'She took Cousin Hettie for a ride in her car and dumped her in a disused quarry.'

'But she says she didn't?'

'"Could I *evah* do such a thing, Lucy? The car stalled, I couldn't restart it, I went to call the RAC and when I came back Cousin Hettie had disappeared. They arrested me a week after they found poor, deah Cousin Hettie's body in the quarry. I could not believe it. They interrogated me and that was dreadful, absolutely dreadful. I had been told by my solicitor not to say anything because I would just tie myself up in knots, so I just had to listen to all those terrible things and say 'no comment'. Of course it would never occur to me to harm anyone."'

'And what do you say to Miss Cowdrey?' Sarah asked.

'I agree with her like crazy!'

'But the jury didn't believe her?'

'She says the judge was a horrible man who misdirected them. Miss Cowdrey describes herself as "a living miscarriage of justice" – the odd thing is I feel frightened the way she says that and I don't know why. But I love her clay modelling classes.'

'Who was the judge?'

'No idea. Miss Cowdrey says that it could never have happened if he'd been "an honourable gentleman like your father, deah".'

Waiting at the railway station, Sarah used her mobile to telephone the assistant prison governor. Having heard her out, he decided to put her through to Governor Mary Heatherington.

'I think Lucy is entitled to know if Miss Cowdrey's trial judge was Marcus Byron,' Sarah insisted.

'It was.'

'According to Lucy, Miss Cowdrey told her that the judge was a terrible man who misdirected the jury. Lucy may be at risk. She may need protection.'

'Miss Cowdrey is a gifted art teacher and harmless,' the Governor said.

'Even though she murdered her Cousin Hettie for her money?'

'The case is going to appeal. She's very protective of Lucy. She doesn't at all resemble some of our rougher, more vengeful ladies who have given Lucy a hard time. It's out of motherly kindness that she hasn't told Lucy that she was sentenced by her father.'

'But Lucy says she finds her frightening.'

'Miss Woods, Lucy is a gifted story teller.'

Sarah was half convinced. Lucy not only loved to fantasise, she enjoyed inventing stories about fantasists like the girl on her wing who claimed to have butchered a young woman. Mary Heatherington's judgment and experience had carried her up to grade 2, and there were rumours that she was to be promoted to head one of the big male prisons.

Sarah caught her train and buried herself in the files of a case due before the Benson Street Youth Court the following day. Luke Grant's sister Selena, whom he had abused before being put in local authority care, was now charged with GBH. A girl of fourteen, Tracey, had been lured to the Grant household, then assaulted by Selena, with the assistance of two male cousins, because of some argument over a boyfriend. Tracey had been hurled across a room, smothered in a blanket, dragged down to the kitchen, hit on the head with a frying pan, hauled back upstairs, and punched on the nose by Selena, causing heavy bleeding, while the two boys pinioned her arms. Tracey fell to the floor where Selena kicked her in the stomach, three or four times. At this juncture Selena told Tracey to beg for mercy and lick the soles of her shoes. The two boys then struck Tracey across the legs with snooker cues, then made her take her trousers down to show the marks.

Lovely stuff. To talk to Selena you'd never guess she was capable of it. She answered politely and looked down modestly. The issue tomorrow would be jurisdiction. Sarah would fight to keep the case in the Youth

Court but it would be touch-and-go, depending on who was sitting on the bench. If the justices decided it was a custodial matter, and possibly worth more than six months, Selena could find herself in the Crown Court before Marcus Byron.

Would he send a character like Selena Grant to keep Lucy company? Sarah could still feel his hand on her knee as they drove to Oak End. He had made a rather touching confession: since his return to the bench, not a single female defendant had been listed when he was sitting.

'Nothing is said, of course,' he chuckled. It was at that moment that Sarah decided that Oliver did not need to know about Marcus's roving hands.

Marcus's second meeting with Ben Diamond had been set up at a different venue – the Buckinghamshire country mansion of a motor racing tycoon who had donated a huge sum of money to the Party's election fund without, of course, the faintest thought of a return on his investment when the Boy got into Number 10.

The Home Secretary arrived with his retinue of officials, an aide carrying his briefcase, police motorcycles throbbing quietly in the tycoon's forecourt. Not that Ben Diamond had lost his populist touch; he could still perform his music hall act from a soap box in Woolwich market, raising steam when he complained that the bureaucrats of Brussels wanted to ban Cox's apples, 'the best in the world'. He never missed a trick: he was always for 'level playing fields' and against 'moving the goal posts'.

'Marcus,' he began now earnestly, 'we intend to take the criminal justice system out of party politics.'

'Like interest rates?'

Ben's smile did not falter. 'Spot on. What we need is coherence on the statute book, concomitance, a clear logic in a clear language. That's why we want your help, Marcus.'

'Or just my name?'

A flutter passed through the crisply ironed shirts (no drip-dries at this level) seated round the table; faintly aghast at such impudence, they were more than faintly relieved that Marcus Byron was turning out to be the lone wolf they didn't want.

'Marcus, I'll be perfectly honest with you—' Ben began but Marcus quietly raised the pinkish palm of his black hand.

'Ben, I'd rather you avoided that.'

'Avoided what?'

'Being "perfectly honest". My sister Wendy recently bought a second-hand car. The salesman finally confided that he was going to be "perfectly honest" with her – this little car was the best bargain to be found anywhere in London.'

Ben had to smile. Then he laughed. He liked the joke, he would tell it himself – if jokes could be copyrighted, Ben would have been sued a thousand times.

'We have been consulting widely,' he told Marcus, 'among the professional bodies. And the pressure groups. We can't make real progress until we win them over.'

Marcus grinned lazily. 'Yeah? NACRO, ASBO,

PONGO and BOZO? Try fast-tracking that lot!' He laughed and slowly drew the Baby's Bottom in his pipe to life. 'What you're really doing, Home Secretary, is consulting the eyes, ears and private parts of the Congress of Justice.'

Ben's Permanent Under Secretary stiffened. 'It's defunct. Doesn't exist.'

'Yeah. As Brigid says, "It's dead and well".'

Ben had been listening to this exchange with a deepening frown.

'The Congress is dead and buried, Marcus.'

Marcus shook his head slowly. 'Call it Lazarus. You only have to lift the right stone.' He drew on his pipe. 'May we talk about whether we want to impose by statute a whole new raft of mandatory sentences on judges?'

Ben was regarding him warily. 'Yes, by all means.'

'I'm a judge. I share the widespread impression that you don't trust judges and magistrates any more than your predecessor Jeremy Darling did.'

Ben's back stiffened. To liken him to Jeremy Darling was the ultimate insult – and everyone was doing it.

'That's not true.'

'I hear that you have in mind to deprive the courts of the power to impose a sentence on youngsters unless it fits a pre-set term: two, four, six, eight, ten, twelve, eighteen or twenty-four months.'

'We must work real consistency into the system,' Ben said.

'Yeah? So what will you have? A ladder with missing rungs. A recidivist youth commits an aggravated domestic burglary. But he pleads guilty. You have to grant a discount for that plea, you'd like to take his sentence down from two years to twenty-one months but no, the statute says there is no rung on the ladder between twenty-four and eighteen months. So he gets eighteen.'

Stony silence round the table.

'I think that may be a fair point,' Ben said. 'Nothing is finalised as yet. That's why we want you to head the Criminal Law Commission. Your knowledge and practical experience will count.'

Marcus wondered. Brigid thought Ben wanted him to dress the shop window.

Now Ben was talking about reform of the Youth Justice system. It had to be done and he would do it – one Action Plan after another. Ben was Action Man and Action Plan Man straight out of Hamley's. Marcus admired the general intention but the more he heard, the more he feared that Ben's zeal and impatience with detail would result in a dog's dinner. Ben was a headliner. If Jeremy Darling was in favour of kicking a beggar once, Ben immediately recommended kicking the beggar twice.

'I do understand your thoughts, Marcus,' the Home Secretary continued. 'Correct me if I'm wrong, but you harbour two main fears – which may boil down to one. You suspect that we may try to do too much too fast, and thus end up by doing too little too slowly. Right?'

'Not exactly, Ben,' Marcus said.

'What then?'

'In my view we already have enough statutes in place

to protect the public. What is needed is a change of attitudes. What is needed is a radical reform of how the criminal justice system works in practice. And that means tackling the vested interests head-on. When did a pre-sentence report from a probation officer or a youth justice worker ever recommend custody? Frankly, the system is waterlogged with professionals who regard custody as an outrage.'

'As I said, we have been consulting widely and—'

Marcus cut in without ceremony. 'If you believe you've got to bring everyone on board in order to get anything done, I'd call that running up the white flag before battle is joined.'

A frowning Ben Diamond called for a break in the formal discussion. The motor racing tycoon's servants promptly appeared with filter coffee, tea and sandwiches. During a moment in which Marcus found himself alone, like a quarantine animal, a young man introduced himself as Edmund Joiner, a junior political adviser to the Home Secretary, 'reporting to Paul Glass' – and, he added, 'an admirer of yours'.

'And may I add, Judge Byron, without being indiscreet, how happy I shall be if you decide to come on board.'

'You're not a career civil servant, then?'

'Heavens, no!' Young Joiner tossed a few salted nuts on to his tongue. 'I used to work for the legal agitator Siegfried Alexander,' he added, 'until I saw the light.'

'Professor Alexander doesn't figure among my admirers.'

'Oh no, dear me no,' Joiner said, 'I can quote all his papal bulls and encyclicals on the great issues of crime and punishment.'

'The man's simply a charlatan,' Marcus growled. 'He fixes his research findings. He ignores or suppresses inconvenient statistics and—'

'And he spends an inordinate amount of time buttering up crackbrains nursing some paranoid obsession – the League for Penal Reform, Women Behind Bars, Common Sense about Drugs, Vengeance is Not Justice, COP—'

'COP? I don't know that one.'

'Close our Prisons.' Edmund Joiner smiled. 'They're lovely people. Then there's SQUAT – more or less self-explanatory – not to mention SCUM, SCREW and Squeegee Bandit Bums. Am I forgetting Bosnian Gypsy Refugees in London and the dear, dear campaigners in Who Killed Wesley Ames?'

'Who was Wesley Ames?' Marcus asked. 'And who did kill him?'

'Wesley was a paranoid schizophrenic who died in a police cell during a violent struggle – three hours after murdering his girlfriend and her two children. According to his supporters, Wesley was innocent of the crimes and simply a victim of police racism.'

Marcus nodded. 'Familiar story.' He leaned towards young Joiner. 'How's the Congress for Justice?'

Joiner's tongue flicked out to ingest a new handful of salted nuts.

'Dead.'

The young man moved deferentially back and away

as Ben Diamond bore down on Marcus, coffee slurping round his saucer. No one followed: a discreet space was left around them.

'Marcus, you have enemies and you behave like a man with enemies. But I'm convinced these talks have dragged on long enough. By nature you're a decision maker. Please let me have your decision now.'

Marcus lowered his baritone's voice. 'If you want me in the job, I'll take it.'

Everyone in the room observed the pumping hand-shake.

Marcus assumed that a handshake was irreversible. Brigid would have reminded him that politicians are like estate agents: they don't mean it until they have to.

A few days later the Boy demonstrated his esteem for Ben by including him in the delegation accompanying the new Prime Minister on his first official visit to America. To meet the President and the Mrs President. To learn how crime had been solved in the USA. To master the doctrine of zero tolerance. To buy a floating prison, second-hand. Maybe two. The *Sentinel*'s Washington correspondent reported that by the time the British party departed, the streets of the capital were knee-deep in Action Plans.

Oliver and Sarah were preparing a meal together, a roast duck, and arguing about men and women, their favourite dish at any hour. Oliver was sporting a butcher's apron.

Sarah, always taller at the close of the day, was prowling round him, a glass of wine in hand.

'So, Oliver Rawl, women are now the majority of the population, but they are still treated like an oppressed minority – right?'

'I hope so.' He checked the oven temperature and timer – someone had to. 'You are about to remind me that long ago, when your great-grandmother was chaining herself to any available railing, the Court of Appeal upheld the Law Society's refusal to let women sit the solicitors' examinations on the ground that women were not "persons".'

'And don't you forget it.'

'Pass the olive oil, your Honour. However—'

'However what?'

'Women are now pouring like molten lava into all the professions, including the law. One third of our profession is now female. Tomorrow two thirds. By the end of the century four thirds. My bones are already bleaching on the beach. Fill my glass.'

'Need I remind you that even today only seven out of ninety-six High Court judges are women, and there is only one female Lord Justice of Appeal out of thirty-five. And all twelve Law Lords are men!' Sarah concluded triumphantly.

'It couldn't be worse in Albania.'

'I don't know why I live with you, Oliver.'

'It's because Ivan can't cook.'

'The fact is, you're a complete philistine.'

'Did you or did you not recently allow yourself to

161

be interviewed and photographed for a *Times* feature on what clothes women lawyers now wear in court?'

'Are allowed to wear,' she corrected him. 'Men have always dictated what women can wear in court. Now women are being heard.'

Though she would never concede as much to Oliver, Sarah felt that too many women played the 'woman' card, or the sexual harassment card, when complaining about lack of promotion. On the other hand, even Oliver could not contest – let him try! – that women solicitors were being paid less than men of the same age and experience. Their own professional association, the Law Society, had commissioned a study of 579 firms. At the higher level of salaried partner, men earned on average £37,000, women only £32,000. Among equity partners, with a share in the business, men earned £51,000 compared to £36,000 for women.

'Which,' Oliver said, dishing out the roast potatoes, 'hasn't stopped you from spending a fortune buying worthless paintings by your former boyfriends at the Chelsea College of Art.'

'Ah! Here it comes again – that painting! You're insanely jealous of Ivan.'

Trouble had begun one winter Saturday when Sarah took herself to the Serpentine Gallery while Oliver skulked by the television watching the England–France rugby match. He had even rented a satellite dish and subscribed to Sky Sport after rugby (and everything involving men tussling over some ball or other) slipped away from the destitute terrestrial channels. Oliver had sworn that he would never subscribe to Sky, like his father would never have bought a German or Japanese car – until he came home one day in a BMW.

Sarah had gone off to the last day of an ultra avant-garde exhibition called 'No Painting' at the Serpentine Gallery. Oliver suspected that she would be bringing home a canvas she'd already bought – probably by the awful Ivan, the star of the show, whose Russian grandfather had known Tatlin and Lissitsky, as Sarah had been impressed to learn when she and Ivan were both students at the Chelsea. He had also been her first serious boyfriend.

Reaching the gallery, Sarah ran into her colleague at Chapman & Burnett, Patty.

'Oliver's crippled by jealousy of Ivan,' Sarah confided.

'Good for you.'

'It's easy not to be jealous of Oliver's own past because he scarcely had one: he was too busy bashing or kicking rubber balls to notice his own.'

'Don't forget to be jealous of his future, though. He's attractive.'

'Oh, do you think so?' Sarah said coolly. 'I must say, I've never seen Oliver as attractive.'

'As what, then?'

'Well – as nothing really. I rather like living with an absolute Nobody.'

'Yeah? When do I bring the van to collect him? Oh go on, Sarah, smile.'

'Oliver's nothing to smile about.'

'So why do you love him? Why do you want to marry him?'

'I don't want to marry anybody!'

'I know. But you want to marry Oliver.'

Oliver, meanwhile, was watching England *v* France on Sky TV, wrapped in concentration, not answering the phone and delighted to have Sarah out of the way.

'Damn! Damn damn damn!'

He'd caught the sound of a taxi's coughing diesel in the street outside, just as the English forwards were bulling forward, and forward again, maul and ruck, for one of their famous pushover tries. He knew what the taxi meant: she had brought home something large from the Serpentine Gallery. And she needed help with the front door. Bang, thump, bell. Imperious. She had timed it deliberately, so he couldn't watch the English pushover. He sidled backwards towards the door while keeping his eye fixed on the television, but only when it was out of sight did he hear the confirming roar of the Twickenham crowd.

His expression was not a pretty one as he let her in.

'Forgot your key?'

'For God's sake give me a hand, Oliver.'

Sarah was clutching a huge flat, rectangular object wrapped in brown paper. Oliver was prepared to give this work of art the benefit of the doubt while it remained a parcel – anything to watch the rest of the match in peace – but peace was not something that Sarah liked to observe him enjoying.

'You're brain dead, Oliver.'

'Well, I know. One sleeps better that way.'

Auriol Johnson is on her best form in the *World*. She has caught wind of Marcus's secret discussions with Ben Diamond.

Is Marcus Byron still a restless soul in search of greater things? Is his restoration to the Crown Court quite enough for his bulging ego? Well-placed sources indicate that the tough black judge may recently have been engaged in clandestine discussions with a senior figure in the Government. This could be another case of *cherchez la femme*, which is French for pillow talk. Marcus's current flame – but will it last? – Brigid Kyle is said to be madly ambitious for her man.

Auriol's view of men boiled down to the epithet 'safety in numbers'. According to Brigid, there were never fewer than three 'in residence' at any one time, but normally, she confided, 'it's more like a club player's golf handicap'.

Not widely understood in 'the Street' was the role of a young man in the bitter quarrel that brought about Auriol's departure from the *Sentinel*. A native of California, with an accent as dry as the local chardonnay, Amos Lewin was on 'sabbatical' or, as he preferred, 'on furlough', from the *Berkeley Voice*, a West Coast paper owned by the Irish racehorse owner Kernan O'Sullivan

– who also happened to be proprietor of the *Sentinel*. Although O'Sullivan was a Catholic father of six – 'and still counting', according to Brigid – the slender and distinctly beautiful freelance journalist Amos Lewin had won what he sardonically called 'the Kernan O'Sullivan Award for Bisexuality'. O'Sullivan, who (to complicate matters further) had once been Brigid's lover in her Dublin days, brought Amos to London.

To do what? To work for the *Sentinel*'s editor, Harvey Trueman (who, whenever O'Sullivan paraded himself as a 'good Catholic', invariably asked, 'What's a good Catholic, I've always wanted to know?') Perhaps. To research British methods of dealing with crime? Yes, certainly. But Amos always carried an aura of ambiguity.

Brigid had taken one look at him and decided that he was going to work for her – a dish for her own table. Amos smiled amiably.

'Fine by me – except that I'm not really planning to do much work over here.'

'So what are you going to do?' The question might have come from Brigid but in fact belonged to a third party who at that moment breezed in, tossing blonde curls. Brigid's assistant, Auriol Johnson, extended a hand to Amos.

'I'm Brigid's gofer,' she explained, seizing his hand. 'I'll show you around.'

Before Brigid could carry him away to lunch, Auriol had carried him away to bed – despite Amos's plea that he was hungry and still suffering from 'jet lag'.

'Sex is good for jet lag,' Auriol told him. 'And so am I. First things first. Are you gay, Amos?'

'At this moment in time,' he sighed, 'not very. I'm not very anything. I like your bed, though. How about I crawl into it, wrestle with my eight-hour jet lag, and then call you? Why do telephones make such a funny sound over here?'

But even as he spoke, Auriol was tossing her underwear at him.

'Well, that's different,' Amos murmured in reluctant admiration.

'What's different?' She unzipped his pants and reached inside like a woman handling ripe fruit in Berwick Street market. 'Let's have a look,' she said. 'Wow!'

'Tell me, Auriol, is this the way all London girls greet jet-lagged Americans?'

The question was scarcely out than his handsome, upturned face was shrouded in bouncing blonde hair, and he heard himself telling a pair of insistent blue eyes that he was their slave.

'For ever?' she wanted to know, fastening a hand on each of his ears.

'Is "for ever" a long time over here?'

'By the way: not a word to Brigid. She's in the grip of the green-eyed monster.'

Auriol told Brigid all about it that same afternoon.

'Your black boy is sleeping off post-coital jet lag. He's a wonderful lay. But you love dull old Marcus, don't you, so you'll never know how wonderful.'

Brigid feigned insouciance but she felt less than

delighted. When Amos showed up a few days later she didn't invite him to lunch.

'Find anyone else in Auriol's bed – or was it a Wednesday?'

'A Wednesday?'

'That's her one-at-a-time day.'

'I think she just likes sex.'

'Well, don't tell her.'

Amos Lewin got the impression that Auriol Johnson would not be working for Brigid Kyle indefinitely.

Marcus Byron, for his part, noticed that Amos was too often on the sharp end of Brigid's tongue.

'You've fallen for this boy?'

'I'm still vertical.'

When Marcus took her to dinner at his favourite restaurant, Chez Victor, she broached the subject of Sarah's message about Lucy.

'Did you ever sentence a woman called Miss Cowdrey?'

'Who? What did she do?'

'She deposited her Cousin Hettie in a disused quarry after she learned that she was the sole beneficiary of the old lady's will.'

'Oh, that one! I do recall. An art teacher, with kind of a mannish haircut – and a terrific liar.' Marcus chuckled. 'It all comes back. Before they found the body in the quarry, Miss Cowdrey had told the police that her Hettie could scarcely walk ten paces so there was no point in imagining she could have shuffled unaided down the dark country lane from the car to the quarry and fallen in. But after Hettie was found in the very same quarry, the good Miss Cowdrey suddenly decided to answer no more questions. Yeah. But she became very eloquent in the witness box. She could have fooled any jury.'

'Except that you didn't let her?'

Marcus stiffened. 'What are you telling me?'

'She's teaching clay modelling to Lucy.'

He shrugged. 'No problem. She's not a violent type.'

'Cousin Hettie might have a different view if she was here to express it.'

'Agatha Cowdrey is straight out of the genteel end of Agatha Christie. They never do anything bad until they do.'

He refilled her glass with Chez Victor's house red, the best in town and only £9.99, pulled from the unfashion-able side of a little, sun-kissed hill east of Beaune.

'You're about to say something horrible,' he drawled. 'You're going to tell me I was a fool to take the job. I can see the snakes seething in that flaming Irish hair.'

She laughed and went into Irish. 'OK. You're nuttin' but a right fool, Marcus Byron. I've always known it. I wouldn't respect you otherwise, would I?'

'I'm going to kick the criminal justice system into the next century,' Marcus growled.

'It's your modesty I love. And did you remind Ben Diamond that we urgently need effective statutory meas-ures against new forms of assault?'

'Not new, Brigid, newly recognised.'

'I stand corrected, your Honour. Like stalking, har-assment, and the wilful transmission of diseases such as Aids.'

'Yeah. We do. But Ben's Permanent Under Secretary cut in. "Aids", he murmured, "is politically sensitive. The notion of the wilful transmission of a sexual disease could be divisive in the gay community."'

'And you almost lost your temper, I suppose?'

'I asked the Permanent Under Secretary since when important reforms offended no one. He became even smoother. "The Government", he said, bending his neck deferentially towards a somewhat bemused Ben, "does not wish to make the mistake of moving in every direction at once. The art of government is to avoid collisions."'

Brigid nodded derisively. 'And the Boy, whom Ben calls the Prime Minister, is looking to the long term – two or three terms of office. The Big Picture takes time to paint.'

Marcus was drinking too fast, eyes rolling: 'I told Ben: "Justice is inconvenient and expensive. But ours is a society that can afford it. This is a nation swimming in money. Take two pence out of private pockets into the public purse and you're there. I may be a famous fascist, but I'm a social fascist. I'd gladly pay ten pence more on my income tax to bring this country of ours on-keel."'

'Marcus, I beg you, stay on the bench. Do the job you know how to do. I'm sorry, I swore to myself I would never—'

'Tell me the truth? Don't ever stop telling me the truth, Brigid. I have no obligation to listen.'

'They do *crême brulée* here?'

'For me, or for you, lady, they'll do the Forth Bridge.'

*   *   *

When Oliver Rawl awoke he needed only one finger to count the blessings in his life: he had not received a snarling, threatening, paranoid phone call from the fugitive Charco Rios since the previous Tuesday.

He was due in Benson Street Youth Court at 9.45 but the first thing to catch his sleepy eye was a long stretch of paper hanging from his fax machine – sure enough, another missive from his other nightmare client, Delia.

'Shit!'

He wouldn't read it. He'd bin it. He'd boil an egg.

He read it.

Delia Atkinson has committed one more overnight murder (Delia's message records) and what is Oliver going to do when the police come for her? Delia commits most of her murders on Blackfriars Bridge and invariably hurls the corpse into the powerful, brown, unforgiving waters below. So she tells Oliver – and the police. Strangulation is the invariable cause of death.

All her victims are male because (she cheerfully explains) she hates all men.

'In that case you might prefer to have a woman solicitor,' Oliver had hopefully suggested more than once.

'Oh no, dear, I think you're a luvvy.'

She rides a man's motorbike, a powerful, noisy black BMW with a broken exhaust temporarily mended by soldering on a Harp lager can.

None of Delia's victims has ever been found by the River Police, and none of the persons she swears she has strangled as a result of her moonlight massacres has ever, actually, gone missing. Delia is nothing if not punctilious about collaborating with the police; she bombards them with faxes – she adores faxes – providing every detail of her depredations, including long and involved statements of grievance against the deceased, each of whom, on inspection, was mainly guilty of not recognising that she was a woman and had never been a man, never been Derek Foster, transsexual.

On a bad day, after a particularly bright full moon, Oliver would receive two or three faxes. So did the victims themselves. Many a distinguished public figure was surprised when his secretary shyly handed him a piece of paper announcing that he had been murdered and dumped in the river the previous night. The victims included the Prime Minister, most of the Cabinet, and leading members of the judiciary. Judge Marcus Byron had been strangled twice.

On the second occasion he took the liberty of phoning Oliver Rawl.

'Is your client a transsexual?'

'Yes, your Honour, though she denies she was ever a man.'

'Big hands, I hear. The sex change didn't involve a new pair of hands?'

'Clearly not.'

'What did she call herself when a man?'

'Derek Foster.'

'Aha? I remember giving him a year inside for seriously assaulting a policeman – GBH, I recall.'

'I didn't know that.'

172

The police records were clear: before her sex-change operation, Delia-Derek had committed a series of serious assaults on prostitutes and policemen, landed up 'sectioned' under the Mental Health Act, exercised his ancient constitutional right to become a she by operation – and was promptly released as no longer a danger to the community.

She now faced more charges than Oliver could remember first thing in the morning. On each occasion Oliver had persuaded the magistrates to grant bail on the ground that Delia was harmless. He now wondered whether he hadn't tried too hard. He suspected that Delia would soon be posting her death threats on an Internet bulletin board.

What takes him to Benson Street Court is Pete McGraw's younger brother Jason, now the leading spirit in a group of tearaways from the Eden Manor estate engaged in firing flaming arrows at cars or hurling scaffolding, bricks and bottles at passing buses. The local bus company is threatening to boycott Eden Manor unless something is done. Communal tension is rising and the staircases are talking about 'dealing with this ourselves' and 'it's estate rules now'. The lynch-mob parents are invariably the same ones whose homes produce violent delinquents.

The McGraw family had insisted that 'Mr Rolls' represent Jason, too, although Oliver thought that one McGraw was more than enough. 'You can trust Mr Rolls,' Jason's mother had loudly informed her little angel in Oliver's office, 'and mind you say exactly what he says.' Oliver tried to explain that it was the client who gave 'instructions', but the lecture did not last long – the lady knew the street, she was right.

Oliver reached Benson Street shortly before 9.45, the deadline for the first batch of cases, but as usual no one had showed up. Only towards eleven would gangs of youths, offenders and supporters begin to surface, smoking and shouting in the street, delaying the moment when they must submit to search by Burns Security guards at the main entrance – and surrender their knives to the metal detectors that ran across truculently twisting limbs.

'Keep still, son.'

'You're fuckin' me up!'

By lunchtime Jason still had not surfaced. The bench routinely issued a warrant not backed for bail. For Oliver, another wasted morning in what was beginning to feel like a wasted life.

At this juncture an official called the Clerk to the Parliaments leapt to unaccustomed prominence when he refused to sanction the legal aid fees of four leading QCs in respect of cases that had gone on appeal to the House of Lords.

'Perfect timing,' Brigid remarked to Marcus. 'I wonder whether the Clerk to the Parliaments knew that you are due to deliver the annual Chancery Bar lecture – and that you intend to question the fees being charged at the top of the profession.'

'Just a coincidence.'

'Marcus, they want you to offend every vested interest, and they're in a hurry.'

Although he could not mention the current cases, which were under appeal to the Lords with the support of the Bar as *amicus curiae*, what particularly delighted Marcus (and Brigid) was that one of the big-earning silks affected was none other than Sandra Golding QC, his erstwhile mistress, a pillar of the Bar, and currently chairperson of the Association of Progressive Lawyers. For Sandra, also a busy journalist and broadcaster, British justice was simply relentless injustice. No IRA bomber could conceivably have blown up a pub full of people, no black could conceivably have murdered a white police-man, no battered wife could conceivably have murdered her husband, even for good reason. No, the evidence had invariably been fixed by the police and the Crown Prosecution Service, with benches of Oxbridge-educated male judges out of Spitting Image nodding and leering in connivance.

In Marcus's view, Sandra was as clear-headed as a beach ball caught in a gale. Now she'd been caught with her hand deep in the public purse – all perfectly legal, of course.

When she defended a senior civil servant from the Department of Defence, who was charged with breaking the Official Secrets Act by sending a storm of classified documents to backbench MPs, no juror was allowed ever to have been in government employment, even as a Post Office clerk. 'What do you think about "my country right or wrong"?' she asked potential jurors. When Sandra represented squatters accused of trespass and vandalism, no juror was acceptable if he or she owned a house. British courts do not allow the unlimited objections permitted in America, so Sandra was always left with a few suspect jurors who may have failed to grasp that they were slaves of the most biased, bigoted and oppressive system known to the modern world. As for the real dictators abroad, they invariably were advised to instruct the expensive Sandra Golding QC to represent them in British courts.

Now it emerged that Sandra had claimed £20,000 from legal aid for a week's preparation of a murder case on appeal and one day in court. This worked out at more than £400 an hour. Sandra had, in the approved fashion, given her fee an 'uplift' of 65 per cent to reflect 'the care, control and conduct' of a case on appeal, then added in expenses and 'rounded it up' to the £20,000.

And the Bar was right behind her.

The Bar's hostility to Marcus was not lessened when he commented during his Chancery Bar lecture that barristers' clerks were expected to put in for what they reckoned their 'governor' was worth. And what he or she was worth depended largely on precedents. The more barristers got, the more they got.

'The fact is that last year barristers put in to the legal aid board for a stupendous total of £286 million in fees, but were granted only £127 million, or less than half. This might suggest that their claims are not considered even fifty per cent credible.'

The reaction was furious and immediate. Antony Laughton QC (whose personal hostility to Marcus was no secret) told *The Times*. 'It is not the Bar which is making this market or assessing these fees. It is the Legal Aid Board which decides what is fair and reasonable remuneration. And if a tiny, one per cent minority of top silks are said to be earning £300,000 in a year from legal aid work, this can be utterly misleading because the sum could well derive from work stretching over three years.'

The Chairman of the Criminal Bar Association informed a conference of young lawyers that the Home Secretary would be making a 'fatal mistake' if he appointed Marcus Byron as Chairman of the Criminal Law Commission.

Brigid knew one cause of Marcus's current distemper about legal fees – he wasn't getting them. He loved money far more than she did. There was also his ongoing divorce. He'd come home to dinner, swallow a few whiskies, and describe his own solicitor as 'a shit'.

'If that guy was a physician, he'd be buying up livers and kidneys from desperately poor donors in the third world.'

'That guy' was the charming Simon Hoare, always an entertaining dinner-table guest. Divorce proceedings involving some nasty property wrangles with Louise had landed Marcus in the clutches of a smart, internationally famous firm of solicitors whose juniors charged £75 an hour. The kind attention of a senior partner like Simon Hoare could cost £300 for the same sixty minutes. Only the best was good enough for Marcus – but now he was becoming restive over the interim bills 'on account'.

On Hoare's desk, when you could get within view of

it, lay a silver blotter from Asprey's, a gift from one of the Arab emirs whose affairs and investments he lovingly managed. Simon was far too civilised to get straight down to business. On being notified of Marcus's arrival, he came straight out to reception with effusive greetings, ushered him to a leather chair within sight of the emir's silver blotter, called for coffee, which arrived on a silver tray, a gift from ex-Queen Tatiana, and solicitously inquired about Marcus's ongoing discussions with the Home Secretary – at five pounds a minute.

'*They* won't thank you, of course, if you take the job on.'

Hoare, an establishment man if ever there was one, with a fine record of discrediting rivals for office within the Law Society, was a great one for 'they' – *they* the politicians, *they* the Bar, *they* the CPS.

'I can imagine the jargon and acronyms you have to wade through when dealing with Home Office officials, Marcus.'

And Marcus, though he would later seethe, could never resist the flattery.

'OK, I'll test you. What's COG?'

'Committee of God?'

'Chief Officers Group. What's PYJMG?'

'Some kind of pygmy?'

'Principal Youth Justice Managers Group.'

'Oh dear oh dear. And *they* will tell you all about "new management teams" and how their district branches may, just may, be broken down into semi-autonomous branch offices.'

'You're right. And the Branch Prosecutor for Great North Crown Court will start talking about "co-terminosity" – by which he may mean harmonising the administrative boundaries of the CPS, the police, the local authorities and the courts. All pie in the sky, of course.'

'Of course. But cherry pie with ice cream.'

Marcus could not resist telling Simon Hoare stories from the criminal courts, often old ones, even though they were the most expensive stories he ever told:

'Yeah, there she is, this bitch, chewing gum in court, sniggering, refusing to give evidence at her boyfriend's trial for murder. She'd made a second statement to the police retracting her earlier evidence. Her counsel is telling me that the bitch is genuinely afraid: "She has been under fear, stress and intimidation."'

Simon Hoare's expression suggests that this is the most *riveting* story he has ever heard.

'What did you do?'

'I gave her two months for contempt. Every liberal pressure group called me a monster. A woman! A mother! Well, they're all mothers! And a man had been murdered. Right in front of her.'

Simon Hoare sighs. 'You're very brave.'

'Yeah.' Marcus glances at his watch. 'I suppose we'd better talk about Louise.'

'Quite right. I can't say I've got good news. Your wife is digging her heels in.'

'She's earning three times my salary,' Marcus growls.

'Ah. That's your view. It's my view. It's not your wife's view.'

'Perhaps we should settle?'

'Never do that. Once you start running, they won't let your feet touch the ground. Frankly, she'll leave you that famous licence plate MB1 if she can get the front wheels of your Rolls.'

Simon Hoare likes to talk in that way. You are never quite sure what he is saying, except that it's going to cost.

On Marcus's way out, Hoare always offered him a lawyers' joke, like restaurants bring a 'free' chocolate with the bill.

'A client makes a nervous inquiry of his solicitor. "*What are your fees?*" "One hundred pounds to answer three questions." "*That's rather steep, isn't it?*" "Yes, now what is your third question?" Ha! Ha ha ha. Ha ha!'

Seven

So much for recent history, the prologue. Now we are back with Jenny Glendower, wife and mother, mother of two, on her knees beside Great North's stagnant canal and weeping in terror.

A lively, questing person, delighted to have a few days to herself, she has merely stepped out of her hotel for a short walk.

But now her body hurts, all of it, from sheer fear. Never before has she been transformed into an object, a non-person, a prisoner, by others immune to pity and foreign to decency. Yes, foreign. How many of these youths had a grandparent born within these shores?

The old cliché keeps somersaulting in her aching head: rape is a fate better than death.

'Please,' she begs, 'please don't.' But she begs without conviction; she is whimpering, not screaming; it's as if they have decided not to understand English.

A few miles away Oliver Rawl, night-duty solicitor, has reached Eden Manor police station and is about to enter the cell holding a new client.

One of the boys, Pete, hurls a stone and she sees rats scampering around a pile of refuse.

It's Charco Rios who forces her to her knees, thrusting his furious, mask-like Aztec face close to hers. His breath smells foul. She can feel his hatred for her – and for the world – like a scorching flame.

'You're asking for it, cunt,' he snarls.

He's clearly the leader of the gang but he's in no hurry to have her. Most of the boys seem to have their hands on her now, exploring her breasts, and up her skirt, pulling at her clothes, jostling, jeering. They haul her up, tossing her about, one to the other, laughing, as if she were a rag doll.

This lady, this mother of two, this English person inhabiting her England.

The little Filipino, Ally, has unzipped and is showing her his cock, grinning. The word 'flashing' flashes; she has heard of it, never seen it, nothing worse than when the TV cameras turn away from a streaker at Twickenham or the Oval.

'You're gonna have nice time, white bitch, yeah?'

These words excite them further. Anything goes with a white bitch, she's asking for it.

Now the biggest of them, and the youngest, the black boy Luke, is getting excited. So far he has been a mere spectator, watching open-mouthed, but now there's this huge, black cannon thrusting, swelling, pulsing and it's taking him over, nothing he can do. To Luke wanting a female's body is like being very thirsty and seeing a beer – you wouldn't ask the beer's permission to open it, to yank back the tab, to get that hiss and whoosh.

'She's mine,' he growls.

The woman is down on her knees again, half-naked now, kneeling at the feet of the big black boy.

'Suck me off,' he demands.

'I . . . I've never done that,' she whispers.

'Yeah?'

'I . . . I don't know how.'

He thrusts his cock in her mouth. 'If you bite me – bitch – I'll kill you.'

Gaston Dubois plucks the tabloid *World* from under the hotel reception desk and begins to study the bare breasts and buttocks. Flipping, he comes across the paper's ace reporter, Auriol Johnson. Her subject is stalkers. She, like Brigid Kyle, is pictured at the head of her column – Auriol's smile suggests to Gaston that if any stalking is on the agenda, she will be doing it. Auriol specialises in 'fury' headlines: FURY OVER FAKE HUSBAND – even if the 'fury' proves, on closer examination, to be a couple of quotes from women's groups.

His thoughts drift back to the blonde lady still out on the streets. But of course! *Merde!* She has hopped straight into a taxi, driven straight to her wealthy lover, and is now safe in his arms, between silken sheets somewhere . . . in Curzon Street, Mayfair, a *beau quartier*!

*   *   *

It's only beginning. Grass, stones, weeds press into her bare back and her head aches as they come on to her, the large and the small, with their special smells, each of which she will remember, until the insides of her legs are sore and the soft lining of her vagina, soaking and spilling alien seeds, screams for an end to it.

Big Luke Grant's hands fondle her breasts.

'Suck me off again,' he growls.

Jenny strives to expel her mind, her consciousness, from her body. Strives to exorcise herself from the agony of the here and now – the pain, shame and degradation. And always the fear, the fear of worse to come. Of death.

Arriving in London for her teachers' conference, she had got through to Oliver's law firm. But not to Mr Rawl. She was informed that Mr Rawl was in court and his mobile had to be switched off but if he was waiting around outside the courtroom with a client he might be reached. Jenny found the word 'client' intimidating; she felt like an idle, West Country woman bothering these busy people with little excuse except an unhappy marriage and no one you could talk to in Yeominster. And what was she really going to say to Oliver? 'It's been a long time since ... since ... '? No, she'd say she'd read about him in the papers and was astonished how little he'd changed.

Oliver, I'm coming to London to have an affair with you. Just a couple of days and then you can forget me all over again.

Was she losing her mind?

Beside the dull waters of the canal, Charco Rios is

raping the white bitch again. His penis feels angrier than the others – as if it's not happy to belong to him.

No. A woman never makes herself attractive by admitting desire, yearning, grief, confusion. Men prefer confident women. How confident she had felt, those many years ago, as a young student!

Charco Rios's hands claw into her hair and bang her head on the hard ground – as if something is her fault. As if he must hurt and punish what excites him.

'Bitch! White bitch! You're asking for it!'

Again she strives to expel her mind from her aching head. To blot herself out. To cease to exist.

She is ashamed to be what they have made of her.

She had phoned him, in court. A voice answered: 'Oliver Rawl.' Her wits returned.

'Do you ever have lunch?' she asked gaily.

He laughed. 'Only QCs have lunch. The lunch hour in court is only an hour and you never know when the court will rise.'

'Oh, I see.'

She was reluctant to suggest an evening. An evening would probably involve the woman.

'Bitch! You're asking for it!'

'Unfortunately I'm duty solicitor on night rota next week,' Oliver was saying. 'I'm being summoned back to court right now. Best thing is, give me the name of your London hotel and I'll leave a message.'

She was shaken. He hadn't once said he would like to see her. It had turned out even worse than she had feared. He sounded too busy to breathe.

Now the little Filipino has moved back in, demanding the same service all over again. Can they never have enough? Her mouth is full of a bitter-tasting fluid. It runs off-white down her chin and she is choking.

But when she reached her conference hotel in Russell Square, there was a message waiting for her at reception. She tore open the envelope, holding her breath. It was a fax:

Dear Jenny,

> *Hope I didn't sound too inhuman. I'd really like to see you and catch up with your news. How about a late lunch on Saturday? If I've been up all night, washing the blood off the hands of a client, you can tell me stories of Yeominster to keep me awake. Please leave a message to confirm at my office.*

She noticed 'at my office' with a twinge of pleasure. Maybe he didn't want the woman he lives with to know about it. Maybe he remembered those red sheets at St Paul de Vence. Her conference ran from Tuesday through Thursday and the hotel was strictly for three nights. She would stay over, find a cheap hotel, send a message to Phil.

No, don't.

It lasts a full hour, although she has lost all sense of time. This is no ordinary hour, not a clock hour. The eight youths drag their naked victim 200 yards back and forth along the banks of the canal, kicking her, striking her, tossing her in the air like a rag doll.

No one comes to help her. No one wants to know.

All the English people in this Englishwoman's England are asleep – or pretending to be.

Across the city, Oliver Rawl has reached Eden Manor police station. The police have arrested a youth whom they insist is really Charco Rios's chum Miguel Garcia, but who claims to be someone else, Cesar Alvarez by name. Oliver has been shown a long, ten-inch blade, wrapped in a Cellophane bag and neatly labelled. Detective Sergeant Doug McIntyre claims to have taken it off the prisoner during a violent struggle on the Eden Manor estate.

The charge, or potential charge, is murder – the unsolved murder of the headmaster, Edward Carr, outside his school gates. Miguel Garcia is one of three suspects who have been on the run since two of them, Miguel and a boy called Gregory, did some talking in a pool hall.

The third and prime suspect is Oliver's lovable client Charco Rios. Charco remains at large.

Detective Sergeant Doug McIntyre is studying Oliver as if he might have committed the murder himself.

'But you don't know where Charco is, we gather,' he says with iron-weighted scepticism.

Oliver stiffens. 'You've brought me here for questioning or to represent a prisoner?'

'Take it easy, Oliver.'

Oliver immediately regrets his tone – Doug is a good fellow if allowed so to be. Naturally they all harbour their doubts about defence lawyers. Life would be a whole lot simpler without them. And convictions easier to obtain.

But Oliver does not altogether regret his tone. There are rules and the rules are the hinges of justice.

Custody Officer Wright is leading him to the cells. You would never guess that Charlie Wright leads a double life. One moment he's a kindly, reassuring uncle in blue, straight out of the Jack Warner mould, and then, no sooner is your back turned, than he is transformed into a fiendishly dedicated football intelligence officer.

Charlie has confided to Oliver that he's disappointed not to have been selected as one of the police spotters who travel abroad when the England team are playing in Europe. He has studied the way the English hooligan leaders from the different clubs get together in pubs to plan riots abroad, and even contact Dutch or German hooligan leaders to fix a venue for the battle of Waterloo or the battle of the Somme.

'Which of course they've never heard of,' Charlie Wright adds scornfully. 'What you've got to understand, Oliver, is that football is the pretext, not the cause of the violence. Millwall hooligans will travel to matches in which the club is not involved. German hooligans will cross the Rhine for a game between England and Belgium.'

'I suppose it's a culture,' Oliver remarked.

Charlie Wright shook his head. 'Oliver, these are not what you'd call cultured people.'

He wouldn't reveal whether he supported a team. 'It might be used in evidence against me.' He couldn't understand Oliver's preference for rugby which remained disappointingly free of hooliganism, except on the pitch.

'How many plainclothes spotters do you have inside Twickenham during an international match or a club cup final?' he asked disdainfully. 'You might as well apply intelligence-led policing to a bowls match between Eastbourne Ladies and Bromley Gadabouts.'

About his lack of 'medals' Charlie was cheerfully philosophical; about his wounds, he was reticent. He had been hospitalised more than once, and recently was off work for two months.

Charlie Wright is taking a long look through the cell door spy-hole at Oliver's new client, Cesar Alvarez, alias Miguel Garcia.

'Shout sooner rather than later,' is his final advice before the cell door closes behind Oliver.

Gaston Dubois has fallen asleep at the reception desk. He dreams of girls as a dog dreams of hares in the open, but it is not a happy sleep and he is fearful lest the girls fleeing across the open countryside of Aquitaine be caught, trapped, destroyed by the pursuing hounds.

The dogs are black. They are not hounds, perhaps Rottweilers. They do not bark, they sneer: Asking for it.

He wakes, lifts his head: the hotel main telephone is ringing. A light on the switchboard indicates an out-side call.

He remembers the lady who went out, alone, and has not come back.

It's the police. An empty handbag with a gold chain has been found in the street by a passing patrol car.

There is nothing inside the bag except a small packet of paper handkerchiefs, one lipstick, a comb, a card bearing the name and address of her hotel – and a notebook containing several handwritten addresses, two of them under the name 'Oliver Rawl'.

'Have any of your guests, almost certainly a woman, not yet returned to the hotel?'

Oh, terrible!

'Yes, sir,' he says. 'A Mrs Glendower. She went out at 0025, alone. Her room key is here. Room 36, sir.'

The telephone rings. Sarah, still awake, reaches for the receiver by her bed, heart hammering: something has happened to Oliver.

It's the police. But not Eden Manor. The call comes from a car patrolling the Great North precinct. They are asking for a Mr Oliver Rawl.

'He set out for Eden Manor police station more than an hour ago,' Sarah says. 'He's duty solicitor tonight.'

'Madam, can you identify a Mrs Jennifer Glendower?'

'No, why?'

'A handbag has been found on the street. It contains Mr Rawl's name and address. We have reason to believe it may belong to Mrs Glendower. We are concerned for the lady's safety. She hasn't returned to her hotel.'

'You can probably reach Mr Rawl at Eden Manor.'

'Thank you, madam. Sorry to have disturbed you at this hour.'

*   *   *

The smell of the youth slouched on the bare cot hits him – a sour odour which might be compounded of cocaine, sweat, hatred.

'I'm Oliver Rawl. I'm the duty solicitor.'

'Yeah?'

'Mind if I sit down?'

No answer.

It isn't clear from the youth's glazed expression whether he does mind or he doesn't. The youth? That's not exactly what Oliver sees. He is immediately reminded of Charco Rios; same racial provenance, same ugly scowl. A face out of a Miltonian allegory. Oliver had opted for *Paradise Lost* at the University of Warwick. It was in that class that he'd met Jenny Glendower.

Later, at law college, Milton was no longer on the curriculum.

Oliver perches on a small stool, wearing his still slightly damp yesterday's shirt, his briefcase close to his feet.

'I'm here to represent you. If you wish.'

Represent? Oliver is conscious that he has been approaching a crisis of belief. The cynicism of the habitual offender is beginning to nauseate him but he conceals the aversion behind protective camouflage.

'Is your name Miguel Garcia?'

'No way.'

'What is your name?'

'Cesar Alvarez.'

'Address?'

'NFA.' No fixed address.

'Where do you sleep then?'

'With a friend.'

'Any member of your family who could come and identify you as Cesar Alvarez?'

'Listen, fucker, whose fucking side are you on? Why you asking the same fucking questions as the fucking pigs?'

'Because,' Oliver replies, 'until you fucking answer these fucking questions you will fucking stay inside.'

'Suits me.'

Oliver almost believes him. Perhaps it suits Cesar Alvarez, alias Miguel Garcia, quite well, for the time being. Perhaps he lives in fear of Charco.

'Chances are, you'll have to face an identity parade,' Oliver says.

'Yeah? What do you know about it, then?'

The point is good. Oliver already knows from his absconding client Charco that there is now a witness in all this, Tony Marquez, who claimed to have overheard Miguel and his pal Gregory boasting in a pool hall about the unsolved murder of Edward Carr. Only yesterday Oliver received another of these snarling Charco-calls, announcing that Charco's pal Gregory had been 'picked up' and 'done over by the pigs' and then positively identified by 'that fucker Marquez, he's dead, dead' at a police identity parade.

Oliver addresses Miguel: 'I ought to tell you that I also represent Charco Rios. Is that a problem for you?'

'Don't know the fucker.'

Oliver waits. No hurry. Miguel is brooding. Doubtless his pride is wounded – he must realise that to go into hiding with friends at Eden Manor and then get involved in something violent is plain careless.

'I know a bastard who wants to get his paws on all that reward money,' Miguel snarls. 'He's dead, the motherfuck.'

'Dead?'

'As good as. Yeah. The pigs have moved the shithead to another estate. Thought they'd be smart.'

'What's his name?'

Silence. Miguel's threats uncannily echo Charco's and now he is regretting having said anything. Sleepless and bored, Oliver yawns.

'The police will want to interrogate you under formal caution as soon as I have taken your instructions – in other words, tonight. I could call in a Forensic Medical Officer on the ground that you are drugged and tired.'

'I don't give a fuck. I ain't saying nothing, got it?'

Oliver's mind settles again on the potential conflict of interests. He shouldn't touch this case. It's ten-to-one that in the long run Charco, Miguel and Gregory will each try to pin the blame on the other, making separate legal representation inevitable. But the 'long run' is money. It's 'charges'. If this evil-smelling youth wishes to pretend that he has never heard of Charco, just as he has never heard of himself, that's his privilege.

'I must warn you that refusal to make a statement can have consequences if you are ever brought to trial.'

'Stuff it.'

Oliver rises, nods, and bangs on the cell door – which opens immediately. Evidently Charlie had been lurking outside.

'Cesar Alvarez,' Oliver tells Doug McIntyre, 'will make a nil statement so long as he is accused of being someone else. In the meantime, I'm requesting an FMO on the ground that he's unfit to make a statement tonight.'

McIntyre writes it down: everything on the record, nice and tidy.

Charlie Wright has a message for Oliver. 'Call your missus back soonest.'

'Thanks.'

Leaving Eden Manor police station, he reluctantly calls Sarah on his mobile. She deserves her sleep.

Sarah repeats the message from the patrol car in Great North. He notices that her tone is rather peremptory – understandable at this hour of the night.

'They found her bag on the street?'

'Evidently.'

'Oh God,' he murmurs.

'An old flame of yours is she, this Jenny Glendower? Sorry, Oliver, I'm tired. Poor woman.'

Oliver telephones Jenny's hotel. A young man with a faintly French accent answers.

'Has Mrs Jenny Glendower returned to the hotel yet?'

'No, no, sir, please contact the police – who is speaking, please?'

Oliver puts a call through to Great North police station and identifies himself.

'We'd be very glad if you could come here right away, Mr Rawl. Your name was found in the handbag.'

'What – what happened to her?'

'We don't know. We're still looking for her. I should warn you that we fear the worst.'

Reluctantly he turns the car towards the east, longing for sleep, longing for home, for a quiet Saturday morning, his heart filled with dread.

He remembers the blood-stained sheets in the French maid's arms, on a morning blazing with Mediterranean sunlight, the blood of love.

Charco and Luke – no, it's all of them – drag her by her matted hair to the edge of the canal, a naked, shivering woman, her skin a mass of cuts and contusions.

'Can the cunt swim?' Ally Leagum chirps.

But Jenny's attention is focused on Charco's deadly slit eyes, which carry the same question. She stares at the dark water, and the lights on the far side, not calculating distances, she's beyond that – she realises they want to destroy what they have defiled.

She can swim. West Country girls of her social class learn to swim – and swim well – from an early age. Abruptly the contours of calculation surface in her numbed head.

'No,' she begs, 'please don't! Please! I'll drown.'

They – four of them – lift her up and toss her naked into the canal. She holds her breath at the last minute. An explosion occurs in her ears as her head strikes the cold water.

Given what she has gone through, she shows amazing presence of mind. She knows it's her last chance to remain alive. Screaming and thrashing, to convince them she is drowning, she allows herself to sink from sight beneath the filthy, muck-filled water. Luckily for her they don't stay to make sure. They run off laughing with her Rolex, her credit cards, her money.

Out of decency they have not taken the engagement and wedding rings from her finger.

Suddenly it's quiet. The cool, dirty water embraces her like a friend. But a false friend. A new wave of panic hits her. She's exhausted. Normally she can swim in calm waters for hours, but now her limbs are weighted down with lead. They refuse to obey her commands. She can't catch her breath. The normal rhythm of her lungs collapses – oh my God, all my tyres are punctured.

She remembers what the instructors taught her on the survival course in North Wales. Don't fight, don't thrash, don't tighten up! Relax, Jenny, relax! Stretch your limbs out! Float! Imagine you are making love to Oliver on a warm summer's night in Provence.

She drifts across to the far bank, searching for steps, because the banks of the canal are too high and sheer for an exhausted woman to climb out. Reaching a row of moored barges, she summons the strength to bang on the sides of the hulls.

A dim light flickers through a window.

She hears a voice, far away. 'Please help me.' The voice may be her own.

Oliver sits beside her bed in Barts Hospital. She's wearing a loose-fitting hospital bed gown, off-white. She has not suffered physical injuries beyond multiple cuts and bruises, but the consultant has insisted on keeping her under observation for two days.

A nurse and a detective constable had taken Oliver aside before he was allowed in to the ward to see her. The nurse warned him about post-rape trauma and advised him to ask Jenny, at the first opportunity, what had happened.

'People tend not to. The victim feels they don't want to know. Then she may feel rejected, unclean. If you find she's blaming herself, don't let her.'

'Loss of self-esteem is always a danger,' the detective constable added.

'Has anyone contacted her husband?' Oliver asked.

'She won't allow it,' the nurse said.

'Normally, we'd get straight through to the next of kin,' the detective constable said. 'But these situations are difficult. You can't play them by the book. You can't ignore the victim's feelings.'

'She'll probably change her mind,' the nurse said. 'They go through very rapid mood swings.'

When he approached Jenny's bed and drew up a chair, she greeted him quite calmly.

'Nice of you to come, Oliver. Oh, what lovely flowers.'

He put them in her hand. He wondered whether to take her hand but didn't.

'I can only imagine what you've been through, Jenny.'

'I'm alive,' she says, 'though they tried to drown me. Do you remember how good at swimming I was when we went to the South of France together? I'd vanish out into the Mediterranean and there'd you be, standing up on the beach, pale and skinny, anxiously scanning the horizon.'

'Skinny!'

'You always wanted to read a book – Milton usually.'

'What happened last night?'

'Didn't the police tell you?'

'The police weren't there. Only you were there.'

'Eight boys. I think there were eight.'

But then the shutter comes down. She doesn't want to talk about it, to go through it all over again.

'Did you catch any of their names, Jenny?'

'There was a huge black boy called Luke. A tiny Filipino called Ally. Another black boy was Pete. The nastiest one, the leader, didn't have a name – yes he did but I can't remember it.'

Oliver hesitates, says nothing.

'Have you spoken to your husband?'

'Phil? He's called Phil. Why should I? What's it got to do with him? He wouldn't care, would he? I'd just be soiled goods to Phil.' She wipes her eyes. 'Sorry.'

Oliver suspects that she has come to London mainly to see him, to unburden herself. But now she can't. You can't discuss your husband's shortcomings when you've just been raped by eight youths for an hour.

'Would you like me to telephone your husband?'

'Oh, I'm sure the police have already done that,' she says in the same suffering tone. Oliver understands: everyone is to blame, a common feature of post-rape trauma.

'What about your children?'

'No need to keep pretending you care, Oliver.' Her eyes are wet. 'Sorry.'

'You keep apologising,' he says. Again he almost takes her hand, but again he doesn't.

Victims, Oliver notes, are never attractive or even appealing, particularly victims of rape. Jenny keeps telling him that it's Saturday morning, that he is tired, that she is wasting his time – that he should go home.

'Well, we won't be having our lunch together today, that's one blessing for you.'

To go out alone like that, after midnight. Why had she done it? Had she been inviting assault, self-destruction? Had it been her way of attracting attention to her unhappiness?

He can't ask. Nothing sounds right when tested on his silent tongue.

'Don't you think your husband should come and collect you when it's time to go home?'

'Get me off your hands.'

'That's not what I mean.'

'I know. I'm not being fair. I don't want to be fair. Did those boys treat me fairly?'

'If you were able to give the police four names, they'll catch the lot.'

'And spend the rest of their lives in jail? Do you think I want that? Just youngsters who . . .'

Should he tell her that he and Sarah between them represent the three boys she has named?

No. He's trapped. It might be his and Sarah's professional duty to 'prove' that one or all of them had been in Timbuctoo the previous night.

Thank God Charco had not been named. Otherwise the police would be interrogating Oliver even as he sat beside Jenny's bed. No, beforehand. Maybe they wouldn't have allowed him to see her.

She says: 'I have to be back in school on Monday. I'm a schoolteacher, did you know that?'

'Yes, I know that, but you can't go straight back to work on Monday.'

'Why not? I have no intention of telling anyone in Yeominster anything. Please tell the doctor I must take the train home tomorrow.'

He almost says, 'You'd be very welcome to spend a few days with Sarah and me.' But both of them would be at work during the day. Both have imminent trials.

No. Couldn't leave Jenny alone in the flat all day.

Anyway – Sarah.

She says: 'They found my clothes – the police. By the

canal.' Her laugh sounds odd, it doesn't belong to her. 'Maybe they'll believe me after all.'

'Of course they believe you.'

'Really? Hysterical woman. Out alone. In a short pink skirt. Asking for it. I bet they're checking out my medical history right now – except I don't have one, apart from two cases of uncomplicated childbirth.'

'Tell me about your children.'

She shakes her head, her eyes far away. 'No, Oliver, you're not interested, you're only being polite. Why did you leave me, Oliver? I've never known because you've never said.'

He glances around the ward without moving his head. Are the other women listening?

Jenny says, 'I've got a photo of us together in the South of France. It was taken by that Arab beach photographer – do you remember?'

'Yes, I remember.'

'No you don't. It's in my travelling bag. The police brought all my things here from the hotel. Would you like to see it? My bag's in the cupboard.'

He brings the bag and lays it on her lap. She rummages, then begins to cry again.

'These are the clothes I was going to wear for our lunch today. I was going to look French – silly, isn't it?'

She finds the photo and thrusts it at him almost in triumph. The young Jenny is smiling gaily at the photographer; he himself looks a bit impatient. He is holding a book in his hand.

'I've changed, haven't I?'

'Not much. I see what you mean about pale and skinny – me, I mean.'

'But you were nice.' Her eyes fill again. 'I loved you. You knew that, didn't you?'

'I didn't know much, at that time, about the emotions. I suppose . . . that when we first . . . we call it "love". But you can't love someone, in the full sense, until you know more about yourself.'

It's quite a speech, forced out of him by the tears in her eyes.

'And what do you know about yourself now, Oliver?'

She must be asking about Sarah. Women, he remembers, are clever at asking questions sideways.

He says: 'I live with someone, Sarah, whose work covers the same ground as mine.'

'That must be cosy.'

'It's not the word I'd apply to legal aid work.'

'Phil's a schoolteacher, too. He does maths.'

'Same school as you?'

'Good heavens, no,' she says, as if Oliver's ignorance is proof that he has no interest in her. 'I teach in a private school for girls. Phil despises me for it. He'd give his life for comprehensive education – though he wouldn't give his life for anything.'

'I see.'

'No, you don't. You don't want to see. You don't want to look at me. I've been watching your eyes.'

'You're giving me a hard time.'

'Haven't I had a hard time?'

'Yes.'

'You're not expecting a woman who's been raped by eight youths and thrown naked in a canal to be fair, are you?'

He tries to guide the conversation back in that direction. 'Would you recognise any of them . . . at an identity parade?'

'Of course. What a silly question.'

'Can you describe the leader of the gang, Jenny?'

'Foreign. Dago. Sort of Aztec – I don't know. I can never tell the difference between South East Asians and South American Indians. Slit eyes. We don't see many of that sort in Yeominster. We don't need them here, do we? They should all be deported.' A pause. 'You think I'm a bigot.'

'We're all bigots, Jenny.'

'I've just remembered his name – the gang leader. Rorco.'

'Rorco?'

'No. Something like that.'

When Sarah woke late that Saturday morning, no head lay on the pillow beside her. She looked in the spare room: empty.

She had always sensed that her judgment was at its frailest first thing in the morning. She tended to feel hurt, angry or confused about things that settled down an hour later.

She knew that Oliver hadn't come home because he was with a woman she had never met, Jenny Glendower.

Arriving home from Barts Hospital in late morning, Oliver fell into an exhausted sleep, scarcely a word to Sarah. He slept through the Saturday lunch he would have had with that woman if she hadn't been raped. Later, yawning and gulping coffee, he informed Sarah that at least two of the rapists (alleged, of course) were 'hers':

'The charming Ally Leagum and the ever-amiable Luke Grant.'

'God, how awful.'

'As of now I can claim only one, Pete McGraw, but Jenny thinks the gang leader's name was something like Rorco. It's not a big jump to Charco.'

'You always said he wasn't interested in sex.'

'I didn't say "not interested". I think he has a problem about girls. As poor Jenny may have discovered. But I also have a hunch.'

Oliver had been pondering his meeting with Miguel Garcia, otherwise Cesar Alvarez, in the cells of Eden Manor police station.

'I should tell you that Miguel mentioned a witness in the case, though not Tony Marquez by name. He said he knew someone who wanted to get his paws on the reward money, someone who was "dead" or "as good as". Miguel also said that the pigs had moved the witness to another estate.'

'Did he say where?'

'No – but I got the impression that he knows. In which case Charco also knows. Miguel claims never to have heard of Charco but I could have been listening to the great snake himself.'

'Oliver, I'm tired. It's Saturday.'

'You still haven't heard from Tony Marquez?'

Sarah shook her head.

'That's odd.'

'Why do you keep on and on about it?'

'I just think it's odd. Want to hear Rawl's latest Sherlock-hunch?'

'If I must.'

'Rawl's hunch is that Charco was assembling some boys to pay a visit to Tony Marquez when they stumbled across a more immediate attraction in the beguiling shape of Jenny Glendower.'

'How can you speak of her like that! You're so cold-blooded, Oliver!'

Later in the afternoon, Oliver returned to the beguiling shape in Barts, bearing a large box of chocolates. Left alone, brooding, Sarah had a premonition that this Jenny Glendower woman had entered her life and intended to stay.

But why was she lying to Oliver about Tony Marquez? Why had she concealed from him not only Tony's original visit to her office, when he was weighing his fear against his greed, but also a subsequent one, when he turned up to complain how plainclothes police had come for him at the pool hall, treating him like a suspect, arresting him in the manager's office, carting him off to Great North police station, then, the following day, hustling him, his mum and his two younger sisters away to a new address. Sarah gathered that the police were promising compensation for his lost job in the pool hall, but only if he stuck to his statement, only if he went all the way to the witness box in the Old Bailey.

'And how did the pigs know I was in on this, about Miguel and Gregory, I mean, 'cos I never said nothing to no one except my mum and you, Miss Woods.'

'You told your mum, Tony?'

'Yeah, but on my mum's name she swears she had nothing to do with it. She's cursing me all over the place.'

And would he ever get the computer tycoon's reward money, not having gone to the police of his own free will?

Sarah merely advised him to collaborate with the police and to keep in touch with her. She knew she had dug herself a hole so deep that no one, not even Oliver – least of all Oliver! – must know.

After Oliver returned to the 'beguiling' Jenny Glendower in Barts, that Saturday evening, with his box of chocolates, Sarah drove to a phone booth a mile away and once again telephoned the Edward Carr police hotline, quoting the reference number of her previous call from memory. On this occasion they treated her with more tact and respect – perhaps her anonymous letter to the Metropolitan Commissioner had got through to them. True or not, they must by now realise that her first call had been well informed.

'I have reason to believe,' she said over the phone, 'that the suspects in this case are aware that Tony Marquez and his family have moved home – and a serious attempt to intimidate the witness, or worse, may be imminent.'

She drove back to an empty flat.

As she drove, the telephone was ringing in the flat.

No answer. Detective Sergeant Doug McIntyre carefully noted down the time of the hotline call, the location of the call box where it had been made, the likely travelling time.

Seconds after she stepped through the door the phone rang again. She took the receiver, a little breathless (McIntyre noted through his headphones). A female voice asked whether she could speak to Sarah Woods.

'Speaking.'

'Sorry to disturb you at this hour, Miss Woods, this is Eden Manor police station. There is some confusion here who is duty solicitor tonight.'

'It's not me, that I can assure you.'

'Might it be Mr Rawl?'

'I have reason to believe it isn't. His rota ended last night as far as I know. He's not here at present but you could try his mobile.'

'Sorry to have troubled you, Miss Woods.'

Doug McIntyre switched off the tape recorder, played back the conversation, played back the recent call to the Edward Carr hotline, and nodded to himself. It was the same woman, it was Tony Marquez's solicitor, Sarah Woods. She had used the same phrase, 'I have reason to believe', in both conversations – very helpful for voice identification tests. And the anonymous letter to the Commissioner, a copy of which lay before McIntyre, reeked, to his practised nostrils, of 'solicitor'. 'An absolute betrayal of promises made to the public', 'an infringement of civil rights', and an 'absolute disgrace' – not the language one might expect from the circles frequented by Tony Marquez.

Either way, the two voice tapes would go to the police lab.

McIntyre carefully wrote a note in the Edward Carr log book. 'Threat to intimidate Marquez. Informant: Sarah Woods. Informant's source probably Oliver Rawl, co-habitant with Woods and solicitor to Charco Rios (warrant) and Miguel Garcia (in custody). Unknown at present: whether Woods passed latest message with Rawl's consent.'

Gaston Dubois resumes his duties as hotel receptionist at eleven p.m. After recent events he has resolved to give up the job, to find an *emploi* in a safer area of London, in the sort of hotel where clients invariably tip you for calling a taxi. The police had not brought the blonde lady back with them; they merely collected her belongings. The hotel manager had been summoned: if anyone should telephone for Mrs Glendower, they were to be advised to call Great North police station. Gaston, who had been thinking about the attractive blonde for hours, was denied the final viewing. The police scarcely questioned him: he was not the prime suspect after all.

Now Mrs Glendower's room has been occupied by a Japanese couple. There was no reason to explain to them why the room had fallen vacant prematurely. 'In the big cities one does not inquire on whose grave one treads', writes Brigid Kyle. Gaston is idly studying the *Sentinel* spread across the reception desk, though the manager prefers paperback novels which can be discreetly laid out of sight when a guest appears.

Gaston has fallen in love with the provocative little portrait at the head of Brigid Kyle's column:

Youth crime is now out of hand. A teenage gang reportedly modelled on the Triads is suspected by police of responsibility for a long list of unsolved crimes ranging across London. These include the ghastly murder of the headmaster Edward Carr, an event which touched the conscience of an entire nation. A plaque was recently unveiled outside his school: LOVE DOES NOT COME TO AN END.

Meanwhile, while love is not coming to an end, an entire nation is demanding retribution.

The gang is known to meet in amusement arcades and pool halls in King's Cross, Great North, Chinatown, and Trafalgar Square. They go routinely armed with lethal knives, swords and martial arts weapons and they perpetrate two or three violent muggings in an average week. A cigarette burn between the thumb and forefinger of the left hand is the badge of membership.

So why do they remain at large? Because no one will talk. No one will take the risk of stepping forward. Because reprisals are swift and violent.

The entire legal system must brace itself to offer real, effective protection to citizens brave enough to give evidence against violent criminals. And our courts must stop shilly-shallying over the carrying of deadly weapons. The courts must never accept that such weapons are carried for 'self-defence'. The sole purpose of combat knives is to cause GBH – Grievous Bodily Harm.

Gaston fervently agrees. So much violence! He sometimes wonders whether, returning home to Bordeaux, he might not study law and become an *avocat*, a lawyer, or a *juge*, an examining magistrate. His eyes close, his head nods. For a moment Brigid Kyle merges with the blonde lady, the hotel guest, who walked out into the night and never returned.

Eight

Marcus and Brigid were invited to Sunday lunch at Paul and Esther Glass's new home in Wandsworth. The family had only recently completed the move from Cambridge, so Esther took Brigid on a tour of the house while Paul and Marcus sat in the garden, sipping wine, gobbling salted nuts and weighing the opposition to Marcus's appointment as Chairman of the Criminal Law Commission.

'How's David?' Marcus inquired.

'He's supposed to be joining us for lunch – though the clock is a fellow-traveller in the life of a teenager.'

'He's still at school?'

Paul nodded. 'First-year A levels. We were worried about him changing schools at this delicate stage, but he seems to like Launcester.'

'Fine school, I hear. Cost you a bit.'

'One doesn't want to leave anything to chance.'

'That's what I thought with Lucy. I was wrong. She hated that posh girls' school of hers. If I'd thrown her into a rough comprehensive she'd probably be taking her A levels.'

Paul's expression registered concern. He and Esther were never sure whether they should mention the tragically absent Lucy.

'David has visited her several times in Oak End,' Paul said. 'I think he finds it extremely painful but he's full of admiration for her courage and good humour.'

'Nice boy, David.'

'Yes. He has the knack of getting involved in all that New Age Traveller business, those tree camps, those sieges of Stonehenge – without allowing the mud to lodge in his head.'

They stood up. The women were joining them.

'It's a gorgeous house, Marcus,' Brigid said. 'I'm crippled by envy. And this garden!'

'Yes, we might be back in Cambridge,' Esther said.

Presently David appeared on the patio, wearing soft moccasins, a small ring without a pendant in his left ear, and his hair tied in a pony tail. He seemed at ease with the adult world, greeting Brigid and Marcus courteously.

Esther led them inside to eat. Hesitantly the conversation came round to Lucy.

Paul leant towards Marcus. 'I may as well report what Ben Diamond is saying about Lucy.'

'Aha?'

'Ben confided to me that if Lucy were released early on parole, her progress could be a powerful message to the young.'

'Test tube teenage delinquent?' David asked caustically – though Marcus noticed that his tone was quieter than the brash inner-city shriek Lucy had cultivated.

'Role model,' Paul said. 'Ben wants to high-profile Lucy's progress through probation and drug Rehab.'

David continued to bridle. 'Just imagine – hand-held cameras tracking Lucy through rehab courses at Cable Street, Crescent House, Ruskin House – all that stuff.'

'I mean, David,' Paul said tightly, 'that Lucy would be demonstrating respect for herself, but also for her . . . parents.'

'For fathers everywhere. I love it,' David said. 'And maybe we can publicise Lucy's progress by working her in with a few of the Boy's favourite pop groups.'

Marcus and Brigid laughed. Everyone at the lunch table knew how sensitive the Government was to the recent adverse publicity surrounding New Downing Street's glitter parties for the New Music. Brigid had written acerbically in the *Sentinel*. 'When will the Prime Minister notice our Nobel laureates? Or aren't they "cool" enough?' The headline was brief: 'Pop Britain?'

'Well, Paul, I admire Ben's plans for Lucy,' Marcus said in his silkiest voice – the amateur baritone who years ago had crossed Bow Street from dreams of the Royal Opera House to the famous courthouse where entry is free. 'But tell Ben Diamond that Lucy may not want to sign up as a role model to the young if she thinks it will advance the career of her vain, conceited and neglectful father. Isn't that so, David?'

David looked uncomfortable. 'I saw Lucy last week. She now has a big bee in her bonnet that may complicate her early release on parole. Lucy has assumed the mantel of Joan of Arc for all women prisoners.'

Marcus laid down his knife and fork. 'Does Sarah Woods know this?'

Lucy was now marked down by the staff of Oak End as a trouble-maker, an agitator.

'The girl has embarked on a crusade rather bigger than she is,' one of the governors told Sarah. 'It began as soon as she met Chelsea Elford. Since that time Lucy has been in solitary three times.'

Chelsea Elford was not an inmate, although she had done time. A case worker for the charity Women Behind Bars, Chelsea believed that no woman should be in prison. It was Miss Cowdrey who had brought Lucy and Chelsea together in association time. Never a trouble-maker herself, a model of rectitude, devoted to her art classes, Miss Cowdrey had secured the support of Women Behind Bars for her pending appeal against conviction.

Miss Cowdrey stood back in the shadows, observing with hooded gaze as Chelsea Elford targeted Lucy. Miss Cowdrey was brooding.

Governor Mary Heatherington had appeared to dismiss Sarah's fears for Lucy, but she had absorbed the message and now suspected that Miss Cowdrey's mothering of the girl concealed a malign purpose. On her instructions, prison officers had twice searched Miss Cowdrey's cell in quest of forbidden items, including weapons.

Miss Cowdrey had wrung her large hands in shocked protest.

'Whatevah do you imagine you will find?'

They found nothing beyond a personal Bible, passages of which, on inspection, proved to be heavily annotated with a green marker pen, the emphasis being on justice and its close cousin vengeance – eyes for eyes, teeth for teeth. Evidently the New Testament was of little interest to Miss Cowdrey. Mary Heatherington had summoned her. The tall, stately spinster stood before her; between them was a large, extremely heavy table, riveted to the floor; flanking Miss Cowdrey were two prison officers.

'I'm returning your Bible, Miss Cowdrey. There is no Prison Department regulation against highlighting the ancient thunderers of the desert.'

'Thank you,' Miss Cowdrey had said with heavy sarcasm. 'I shall report this intrusion to the authorities and to the European Court of Human Rights.'

'One other matter. These three letters you see in my hand were found tucked into your Bible – the book of Leviticus to be precise.'

'Those are mine! They belong to me!'

'All three letters are written in the same hand and appear to be in code. They are signed "D". Each ends with the words "Justice on Blackfriars Bridge". Can you explain them?'

Miss Cowdrey's bosom was heaving, her large hands were restless.

'These letters, Governor, are sent by a vital witness in my case. As such, they are privileged and confidential.'

'Has your lawyer seen them?'

215

'There are some things, Governor, one does not divulge.'

Sarah Woods learned all this from one of Oak End's assistant governors. She made a mental note to inform Oliver about 'D' and 'Blackfriars Bridge' – the hallmark of his transsexual fax maniac Delia Atkinson.

'Did the Governor return the letters to Miss Cowdrey?' Sarah asked the assistant governor.

'Yes – but we made photocopies.'

Of all this Lucy probably knew little or nothing, beyond the fact that Miss Cowdrey's Bible had been 'seized by the fascist regime'. It was Chelsea Elford who dominated Lucy's conversation when Sarah visited. Chelsea had been sentenced to five years for armed robbery after her boyfriend made her act as lookout. 'Whenever he ran short of money for heroin Chelsea got beaten up.'

'Yes, Lucy, but you—'

'And when they brought Chelsea into the dock she felt total isolation as a woman. Everybody in court was male, the judge, the barristers, the officials. Men had control of her life.'

'What about the jury?' Sarah asked.

'What?'

'There must have been women on the jury?'

'I expect there were a few token women. You know the sort, smug suburban housewives in costume jewellery. *They'd* never rob a bank.'

Lucy showed Sarah a sheaf of press cuttings supplied by Chelsea. 'Guilty of Being a Woman' was the *Guardian* headline. Glancing through the cuttings, Sarah noted that they all proved that courts were harsher on women than men.

'Chelsea says it's because the women have offended cherished male myths of suitable female behaviour,' Lucy told her.

Sarah didn't want to get into an argument. Oliver was for arguing with. That's why he had been born.

'You're part of the system, aren't you?' Lucy challenged her. Electric charges were sparking in her wiry hair.

'Lucy, your interests and your release on parole are what concerns me.'

'Yeah? Only because his Honour, the great Marcus, is set to run the country and bung thousands of women inside – women like Chelsea's friend Tessa who was given twenty-eight days for throwing empty bottles during a demo. They wouldn't even grant her bail.'

Sarah nodded patiently. There was usually more to it than the women admitted in their stories. They never told the whole truth – especially the druggies. Lucy was particularly excited by Chelsea Elford's efforts on behalf of the Nigerian drug smugglers in Oak End, beleaguered women who had no visitors and wept every night for their lost children. Sarah and Oliver both represented several of these 'drug mules', who were paid by Nigerian suppliers to swallow the packets then take the plane from Lagos to London. They were sitting ducks – Customs officers could smell them coming at 10,000 feet above the ground.

'Chelsea says they should all be released and deported,'

217

Lucy said. 'Miss Cowdrey agrees. She prays with these women for their lost children. I'm trying to get them to go on hunger strike.'

Sarah wanted to talk about early parole and the conduct most likely to earn it, but Lucy scornfully told her to forget it.

'Every prisoner here is a political prisoner! OK? You're either for women or against them. If you don't agree, you're no longer my solicitor. Got it?'

Sarah rose. Time was up. Taking on Lucy Byron as a client had perhaps not been one of her wiser decisions.

Word reached Marcus from Paul Glass of mounting opposition – 'from certain well-orchestrated quarters' – to his appointment as Chairman of the Criminal Law Commission. The Home Secretary had urgently summoned Paul and Edmund Joiner to confer with him at his heavily, but unobtrusively, guarded private residence.

'I believe I have to bite the bullet and announce Marcus's appointment to the House without further delay. Frankly, strictly between ourselves, the Prime Minister is growing restless about the endless speculation in the press.'

Edmund Joiner handed him a list of organisations, headed by the Bar Council, the Criminal Bar Association, the Association of Progressive Lawyers and the Probation Service, all of them now on record as vigorously opposing Marcus's appointment.

'If we want to reform the entire criminal justice system,' Joiner added, 'it won't help if we start by alienating the Bar.'

Ben snorted. 'How do you reform the system without alienating the Bar? Anyone with such powerful enemies as Marcus Byron must be right. As Marcus says, we want an end to "revolving door" justice in the magistrates courts, where young offenders pass in, pass out, re-offend. The whole system has to be fast-tracked and given backbone: Reparation Order, Action Plan Order, Supervision Order. I have promised the nation that everything is going to move along at the double. "We're taking off", I announced in the House. "Every case in the Youth Court must be resolved within two months of charges being laid."'

Edmund Joiner then reported from the Whips' office on mounting opposition within the parliamentary party to Marcus Byron's appointment.

'You may have to settle for Byron's policies without Byron himself, Home Secretary.'

'I thought you were an admirer of his, Edmund.'

'I am. But I am not the legal and political establishment.'

Ben Diamond turned to Paul Glass. 'You're unusually quiet, Paul.'

'I have to admit the situation is not good and not improving. The Bar considers Marcus's recent attack on legal fees to have been extremely ill timed. A solid block of opposition to his appointment has now formed within the House Home Affairs Committee.'

'Marcus Byron is always going to be a pro-active fig-ure, and a highly contentious one. That's one reason why I want him to chair the new Criminal Law Commission.'

Paul Glass nodded. 'But Byron is also a man with a daughter who may not long hence emerge from an open prison on parole.'

'Lucy? She's to be a model of rehab. We all agree on that.'

'But does Lucy agree? She's notoriously hostile to her father – as her trial rather stunningly revealed.'

'Your David knows her well. Is it true that she remains in the grip of a drug habit?'

'No, David assures me that she has kicked it. And Marcus himself tells me he's confident of getting his daughter on-side.'

'How confident?' Ben Diamond snapped.

Paul Glass turned to Edmund Joiner, who had fallen silent – as befitted a junior. 'What do you think, Edmund? You see David whenever you visit us.'

'I . . . I hesitate to give an opinion.'

'Why?'

'Because, frankly, David himself isn't sure of Lucy.'

Marcus and Brigid were heading for a weekend they had long promised themselves at a pleasant little 3-star hotel in Dorset. Cruising down the M3 in his beloved Rolls, blacker than normal against the ivory leather upholstery, never more than one hand on the wheel, the other light-ing cigars or venturing into playful indecencies, Marcus remained oblivious to the powerful BMW motorbike which had been tracking MB1 ever since they crossed Earl's Court Road and headed west towards the Hogarth Roundabout.

'So what do you hear from the Lord Chancellor's Department, Marcus?'

'About what?'

'About your attack on exorbitant legal fees.'

'Yeah, well. I gather that Tommy favours a warning shot across the Bar's bows, or some such claptrap, but no real action – for the time being.'

'Stop referring to our new Lord Chancellor as Tommy, Marcus. It's rather insiderish. It sounds as if you've already entered the charmed circle of winks, nods, croneyism, insider-lobbying—'

'It was Tommy who restored me to the Bench.'

'Yes, dear. But Tommy was until recently a fat-cat QC. Since taking office he's spent a fortune – the public's fortune – on wallpaper for his official bedroom. The Government's spin doctors are now fully employed desperately explaining that the Lord Chancellor's wall-paper, the new £25,000 oak dining table, three *chaises longues*, two wardrobes, a sideboard, and a total cost of refurbishment estimated at £650,000 – is all part of a ten-year "rolling programme" of work begun long before Tommy sat on the Woolsack.'

Marcus nodded – though nodding against the leather headrest of a Rolls is a fine art. 'OK.'

'As for Tommy's new custom-built oak dining table,' she went on, 'we are told that it can seat ten and is "very good value for money" – that's £2,500 per head.'

'So what?'

'So Tommy has to listen when they bad-mouth you. He has to listen to the 11,500 staff in the Lord Chancellor's Department and the Court Service Agency – not a few of whom hate your guts every bit as much as Ben's senior officials do.'

Marcus sighed deeply. 'Right now I feel like an untethered cargo in the hold of a leaking boat caught in a storm.'

'Stay out of it, Marcus. Stay on the bench.'

They were now following the A30 south-west. Marcus's attention was fixed on the motorbike that had been in his mirror for too long. It slowed whenever he slowed, keeping a uniform distance, and accelerated whenever he put his foot down.

'Hold on. We're stopping.'

Abruptly he pulled into a lay-by and jumped out with a speed surprising in such a heavy man. The BMW roared past them. There was no way of identifying the rider swaddled in helmet and black leather but Marcus got the registration number: M245 KRD.

'Fractured exhaust pipe,' Marcus reported as he refastened his seat belt.

Checking in to the 3-star hotel, housed in an Edwardian seaside mansion, Marcus offered the manager his routine complaints about the stairs, fire doors which swung back in your face as you carried luggage, the mattress, the view from the bedroom.

'You want five stars for the price of three,' Brigid said after the bemused manager had departed, browbeaten into offering a concessionary rate if they undertook to dine-in on both evenings.

Marcus chuckled. 'You have to get your retaliation in first, my Uncle Jeremiah always taught me. Anyway, I've got a five-star woman for the price of three.'

She moved to slap him but merely found herself on her back across the bed, with Marcus already removing his trousers.

'Marcus, wait! The manager may come back with another concession.'

'I've been waiting for two hours on that damn road.'

'They should bring Dorset nearer to London when they know you're coming, is that it?'

He flipped her over on to her stomach but she didn't mind. Marcus liked to rape a woman before he settled down to making love to her. A woman was 'asking for it' until he'd discharged that little bullying ritual. Never wear one of your better outfits on arrival; you could more or less count on writing it off. Complaints were met by a casual promise that damages were covered by Marcus's All Risks insurance policy. Apparently Louise hadn't been so keen on the 'you're asking for it' routine – one of the several difficulties in the marriage now greasing the smiling pockets of Marcus's solicitor, Simon Hoare.

Half an hour later Brigid glanced down from their bedroom window to the hotel forecourt. Several cars were parked there, including MB1 and, next to it, the large black motorbike whose registration number Marcus had noted down when it passed them on the road. Something resembling a beer can seemed to have been attached to a broken exhaust pipe.

Later, when they had dinner, the table next to theirs was occupied by a lady who sat alone, remorselessly smiling at them and nodding agreement with every word they said.

Brigid noticed that her hands were exceptionally large for a woman. Finally driven to exasperation by the inexorable eavesdropping and the relentless smile, Marcus abruptly turned to their neighbour after the main course had been cleared away.

'My name's Marcus Byron,' he said. 'What's yours?'

'Oh, you know it, dear,' the woman said in a deep yet ladylike voice. 'In fact, we're close friends, you and I, Judge, very close.'

'I've seen you in court?'

'Oh yes, very much so. And my poor sister, too.'

'What's your sister's name?'

'Oh, you know that one, too, dear. So does someone very precious to you.'

With that she delicately wiped her lipsticked mouth with her napkin, rose, and trotted out of the dining room, vainly attempting to suppress (Brigid noticed) a manly stride.

While Marcus took his pipe for a stroll in the garden, Brigid made an inquiry of the manager, who with some reluctance consulted the hotel register and identified the lady as an unscheduled guest occupying Room 19.

'A Miss Agatha Cowdrey, madam.'

Brigid stared at him. 'Did she enter her permanent address?'

The Manager studied the register again. His expression changed. 'The address given is "Blackfriars Bridge".'

'Rather unusual?'

'Very!'

'Maybe you and I should pay a visit to Room 19.'

After some hesitation he consented and she followed him up a rear stairway, he holding a spare room key. After knocking in vain, he inserted the key in the lock. The door opened. The room had been vacated.

The BMW was no longer to be found in the hotel car park.

'Very unusual,' the manager repeated, 'and this Miss Cowdrey did not pay for her dinner.'

Brigid went straight up to their own room. Tucked under the door was a sheet of fax paper. A message had been neatly written in childlike capitals: AGATHA NEVER FORGETS AND NEVER FORGIVES, JUDGE. THINK OF YOUR DAUGHTER BEFORE IT'S TOO LATE. SAY NO TO THE JOB. LOVE, AGATHA COWDREY.

'We should inform the police, Marcus. And Governor Heatherington.'

Marcus nodded grimly.

A phone call to Oak End Prison merely confirmed that Agatha Cowdrey was where she should be, and would long remain – in her cell.

Brigid lies awake listening to the gentle wash of the sea

on the Dorset coast, convinced that the motorbike with the broken exhaust will come back. Beside her Marcus is asleep. Occasionally he tosses and groans, kicking the duvet from the bed as if fighting off an attack. Brigid is tempted to lay a hand on his forehead, to ease him out of his nightmare, but she decides it goes with the job, the job he refuses to reject.

And will not, she increasingly suspects, get.

In Marcus's dream they – his enemies – are meeting in the crypt of an East London church. Although now semi-derelict through disuse, the church is famous to students of architecture for its unfinished Hawksmoor tower and for the magnificent headstones in its overgrown graveyard. The vicar, an ardent member of Liberty and of the Howard League for Penal Reform, is fighting against the closure of the church threatened by the Bishop – a fierce battle sharpened by the Bishop's conviction that the vicar wishes to keep the church open not to worship God, but to provide a place of refuge for terrorists and paedophiles on the run.

They meet by candlelight. Only carefully filtered and totally dedicated Progressives have been invited. Everything they stand for remains in peril. The new Government promises to be tougher, harsher, more punitive on crime than its predecessor. It is building prisons at a furious rate. It is threatening to merge the Probation Service with the Prison Service. It is poised to throw twelve-year-olds behind bars, girls as well as boys. It has refused to raise the age of criminal responsibility from ten to fourteen. It listens to senior police officers. It rules out the de-criminalisation of cannabis. It plans to introduce a dangerous new category of 'collective crime'. It believes in mandatory sentences.

Most threatening of all, Ben Diamond is determined to elevate Marcus Byron, the deadly enemy of the Progressives, to his right hand.

Only those who ignore history are doomed to repeat it.

Governor Mary Heatherington wanted Lucy out of Oak End – as she was making clear to Sarah Woods.

'She's doing herself no good here. All this permanent agitation is merely getting everyone excited and setting back Lucy's own chances of an early parole. An open prison would help her negotiate her passage to freedom.'

Sarah agreed but had little say in the matter. It was Lucy herself who could call the shots. She kicked and screamed and claimed that it was a 'political decision' to remove her from her 'sisters' in Oak End. She threatened to abscond from any open prison within an hour – forcing Governor Mary Heatherington to yield.

'A prisoner can be transferred to an open prison only by her consent,' she reminded the national Director of Prisons by telephone.

An hour later he called back after conferring 'at the highest level'. With whom, he did not choose to say. He gave Governor Heatherington a clear instruction: to receive Lucy's boyfriend, young David Glass, at noon the following Tuesday and to leave him alone, 'utterly alone, no observers', with Lucy Byron.

'He is not to be searched on arrival,' the Director of Prisons added.

'I'll need that in writing,' the Governor snapped back. 'If things go wrong, you carry the candle.'

'Agreed.'

The Director saw no reason to add that he had taken care to obtain the same written authorisation from the Home Secretary – through the good offices of Dr Paul Glass.

What Agatha Cowdrey feels for Lucy is simply love. But she had also loved Cousin Hettie – though the emotions involved were somewhat different. All the people whom Agatha Cowdrey had loved possessed something which they ought to give her freely, in recognition of her 'friendship', something they refused to give. It could be money, it could be passionate kisses on the mouth. She always waited in vain. Finally her love soured and twisted like a withered vine into a murderous love.

Miss Cowdrey has discovered that Lucy is to be released the following Tuesday. She has overheard a murmured conversation between two prison officers. But word had already reached her from another source, her very dear sister. Who had once been her brother. She had always loved her younger brother Derek, even when he ran away from home, vanished, and news reached her that he had adopted the name Foster. She always forgave his violence; after all Derek, like she herself, suffered from the refusal of cruel, heartless people to return his love. When he became a woman, brother and sister were reunited as sister and sister. They shared so much in common, she and 'Delia Atkinson', though Delia adored powerful motorbikes while she stuck to four wheels. They sent each other loving faxes.

Of course Delia's lifestyle remained rather different from her own. He was always in trouble with the police (for things he had not done), she never. That didn't seem fair. Derek-Delia needed money far more urgently than she did. Naturally Cousin Hettie had rejected the reprobate even before his-her scandalous sex-change; only Agatha nestled within the comforting paragraphs of Cousin Hettie's will. That was nice, it might even be construed as love reciprocated – except what use was it while Cousin Hettie refused the ultimate act of love, to die?

Now that the forces of injustice had locked up Agatha, Delia was bravely carrying the candle for justice. And what is justice if not righteous vengeance?

And now Lucy intended to betray her love by secretly slipping away. That wasn't at all nice. So much loyalty and kindness betrayed. It wasn't acceptable, not at all.

Miss Cowdrey and Lucy are alone together in the modelling room, no other prisoner or member of staff in sight. Lucy is at work on a vase in the Etruscan style, working from one of the illustrated books donated by Art Inside.

Miss Cowdrey has been unusually silent this evening.

She seems to be watching Lucy's efforts at producing a graceful, symmetrical vase with something worse than disapproval.

'You're not really trying, are you?'

'Oh, I am, Miss Cowdrey.'

'You have been listening to stories about me, haven't you?'

Lucy's mucky hands freeze. The light in Miss Cowdrey's grey eyes is hard and manic.

'Stories, Miss Cowdrey?'

'Don't pretend, deah. You don't believe in my innocence, I can tell. I've always known you were deceiving me. Just like your father.'

Miss Cowdrey is standing over Lucy, staring down with the blank, expressionless gaze that gives Lucy nightmares in her claustrophobic cell. At home you could run down to the kitchen, make yourself a cup of something, but here there's no way out of your cell all night long unless it's the toilet. Thirteen hours of screaming panic.

'Let me give you a little advice, deah. Never talk about your father, not in this prison.'

'But I don't,' Lucy whispers.

'Oh but you do, I've heard you. You go around boasting about your famous father, the judge.'

'No.'

'Yes. You've been deceiving me all along, haven't you? You know I'm preparing a second appeal and your father is determined I shan't succeed. But I shall succeed, shan't I, Lucy? And you're not going to stop me.'

The would-be Etruscan vase fell to the floor as the

large hands fastened around Lucy's throat. The girl thrashed her legs and struggled to free herself but she was no match in weight or strength for the tall, posh lady who hadn't dumped Cousin Hettie in the quarry.

The door swung open. Governor Heatherington had put Lucy's classes with Miss Cowdrey under covert observation ever since she had heard Sarah Woods's concerns. It took two prison officers to wrestle Miss Cowdrey's hands from the choking girl's frail neck.

David Glass usually made the journey to Oak End by train, hitching a lift to save the taxi fare when he could, but on this occasion an official car brought him, parking discreetly some distance from the prison gates.

Monitored on closed-circuit television, the young man in jeans, Indian cotton shirt and moccasins strode towards the prison gates, a small denim satchel on his back – yet not too small to be carrying enough cannabis, crack and heroin to keep the women of Oak End happy to the end of time. The Governor's deputy had positioned herself at the first gate, but David passed through without a search, contrary to every regulation. She accompanied him across a courtyard decorated with hanging flowers to the second gate; again no search.

They knew what was in the satchel.

Lucy was waiting for him. They were left alone in a large, pleasantly furnished reception room normally reserved for VIPs inspecting the prison.

He offered her a spliff of cannabis, and later another.

He told her that she could only beat the system, expose the system, when she regained her liberty. She could then join Chelsea Elford and the sisters of Women Behind Bars in open agitation. Lucy argued, sulked, resisted, but the grass gradually eased her head and set her feet dancing.

'Let's take a trip, Lucy,' he said.

'Yeah. Just me and you – and everyone.'

An hour after his arrival, she and David drifted in a pleasant, smiling haze through the huge, impenetrable gates of Oak End and into this silly posh car which seemed to be waiting for them with some kind of chauffeur who never said a word. Lucy knew that she was 'escaping' with David into freedom, into their own space, and their own 'thing'.

All her belongings were already stowed in the boot of the car, but she didn't give it a thought.

They drove at great speed. Lucy never saw the police outriders forcing a path through traffic and traffic lights.

'We're flying,' she murmured.

'And we'll never stop flying, Lucy.'

The back of the car was thick with marijuana and happiness and cuddles – all the way to Milton Grange open prison, set in beautiful Sussex countryside, with pigsties, stables, cow sheds and large greenhouses, where prisoners cultivated flowers for exhibitions and banquets.

Lucy arrived sky-high. 'Where are we, David?'

'This is the nice house where you're going to live for a few weeks.'

'With you?'

'I'll come and see you. I always do, don't I?'

'Yes, but—'

'Look, Lucy, cows and horses. You love cows and horses, don't you?'

'Yes, but—'

'You can milk the cows and grow organic vegetables here.' He smiled. 'You can do virtually anything you like here – except run away. You won't run away, will you?'

Alighting from the car, she tottered on liquid legs and leant on David for support.

'Listen to the birds,' she sighed.

'The birds are you and me.'

They took her to a special room, with only one bed, crisp white sheets and a little teddy bear lying on the soft pillow. A bowl of white grapes and a vase of marigolds, yellow and copper-coloured, stood beside the bed. When she reached out to embrace David again, her arms clutched thin air. He was gone. Lucy was alone and in the very special, tender care of the State.

The Home Secretary had adjusted his busy diary to monitor Lucy Byron's journey from Oak End to Milton Grange. Even the Boy had politely excused himself during a meeting with the Prime Minister of Japan in order to hear the latest progress report.

'So far so good,' Ben Diamond advised him by direct line. 'Milton Grange should suit Lucy. She made a point of tending the goats and working in the garden at Oak End, and she might even like the communal bedrooms, eight or ten to a room, with their big windows overlooking the countryside.'

'She's going to be a role model, remember?' the Boy said with just that touch of friendly menace that Big Ben found enthralling.

'Yes, Prime Minister, exactly as you say – a role model.' Ben did not add that what most of the women in Milton Grange hated was the difficulty of visits. The five miles from the nearest railway station had to be covered by taxi following an hour's train journey from Charing Cross. The families of the poorer women couldn't afford it – and they felt alien, particularly the black ones, in so much lush, all-white Sussex countryside.

But Lucy Byron wasn't poor; and if black, a special kind of black.

'So get her off the drugs,' the Boy was saying crisply over the phone. 'I want a clean Lucy. Total detox. And then – but only then – will you announce Marcus Byron's appointment.'

'Yes, Chief.'

Ben hurried from his office by limousine to the reception he was staging in Lancaster House to mark his return from the United States as a member of the Prime Minister's retinue. Leading journalists had been invited. Ben made a short speech about successful American experiments in 'zero tolerance' towards petty street crime.

'It's certainly something that we in this country need to study closely.'

'What about vehicle crime?' he was asked by Auriol Johnson. The journalists smiled – everyone knew that Ben himself had been the victim of car crime five times in five years.

'Yes,' Ben responded earnestly, 'car thefts cost us two billion pounds every year. Britain has the highest figures for car crime in Europe, 1,400 cars stolen every day. Of which 150,000 are never recovered. Yes, that's something this Government intends to stamp on.'

Later, circulating among his guests, Ben seemed less preoccupied by law enforcement than by the lavish banquets laid on in Washington for the British visitors.

'Blitz-glitz is more fun than zero tolerance?' Brigid Kyle asked him. Ben regarded her cautiously. Kyle was to his eye the most attractive assassin on the Street, but she was also Mrs Marcus Byron – though no priest had as yet been invited to agree.

'Don't be cynical, Brigid. It's definitely a new transatlantic relationship. Our visit was the hottest ticket in town, everyone wanted to be there, from the computer magnates of Silicon Valley to Hollywood stars such as Steven Spielberg, Tom Hanks, Barbra Streisand, Harrison Ford.'

'And no mention of oral sex?'

Ben decided not to hear the question. 'The President achieved a perfect mix of youth and achievement, high tech and commitment to the future.'

'I hope the furniture was up to standards acceptable to our new Lord Chancellor,' Brigid said.

'Well, as you know, Tommy wasn't invited, much to his annoyance,' Ben chuckled. 'Tables in the East Room were set with Eisenhower gold plates, terracotta damask tablecloths, and some strikingly beautiful stuff from the Kennedy era. Silver candelabra holding gold tapered candles . . . I have to admit I don't have much of an eye for furniture.'

'What did you eat?' Auriol Johnson asked innocently.

'Basically an Anglo-American menu,' Ben replied solemnly. 'Honey mango glazed chicken, grilled salmon with oven-seared Portobello mushrooms, roasted artichokes, strawberries and cream with brandy snaps accompanied by Newton Chardonnay, Swanson Sangiovese and Mumm from the Napa Valley.'

'Well, don't say a word about it next time you stand on a soap box in Woolwich market.' Auriol smiled.

'I really believe that our people expect their elected leaders to be treated with dignity when they travel abroad,' Ben told her.

'You might get more "dignity" in a Tibetan monastery.'

Ben carried the expression of a man suffering insult with forbearance. Finding Marcus, he shook his hand with an air of embarrassment. Everyone was monitoring the inter-action between them.

'I don't give up easily, Marcus,' Ben murmured in his ear. 'I'm meeting resistance to your appointment, but I'm a fighter. You know that, don't you?'

The Home Secretary moved on without waiting for the answer.

Auriol Johnson closed in on Marcus. 'What did Ben say to you?'

'He said he admired my fob watch.'

'I bet you'll tell Brigid what he said.'

'Yeah?'

'Marcus Byron used to divide the nation. Now he merely divides the Government. How about that, Marcus?'

Among the journalists, Marcus was now the centre of attention. They wanted to know why his rumoured appointment had been delayed. Was it because the crime policies he recommended in private to Ben Diamond were too radical? A woman from the *Guardian* asked him about plans to reduce school truancy by punishing the parents.

He bent to her with grave courtesy.

'I favour legal penalties for aggravated truancy provided you punish the parents first.'

'But aren't the kids who go truant generally from families that cannot control them?' the *Guardian* pressed.

'Cannot or don't?' Marcus came back. 'I think it would be up to the court to decide on the merits of the case. Maybe we would discover that a whole lot of parents who "cannot" suddenly "can" if they face a fine of up to one thousand pounds.'

The woman from the *Guardian* wore an expression of disgust. 'And what happens to the single mother living on benefit with six kids?'

He nodded politely. 'Quite so. I think magistrates are sensible people. That's why they're there. And don't forget that sociologists have shown that an early phase of truancy is often associated with missing school as part of a family holiday. In the case of immigrant families, you might get a six-month visit to Pakistan or three months in Jamaica – quite deliberate, no question of inability to control the child.'

'Who would prosecute the parents?'

'The local education authority. Now you must excuse me, Brigid and I are due at the opera.'

'*Don Giovanni*?' Auriol asked.

Nine

The police now had eight boys in the bag for the rape of Jenny Glendower. After a week of frustration, the detectives on the case had been granted a lucky break.

From Jenny herself Oliver had heard nothing since her discharge from Barts Hospital. She had insisted on making her way back to Yeominster alone, a band of pale skin on her wrist where her Rolex had been, and only reluctantly allowed Oliver to lend her money for the fare. He received a cheque through the post – but no message. He hadn't cashed the cheque.

The arrests began after one of the boys, Timothy Malvinas, finally half confessed to his mother – 'I've got to tell you something but I can't because you're going to get upset.' He swore to her that he'd had no part in it, not laid a finger on the blonde woman, merely been a bystander. Believing him – her own son! – Mrs Malvinas had gone straight to Great North police station.

'My Timothy would never do anything, never,' she told the duty officer. 'I have brought him up good.'

But not 'good' enough to avoid a long list of criminal convictions, a few serious. Known at school as the

'Governor', Timothy had once broken a boy's nose and forced his terrified victim to thank him.

The police showed him a video recording of a gang of boys accompanying a woman along a darkened street – the camera sited above the off-licence, near the Chinese take-away. Timothy was one of them. He began to name names, still protesting his own innocence.

Rapidly they picked up Pete McGraw and little Ally Leagum. They found Luke Grant fast asleep in Catherine House, where he lived in the care of Sedge Hill social services. Although over six foot and said to weigh seventeen stone, the fourteen-year-old boy was too sleepy to resist – until it was too late, and they had him in the van, cuffed.

Finally they grabbed the prize catch, Charco Rios, already wanted for the murder of Edward Carr. During the small hours of the night the fugitive Charco had walked into a police trap outside the temporary home of Tony Marquez, the former pool hall assistant he had declared 'dead' or 'as good as'. Charco was carrying a lethal blade.

Sarah and Oliver were called to the police station, she to represent Luke and Ally, he to represent Charco. It was to be Oliver's first meeting with Charco Rios since the boy had broken bail and vanished.

The police offered the solicitors a brief résumé of the facts. The alleged facts. A number of bladed weapons were on display, each neatly labelled and wrapped in Cellophane.

They were taken down to the cells. Sarah found the great hulk of Luke slumped on the floor, half asleep.

'Hello, Luke, long time no see.'

'Yeah.'

'So what's all this about?'

'Dunno.'

'Attempted murder and rape are two of the most serious charges in the book, Luke.'

'I never done any of what they said. I told the others to lay off her but they wouldn't listen.'

'So you agree you were there?'

'Yeah.'

'As you know, I shall need to hear your version before I advise you whether to make a statement to the police.'

'I'm not saying nothing. They just try and stitch you up.'

'Under the new law, refusal to make a statement is likely to be held against you when you appear in court.'

'Yeah.'

Looking at this despondent kid, at the sleepy-sullen eyes which never met hers, she had difficulty in imagining him doing anything so terrible, so callous, so brutal, so inhuman. But Sarah Woods had experienced similar incredulity too often to take her feelings seriously.

Two cells along, Oliver was having a harder time. As usual Charco took refuge in a high pitch of rage and launched into a welter of accusations.

'I was fucking set up!'

'How?'

'The pigs were waiting for me. Gotcha, sonny, just as we thought, intimidation of witness and all that shit.'

Oliver shrugged. 'If the police take the trouble to

241

arrange new accommodation for a witness, they're likely to keep an eye on him.'

'Oh yeah? I bet that shithead Miguel Garcia sang to the fuckin' pigs, that motherfuck.'

'One thing I must tell you, Charco. After his arrest, Miguel insisted he'd never heard of you.'

'Yeah? If it was you that shopped me to the pigs, fucker, you're dead!'

'That's untrue and nonsense.'

'Yeah, you say.'

Oliver had said nothing to the police. Not to anyone, apart from Dodgett – and Sarah. But talking to Sarah was as intimate and fail-safe as talking to himself.

HOW MANY LIVES HAD TONY MARQUEZ? HOW MANY LIVES HAS OLIVER RAWL?

Now that Charco was a rat in the bag and heading for the Central Criminal Court at the Old Bailey, it seemed to Oliver inevitable that he would have to drop Miguel in the Edward Carr murder case. The three separate charges against Charco – the murder of Edward Carr, attempted witness intimidation, and the gang rape of Jenny Glendower – made him the perfect client for Hawthorne & Moss.

'Let's hope Charco pleads Not Guilty,' Dodgett would inevitably murmur, his eyebrows at prayer. You could bet on that.

Leaving Charco's cell, Oliver wearily interviewed a despondent but stoical Pete McGraw.

'So what happened, Pete?'

'You've always stood by me, Mr Rolls.'

'What happened?'

'Ask Charco. I didn't have nothing to do with it.'

'Pete, haven't we been here before? Remember Jackson Saint and the gang rape of two schoolgirls? If I recall, you had nothing to do with that, either – until the identification evidence could no longer be resisted.'

'You're supposed to believe me, Mr Rolls! That's your job!' Pete almost howled in anguish.

Oliver left the cell convinced that he would have to part company with Pete in the Jenny Glendower case – though few boys had been 'better' clients for Hawthorne & Moss. Charco was one of the few. He was in a league of his own.

Hubert Hare was the Youth Justice officer sent to collect Lucy and her bag from Milton Grange open prison. Her parole had been accelerated and she was now released on probation. Hubert Hare had been instructed to drive her straight to Ruskin House, the drug rehabilitation unit in West London, where a bed awaited her.

The previous day Ben Diamond had announced a new, 'last chance' opportunity for prisoners deemed by the parole board to be no threat to the public. But in case anyone thought Ben was going soft, he also announced that prisoners on parole would be electronically tagged.

'Sorry to be leaving Milton Grange, Lucy?' Hubert asked.

Lucy blinked behind her glasses. 'This is a lot of daylight.'

Hubert laughed. 'We're sure you'll really enjoy Ruskin House, Lucy.'

'Yeah.'

'Make the most of life's chances.'

'When will I see David?'

'Shouldn't be long. Just a day or two to settle you in.'

Lucy had read the Ruskin House leaflets, signed the forms. *Clients must be 24-hour drug and alcohol free before they can be interviewed. They must have completed their detox. Ruskin House is a six-month therapeutic programme for re-establishing themselves within the wider community.*

Lucy was gazing out of Hubert's car at fields, trees, pubs, advertisements – things she had seen little of for almost eight months.

'Have you got a spliff, Hubert?'

Of course he had. Hubert Hare never travelled far without cannabis. He was tempted but he knew his duty.

'Lucy, if you don't believe in your own future, who else will?'

'Yeah.'

'When did you last have a spliff, Lucy?'

'Ages ago. I haven't touched a thing since they sent me to the open.'

'Good for you, Lucy. They're likely to give you a test as soon as you step in the door of Ruskin House.'

'I still think cannabis should be legal.'

He nodded in silent agreement. Criminalising cannabis merely 'demonised' the smoker.

'I mean,' Lucy went on, 'it's all about vested interests, isn't it? The Home Office, the politicians, the Drugs Squad, Customs and Excise, the legal system, educationists – they're all in it together.'

Hubert decided to step carefully. This girl was the daughter of Marcus Byron and not to be trusted. He remembered Byron's intervention during a conference of the London Drugs Forum. The progressive criminologist Professor Siegfried Alexander had lucidly demonstrated how the tax revenues generated by legal sales of cannabis could be used for better control and treatment of hard drugs.

'You may be shaken to learn', Alexander had told the Forum, 'that during the past twenty-five years, no fewer than half a million people have been prosecuted for cannabis use – some 60,000 arrests in the most recently available statistical year.'

During the lunch break Alexander's carefully vetted disciples, who included Hubert and Edmund Joiner, withdrew to a specially reserved room, where the professor lectured on 'Pavlovian Therapy – the Theory of Conditioned Reflex'. Professor Alexander emphasised his points by vigorously shaking a small head from a long neck; Hubert's partner in life, Edmund Joiner, who had worked for Alexander, and was now his mole in the Home Office, likened his appearance to a turkey's. 'And never mention Christmas to him,' Edmund drawled.

'Some ignorant people speak of electric shocks', Alexander rebuked his audience, 'but the correct term is "reinforcement therapy". Science is science, my friends. This, after all, is how I solve the problems of the filthy, verminous, debased young delinquents who are put in my care at the Blackhead Road Clinic. Much more effective than prison. Much more efficacious than "anger management" or the "cognitive model of delinquency prevention and offender rehabilitation" that you – our worthy social workers and probation officers – are required to sell to unsuspecting magistrates.'

This had been met with a tense silence. As a member of one of Ben Diamond's new YOTs – Youth Offending Teams – Hubert was deeply committed to a 'multi-faceted programme for fostering socio-cognitive skills'. This involved 'values enhancement' and 'emotional management', even if that required an expensive, self-esteem-building trip down one of Africa's great rivers. Alexander's passion for Pavlovian conditioning and his insistence that 'everything is physical' filled Hubert with dismay – and yet, as Edmund insisted, 'Without Alex's leadership we would be at the mercy of the Ben Diamonds and the Marcus Byrons. The hangers and floggers. The prison addicts. And then the whole edifice of progress might be destroyed, my dear Hubert.'

After lunch they had rejoined the main meeting. Late in the afternoon Marcus Byron stood up in the audience, disdaining the microphone passed to him – his rich baritone voice could fill any hall:

'Ask any case worker in any London drugs clinic. He

or she will tell you that any clear line between "hard" and "soft" drugs vanishes on the street. The dealers often mix a fragment of heroin in with cannabis, to foster addiction. Many kids smoke over seventy spliffs of cannabis a week and become really fractious if they can't get it. And they don't know what they're getting. Legalising pure cannabis wouldn't affect that market.'

Hubert and other hecklers at the Forum loudly urged Judge Byron to sit down. Edmund was seething. Hubert's gentle temperament could not match Edmund's hatred of Ben Diamond, Paul Glass and Marcus Byron – and everything they stood for. 'Homophobes', he called them. All their powerful enemies within the criminal justice system knew Edmund's mobile telephone number, not forgetting the dots and forward slashes for the Joiner.UK private e-mail correspondence which Hubert couldn't help reading.

Now, driving north through Sussex, it wasn't lost on Hubert that the thin, wide-eyed girl seated beside him was the judge's daughter. Sorely tempted to offer her (and himself) a spliff, he resisted. Hubert Hare knew only the general outline of Operation Lucy. Edmund knew more. And Keith, too. Keith Mariner.

An hour later Hubert's car was threading through the semi-dilapidated, inner-city streets of Great North where winos, druggies and beggars wandered and lurched, each in his own haze. Knots of idle young men stood about at corners and intersections, some of them well known to the affable Youth Justice officer, Hubert Hare.

His clients, their pockets loaded with blades and the

conditional discharges which his pre-sentence reports invariably recommended to the courts.

He parked in front of Ruskin House. Keith Mariner was waiting for Lucy in the front office.

Lucy was assigned a room with two other women, one of whom, Fiona Sheehy, claimed to be in her late twenties but looked ten years older. Her natural beauty had been sorely ravaged by addiction and abuse, as Keith Mariner pointed out to Lucy in Fiona's presence:

'Let Fiona be a lesson to any young woman,' he said.

Fiona nodded meekly. Natural pride seemed to have deserted her. She had been in Ruskin House for a couple of months and was now allowed out twice a week but always under supervision. She wept a lot, when awake and when asleep. What Lucy longed for was a room of her own, a space where no one intruded, where she could place a jug of flowers, the colours she liked – and a mirror. She yearned for a mirror. You never caught sight of yourself in Holloway, Oak End or Milton Grange. And, yeah, same again at Ruskin House. Mirrors were dangerous.

There were no iron bars and very few locks at Ruskin House, but you weren't free to leave the building, not until Keith said you could.

Keith Mariner was Lucy's 'keyworker' – the new jailer in her life. An ex-con himself, and proud of it, a reformed criminal and addict (he said), black as her dad, shaven head, funky T-shirts, Keith was into 'rehab', the music scene, and serious films: Godard, Fellini, Angelopoulos. Keith was the street, but reformed. Keith would sit you all down in the Garden Room, the new residents, and talk about 'the Ruskin' while pumping his arm muscles.

With Keith it was warnings, warnings. You might be on rehab but you were always a short step from hell.

'Don't forget, Lucy, that anyone convicted of dealing in Class A drugs on two or more occasions now gets a mandatory sentence. Minimum of seven years. That could be a long time.'

He made Lucy nervous. Too pleased with himself. Gosh gosh, just look at those reformed biceps. She always wanted to have a go at him. She wanted to say, 'Keith, could you kindly reduce your body language. As a woman, I find it oppressive.' She could imagine his laconic response.

'What's your problem, Lucy?'

'Your balls are hanging out of your trousers, Keith,' she'd say.

But she didn't. She sat on the sofa wedged in between two other initiates, silent and seething. Keith Mariner cultivated that special kind of tolerant professional smile you got from Hubert Hare and all the other products of 'sixties sociology within the criminal justice system. Her own father was a pig but a pig with a straight tail. She felt sure that Keith's tail wasn't straight.

Anyway, off he goes into his 'background lecture', his massive thighs flexing beneath his jeans.

'What's the knowledge I want to share with you?

Frankly' – and here he addresses each of them by name – 'frankly, I call it survival knowledge.'

Keith pauses, waits, special smile. Let it sink in.

'So here's a spot of history. Don't let's imagine that history is just castles and the Tower of London. Our cities have a history. You and me, we have histories.'

'I never knew that,' Lucy wants to say. 'I thought history was Henry VIII and the Gunpowder Plot.'

But she sits tight and on he goes.

'In the 'sixties the drug scene was mainly acid and barbiturates – they're the worst killers. About 1964 the Chinese began to import a lot of heroin. Cocaine like opium had been around since Victorian times. So in the 'seventies you had young smackheads and scagheads, mainly people in their early twenties, but by the end of the decade younger people were in. In the 'eighties the streets were saturated with heroin – chasing the dragon. Then Ecstasy hit the teenagers and young adults, not an addictional drug, mainly the dance and rave scene.'

'"Addictional"?' Lucy wonders. Does he mean 'addictive'? But she isn't sure of the dictionary in her head and never uses any other kind. She senses that if she releases the latch of restraint just once, Keith might bring up all her other unspoken challenges. He might say: 'There are other people in this room, Lucy, and they may wonder why you're doing all the talking. Is it because you're a famous judge's daughter?'

Lucy is simmering, coiled tight. She hasn't said a thing!

Keith's technique for achieving lasting rehab involves

a kind of forced march, again and again, through the nightmare jungle of addiction.

'Believe me, there are people here, in the Ruskin, who have known the horror of simultaneous addiction. They'll rob and even kill to get the £1,000 a week their crack habit demands. Are you interested, Lucy?'

Keith has been watching her as he speaks. He is well aware that Miss Agatha Cowdrey 'almost murdered' Lucy in Oak End – to frighten Judge Byron following the message slipped under his hotel bedroom door in Dorset by Delia. A dead Lucy was of no use to Operation Lucy – not yet, anyway.

'Is that what you did, Keith?' Lucy asks. 'Kill people to feed your habit?' The latch of her restraint has come unfastened. The more vivid Keith's descriptions of drug abuse, of desperate degradation, the more he seems to take pride in his own involvement.

'I wouldn't be here if I'd killed anybody, Lucy.' She cannot argue with that, though she no longer believes anything he says. 'I'll be frank with you,' he says, as if bestowing a gift, 'because I know you're intelligent people. Here at Ruskin House about thirty-two per cent last the course. We allow only one relapse.' He pauses, watches them. 'Some of our staff don't think it helps to divulge this painful information to newcomers but I do.'

Lucy thinks: he's been taking advantage of Fiona's drug habit. He saunters into their bedroom with that relaxed, muscular style of his, then sprawls across Fiona's bed in a display of possessive body language that makes the snakes dance in Lucy's hair. There are no locks on the doors. On Lucy's first day in Ruskin House, Keith had explained to the newcomers that this was a mixed-sex rehabilitation unit with no rules about sexual relations.

'The only rule is consent. Any case of harassment and that person is shown the door.'

Fiona had started on heroin at the age of fifteen; for the past four years it had been cocaine. She spoke passionately of her pain about her family and schooling.

'My dad showed me no love. I went with men for love. I went to a rehab to get out of a prison sentence. I'm on a two year suspended. You can get off drugs. The problem is staying off. If I flunk it here, if I touch anything, I'm back in there.'

Fiona Sheehy and the addict within her were in constant conflict. She told Lucy how she'd go to Woolworth's and steal a sachet of batteries worth seven quid, sell them at the corner shop for £2.50, then steal supermarket meat to sell to single-parent families on the estates.

'Then you go and spend twenty on a rock. That stops you clucking. But it's gone within ten minutes.'

Fiona talked about sex a lot – but it was always 'sex', not a particular bloke. 'When I need stuff I'd give my body for a ten-pound note.' She regarded herself as hopelessly promiscuous and blamed her dad for never loving her.

Keith would join them in the garden, but briefly, always restless, always prowling, always (as he liked to put it) 'making the house rules stick'. Keith tended to talk about Fiona as a 'case', as a recidivist, as a woman on 'the last chance diving-board'.

'Now take Fiona here. If I see her watching a film too quietly I'll urine test her straight away – won't I, Fiona?'

Fiona was always completely passive in Keith's company. 'If I screw up this time I won't get funded again,' she whispers to Lucy after Keith has left them.

Hubert Hare gave little dinner parties. The Youth Justice officer shared an apartment in a Battersea mansion block with an equally elegant young man of his own generation, Edmund Joiner. The furnishing was sparing but beautiful: Hubert and Edmund haunted the Lots Road auction rooms at weekends. Sarah and Oliver were surprised to be invited for 'nine-ish' on a weekday evening – 'Ten-ish is my bed-ish time,' Oliver complained – and were even more disconcerted when, arriving hungry on the dot of nine, they were greeted by Hubert wearing a primrose-yellow bath robe.

No sign of other guests.

'Darlings, you're an hour early! Never mind! Edmund is decent and already fighting to extract the ice-tray from the freezer. Edmund! Edmund!'

Wearing dour, middle-aged expressions, Sarah and Oliver noticed a mass of Sainsbury's carrier bags littering the kitchen doorway and clearly still containing tonight's dinner.

'Hubert's supposed to be our cook tonight,' Edmund Joiner sighed as he poured their drinks, 'but he can never bring himself to peel a clove of garlic until he's washed his hair. So everything hangs on the question, "Where, oh where, is the Mitchell's conditioner for hair of African provenance?" I am invariably accused of hiding it. As if I would. I mean, why should I? I want to eat. Sarah and Oliver here look ravenous – you haven't been starving yourselves deliberately, have you?'

Oliver and Sarah gradually became aware that they were not the only living creatures in the room. From time to time strange, stealthy sounds reached them, emanating (Oliver insisted) from a long, rectangular glass tank half covered by a black velvet cloth which stood in a corner between the dining table and a window. A vase of artificial flowers stood on the tank.

Finally Oliver took a look and cautiously lifted the near side of the velvet cloth.

'Hm. Seems we weren't the first guests to arrive after all. The others have been eaten.'

'Eaten?'

At that moment Edmund breezed back from the kitchen to replenish the ice bucket.

'Ah yes, so you've met Ka and Ma.'

'Where are they from? The Congo?' Oliver asked. 'I can see two heads but everything else seems to belong to both of them.'

'They'll soon sort that out when they get their dinner,' Edmund said.

Two other guests arrived separately towards ten. Edmund introduced the first, a black American journalist called Amos Lewin, but Hubert had to be brought fluttering from the kitchen to introduce Keith Mariner, a social worker from Ruskin House, not only to Sarah and Oliver but also to Edmund.

'Sarah, meet Keith. You, Keith and I have a client in common, the remarkable Lucy Byron.'

'Yes, we've been expecting a visit from you,' Keith told her. He stood with feet planted wide, as if about to call the roll.

'I thought it best to let Lucy settle in,' Sarah said. 'How is she?'

'Fine, just fine.'

There was something ultra-theatrical about Hubert's introduction of Keith to Edmund.

'So pleased to meet you, Keith. Hubert mentioned that you work in a detox unit.'

'Rehab,' Keith corrected Edmund.

'Oh, apologies. Detox and rehab, I really must get them right.'

Keith immediately launched into a lecture that sounded to Sarah as if it had been tape-recorded.

'I've been trying to get the facts of drug life across to Lucy. I've warned her that a £15 crack rock lasts only ten minutes – if you're clever. You need £180 to £1,200 a day to feed the habit. The dealers work from mobile phones. The street price has gone down although the quality remains high. Crack is a binge drug. There is no substitute like methadone is for heroin. The typical user starts his day by obtaining the money. He meets friends. He scores drugs. He takes drugs. A typical heroin addiction can cost £30 – £60 a day for half to one gramme. The average period of addiction is twelve years including various interventions. That's what we're trying to impact on in Ruskin House.'

Oliver was fighting a yawn.

'Bored, Oliver?' Keith flexed various muscles.

Sarah could imagine Keith dressing down Lucy in Ruskin House for inattention, giving his biceps an extra-twitch.

Oliver tried a brave smile. 'Just hungry. Like Edmund's pythons Ma and Ka, by the sound of them.'

'And we all know the conventional medical answer to heroin,' Keith continued. 'Methadone. But here's the problem. Methadone impacts strong. Doctors prescribe a hundred mils when it should be forty. There are thousands on it in Liverpool Toxteth, crawling around like slugs – give them the green medicine.'

Edmund could no longer suppress his irritation: 'Oh come, Keith, not again, not at this hour, please.'

'Not again!' Sarah and Oliver exchanged a glance. Why had Hubert been so over-elaborate about Edmund never having met Keith before?

Much more appealing to Sarah was Edmund's guest, Amos Lewin, who quizzed her and Oliver about their work as if genuinely interested. Evidently he was in England to study the criminal justice system 'under the wing' (as he put it), of 'the redoubtable Brigid'.

'That woman is frightening,' screamed Hubert Hare, scampering back and forth to the kitchen. 'She hates all of us. Can't imagine how you can *breathe* in her company, Amos.'

'She's simply the mouthpiece of Marcus Byron, the

archetypical Uncle Tom,' Keith Mariner declared. 'He hates his own kind. He wants to be white.'

'In that case, he fooled me,' Amos said.

'You're talking pernicious nonsense,' Sarah snapped at Keith.

'Oh, he knows how to charm the ladies,' Keith smiled patronisingly. 'Byron is the big baron among judicial drug dealers. The opium he trades in is called punishment. He feeds the idiot public's addiction for vengeance.'

'Nicely put, Keith,' Hubert called from the kitchen. 'Keith knows all about drug barons – he used to be one himself.'

Encouraged, Keith warmed to his theme, marching his big thighs about the room.

'It's easy money. A consignment comes in magnetised to the exterior of the ship below the water line. The diver goes down by night and that's it. Worth millions. You have a hierarchy of dealers, each cutting it into smaller quantities. The raw heroin comes in about seventy per cent proof. The next stage is mixed with baking powder to fifty per cent, then forty. On the street it's twenty to thirty per cent. Pyramid selling is also imitated by kids.'

'What per cent proof is Marcus Byron?' Oliver asked.

At this juncture Edmund opened the french window and stepped outside to a small, paved garden, returning with a hessian sack containing writhing, squealing creatures. Edmund was now wearing a pair of large, reinforced gardening gloves.

'Sarah, would you mind?' he smiled, indicating that

she should remove the artificial flowers and the velvet cloth from the pythons' tank.

She recoiled. 'What are they?'

'Rats, dear. Dinner time for Ma and Ka.'

'But they're alive!'

'Of course. Would you want to dine off a dead rat?'

'But it's so cruel!' she protested.

'Where Ma and Ka come from, compassion is not a major concept.'

'I'm afraid I'm going to have to leave the room,' she said, disappearing to the toilet.

'I'd leave too if I could,' Oliver said as Edmund tossed several furiously thrashing rats into the glass tank. It was five minutes before the laws of the jungle finally asserted themselves within the tank.

'You can come out, Sarah,' Edmund called, replacing the black cloth and the flowers. 'It's all over.'

It was almost all over for Oliver, too. Sodden on Edmund's lethal martinis and very pale, he sat slumped with leaden eyelids which refused to stay open. Sarah, herself exhausted but determined not to succumb to a similar indignity, gallantly asked Edmund about his work.

'What do you do when you're not feeding rats to pythons?'

'If you must know, I am involved in interminable communion with the most boring people in the world.'

'You must be a solicitor, the lowest of the low,' Oliver murmured, then fell irredeemably asleep.

'Oh dear,' sighed Hubert, bending over Oliver, 'He does look terribly ill. Should we call the morgue?'

The first course was served shortly before midnight, by which time Sarah had packed Oliver into a minicab with the help of the muscular Keith. She scribbled the address on a leaf from her diary and handed it to the driver, together with the fare. The driver, an Asian, reminded her of a character involved in one of Oliver's rape cases – perhaps it was the same man, for whom Oliver had 'miraculously' (he said) obtained bail with the help of a £10,000 surety from the family.

She didn't bother to tell the comatose Oliver that she loved him. She didn't. Who would, or could? The pathetic Jenny Glendower?

Staunchly she fought her way through a brilliant meal that came like the acts of an opera whose overture had been delayed three hours by the diva's indisposal. Each 'act' of the meal was punctuated with twenty-minute intervals, until, offered coffee at two in the morning, Sarah finally wilted. By that time she had discovered a few facts about Edmund Joiner.

Or had she? He spoke in verses not chapters. Every fragment of autobiography arrived wrapped in jest and self-mockery. He had taken a first-class law degree from Cambridge 'without ever opening a book'. Later he had been recruited by the eminent criminologist Professor Siegfried Alexander 'as he rather improbably styles himself'.

'How should he style himself?' Sarah asked with more than a hint of irritation.

'Oh dear, that would be telling.'

Here Hubert intervened from the other end of the

table. 'Don't provoke Sarah, Edmund, we kept her waiting three hours for her dinner, poor girl.'

Edmund feigned contrition. 'Frankly, Alex is a complete charlatan. All his "research findings" are fixed in advance. He will soon "prove" that crime is a figment of the conservative imagination. No wonder he detests my new boss.'

'Edmund now works for the Government,' Hubert told Sarah, returning from the kitchen bearing a soufflé in the prime of life.

'Doing what?' Sarah asked.

'He's a member of Ben Diamond's kitchen cabinet.'

'Hubert!' exclaimed Edmund. 'You're incorrigibly indiscreet, dear!'

'That's how I met Edmund,' Amos Lewin cut in. 'I turned up at the Home Office to interview Paul Glass. He was held up in a meeting so I was entertained by this beautiful boy.'

'Their tête-à-tête was later resumed in Amsterdam,' Hubert said with asperity. 'Fortunately I am foreign to jealousy – up to a point. Tell me, Amos, did Edmund prefer the "crucifixion" position when in the land of the tulips, or was it "cross-bow"?'

Amos did not respond but Edmund did, turning to Sarah. 'Hubert's frightfully upset because half his case load is suspected of having raped some woman before throwing her in a canal in Great North. A respectable mother of two, such bad taste. I told him, "Hubert, she must have been asking for it" – but he's inconsolable. Oh dear, I forgot: Hubert's clients are also yours.'

Sarah ignored this. 'Will Marcus get the Criminal Law Commission job?' she asked Edmund.

'Oh, I'm sure there will be a happy ending, dear. I'm told that you represent young David Glass, such a nice boy, he and I sometimes play chess. He adores Lucy, of course. Tell me, does representing little Lucy bring you into heavy-duty contact with the great Marcus?'

'I don't know him at all well.'

'But you do, you do,' Hubert corrected her. 'And there are rumours flying about.'

'What rumours?'

'Oh, don't look so fierce, dear, I grovel.'

'Well, go on, Sarah,' Edmund said sarcastically, 'sing for your supper and tell us what part of your thigh the legendary judge likes to squee-eeze. And does he still imagine himself to be the Number One Target of the Great Progressive Conspiracy?'

It was now shortly after two. Stunned by this outburst, Sarah declined coffee and made her escape. The nice American, Amos Lewin, offered to see her to a cab.

'Bad things are going to happen,' he murmured when they reached the street.

'To—'

'To Lucy. And David. And Judge Byron.'

Half an hour later she found Oliver stretched out on the sitting-room floor, snoring loudly, and only half undressed. A ghastly sight to finish a ghastly evening.

*   *   *

Marcus Byron's enemies now struck hard. He was summoned, at short notice, to appear before the House of Commons Select Committee on Legal Affairs by its bullish chairman, Willy Braithwaite. Marcus was taken by surprise. Had Ben Diamond actually announced Marcus's appointment as Chairman of the Criminal Law Commission, then a grilling by the Legal Affairs Committee was to be expected. But the Home Secretary had made no such announcement – a deafening silence.

Marcus remained, simply, a Crown Court judge – and judges were never brought before Parliament. Their independence was inviolate. They need never answer for their decisions or opinions.

What was Braithwaite up to? Why had a majority of his committee endorsed the summons? Brigid reckoned she could name at least three members of the Committee, apart from Braithwaite himself, who were long-time supporters of the Congress for Justice – which, of course, no longer existed.

A message from the Lord Chancellor's office not only advised Marcus to decline the summons, but promised a strong statement affirming the independence of the judiciary. Ben Diamond telephoned Marcus at home.

'Stay away, Marcus. As Tommy has told you, you have every right to decline. Plead privilege.'

'I'm not keen on pleading.'

'They've dug a hole for you. Don't jump in.'

Brigid fervently begged Marcus to listen to the two senior politicians in whose hands his future lay.

'Be careful, my darling. If the Lord Chancellor tells

you to stay silent, you must. He's your boss. It was he who restored you to the bench.'

'Oh yeah? They've got me coming and they've got me going. "BYRON LIES LOW" yells Auriol Johnson in the *World*. "BYRON DEFIES PARLIAMENT" is the *Guardian* headline. "BYRON PLEADS PRIVILEGE" says *The Times*. The *Telegraph* will tell its readers that it's high time Marcus Byron faced down his critics in open confrontation. "LOST YOUR BALLS, MARCUS?" is the question on page one of the *Sun*.'

Brigid laid her fiery head on his shoulder. 'The first art of war is to choose the time and place for battle. You will find yourself hamstrung by Ben's silence.'

'I'll wear my new suit from Simpson's,' he chuckled. 'And my fob watch.'

Brigid took Amos Lewin along to the House committee room. Amos had not been a frequent visitor to the offices of the *Sentinel*. A postcard from Amsterdam announced that he had found 'happiness on a white bicycle but, alas, both wheels are rolling inexorably back towards the great wen, where duty lies'. Happiness? She wondered in whose company. He didn't say, even when asked. Nor was he to be chided about absenteeism. Enjoying his furlough from the *Berkeley Voice*, Amos took a relaxed view of his obligations to Mr O'Sullivan, proprietor of the *Sentinel*. He would study the British penal system 'in depth' – but in his own good time. Amos had begun his research by laying his handsome head on more pillows than even the liberated Brigid thought appropriate.

Particularly if one of the pillows belonged to Auriol Johnson. Here was a woman without fear of hell, being already in residence.

Amos liked to tease Brigid about her distant personal relationship with their boss.

'I hear you and Mr O'Sullivan both featured in Molly Bloom's day,' he said slyly, by way of reference to her favourite Dublin novel, James Joyce's *Ulysses*.

'Well, don't tell Marcus. When I gave him Molly's monologue to read his reaction was, to say the least, mixed. He's a tremendous puritan.'

'I hadn't heard that one!'

'Well, let's say he's a puritan regarding everyone but himself.'

She enjoyed the teasing. She was perhaps a little bit in love with Amos – everyone was – and she decided to believe him when he assured her that he no longer 'messed about' with Auriol.

'White bikes in Amsterdam are better?'

'Aha.'

'Who was it, Amos?'

'I plead the Fifth Amendment.'

'Someone I know?'

'Someone you met once, according to my fragile information.'

'Male or female?'

To that she never got an answer. Being angry with Amos was uphill work, not least because he and Marcus had hit it off from their first meeting. The young journalist would sit at Marcus's feet, metaphorically and sometimes literally, attentively tapping notes into a laptop. What surprised Brigid was Amos's respect for Marcus's tough stance on crime. It didn't fit in with the rest of Amos, a true product of California's laid-back liberal sunshine.

Progressives [wrote Amos Lewin in the *Sentinel*] tend to regard Marcus Byron as a square and a bore and almost certainly psychopathic – but are the Progressives wrong?

'The idea of zero tolerance', he told me, 'comes from the conviction that serious crime very often emerges opportunistically from lesser crime. The devil will indeed make work for idle hands and if people are permitted to hang around on street corners drinking, being abusive, playing truant, then it is virtually certain that more homes in that area will be burgled, more cars broken into, more people assaulted.'

He seemed, at that juncture, to expect a comment – and most probably a hostile one. He gave me a slow look. 'What we have to confront head-on, Mr Lewin, is the liberal orthodoxy that crime is an inevitable by-product of poverty, inequality and poor education. Here in Britain that permissive message has got through to both the inner city poor and the police. The young men came to believe they could do what they liked because they were "victims of society" and victims of "institutionalised racism". And the police merely waved the stolen vehicles through the red lights.'

'That's a striking image', I commented, 'for the permissive society.'

'As you know, my thesis is this: One window is smashed in an empty building. No one repairs it. No one is held accountable for the damage. The word goes out that the building is easy game for vandals. Soon other windows are broken. Now dilapidated, the building becomes a haunt for dossers and drug dealers. The drugs draw crime into the locality. Respectable families begin to move out. Delinquency becomes the norm. The criminal element gains the ascendancy. The police strategically withdraw, citing the need to avoid confrontation.'

'How have people reacted to your argument?' I asked him. 'The police, for example?'

Marcus Byron offered me the patient smile of an embattled law enforcer.

'The initial police response to "Broken Windows" was cool. The cops reckoned they had enough to do without pursuing litter louts and lippy kids playing loud radios. As it happened, the test bed for zero tolerance came to be Metropolitan London after Mike Price took over as Police Commissioner. Superintendents and Chief Inspectors were ordered to clear parks of winos, the streets of teenagers carrying screaming hi-fis, and the intersections of windscreen-washing squeegee men. Minor delinquents hauled in led the police to more serious offenders. The Crime Festival was over.'

(Judge Byron is a man of few doubts – but if

we could interview the great prophets of the Old Testament, we might find even fewer.)

'And Britain's prison population has soared to record figures?' I asked.

'Draw your own conclusions,' Marcus Byron concluded dryly.

Marcus Byron sat, upright and smartly attired, before the Select Committee, hands folded.

Following the usual courtesies, perfunctory on this occasion, the veteran war horse Willy Braithwaite asked Marcus, point-blank, whether the Home Secretary had invited him to chair the Criminal Law Commission.

'You must ask the Home Secretary,' Marcus said.

'I'm asking you, Judge Byron.'

'I must plead *doli incapax*.'

This produced laughter from those members of the Committee and the press who understood – but not from Braithwaite.

'The language of this Parliament is English, Judge Byron.'

'*Doli incapax* means I'm too young to understand what's going on,' Marcus drawled. 'It normally applies to kids between the ages of ten and thirteen – but that's just about my age when it comes to affairs of state.'

'You're on record,' Braithwaite said, 'as recommending an erosion of our ancient right to trial by jury. Correct?'

'What proportion of contested criminal cases go to trial by jury?'

'I am asking the questions, Judge Byron.'

'In my opinion, too many defence lawyers are abusing the right to a Crown Court jury trial in "either way" cases.'

'"Abusing"? Isn't that a dangerously strong word?'

'The facts are clear. Every year 120,000 cases are sent up from the magistrates' courts to the Crown Courts. It should be fewer. Why? Of these, 22,000 cases are indictable and the magistrates therefore have no option but to commit to the Crown Court. The rest – 98,000 – are "either way" cases where the magistrates enjoy discretion. Of these, 62,000 are committed to the Crown Court by decision of the magistrates. But in the remaining 36,000 cases, where the magistrates were prepared to retain jurisdiction and hear the case, the defendant exercises his right to a jury trial.'

'And that's what you want to put a stop to?' Braithwaite boomed.

'I'm saying that in "either way" cases, only the magistrates should decide on jurisdiction. That's what happens in the Youth Court. And let's not forget that eighty-two per cent of defendants who opt for jury trial never see a jury because they plead guilty before they come to trial. The expense is enormous and everyone's time is wasted – except the lawyers' time.'

'If you were Chairman of the Criminal Law Commission, what, precisely, would you propose?' Braithwaite pressed him.

'I would propose that the automatic right to jury trial be removed from such offences as assault, ABH, theft, handling stolen goods and some indecency offences.

The result could be an additional 18,000 cases a year heard by magistrates rather than the Crown Court. One could go further and include possession of an offensive weapon, possession of class B drugs, and burglary from non-domestic premises.'

Another member of the Committee, one of Brigid's 'suspects', took up the questioning:

'Are you aware, Judge Byron, that the Bar has utterly rejected any such proposal as "prejudicial to justice" and "the loss of an ancient liberty"?'

'Yeah. They would say that, wouldn't they?'

'And are you aware that the Law Society, in a rare show of solidarity with the Bar, has also expressed outright opposition. Both bodies have expressed staunch devotion to an Englishman's ancient right to jury trial.'

Marcus played with his fob watch. 'As I said, no such right exists with regard to a whole swathe of minor charges. I merely propose extending that swathe.'

A third member of the Committee took him up on the issue of Community sentences.

'Would you describe yourself as a declared enemy of the Probation Service, Judge Byron?'

'Certainly not. A fine body of men and women whose sincere dedication is too often vitiated by mistaken attitudes and policies.'

'That might amount to what I said?'

'Listen, some 12,000 summonses are currently outstanding against offenders who have breached community or probation orders. Thousands of others, who were given community service orders as a humane alternative to custody, have simply dropped out. Vanished. Goodbye. Behind the 20,000 summonses for breach issued in a single year, you can find many thousands more who have simply flouted their sentences and are never going to be brought back to court.'

Braithwaite came again: 'Are you in favour of sending fine defaulters to prison?'

'Shall I tell you something, Chairman? Many convicted offenders will go to the cinema this evening rather than come to court to explain why they cannot afford to pay five pounds a week towards a fine. The fine is not regarded as the primary obligation in a personal or family budget. It not only ranks below the electricity bill, it ranks below Darren's new Adidas trainers, three pints of beer and a cinema ticket. So yes, in the end you have no alternative but to send them to prison.'

Another member of the Committee, a practising QC and high on Brigid's list, intervened smoothly:

'As I understand it, you are proposing to deprive the Bar of its ancient entitlement to Crown Court prosecutions?'

'Of its monopoly.'

'You wish to extend the rights of audience – in plain language, the right to be heard – in the Crown Court to lawyers employed by the Crown Prosecution Service?'

'Yes. And so does the Director of Public Prosecutions.'

'Do we want state prosecutors in this country?'

'That phrase is mere rhetoric from the Bar. CPS costs

could be reduced substantially by transferring routine cases from expensive barristers to CPS staff.'

'Ah. "Routine cases" – how would you define them?'

'I mean plea and directions hearings. CPS solicitors can handle these perfectly competently – as they do in the magistrates courts. No jury is present.'

'But you would go further?'

'Barristers employed by the CPS should be granted rights of audience on any case appropriate to their individual experience.'

'Including jury trials?'

'Yes. The Bar has been sitting on this proposal for too long. They'll sit on it for ever if allowed to do so. Every barrister, independent or employed, is a member of the Bar – which is why the Bar rules.'

'Judge Byron, you are aware that in jury trials barristers employed by the CPS may only sit as junior advocate to a senior one?'

'I am indeed aware, sir. And what has been happening? Thanks to the National Audit Office, we know. In three cases out of four the independent barrister returns the brief to the CPS at the eleventh hour, when something more lucrative turns up on his plate. So what happens then? A junior counsel is hastily brought in, usually at the last minute. The result is sub-standard.'

'You have also complained about antiquated dress codes in the courts? Would you not agree with the Chairman of the Bar's public affairs committee, Cynthia Miles, that wigs and gowns lend authority to the proceedings in the criminal courts?'

'Mrs Miles has a problem.'

Marcus waited – his old trick.

'Ninety-five per cent of criminal cases in this country are resolved by wigless and gownless magistrates in courts where the lawyers, too, wear ordinary clothes. Without apparent loss of authority. That's Mrs Miles's problem. But there is a deeper one. When the Bar speaks high principle it usually means money.'

'I regard that as a despicable remark,' commented the QC, 'but thank you for so freely and frankly revealing to this Committee the way your mind works.'

'Yeah. I'd like to be a citizen of a country where the punishment fits the crime.'

Ten

BYRON CHALLENGES RIGHT TO JURY TRIAL
(*Sentinel*)

Eight youths were brought before Benson Street Youth Court on a first appearance, charged with rape and the attempted murder of an unnamed woman in Great North. The press turned out in force and a tall TV gantry was parked across the street. Given the seriousness of the charges, legal aid had immediately been granted to engage barristers.

All but one barrister took the view that an application for bail would be merely routine: no chance. But Sarah's barrister Bob Jolly, representing Luke, took a different line, insisting that 'my job is to fight for my client's liberty all the way'.

'But is liberty in Luke's interest?' Sarah argued during a ten-minute visit to Jolly's chambers. 'He's only fourteen. Free to come and go from Catherine House, Luke has got himself into one crime after another. He finds nothing to occupy him day and night. They sent him to a special needs school but he was expelled for bullying and stealing cash from the canteen. In my view he needs secure accommodation for his own good. I mean, look what he's done.'

'Alleged to have done,' Jolly corrected her.

'That's all the magistrates need consider on a bail application.'

'What *I* need to consider, Sarah, is what our client's instructions are. He's asking for bail, isn't he?'

'Yes he is. But Sedge Hill social services, who are very clearly in *loco parentis*, do not support bail. They're saying they don't want him.'

The small room in the Youth Court was jam-packed. Sarah and Oliver wriggled in behind their respective barristers, only two places apart.

The chairman of the bench reminded the reporters present that they would hear the names and addresses of the accused in court but must on no account publish them. The identity of the victim was not listed – but the same prohibition applied.

The Crown Prosecutor read out the alleged facts and said they applied equally to all eight defendants.

One by one the defending barristers went through the form. There was as yet no identification evidence from the victim and the video film was of poor quality. No ID parade had been held. There was as yet no forensic analysis, therefore no forensic evidence. There had been no eyewitnesses.

So: bail, please.

The only marginal exception was Charco's barrister, Nathan Shayles, who mentioned that bail for his client would be nominal since he was already in custody 'on another matter'. Everyone knew the other matter: the murder of Edward Carr.

Case by case the magistrates remanded the boys in custody. Only Luke and Ally Leagum, at fourteen, were too young for custody. In their case it would have to be secure accommodation.

By five in the afternoon the court was empty of defendants and lawyers except for Jolly, Sarah – and Luke Grant himself. The huge boy sat blank-faced and stricken between two green-shirted Securicor guards, with two more posted at the doors.

The prosecutor told the court that Luke had been absent from Catherine House on the night of the attack on the woman, returning at 4.05 a.m. It emerged that in January and again in May, Luke had been charged with robbery and pleaded NG on both occasions. While on bail, he had robbed a man of £20 in Great North. Luke carried unexplained burns and cuts – in particular a scar on his hand which he was inclined to display proudly, with a grin.

Bob Jolly began by reminding the magistrates that Luke had not been remanded to local authority accommodation on the basis of a criminal conviction. Luke had been the victim of 'wholly inadequate parenting'. Jolly then applied for bail with conditions: a curfew; to stay away from Great North; not to associate with the co-defendants; and not to seek any contact with the victim.

Sedge Hill's social services were represented in court by two senior staff.

'We have to consider the public interest but this court is also charged with responsibility for Luke's welfare, you understand,' the chairman told the social workers.

'Yes, madam.'

Linda Manley, a Sedge Hill social worker, testified that Luke had been taken into care after his mother complained that he was out of control and in constant trouble with the police. Catherine House, too, had found him difficult to handle, although he was well liked in the home and never showed aggression towards members of the staff. He stayed out late, three or four times a week, sometimes until 4 a.m.

'No member of staff can enforce any curfew imposed on Luke by the courts,' Linda Manley told the magistrates. She was now applying for secure accommodation under section 25 of the Children's Act on the ground that Luke was likely to cause harm to himself or others. Secure accommodation, she added, was available.

The bench knew what it was going to do. Sarah knew what it was going to do. Maybe Bob Jolly did, too – but he wouldn't enjoy his dinner unless he'd earned it. He fought secure accommodation for an hour.

'Madam,' he said, 'the CPS has simply slapped a charge of attempted murder on top of the rape charge.'

Sarah wondered whether he would have adopted this line before a stipendiary or a Crown Court judge. The rape charge alone was sufficient to refuse bail. The three lay magistrates maintained neutral expressions, carefully guarding their own thoughts until they could consult their clerk in the retiring room.

Linda Manley's position remained unshaken by Jolly's cross-examination. Geoffrey Costello, Sedge Hill's Children and Family Team Manager, confirmed that Catherine House would be incapable of enforcing any new bail conditions that the court might impose on Luke.

'But you should and you must,' Jolly pressed him.

'Catherine House is not secure accommodation. We do not lock our children up.'

Luke began to weep silently when Costello was forced by the barrister's intransigence to go further into the boy's history than he wanted to. Before Luke was put in care, there had been an incident of grave sexual assault – involving penetration – on a young male cousin. Only after he was put in care had Luke's siblings been removed from the register of children at risk.

Sarah glanced at the weeping Luke. 'I advise you to rest your case,' she whispered to Jolly.

To her surprise he did. Later he despatched a vast bunch of flowers, with a note. 'You were right, Sarah. I try to keep faith with myself by refusing to accept the inevitable. But I was guilty of forgetting that Luke is a child. Sorry for the distress I caused him – and you.'

Still confined within Ruskin House, Lucy read the newspaper reports with restless interest. They were full of speculation about her dad and his future. Marcus this Marcus that. Some big job in the offing. Maybe. His Honour was constantly interviewed. What he would do if. Lucy knew by heart all the boring things he would do if, but David had begged her to stop hating her father; he called it self-mutilating; she listened to David; and she no longer found within herself the old furies. Yeah, let Marcus claim a knighthood by opening up more secure institutions for incurable offenders below the age of fifteen. Let him instruct police forces to practise zero tolerance if a kid dropped a chocolate wrapper on the pavement. Let him inflict community punishments on what Ben Diamond called 'families from hell' – often the poorest in the land. Let him abolish conditional discharges.

Yeah. Arise, Sir Big Mouth.

Yeah. That was Dad's style, with a little greasing of the engine by Brigid. Oh, how the two of them loved to parade together at the opera. Marcus never missed a performance of *Rigoletto*, his all-time favourite, although – as Brigid liked to jest – it should have been *Don Giovanni* with Marcus singing the title role. That flame-haired bitch, so confident of her hold on him. She'll learn. As soon as he gets the Big Job he'll move on to younger boobs like Sarah Woods's. Lucy can tell, she can always tell when his pants are hot. She'd known from the first time Marcus and Sarah visited her together in Oak End. Oh yeah. Sarah will say no all the way to one of his king-size beds.

There was no shortage of earnest discussion groups in Ruskin House to pass the time, many of them conducted by Keith. Black Consciousness. Being a Woman. Reason and Masculinity. Crime and Responsibility. Yeah, Keith and his bulging biceps were now urging Lucy to 'access' the acupuncture lessons – 'a very important relaxation weapon, Lucy.'

Keith made his 'clients' in Ruskin House write REASON in large letters at the head of a blank sheet of paper. He conducted classes on REASON. He said that no sooner had the ancient philosopher Plato 'accessed' true REASON, than true WISDOM had 'impacted' on Plato. As far as Lucy could gather, REASON was 'not getting confused all the time'.

'To help you get your REASON faculty warmed up this morning, I'm offering you what I call "cognitive quickies". OK? Here's one:

'Two sheep are in a field. One is looking north and the other south, yet they can see each other without turning round? How is that possible?'

Lucy couldn't solve it. She wasn't sure she wanted to. She felt Keith was cheating, like detective writers cheat by offering clues you could never get. At the end the great detective sums up, making everyone feel thick and stupid.

It turned out that the north-facing sheep was standing to the south of the south-facing sheep.

When Sarah visited her in Ruskin House, invariably so nicely-nicely dressed, always so sane and sensible, the bitch, she urged Lucy to be patient. But Sarah was not suffering constant hectoring from the biceps about 'attendance and punctuality'. Unlike Lucy, Sarah was not receiving a storm of 'spoken warnings' followed by 'written warnings'. Sarah didn't have Plato on her daily agenda.

One morning after breakfast Keith instructed Lucy and two others on parole to assemble in the Garden Room. He informed them that the Trustees of Ruskin House had authorised a visit by selected journalists.

'The Home Office has given the green light. You are free to talk to them or not talk to them. It's your choice, my friends. And if you do talk to them, your names will not be disclosed. They'll describe you by pseudonyms.'

'Who are they?' Lucy asked.

Keith shrugged. 'I don't have their names. I didn't arrange it, Lucy. I'm told all three are respected print journalists. There will be no microphones or tape recorders.'

Lucy knew it would be wiser to refuse, but she couldn't resist it. She was bored and fretful. Her first promised outing into the real world still lay a week ahead. She hated the electronic tag round her wrist. A member of staff had only to glance at the control panel to confirm that Lucy had or hadn't walked out of Ruskin House. (The front door was locked against intruders; anyone could walk out.)

Call it providence, but the journalist assigned to interview Lucy happened to be Auriol Johnson of the *World*. It was a fine day and they sat in the garden, sipping lemonade. Auriol offered her a cigarette. 'Have the packet.'

'Don't smoke menthols.'

Auriol lit up. 'What should I call you? I'm not allowed to know your real name.'

'No need to call me anything. When you're a prisoner, you're nobody.'

'Fine.'

Lucy adopted her wounded look – eyes large and staring as if stretched by grief. 'Nothing's "fine" for me.'

Auriol produced a notebook. 'Is that because you're off drugs?'

'It's because you can walk out of here but I can't.'

'Good point. Better than prison, isn't it?'

'Yeah.'

It was a hot day and Lucy was wearing a short-sleeved pink vest with the word 'Scum' woven across her small breasts. Auriol asked her about the tag attached to her wrist.

'Was it a condition of early release from prison?'

'Yeah. Keeping me inside cost them £23,000 a year.'

'What's the cost of administering a tagging order?'

'They told me it's only £1,900 a year.'

'Who told you?'

'The Governor of Milton Grange, the day I got out. Such a nice little smile the bitch gave me. Bye bye, Polly.'

Auriol nimbly suppressed her surprise at the 'Polly'. Smart little girl.

'Does the tag bug you?' she asked.

'It's a bug, isn't it?' Lucy said fiercely.

Auriol was aware that tagging had been an enormous success for the Home Office during the three years since regional trials began. Nearly one thousand offenders had been tagged – and always 'voluntarily'.

'I suppose they'll always think up something new,' Auriol said.

'"They"? You're "they".'

'Want to talk about yourself?'

'Why I'm here, you mean?'

'Anything you like. What about your family?'

Lucy shot her a glance. 'What's my name?'

'Sorry, no idea. As I told you, we're not allowed to know.'

'Yeah?'

'Don't you believe me?'

Lucy was in an agony of hesitation. She wanted this journalist to know who she was – and she didn't. She didn't trust Keith either: you could bet he'd sold a story to this nasty blonde bitch, chewing gum and smoking menthols. Lucy knew all about fees for tip-offs.

Auriol was listening to Lucy's silence. Shy little girl with an unusual history – capable of breaking loose, going wild. Auriol's source had informed her that 'the System' was hoping that Lucy's rehab would offer a model to the young. Auriol's source was Keith Mariner. Keith liked money. He didn't like Marcus Byron 'and all that get-tough shit'. Auriol suspected that Keith might even be hooked into the Stop Byron movement.

Lucy Byron could be a story in the making – and Auriol's job was to make stories happen as well as write them.

'So when will they let you take your first outing?'

'Next week. But when's next week?'

'Got a boyfriend, have you?'

Lucy's eyes caught light. 'He's taking his A levels next year, poor sod.'

'Where did you meet him?'

'Tree camp. Fighting the new road.'

'Looking forward to going out with him again?'

'I've been thinking about that. It wouldn't be easy coming back here afterwards. You have to be in by ten.'

Auriol sighed sympathetically. 'The more liberty you get, the harder not having it all.' Then she said, 'Good luck.'

'Would you like to see something I've written?'

'Written?'

'I'd like to go into journalism.' She ran up to her room, hoping to catch Keith and Fiona 'at it' when they thought she was safely out of the way, and, finding no one, brought back a single sheet of folded paper. Auriol's eyes scanned it rapidly.

It had to happen, the backlash against last year's chichi frippery and prissy sweetness. The law-abiding deb look is out, the Bad Girl snarl is what it's about. This means lived-in lipstick, smudgy eyes, torn tights and all-night drinking dens of dirty dancing . . .

'Hey! Talent! But I'm not allowed to know your name!'

'I wrote it for the "Teen Scene" page of *Hello!* before I was awarded Her Majesty's hospitality.'

'But they didn't use it?'

'They didn't use anything I sent them.'

'Well, it's good. It feels professional.'

'Why don't you publish it, then?'

'It's a year out of date.'

'Commission me to do an update.'

'OK. But only when you come out and I know who you are.'

Leaving Ruskin House, Auriol flashed her blonde curls and neat, tightly packaged hips at Keith, beckoning him to follow her out into the street. They left the building separately.

Observed by Fiona.

Auriol was waiting for him beside her Audi.

'Who's Lucy Byron's boyfriend?' she asked.

Keith flexed his thighs, crossed his arms, and displayed the biceps bulging beneath his T-shirt.

'Who's yours?'

She said: 'Don't be a bore, Keith.'

'I'm free for an hour. How about you?'

'I could report you.'

'Yeah?'

'I never sell myself, Keith – not below Cabinet level.'

He was still smiling. 'Sell? You'd be buying yourself the best screw in London Town.'

'Forget it, Keith.'

'OK,' he said, 'but the boyfriend's name is worth four figures. Dynamite.'

'Knock off a zero, Keith, and stay in your job.'

'You're a hard little bitch, Auriol. There's more to this than a boy's name.'

'Aha?'

'There's a story here.'

'So you said.'

'It could be yours. Or it could be the *Sun*'s. Or the *Mirror*'s.'

Her expression tightened. 'I deal in exclusives, you know that.'

He smiled broadly. 'I need your knickers, Auriol. I might go to Brigid Kyle and then there'd be a different kind of story.'

'Brigid? She wouldn't believe you.'

'Believe what? That's your problem, Auriol, you don't know what's cooking in the pot.'

'Too many needles in your life, Keith. You might be HIV positive. That big arm of yours is like a pin cushion.'

'No shortage of condoms in Ruskin House.'

'I'll talk to my boss about money. But I need a peep into the pot first.'

'Yeah? A little lady called Lucy is out on parole. You've just met her. She's well connected. Her rehab will be a model to the nation's young. But someone doesn't want that to happen.'

'Lucy herself? That's not worth my knickers.'

'Not Lucy. Someone big.'

'How big?'

'How long's a piece of string, Auriol?'

Observing Keith stride back to Ruskin House, Fiona Sheehy, otherwise Detective Sergeant Helen Winter, felt tempted to warn Lucy. But Helen Winter worked to a strict remit under the ultimate personal authority of

Metropolitan Commissioner Mike Price. Warning Lucy about anything was not part of that remit. Only 'reporting out'.

Reports were reaching Ben Diamond that Marcus Byron had recently been in secret conclave with senior police-men, some of whom were suspected members of Masonic Lodge 9179, otherwise known as the Manor of St James, an imposing sandstone building which might at first glance resemble any of the gentlemen's clubs in Pall Mall and St James's Street. But (Ben was informed by his junior political advisor, Edmund Joiner), Masonic Lodge 9179 was a very unusual club.

'Gentlemen arrive carrying a special regalia, Home Secretary: blue lambskin aprons and wands carried in flat black briefcases.' Delicately Edmund – who had spent the morning doodling versions of Amos Lewin's tumescent penis on a scratch pad – laid before his master a photograph showing a large number of senior police-men wearing the white gloves, embroidered sashes and lambskin aprons of the Worshipful Order of Masonry.

'Among them we can identify two Assistant Com-missioners, two Deputy Assistant Commissioners, and twelve Commanders.'

'Are you saying that Marcus Byron has been sighted entering the building?'

'Not confirmed as yet, Home Secretary.'

The Home Secretary sighed. 'But you believe that Marcus Byron is a Mason? Has he ever said as much?'

'They never do – do they?'

Edmund Joiner was aware that one of Ben Diamond's uncles, a police officer who'd believed himself morally bound to arrange alibis and cover-ups for other members of his Lodge, had been sent to prison. As a boy Ben had developed a lifelong suspicion of Masons. When a student at the University of Lancaster he'd even circulated a petition calling for their banishment. Edmund had made a careful study of the Home Secretary's biography, particularly the grey chapters that did not appear in *Who's Who*. As Siegfried Alexander used to tell him, 'the grey chapters are where the truffles grow'.

Ben Diamond was now under mounting pressure to expose Masonic influence in the judiciary and police. The Association of Progressive Lawyers had written demanding that judges, magistrates and policemen must be forced to disclose membership of the Worshipful Order of Freemasonry. The letter had been drafted by Professor Siegfried Alexander but it carried no hint of its provenance. Signed 'Sandra Golding QC' on behalf of the Association, it exposed 'a huge conspiracy'. No fewer than sixteen of sixty-four judges on the North East Circuit were known to be Masons; the same was proven about eleven of the eighty-eight magistrates in south-east Hampshire.

The nation's leading police chiefs now requested an urgent audience with the Home Secretary. On the advice of his officials he delayed the meeting, insisting on a detailed advance agenda, and confining his visitors to a delegation of three. One particular item on their agenda infuriated him – the demand that he confirm Marcus Byron's appointment as Chairman of the Criminal Law Commission. The Home Secretary regarded this as a matter for the civil power alone.

A few days after this meeting an anonymous article appeared in the weekly *Law Forum* (edited by Prof. S. Alexander). Edmund Joiner sent it on without comment to Ben Diamond, 'Attention Home Secretary' – though he did take the trouble to underline one sentence: *It can no longer be doubted that Judge Marcus Byron and his silver-braided friends of the Masonic Order have dangerous ambitions.*

Marcus Byron holds out his empty whisky glass to Brigid. 'A horse doesn't win the Derby if it languishes in the stall.'

'What are you talking about?'

Marcus's eyes rolled. 'Lang . . . wish.'

'You've had enough, Marcus. Frankly, you've had enough too often these last weeks. OK, last one until the Ten O'Clock News drives you mad all over again.'

'I had a call from Metropolitan Commissioner Mike Price. He warned me about Lucy.'

'Lucy?'

'The Met have a listening post inside Ruskin House. They don't like what they're hearing.'

'A bugging device or a person?'

'A young woman who goes by the false name of Fiona. She shares a room with Lucy. According to Mike, she's one of the most dedicated undercover policewomen within the entire Met. Prepared to go to any length, including intermittent drug addiction. She's now advising her superiors that they are planning to dish me through Lucy.'

'"They", Marcus?'

'As you always say, the Congress for Justice is dead and well. As a good Hindu, I must believe in reincarnation.'

The *World*'s ace investigator, Auriol Johnson, was expecting the anonymous call. Keith had tipped her off that it was imminent. An unidentified male voice would inform her that he supported West Ham United – and she must reply, 'I prefer Brentford.'

When the call finally came she heard an educated voice, with more than a hint of camp. Not a likely football fanatic – but a voice worth recording. Unlike most of her informants, he clearly wasn't interested in a pay-out, or her knickers. She guessed that Y-fronts would be more his territory.

'A pub in Wandsworth, you say?'

'Golden Dragon, at the corner of St John's Hill and Newcomb Street. Be there by seven-thirty. Take a female colleague. Look for a young man at the bar wearing a West Ham scarf.'

'He'll be expecting me?'

'He'll have been told that two female hitchhikers can afford thirty pounds' worth of cannabis.'

'Cannabis? That's not a story. Can't he push me some hard stuff?'

'The story is who he is.'

'Why are you setting him up?'

'Too many questions, Miss Johnson. Just tug his scarf and say, "I prefer Brentford".'

The man rang off.

Auriol was sceptical. Heroin, crack cocaine or even Ecstasy tablets would be a whole lot better. She decided to take along Liz Heath, who worked in the picture department and was expert in the use of miniature cameras.

Two young women hitchhikers wearing jeans, light anoraks, and carrying backpacks.

'Who are you setting up?' Liz asked as Auriol's Audi crossed Vauxhall Bridge.

'Dunno.'

'Sorry I asked.'

'I'm fucking serious, pussycat: I-do-not-know.'

She parked the car at a prudent distance from the Golden Dragon – hitchhikers don't drive Audis. Auriol sent Liz in first to recce, carrying a rucksack. That pert little Auriol Johnson face which perched on the neck and shoulders of her daily outpouring of scandal, exposure and plain vitriol was now dangerously famous. Despite her dark glasses, which she wore even in the rain, people often stopped her in the street as if she were a TV soap star. She had always fancied herself as a bit of an actress, and got a pleasant vibe every time she went undercover. Crooked businessmen, tyrannical bosses and bungling bureaucrats rarely suspected that an innocent blonde with a high, squeaky voice was turning them over.

Gotcha!

Liz came out of the pub after less than a minute and crossed the road to the bench where Auriol was fending off a couple of Irishmen.

'A lad in a West Ham scarf is standing at the bar.'

'Lad?'

'Not more than seventeen or eighteen.'

'Describe.'

'Nice looking. Ponytail. Ring in left ear, no pendant. Quiet clothes.'

'Is he alone?'

'He has a bird with him.'

'He does? Describe bird, Liz.'

'Same age. Small, thinnish, mixed-race parentage. White and Afro-Caribbean. Might be wearing contact lenses.'

'Shit! That dumb fucking idiot, Keith! I've met the girl, she'll recognise me. You'll have to do this alone, Liz.'

'So it's me who "prefers Brentford"? Whatever you say. Makes taking pics harder.'

'Give me your fucking Minolta.'

'Remember: light's the essence. Not the light where you are, but where the subject is.'

The two women exchanged gadgets. Auriol handed over her miniature Sony tape recorder. 'Fastens in top of boot. Voice-activated. No friction when you're seated – but don't move your foot – sounds like Hiroshima.'

Liz went back inside, assessed the crowded bar once more, pushed up to the young man and gave his scarf a gentle tug. He turned his head a fraction.

'I prefer Brentford,' she said.

'Only one of you?'

'My friend's not feeling well.'

He led Liz to a corner table, his girlfriend following.

'What will you drink?'

'Shandy. Half.'

He returned to the bar, leaving Liz with the girlfriend, who seemed tense, even suspicious. 'Friend of David, are you?' she asked.

'Is that his name? Never met him. I heard about him on the grapevine.'

'Heard what?'

'You're not part of the scene, then?'

'What scene?'

'Never mind.' Liz offered her a cigarette, which the girl grabbed and lit nervously. Her eyes never rested for a moment.

The young man brought Liz's shandy. The three of them discussed New Age Travellers, music festivals, rock concerts and which celebrities took cocaine. He was clearly into music and seemed quite relaxed. While they chatted his hands were calmly rolling three smokes of cannabis. He lit one, inhaled, handed it to the girl. She frowned, shook her head, took it, her nerves evidently too tight to refuse.

He offered the third spliff to Liz. 'This is what you'll be getting.'

Auriol had now entered the pub, wearing a headscarf and very large dark glasses, her rucksack discarded. She placed herself in the shadows by the cigarette machine. She recognised Lucy but not the young man. Who was he? This must be the first evening of freedom Lucy had known in many months and there she was, smoking grass in flagrant violation of her parole. No wonder she looked as if she was sitting on hot needles.

Auriol was focusing the miniature Minolta GV-777. Daren't use a flash.

'Still at school, are you?' Liz asked her companions. The girl merely scowled but the young man responded readily.

'A Levels. History, politics and the philosophy of law.'

'Better you than me,' Liz laughed. 'I had difficulty scraping together a few lousy GCSEs.'

Then he said: 'I hear you might be looking for some stuff?'

'If we can afford it,' Liz said. 'My friend and I are hitching to Portugal and some stuff might ease the long hours by the roadside.'

'I'm selling at tens.'

'Ten pounds?'

He nodded coolly. 'And each batch likely to run to ten joints.'

'I can pay thirty pounds.'

The girlfriend was becoming increasingly agitated, clutching at his arm and close to tears. 'Don't be stupid, David!' she whispered.

'No risk,' he murmured.

'You don't need the money! Think of your dad!'

David took a small packet from his pocket and displayed it in the palm of his hand.

'That's 1.89 grams and you can have three for thirty. One hundred pounds for twenty-eight grammes is the standard price. It's very good stuff, good strong hash. I can guarantee its quality, I use it myself.' He smiled charmingly. 'And you're smoking it now.'

The girl was twitching as if she had fleas. Liz reached into her wallet belt but David abruptly stood up.

'Outside the pub is better. You never know.'

Liz began to lift her rucksack.

'I'm staying here,' the girl said, not budging.

Observing this choreography, Auriol was worried by Lucy Byron's resistance. She needed both of them out there, in the daylight. Auriol began to move towards the door.

Liz shouldered her rucksack and followed David outside, relieved to be offering the miniature Minolta more light – provided fucking Auriol didn't fuck it up. The girl came in pursuit of her boyfriend, trying to pull him back. Now that they were all outside on St John's Hill, Liz noticed that they were standing directly opposite a magistrates court.

David's eye followed hers. He smiled gently. 'They close at five.'

As the cannabis and the money changed hands, Lucy buried her face in her hands. 'Wonderful, great,' Auriol murmured to herself as the Minolta raced.

Then David astonished Liz by writing down his full name and telephone number on a scrap of paper.

'In case you should want some more after you get back from Portugal. But if I'm not in, never leave a message.'

The girl was in tears. 'David! Why are you doing this?'

Five minutes later the two female reporters from the *World* were inside Auriol Johnson's Audi. Both lit cigarettes.

'Get the fucking pics?' Liz asked.

'Let's hope.'

'We have more than murky pics, darling.' She handed Auriol the scrap of paper containing the young man's name and phone number. 'The boy's crazy. Can he be that short of money?'

'Holy fucking cow!' exclaimed Auriol. 'Do you realise who this young fuck is? And the girl! Do you realise what a story we've got!'

Later that evening Auriol telephoned Keith at Ruskin House. Keith had a mobile for 'private calls'.

'Has she come back yet?'

'She arrived a few minutes before ten. She looked bad.'

'Bad?'

'Upset. Tearful. I demanded a urine sample. She refused. A refusal is deep trouble.'

'Keith, what the hell is really going on?'

There was merely a dark chuckle at the other end of the line. 'I'm still waiting for my money, pussycat.'

Eleven

Jenny Glendower sits in the waiting room of a police identification centre, flanked by two solicitous CID officers. If her tongue runs over her lip, they run for a glass of water. Her journey from Yeominster and her hotel accommodation is at the police's expense. These two policemen in plainclothes had met her train at Paddington, both the soul of courtesy, grateful for her continued co-operation and apologetic for what they called her coming 'ordeal'. Seizing her small suitcase, they introduced themselves as Detective Inspector Paul Gibbs and Detective Sergeant Doug McIntyre.

She had wondered what she should wear. Not only was she going to see the boys who had raped her but they (she thought) were going to see her.

'No they won't,' Gibbs reassured her as soon as he was seated beside her in the back of a police car, McIntyre driving. 'You'll be looking through one-way glass, Mrs Glendower.'

Anyway, she had chosen a trouser suit in a dark blue cloth. No more screaming pinks and short skirts. She had also told them in advance that she wished to stay again in the Winfield Hotel, if possible room 36. Unknown to her, this generated alarm and concern within the CID; it was held to be symptomatic of protracted hysteria. McIntyre was convinced it also belonged to the 'death wish' syndrome common among victims returning to the scene of their ordeal.

'As soon as our backs are turned, she'll go walk-about in the streets of Great North, on her own, at night, all the way to the canal,' Gibbs warned his superiors.

The decision was taken that the Winfield was fully booked, no rooms available. So was every other hotel in Great North. Bloomsbury would do nicely.

Gibbs is preparing her for the identity parade.

'You've told us that four of your attackers were black Afro-Caribbeans. So the first "parade" will consist entirely of black youths aged fifteen to twenty.'

'Yes, I understand. Pete and Luke were black. I didn't catch the names of the two others.'

'Then you mentioned two who you thought might be Filipinos.' Gibbs smiles faintly. 'So we might call the next parade a "Far Eastern journey".'

'The very little one?'

Gibbs offers no comment. 'Two you described as white.'

'But I don't think either was English.'

'We've chosen a variety of Europeans. Finally, the one you thought was the leader—'

'Rorco? He reminded me of one of those old engravings of the Aztecs.'

'We're short of boys born at the time of the Spanish conquest of Mexico but we've done our best.'

'What you have to understand, Mrs Glendower,' McIntyre adds, 'is that we have arrested eight boys who broadly fit your descriptions. The street video shot is too distant and blurred to be conclusive but it also helps.'

Neither Gibbs nor McIntyre is going to tell her that defence solicitors will be present to monitor the proceedings. But Oliver Rawl's name had been found in her abandoned handbag; Rawl had visited her in hospital; the firm of Hawthorne & Moss will therefore not be represented by Mr Rawl at the parade. After some consultation it was also agreed with Chapman & Burnett that Ms Woods would be represented by a nominee.

Gibbs touches her hand. 'Nothing to worry about, Mrs Glendower. We'll walk down the line slowly, Mrs Glendower, no hurry, look carefully at each one, then walk back again. Then repeat the procedure. Take your time.'

Jenny nods, mute.

'There's always a temptation,' Detective Sergeant Doug McIntyre adds, 'to snatch at it. Suppose you feel sure. "That's the one! That's him!" So why bother with the others? However convinced you feel, Mrs Glendower, remember that a lot of lads look like a lot of other lads – and you never saw them by daylight, did you?'

'Yes, I understand.'

Gibbs nods. 'It's going to be a bit of an ordeal for you, but you're a brave woman, all of us know that.'

'There's one thing I've wanted to ask: where do the others come from, I mean—?'

'The others in the line? Some are boys we recruited an hour ago down at the local Social Services hostel plus a few straight off the street – five quid an hour and they leap at it.'

'Oh.'

'What you have to remember is that we fit them up a bit.'

'Fit them up?'

Gibbs glances at her. Her voice has risen.

'The rules about identification now prevailing, Mrs Glendower, God bless the Home Office, are somewhat baffling. For instance, you have told us that your lads mostly displayed burn scars on their hands.'

'Yes, they did.'

Jenny recalls the huge black boy displaying his left hand with a grin, the scorch mark between thumb and forefinger which had turned into a scar at the point where the charcoal skin on the back of his hand merged with the pink-grained palm. All the lads had shown her their burns, as if keen for her admiration, all except their leader, who disdained her attention . . .

'So all the lads we show you will be wearing gloves,' Gibbs informs her.

'But why? Why!'

'Because Mrs Glendower, it's quite a common initiation ritual among the gangs and if you snatch at burn scars you could be making a mistake.'

'But—'

'And then you told us there was a very large black boy.'

'Yes, broad-shouldered and tall. Luke.'

'Madam, any small person like yourself who gets set upon is liable to see her attacker as taller than he is. So if we had them all standing up you might, out of the goodness of your mind's eye, just go for the tallest.'

Her common sense rises in protest. Do they want her to identify her tormentors or not? Whose side are these two nice men really on?

'But I told you,' she exclaims, 'one of them, a Filipino, he was smaller than me.'

'So you might just go for any very small lad. Better to have them seated.'

'But—'

'Then you mentioned a black lad whose wiry hair was dyed bright yellow beneath his baseball cap.'

'Yes, Pete.'

'So we could have all the black lads wearing identical red baseball caps – or none. An innocent lad might be wearing the cap more the way you remember it. You end up accusing a baseball cap.'

'But doesn't it help you at all that I remembered four of their names?'

'Yes,' Gibbs agrees, 'that's vital evidence. But it can't be conclusive. Believe me, we do understand your feelings, Mrs Glendower. We have discussions among ourselves, particularly about scars, dreadlocks and dyed hair. But the first thing a boy on the run does is get rid of his hair-style. So let's forget the hair, shall we? Each boy will be wearing a white skull cap.'

Jenny looks crestfallen.

'Mrs Glendower,' McIntyre says in his reassuring Scottish way, 'you'll be fine, just fine. You're a heroine to us, madam, and don't you forget it.'

She smiles: nice man. 'Thank you,' she says.

After further delay, they start with a parade of Afro-Caribbeans. Flanked by Gibbs and McIntyre, she can't help noticing four men following at a discreet distance with notebooks.

'Who are they?' she whispers to McIntyre. Gibbs is nice but just a bit smooth – she prefers McIntyre.

'Defence solicitors observing,' McIntyre says. 'Kindly ignore them.'

'Sorry.'

Jenny finds herself staring through one-way glass at eight black peas in a pod. Each youth wears a white, close-fitting cap down to his ears and gloves on his hands. She's reminded of the surgeons bending over her just before she was delivered of her second child by Caesarean section.

She stops, whispers. Gibbs tells her to point and speak loudly. 'They can neither see nor hear you,' he reminds her.

'Number four,' she says, 'that's Luke.' He's seated but she recognises his muscular bulk. He's staring blankly into space, wearing an expression of hurt innocence.

To her surprise, McIntyre repeats her words loudly, as if addressing a public meeting. She notices the four men following scribbling in their notebooks.

She comes back down the line, trying to concentrate, to remember. Suddenly all blacks, like all proverbial Chinese, look alike.

'Take your time,' she hears.

'Number seven,' she says, 'I think that's Pete.'

'You have to decide,' Gibbs says. 'Otherwise it's a qualified identification.'

'"Qualified"?'

'You must be certain, madam.'

'He kept asking me for a kiss – I mean before they all—'

'Take your time. There's no hurry.'

'Number seven is Pete,' she says angrily.

McIntyre repeats it loudly. The four defence solicitors scribble.

She walks down the line again. All those pairs of eyes beneath those white plastic caps seem so docile, passive, defeated, nothing like what she saw in their faces when they raped her. She has shots at the two other black boys, but she isn't sure. The solicitors scribble: the lady is not sure.

'I don't know,' she tells Doug McIntyre. 'I'm rather tired. Sorry.'

Thirty minutes later she drags herself through a second identity parade. This time it's the 'Aztecs'. She has no problem, her heart leaps in a fiery mix of fear and hatred. His is the most evil face she has ever seen. The young years seem to have been expelled from it by a corrosive acid of permanent rage. She remembers him lighting a cannabis spliff with a big gas lighter whose whooshing flame threw his evil face and cat's eyes into stark relief. Now she sees him in a cage whose glass wall cannot hold him; he's about to leap out on her and knife her through the heart.

She controls her voice. 'Number three is the leader of the gang, Rorco. Yes, I'm certain.'

McIntyre shouts it out. He's not worried by her continued mis-remembrance of Charco Rios's name. Oliver Rawl and his counsel may try to make a meal of it but no jury will be swayed. No jury believes a woman is writing names in a notebook while she's being raped.

Later she spears Ally Leagum with equal confidence, then one of the white boys who had drifted along silently with the gang – but she could still feel his rising heartbeat and racing breath as he took his turn by the canal.

'I'm tired,' she murmurs.

They take her inside the waiting room for a cup of tea. McIntyre gravely apologises: he has forgotten whether she takes sugar.

'Well?' she asks him. 'Did I get all eight suspects?'

Gibbs hesitates but McIntyre is responsive. 'Five out of eight, Mrs Glendower.'

'Only five? You mean I got three wrong?'

'Don't let it trouble you. Believe me, five out of eight is remarkable.'

'But three will get off!'

'I doubt it. We have other evidence.'

'Tell me the names of the five.'

'Regrettably,' Gibbs cuts in, 'we're not allowed to do that. You will be the prime prosecution witness in this case, madam, and a witness must not be told anything that she does not know on her own account.'

It is late on a late-summer afternoon when they reach her hotel. The parting between herself and the two police officers is brief, perfunctory. They have all had enough of each other's company. The job is done. She assures them that she will dine in the hotel, go to bed early, catch the first morning train back to Yeominster.

McIntyre reminds her that the police will pay for her taxi – and then she is alone.

Up in her room, she fiddles with her address book, dithers, then dials Oliver's home number. His recorded voice invites her to leave a message after the tone.

Auriol had sent the little Cellophane packet straight to the *World*'s lab. By morning she had confirmation that the substance was indeed cannabis. She immediately telephoned Paul Glass's office.

'Who's calling, please?'

'Auriol Johnson of the *World*.'

'Dr Glass is tied up in a meeting. Perhaps you'd like to speak to our press officer?'

'This is very personal and urgent. It concerns his son David.'

Paul Glass himself was on the line within ten minutes, tense and brusque. 'I have a busy morning. Just tell me what you wish to tell me.'

She was tape recording the conversation and she knew that modern law obliged her to warn him of the fact, but

Auriol treated the law as an ass when it inconvenienced her. Her telephone had been doctored to suppress the warning bleep and the intermittent bleep at fifteen-second intervals which – again by law – warns the other party that they are on tape.

She gave him a brief account of what had happened. His son had sold her colleague cannabis worth £30. Laboratory tests confirmed that the substance was genuine.

'Dr Glass, we believe this is a matter of public interest – in view of the position you hold as Special Adviser to the Criminal Policy Directorate.'

Paul Glass sounded incredulous, shaken. Well, he would be, wouldn't he? It's a long road back to Cambridge from Whitehall.

Auriol didn't mention Lucy. She was waiting for Glass to ask whether David had been alone in the pub, whether there were any witnesses apart from the two journalists. But he didn't ask. She was absorbing Dr Glass's silences.

'Your son was with Lucy Byron,' she said.

His voice almost choked. 'It doesn't surprise me.'

'Meaning?'

'I can't say more.'

'Lucy Byron was trying to restrain David. She didn't want him to do it.'

His voice cracked. 'I must have time to speak to my son. No more questions.' The line went dead.

Half an hour passed before Auriol's editor received a call from the Home Office, begging him not to release the story pending 'further inquiries'.

The Home Secretary himself telephoned Marcus Byron at Great North Crown Court during the lunch break. Ben rapidly outlined the story.

'We're facing a disaster, Marcus. That bitch Auriol Johnson has us by the short hairs. I had a word with the Prime Minister. His instructions are clear.'

'Yeah?'

'"Damage limitation" is the name of the game. And we are going to need your co-operation.'

'I'm not understanding a word of this. Are you talking to me about my Lucy?'

'Your Lucy and David Glass. Talk to Paul. You and he are the fathers in the case. You'd better get your act together.'

Marcus then attempted to reach Lucy's solicitor at Chapman & Burnett, but Sarah Woods was out. He left a message and tried Sarah's mobile but it had been switched off. Unknown to Marcus, Sarah had been plucked from her office at short notice by Paul Glass.

Early in the afternoon David Glass was granted permission by his Headmaster to meet his father and solicitor at St John's Hill police station. The three of them convened for a tense conference on the street outside. Sarah would have liked ten minutes alone with David, but Paul Glass, Special Adviser to the Criminal Policy Directorate, dark-suited and authoritative, remained glued to his son.

'Do you agree the facts, David? Is it true?' he demanded.

'Yes. Sorry, Dad.'

'It's a bit late to be sorry, isn't it?'

David turned to Sarah. 'I have to make a statement to the police straight away – for Dad's sake.'

'No you don't. I want to know every detail of what happened.'

'Forget it, Sarah.'

'Were you alone in the pub when you sold the cannabis – if you did?'

'I was with Lucy.'

'Lucy! My God, how could you do that?' She turned to Paul Glass. 'Have you spoken to Marcus Byron?'

His jaw was set tight. 'He has been informed.'

'But has Lucy been informed?'

'That's up to her father.'

She bridled. She had always been led to believe that Paul Glass and Marcus Byron were old friends. David and Lucy clearly loved one another. Was Paul Glass now solely concerned to save his own son – or, the thought dawned, his own career?

'I have to remind you both that I also represent Lucy.'

'I want to keep Lucy out of this,' David said.

'Fat chance, David! You're in the hands of Auriol Johnson, remember?'

'That's news to me,' David said sulkily.

'You honestly thought you were selling the stuff to a hitchhiker?'

David nodded, mute.

'I want to speak to Lucy before David makes a statement to the police,' Sarah insisted. 'Don't you both understand what this could mean for her?'

David looked crushed. 'Let's wait, Dad.'

But Paul Glass was in no mood to be swayed by sentiment. He knew the meaning of the legal phrase, 'at the first opportunity'.

'David and I are now going inside,' he informed Sarah. 'If you don't wish to accompany us, that's your right. I am perfectly capable of safeguarding David's legal rights.'

Sarah could not desert David. Entering the police station, she lost no time in reminding the duty sergeant that David's name could not be published because of his age, nor could his father be identified because that was tantamount to exposing David.

'That's agreed, Miss Woods. But if, as Dr Glass tells me, the *World* has already got hold of the story, it's going to be difficult to keep the bug in the bottle.'

Sarah listened as David dictated a statement. It was the first time that she had heard a full account. She noticed gaps in the story – and so did the duty sergeant.

'You say you believed this woman was a hitchhiker?'

'Yes.'

'You'd never met her before?'

'No.'

'She approached you when you were standing at the bar?'

'Yes.'

'Why did you know she wanted to buy cannabis?'

'I'd been tipped off by my supplier.'

'You've been doing this regularly?'

'Not regularly. Once or twice.'

'Who is your supplier?'

David's gaze fell. 'I don't know his name.'

No one present believed he was telling the truth.

'Were you alone with the "hitchhiker" throughout the incident?'

David seemed to shrivel. 'Yes.'

'He was with his girlfriend,' Paul Glass cut in. 'Naturally he's anxious to protect her.'

The sergeant looked from father to son as policemen look. Sarah was choking.

'Was your girlfriend involved in the sale of this substance?' the sergeant asked David.

'No, not at all.'

'Is she also a juvenile – under eighteen?'

'Yes, seventeen – like me.'

'In that case I don't think I need to know her identity – at this stage. It's not for me to predict, but no further steps may be taken in this matter. Or the incident may be dealt with by way of a caution.'

A few moments later David was formally arrested – but not charged. He seemed surprised, almost indignant, reminding Sarah of his principled stand when arrested for trespass at the New Age Travellers' tree camp: the worse the better.

'Aren't you going to charge me?' David asked the duty sergeant.

'We have to review the facts and the circumstances. As of now, we have no evidence beyond what you have told us. Police bail will be granted without conditions.'

When the three emerged from St John's Hill police

station, Sarah again requested an opportunity to speak to David alone – but Paul immediately sent his son back to school on the bus.

David gripped Sarah by the arm before he took his leave: 'Whatever happens, Sarah, I want you to represent me. You're the best.'

Paul walked her to her car. 'In my view, Sarah, you will find it difficult to represent both David and Lucy from now on. Probably impossible.'

She didn't reply. Her heart was hammering with anxiety.

'My son,' Paul continued, 'is too naïve and decent to see what I can see and you should see – a clear conflict of interests.'

'Why?'

'Lucy is a potential witness against David in this case.'

'But the facts are admitted!'

'There may be more to this than David has admitted to the police or to us. I myself am convinced that David was selling cannabis to help pay for Lucy's continuing addiction to Class A drugs.'

Sarah strove to contain her rising anger. 'Lucy has not touched drugs since she left Oak End. She was clean at Milton Grange and she's clean at Ruskin House.'

'But she wasn't clean last night at the Golden Dragon public house.'

'So you want me to drop Lucy?'

'You must choose but the choice has to be made.'

Sarah Woods slammed the door of her car. She drove

straight to Lincoln's Inn, where she briefed Bob Jolly QC to seek an immediate injunction banning the *World* (and any other paper) from naming either David Glass or his father or his father's job. Bob Jolly listened intently.

'We may be up against a technical difficulty, Sarah. If we go for an injunction under section 49 of the 1933 Children and Young Persons Act, the *World* may argue that the Act protects the anonymity of young persons only if they have been charged with a criminal offence.'

'And David hasn't been charged yet.'

'Precisely. We could argue that he may yet be charged, and that the law is an ass if it allows this loophole.'

'We could try the 1981 Contempt of Court Act.'

Bob Jolly nodded. 'We could. The ambiguity there again is whether it comes into operation when a person is arrested, or only when charged. We'd have to argue that legal proceedings are active from the moment of David's arrest – and so he cannot be named. It's our only hope – though a faint one.'

Late in the afternoon Marcus Byron finally got through to Sarah when she was driving back to her office, his mood belligerent, even accusatory.

'Where the hell have you been? Shining Paul Glass's shoes, I assume.'

She marvelled how the two fathers, though old friends, had abruptly broken ranks – as any experienced lawyer would.

'May I call you back?' She disliked driving with one hand in heavy traffic or any traffic. Oliver could do it but nothing was beyond Oliver.

'Yeah? When? You'd better get one thing straight – you can no longer represent my Lucy *and* David Glass. Is that clear? It's one or the other.'

Later, incensed and distraught, Sarah poured herself a half pint of chianti and unburdened her miserable day to an attentive Oliver. She was quite in the mood to quarrel with him, too, but this evening's Oliver was the nice one, sympathetic and solicitous, though he insisted on ironing his shirts while she talked.

'Paul Glass talks about Lucy's continuing addiction to Class A drugs. Yet she has been subject to almost daily urine tests in Ruskin House and she has a clean bill of health. Clean! Do you get that, clean?'

'I don't like the sound of Paul Glass's agenda. He's determined to save his career, whatever the price.'

'These bloody men! These ego-fired potentates! What do they care about their children?'

'I doubt that's fair if applied to Marcus and Lucy.'

'I don't want to be fair! My head's splitting! I have a ten-megaton migraine!'

The legal situation, moreover, was little better than the human one. Bob Jolly had gone before Judge Sawyer in chambers and obtained an injunction on behalf of David Glass – but Jolly did not expect it could be sustained for long. You couldn't suppress high-voltage public scandal these days. Not with Auriol Johnson pressing the buttons.

Oliver agreed. 'Frankly, the law protecting the anonymity of juveniles is an ass all-round. A boy of fourteen gets thrown out of school, teachers refuse to work if the

LEA restores him, mums demonstrate against him at the school gates – and his name can be splashed all over the front pages, alongside his scowling mug. Whereas if he were to be charged with stealing a packet of biscuits, no name, no face.'

'Oliver!'

'Yes?'

'Never mind the packet of biscuits, we're talking about David and Lucy.'

'You won't be able to represent both of them. It's either one – or neither.'

'David told me he wanted me, right in front of his father. It sounded like a cry for help. And I'm not going to desert Lucy either!'

'There's more to this case than meets the eye. Who tipped off Auriol Johnson? That's the question.'

'She doesn't know.'

'She says she doesn't know. Is she likely to be granted the OBE for integrity?'

'Actually, I believe her.'

Despite Judge Sawyer's injunction, Auriol Johnson lost no time in reporting to readers of the *World* from David's private school, Launcester – though without naming David. 'Can you confirm that the school has a policy of zero tolerance towards drug possession?' she had asked the Headmaster. He had fended her off: 'The law does not allow me to offer any comment which might affect the rights of an individual.' But pupils passing through the

school gates were not so shy. A boy told Auriol: '****
is very nice but a bit shy, a bit held-back. Maybe he felt
a need to prove himself. I feel sorry for him.'

> The Crime and Disorder Bill [writes Auriol Johnson]
> follows Ben Diamond's White Paper, *No More
> Excuses.* What excuses will be offered for the conduct
> of a youth reliably reported to be the son of a senior
> figure in Diamond's new legal set-up? And for his
> girlfriend, currently on parole, the daughter of a
> legal figure no less eminent?

'What use a bloody injunction?' Sarah yelled at Oliver
across the breakfast table, staring at the front pages of
half-a-dozen newspapers. Every newspaper reported that
an unnamed boy's highly placed father had taken him to
the police to make a statement. 'A prominent legal official
has marched his son into a police station and made him
own up to drug dealing. It is understood that the boy is
anxious to protect the identity of his girlfriend, who was
also present.'

What most worried Sarah and Bob Jolly about the
situation was the steady erosion of David's right to plead
Not Guilty if the CPS went ahead with a prosecution.
Both lawyers now suspected that David had acted under
'duress', and duress is a defence even if the facts have been
admitted.

Marcus and Sarah held a tense, ten-minute conference

in MB1 before going inside Ruskin House to meet Lucy. Marcus listened with grave concentration as Sarah reported everything that Paul and David Glass had said and done from the moment she was summoned to meet them outside St John's Hill police station.

'So Paul insists that you can't represent both Lucy and David?'

'He regards them as potential witnesses against each other.'

'What can Lucy tell the police that David himself hasn't already told them?'

Sarah hesitated. 'Paul claims that David was selling dope to pay for Lucy's habit.'

'Jesus!' Marcus raged. 'The girl is clean! Every test shows that!'

Sarah was close to tears but Marcus was relentless.

'And I'll tell you how the Boy and Ben Diamond see it. What terrifies them is the accusation of a Government cover-up to protect a senior official. They're pressing Paul Glass to make a public statement. They also want the Attorney General to appear before Judge Sawyer with a request that the injunction be lifted in the public interest.'

'Bob Jolly and I will fight that.'

'But Paul won't. And supposing David goes along with his dad – as he certainly will? In that case you and Bob Jolly will be attempting to walk on water.'

Entering Ruskin House, Marcus and Sarah were met by a deeply concerned Keith Mariner. He pumped Marcus's hand in a big display of commiseration.

'I've got bad news, Judge Byron. When Lucy returned

from her first evening at liberty, she refused a urine test. She's still refusing. As you know – and Lucy knows – cannabis can be detected for up to a month.'

'Why did you want to test her?' Sarah asked.

'Hey, Miss Woods, isn't it obvious?'

What wasn't obvious to Marcus was how much Keith knew about Lucy's evening out with David Glass.

'Of course Lucy's refusal is serious,' Keith went on. 'It means automatic suspension of future exeats, and it has to be reported to the Parole Board. A refusal is tantamount to a positive.'

Marcus didn't care for Keith. After a further private conversation with Metropolitan Commissioner Mike Price, he was convinced that Lucy and David had been set up for a sting with the connivance of someone who had known when she would be allowed her first full evening away from Ruskin House.

'Miss Woods and I wish to talk to Lucy privately,' Marcus said.

'Fine. We can offer you the Garden Room or, if you prefer, the garden itself.'

'The garden,' Marcus said.

When Lucy joined them she kissed Sarah but couldn't look at Marcus. Both noticed the electronic tag back on Lucy's wrist.

'Say nothing!' Marcus instructed, pointing to the tag. Grasping Lucy's hand, he led her back through the open french window until he found Keith.

'I'd like Lucy's tag removed during her interview with her solicitor. You can restore it as soon as we've departed.'

Keith gave him a slow look. 'Any special reason, Judge?'

'I never make requests without reason.'

'But the tag does no more than establish where she is.'

'Yeah. She'll be with us in the garden.'

Keith removed the tag. Marcus and Lucy rejoined Sarah in the garden. Sarah's expression indicated puzzlement but Marcus had no wish to explain his fantasies about miniature tape recorders disguised as electronic tags.

'I let you both down,' Lucy said in a flat voice.

'No, you didn't,' Marcus said. 'You are innocent in this affair.'

'Did Keith tell you I refused a urine test? Know why? When David offered me a spliff in the pub, I took it.'

'Lucy, did this happen in the presence of—'

'Yes. That "hitchhiker" woman was sitting with us. I didn't like her from the start. I can smell phoney. I only took the spliff because I was nervous. I couldn't understand how David could be so naïve. I kept trying to stop him selling the stuff but he—'

Marcus firmly took Lucy's hand. 'Lucy, before this woman "hitchhiker" showed up, did David warn you that he was expecting someone?'

'No. We were just having a good time, my first evening out.'

Marcus was pacing the garden like a caged beast. He turned to Sarah:

'You'd better tell her.'

'Tell me what?' Lucy asked.

'Lucy,' Sarah said gently, 'Paul Glass insists that I cannot continue to represent both David and you.'

'Why?'

'Paul believes that what David told the police was less than the whole truth.'

Lucy looked from her solicitor to her father, trembling and bewildered.

'What's the "whole truth"?' she whispered.

Sarah told her.

Lucy clutched her own face as if to tear it. 'No! No! That's not true! David would never tell Paul that!'

'No one's saying he did,' Sarah said quietly.

'I don't understand any of this!'

They sat in silence. Then Marcus banged his fist on his knee:

'Paul Glass is right – and I was right, Sarah. You cannot continue to represent both Lucy and David.'

'Yes, she can!' Lucy cried. 'She must!'

Marcus sighed. 'I take the view that Sarah is already representing David in the courts on this case, so I'm going to find another solicitor for you.'

'Lucy,' Sarah said, 'you're more than a client to me, you're a dear friend – and I love you. But your dad is right. It's horrible but it's true.'

She kissed Lucy on both cheeks then hurried from the garden, leaving father and daughter alone, wrapped in silence. Never had Marcus felt closer to Lucy.

* * *

Oliver's first remark on climbing out of bed was normally, 'What do I need today? I need a fax from Delia.'

But this time it wasn't a fax. It was a headline in the *Sentinel*: WOMAN POINTS GUN AT JUDGE

A woman was on the run last night after she threatened Judge Marcus Byron with a gun and started a big security alert in Great North Crown Court. The Victorian gothic building was sealed off for more than four hours as police armed with submachine-guns searched corridors in a fruitless hunt for the woman. Bewigged judges, barristers and court officials spilled out on to the pavement as the building was evacuated. The search relied on blueprints of the 1871 building designed by George Street.

The incident occurred in oak-panelled Court No. 7. At about 12.20 the woman, wearing a green anorak, ran from the public gallery (according to one version) or came through a door normally used by solicitors (according to another) holding the gun in front of her in a double-handed, police-style grip and shouting, 'I want my appeal heard now. I want to be a woman. If I'm not heard, I will shoot this black bastard.'

When the court registrar moved towards her and offered to take down details of her case, she pointed the gun at him and said: 'If anyone moves you will all get shot.' A barrister later commented that the gun may not have been real. After about three minutes the woman slipped out by the same door and disappeared in the labyrinth of corridors. The woman is believed to have undergone a sex-change operation.

Well at least it can't be Delia this time, Oliver thought. She didn't use guns. Strangulation was her thing. And there was no mention of Blackfriars Bridge.

But even as he replaced the lid on the marmalade, Delia was returning to the scene of the crime. Once wasn't enough for so much fun. This time she was nabbed immediately. A furious struggle took place. One of the security guards later told the *World*, 'I've never known a woman with hands like those. I thought I was a goner.' The pistol turned out to be a fake Beretta.

Called to Great North police station, Oliver found Delia in a serene mood. The police had given her a cup of tea, which she was holding quite daintily in her huge hands.

'Who are you really, Oliver?' she smiled flirtatiously.

'I'm your solicitor.'

'Oh I know that, dear, but who are you really? One of *them*?'

'Why did you do whatever you are alleged to have done but didn't do?'

'That black bastard Marcus Byron thinks he can get away with his wicked work. He bad-eyed me in Dorset, you know.'

'In Dorset?'

Delia smiled enigmatically. 'I had been sent.'

It sounded faintly religious.

'Sent?'

'By the avenging angels. But he didn't heed the message, didn't cease his evil work, even though he had imprisoned my innocent sister.'

'Your sister, Delia? I didn't know you have a sister.'

Delia smiled enigmatically.

'What's your sister's name?'

'That would be telling. Yes, dear, so they sent me again.'

Now, in Oliver's presence, Delia was charged with two counts of possessing an imitation firearm with intent to cause fear of violence.

'No statement,' Oliver informed the Custody Officer, 'until she has seen a doctor.'

'So what kind of a prison is "she" heading for, Mr Rawl? Male or female?'

Oliver emerged angry and alarmed by his latest interview with Charco Rios in Downton Juvenile Offenders Institution. Charco still had friends out there, and gang law was vindictive. He continued to insist that Oliver had fucking shopped him to the fucking pigs. Charco was convinced.

Oliver took Sarah to Pasta & Basta with the intention of getting to the bottom of it. When she began talking about David and Lucy, he cut her short.

'We're in trouble, you and I. Your clients and mine are potentially hostile witnesses to each other.'

'Maybe, Oliver, but I don't like your tone.'

'Each of the eight statements to the police says in effect, "It was the others who had her, not me."'

'It's early days. Who knows? I still don't like your tone. It's not my fault that your former girlfriend decided to walk alone at night in Great North.'

'True. But what about Charco Rios? The CPS are bound to bring a subsidiary charge to the murder one: attempted interference with the course of justice.'

'So? That's the least serious of the three charges he faces.'

'Oddly, it's the one that most obsesses him – because that's how they got him. Charco comes from a Mafia culture where betrayal and revenge are almost religious rituals.'

'That won't impress a QC like Antony Laughton.'

'Oh but it does. Laughton is determined to force the prosecution to disclose the information that led them to place Tony Marquez and his family under round-the-clock surveillance.'

'"Information"? Once they'd moved him to a safe house the protection becomes mere police routine.'

'Perhaps – but what led the police to Tony Marquez in the first place?'

She shrugged. Oliver's temper frayed.

'I was summoned to Dick Dodgett's office. Dick asked whether I'd informed anyone else about Charco's threats against Tony Marquez. "Only yourself," I told him. "What about Sarah?" he asked.'

As he spoke, Oliver's angry gaze had been fixed intently on his plate. But now he looked up.

'I denied it to Dodgett. I lied to my boss.'

'And why are you looking at me like that?'

'If you went to the police, Sarah, fine. If you thought I shouldn't know, fine. But now you have to tell me the truth.'

Sarah laid down her fork, wrapped in congealing tagliatelle. 'I can't eat. I can't sit here with someone who doesn't trust me.'

Informed that Lucy Byron had been involved in the 'David Glass incident', and had refused a urine test after her return to Ruskin House, the Home Secretary could no longer resist the conclusion that Edmund Joiner and his own senior officials had been right all along: the Byron family were a liability.

In the House he faced merciless taunting from the Opposition. Opening a Commons debate in his best Big Ben style, leaning forward across the despatch box and periodically punching the air, Ben Diamond unveiled a tough new Community Safety Order, allowing courts to impose curfews and exclusions on 'neighbours from hell'.

'Madam Speaker, you go to the police, you get another brick through your window, you withdraw your complaint. Let me give the House one recent example out of many. I am quoting a report in yesterday's *Sentinel*:

'"'You're an effing bitch and you're effing dead and I'll be back tonight to effing kill you,' yelled Ted Batty. Covertly filmed video showed Batty making repeated attempts to board up a neighbour's house and set fire to it with the owner and his two young daughters inside."

'For the future, Madam Speaker, the Government proposes an injunction to be obtained in the County Court on a lower standard of proof than the one prevailing in the criminal courts. Police officers will be able to testify that complaints have been received without naming the complainants. In addition, professional witnesses like private detectives may be used to gather evidence of harassment or intimidation on a round-the-clock basis.

'Those who fail to comply with injunctions will be liable to a maximum penalty of four years' imprisonment. What I am proposing is that delinquent families be treated and punished as a unit.'

By this time not only the Opposition ranks across the floor but also Ben's own backbenches were heaving.

The Shadow Home Secretary, the Rt Hon Jeremy Darling, was up. 'Madam Speaker, would the Home Secretary confirm that what he is offering the House is Byronism without Byron?'

Ben was duly stung. 'I anticipate criticism from those whose first care is always to tuck up the wrongdoer in bed with a cup of hot chocolate.'

Behind Ben, Willy Braithwaite, once a probation officer, caught the Speaker's eye.

'Does the Home Secretary not agree that the parents of young offenders are generally on benefit and struggling to cope? Does he not understand that fines and curfews will only increase feelings of inadequacy?'

Cheers. Jeremy Darling jumped up again.

'Will the Home Secretary confirm that he shook Judge Byron's hand on appointing him to Chair the Criminal Law Commission, and has ever since been trying to unshake the judge's hand?'

Gales of merriment swept the Commons, even the Government's backbenches. Ben's face was a study in chagrin. Beside him the Boy – of late a rare visitor to the Commons – sat stone-faced.

'And will the Home Secretary tell us,' Darling continued, 'why the Government has attempted to hush up an alleged scandal that might well affect the standing of two prominent persons whom I of course cannot possibly name—' (rising uproar, shouts of 'Hypocrite!') '—cannot possibly name, Madam Speaker, because it is not for me to ignore a judicial injunction designed to protect the anonymity of young persons—' (uproar, cries of 'Order!' from the Speaker) '—even though, Madam Speaker, such an injunction cannot be imposed on this House and—!'

Darling did not need to finish. He sat down, beaming.

Ben rose again, quivering with rage. 'If the Right Honourable Gentleman wishes to play the clown, none can outdo him in that role.'

Uproar.

The siren's call on her mobile phone came as Sarah Woods left Benson Street Youth Court for the lunch break. Passing the Burns security guards at the entrance, she had rapidly surveyed the scene on the street, then reached into her bag to activate her cellnet. The lunch hour was as good a time as any to get mugged, with so many restless or aggrieved young offenders hanging around. A recent Brigid Kyle column had quoted a passage from *The Winter's Tale*: 'I would there were no age between sixteen and three-and-twenty – for there is nothing in the between but getting wenches with child, wronging the ancestry, stealing, fighting.'

Brigid had commented that Shakespeare, on a return visit to his native isle, might very well amend 'sixteen' to 'fourteen' or 'twelve'.

All morning Sarah had wrestled with the destructive bravado of these boys in the cells and corridors of Benson Street. As soon as their pals showed up in the visitors' waiting area, you couldn't get the defendants' attention, it was all show and macho and endless expletives about being kept waiting – as if a court were a pop concert that had failed to start on time. But she did feel sorry for the mums who sat there for hours worrying about the younger children.

In the Youth Court friends were not allowed into the courtrooms, though that didn't stop them trying. One of Oliver's colleagues at Hawthorne & Moss had been seriously assaulted by his own client at Benson Street when being taken down to the cells. On another occasion Sarah had witnessed a female defendant of hers jerk out a leg and trip up the prosecutor, a small Asian woman, as she passed. Although closed circuit television had now been installed at Benson Street, it was still a major issue whether to return weapons confiscated by the Burns guards at the entrance.

Sarah had tossed that one to an incredulous Brigid Kyle. It had surfaced in the *Sentinel* the following day. But the siren's call now sounding on Sarah's cellnet as she walked rapidly towards Luigi's sandwich bar was not from Brigid. The voice competing with the heavy traffic belonged to Auriol Johnson.

'Have lunch with me at Mirabelle. I know you think I'm a bitch but I have a soft spot for Lucy. I want to help.'

'I no longer represent Lucy,' Sarah replied tersely.

'So I hear. But you're fond of her. Just lunch. I talk, you listen. I won't be eating you.'

'I'm not sure it would be ethical.'

'Well, deah, how many rapists do I represent?'

'I – I really have to consult my seniors first.'

'Fine! I may have played tennis with the males among them. And why not bring your other half, the reportedly charming Oliver Rawl? He can be your long spoon.'

'I'll speak to him this evening.'

By the time Sarah got home she found Oliver in the kitchen, wearing his butcher's apron, a half-empty bottle of chianti at his side.

'It's half-full, not half-empty,' he said quickly.

Having had a good day (no faxes from Delia, no news of Charco Rios), he had decided on impulse to call at Sainsbury's and cook his 'special', frankfurters, desalinated sauerkraut and onioned mashed potatoes, plus the mild mustard sauce for whose exact formula every leading chef in London would have given his liver.

Sarah entered the kitchen weighed down by plastic bags of her own.

'You might have told me, Oliver!'

'I thought we might discuss Ivan's painting.'

'God, not again!'

'Better still, we might discuss the entire history of Western art from Cyrus of Cyprus to Chagall – and how Ivan fits in, if he does.'

'Can't you ever cook frankfurters without getting drunk?'

Ivan's painting had emerged from its brown paper wrapping on that winter Saturday afternoon when Oliver had wanted to watch rugby on Sky Sport. The 'painting' – Oliver could convey quotation marks by a peculiarly vicious slide of his tongue – was a uniform crimson from start to finish, head to toe, and unframed.

'You may think it's unfinished,' Sarah had said defensively, 'but you'd be wrong.'

'I'd say it is unbegun.'

'I think it's brilliant. Completely compelling.'

'What is it?'

'It's a No Painting. It's a breakthrough. Ivan has transcended all formal constraints.'

'I won't ask you how much it cost.'

Sarah had confronted him, eyes alight, hands on hips, chest thrust out. 'Two thousand.'

Later, having chosen a wall for Ivan's all-crimson No Painting – or, as Oliver put it, having sacrificed a 'perfectly innocent wall' – Sarah set about painting the wall to the same shade of crimson.

'Oh!' she had cried, 'it's so hard getting it right! But Ivan says it has to be done.'

'The painting refuses to disappear entirely, is that the problem? You spent two thousand on a work of art which refuses to vanish entirely?'

'You're such an utter philistine, Oliver. Ivan's point is that the eye has to find the painting. Find it! Ivan says that our eyes are congenitally lazy and conventional. That's why he despises frames. The frame is nothing other than a banal signal to the bourgeois viewer as to where he can safely stop looking. But Ivan says we have to look everywhere – and nowhere.'

'Hard work.'

'And only when the eye cannot find it, does it become a No Painting.'

'Supposing the eye doesn't want to find it?'

'Oliver, you won't upset me. Though you're free to keep trying.'

'Presumably, if a wall and a painting are indistinguish-able, the wall becomes as valuable as the painting – except that it's harder to auction it?'

'Yes, Oliver,' she had said with elaborate patience.

'In that case the wall was a shrewd investment. Ivan has made me a rich man.'

'It's not your wall. I have been working on this wall for hours. I have given it my labour. It's mine. Morally.'

That was six months ago. But now, with the aroma of frankfurters, sauerkraut, onioned mashed potatoes and mustard sauce filling the kitchen – and a noticeably depleted bottle of chianti at his side – Oliver was still going on about it.

Why? Was the painting the real subject of contention?

'Oliver, Auriol Johnson is suggesting lunch with us.'

'Us?'

'You as well – I expect she wants to have your trousers off, she's famous for it.'

'Good idea. Lay the table.'

For Oliver it turned out to be easier, in the heat of the working week, to find time for lunch with Auriol Johnson than it had with Jenny Glendower. He and Sarah belonged to a new generation of solicitors increasingly adept at using the press in their client's cause, sometimes loudly, when leaving a court, more often by discreet exchanges of information off the record. Judges were incensed by this new tactic, the Lord Chief Justice himself having deplored it in a speech to his assembled Commonwealth colleagues. The elders of the Law Society didn't approve either – or felt constrained to say so.

'Well, fuck 'em,' Auriol laughed, clinking her glass against Sarah's when she, Sarah and Oliver met in Mirabelle, in Curzon Street. 'Do you pass this Chablis as chilled enough, Oliver?'

'It's fine,' he said. 'Who is it we're supposed to fuck? The Law Society?'

'Oh he's lovely,' Auriol told Sarah. 'And God, the villains he represents! The notorious fax-murderer Delia Atkinson who recently waved a gun at Marcus Byron in Great North Crown Court! The gang rapist Pete

McGraw! His sweet little brother Jason, specialist in dropping concrete blocks on buses passing beneath! And Charco Rios, oh what a lovely lad! How do you manage to breathe in their presence, Oliver?'

'In their alleged presence,' Oliver corrected her.

Auriol laughed, bug-eyed. 'You've got some beauties, too, Sarah, haven't you? So why did you part company with dear little Lucy Byron?'

Sarah glanced at Oliver who frowned. Their backs were up already.

'You're supposed to do the talking,' Sarah told Auriol.

'I only want to help Lucy, my dears.'

'Then why not speak to her father?' Oliver said.

Auriol brushed this aside with a motion of her flashily braceleted wrist.

'Marcus? Because of his taste in mistresses. Didn't you know about me and Brigid? I was her assistant. I was better at her job than she was. She tried to get me busted by putting it about that I was inventing the evidence for my stories.'

Auriol lit another cigarette, then reached into her Gucci bag and extracted a miniature cassette.

'The point is, my dears, that nasty Auriol Johnson stumbled into this David Glass story half innocent. And even after the meeting in the pub my editor and I thought we had nothing bigger than a minor embarrassment to the Government. But now I realise that Lucy wasn't with David on that "fateful evening", as they say, by chance. No way!'

'I cannot comment,' Sarah said. 'I represent David.'

'It was little Lucy who was being set up, she was the real target of the sting, right?'

Silence.

'Set her up in a compromising situation. Get her to smoke pot in front of two journalists. So she refuses a urine test a couple of hours later, is confined to Ruskin House, and gets reported to the Parole Board. Very neat. But who dunnit?'

Silence at the table.

'Isn't that what Marcus Byron believes happened?' Auriol pressed. 'Isn't he right?' She prodded a painted nail at Sarah. 'And why did Paul Glass run to the police – I have an impeccable source in the Met – to explain that gallant David was merely financing Lucy's bad drug habit?'

Silence at the table.

Auriol was studying Sarah. 'You did know that, darling? Or perhaps you didn't? We're off the record,' she smiled.

'I'm sure you understand,' Oliver said, 'that Sarah's relationship with David must remain confidential. That's bound to extend to David's father.'

Auriol made an impish face at him as if to say 'prig'.

'But does this little tape in my tiny hand remain confidential?'

'What is it?' Sarah asked bleakly. She had never enjoyed a good lunch less, and had scarcely touched her food.

'I'll tell you the truth, Sarah, though I haven't made a lifelong habit of it. I took myself to the Golden Dragon because of an anonymous tip-off. The same voice had spoken to me before, putting me on stand-by for what he called "the right occasion".'

She juggled the tape in her hand.

'This is his voice,' she said. 'But we still don't know who it is.'

Sarah was twisting the napkin in her lap. She could no longer eat. Auriol was smoking serenely. Oliver continued to plough through the dishes set before him, hospitality of the *World*, as if this was his last meal.

'I expect you're taping this conversation, too,' he said.

'God, your man is protective, Sarah. Can I borrow him? I always return men to lender, with the right post-age.' She winked long, mascara'ed lashes. 'I even thought of going to law college myself but they told me I'd be overpaid in your profession.'

'So you decided you'd rather spend your life discovering the truth rather than concealing it?' Oliver said.

'Know something, Sarah? This whole story isn't about a senior official's son who sold thirty quids' worth of grass to a journalist he believed was a hitchhiker. I thought it was! But it wasn't and it isn't.' She lit another cigarette. 'Marcus Byron is of the same opinion, isn't he, Sarah?'

'You must ask him. I represent David Glass.'

'You keep saying that – so tedious. And what about poor little Lucy – who you love so much? This whole sting operation is directed at her, and through her at his Honour Judge Marcus Byron – the man they don't want to head the Criminal Law Commission. That's what all this "is he a secret Mason?" rubbish is also about.' Auriol paused. 'By the way, *is* he a secret Mason?'

'No idea,' Sarah said, nervously sipping at her Evian.

Auriol handed her the cassette. 'What I want to do is commission a voice-printing test from Voice Identification Services. They make spectrograms as a basis for comparison.'

'Comparison with what?' Sarah asked.

'That's the problem, darling. Until someone recognises the voice on my telephone tape, I've got nothing to compare. So do please bend your ear to this cassette.'

'Why should either of us know the man?'

'Because you have been representing Lucy and David, that's why. Because I am convinced that this is an inside job.'

'Inside what?' Sarah asked coldly.

Auriol smiled faintly and called for the bill. Leaving Mirabelle, Oliver flagged a taxi and opened the door for Auriol. 'Thanks for lunch.' But Auriol, tossing her Formula One hairdo, announced that she would walk and prodded Sarah into the cab, which sped away.

Auriol's arm tucked into Oliver's, her rapacious, bug-eyed gaze settling on him. 'I'm going to eat you.'

'I thought we'd had lunch.'

'Tell me about this dreadful rape case. It must be odd for you and Sarah to find yourselves both involved.'

'Nothing's odd in our line of business.'

'Who was the woman – the victim?'

'Victims of rape cannot be—'

'Yes, yes, Oliver, but who was she? How did she come to be out alone, at night, in the streets of Great North?'

'No idea.'

'A friendly policeman told me that your name and number were found in her discarded handbag. You were her only visitor in Barts. Old flame? I didn't like to ask in front of Sarah. I mean, she's rather conventional, isn't she?'

'If your policeman was that friendly,' Oliver said stiffly, 'he no doubt told you the victim's name as well.'

'No, Oliver. He naïvely thought you might be representing her – rather than the rapists. Don't look so cross, darling. Want to see my flat?'

'Now?'

'Now is my favourite time.'

Auriol's flat turned out to be located on the tenth floor of an ultra-mod mansion block – the sort of grandiose building you hurried past, with its liveried doorman, aroma of cigars, and painted old ladies speaking angry Italian; people who chose to live in an ocean liner in dry dock. The corridors were thickly carpeted and hummed with a sinister blend of air conditioning and telephone music piped through hidden vents.

'It's quite vulgar, you're thinking, Oliver.'

'Yes.'

'But comfortable and convenient – like a lawyer's conscience.'

Auriol insisted on playing him the tape of the telephone voice that had summoned her to the Golden Dragon.

'*Golden Dragon, at the corner of St John's Hill and Newcomb Street. Be there by seven-thirty. Take a female colleague. Look for a young man at the bar wearing a West Ham scarf.*'

'Recognise, darling?'

'It's familiar.'

'Try harder, Mr Rawl.'

He tried harder for the hour following – though one tended to lose track of time (and of Hawthorne & Moss) in Auriol's bed.

'I don't suppose,' he said, 'you've run into an American journalist called Amos . . . I forget his second name.'

'Lewin?' She smiled. 'Black?'

'That's him. If I were you, I'd ask him to listen to your tape.'

Oliver vaguely remembered bits and pieces of the dinner party given by Hubert Hare and the other bloke, whose name escaped Oliver, the night he'd been shipped home dead drunk and fast asleep in a taxi; he remembered liking the black American journalist; but he did not suspect that Amos Lewin had occupied this same, super-king-size bed and Auriol's unique attentions only forty-eight hours ago. He did not suspect that as a consequence of that coupling – and Amos's professionally expert intervention – Voice Identification Services had already nailed the voice on the tape.

Indeed, Oliver did not suspect that the whole purpose of his erotic afternoon, and of the lunch *à trois* that preceded it, had been Auriol's determination to get to the victim of the sensational gang-rape ahead of the field. Who was she? Oliver Rawl knew. The rest, the cassette stuff, had been dust in the eye.

Twelve

Auriol Johnson bided her time, waiting for the trial to appear on the Old Bailey listings. Only then did she track the husband down to his mother's terraced home in a quiet Yeominster suburb. Auriol chose a Sunday afternoon. A few kids were kicking a ball around but otherwise this modest street was fast asleep.

Pushing at the half-open wooden gate, and avoiding a row of empty milk bottles – they still had milk delivered by electric cart and in bottles! – she could see a television flickering through the living-room window. The roar of engines and the yelling voice of the commentator indicated that Phil Glendower preferred Formula One to Epsom races or the solemn hush of golfers sinking their putts. She tried the bell but heard no ring from within; stepping back to make her bouncing blonde hair visible, she presently became conscious of an unshaven face glaring at her through the window.

The door opened. The man's expression was guarded, hostile even, but she sensed at once something vulnerable, self-pitying, beneath the scowl. Phil Glendower was a man

ANONYMOUS

balding before his time. Even at five yards his breath
signalled alcohol.

'Mr Glendower?'

No answer.

'My name is Auriol Johnson. I work for the *World*
newspaper. May I talk to you, Mr Glendower?'

'Tabloid scum, are you?' His accent was West Country,
softer than his words, not so much working class as
wanting to be.

She smiled sweetly. 'Do I look like scum?'

'I know your column. I see it in the school common
room.'

'I hear you're an important figure in the local Labour
Party.'

'Do you?'

'Chairman of the District party and a local councillor, too.'

'That's not why you're here. It's because of her.'

Auriol noted the yards of enmity in that 'her'.

'My editor thinks this is a big story and one for which
we'd be prepared to pay generously.'

'What do you take me for?'

She took several steps towards him, her large eyes
beaming innocence.

'Because your wife can never be identified, Mr
Glendower, we'd be obliged by law not to identify you
either. Not even the city where you live.'

'If you don't take off, I'm going to slam the door on
your famous foot.'

Auriol stepped back, making noisy contact with the

milk bottles. 'My God, can the things they're saying about you be true?'

He hesitated. 'Who's they?'

Fifteen minutes later his aggression was mouldering into self-pity. Two or three empty beer cans sat on the floor, near the sofa. He consented to turn the Formula One commentary down, but insisted on keeping the picture up, a corner of his clouded eye monitoring the toy-like cars as they hurtled, red, blue, yellow, round and round some foreign track.

'Are those your kids playing in the street?'

'You can leave the kids out of it.'

Full of concern and understanding, she began to coax the story out of him with little sighs of sympathy. Clearly he wanted to talk. There had been no one (she discovered) to talk to. He was a lonely man. Auriol was an expert on lonely men.

He recalled how six months ago he had returned home from the school where he taught maths to find a battered wife.

'It was a Monday evening. I remember that. It was a Monday. She was supposed to be back on the Sunday but she didn't show up and sent no message.'

'Were you very worried?'

'I had no contact address in London. She'd called me once, during her conference, to ask after the kids, and to say she'd decided to stay on a few days. I think she must have moved out of the conference hotel – well, I know she did, don't I?'

'How did she look when she came home?'

'I remember I came through the front door and she came out of the bathroom. She looked me in the eye helplessly and asked, "Do you still love me?" I saw the cuts and bruises on her face. "Have you been mugged?" I asked. Then she started to tell me that she had been attacked by a gang of youths in London.'

'"Attacked"? Was that the word she used?'

'She said "attacked".'

'What did you think she meant?'

'I don't know what I thought. Then she said, "Phil, they raped me one by one – eight of them."'

'What was your immediate reaction?'

'She was trying to hold me. She was in her bathrobe. The kids were having their tea in the kitchen, I remember that. I pulled away from her. She felt dirty and I experienced . . .'

'What?'

'Frankly, revulsion. I took the dog for a walk.'

'Did Jenny ever break down?'

The sudden use of his wife's name disturbed him. Auriol noticed that he couldn't bring himself to say the name – his wife was always 'she'.

'No, she never cried, if that's what you mean, never. She went back to her school two days later as if nothing had happened.'

'Did Jenny tell her Headmistress the truth?'

'No idea. We were barely talking to each other. Why had she been walking alone at that time of night in London? The question turned over and over in my mind.'

'But you didn't ask her?'

Phil Glendower shook his head.

'Weren't you moved to pity by what she must have suffered?'

'Why had she moved to a hotel in Great North without telling me?'

'That I don't know, Mr Glendower.'

'I felt she was to blame, you see. I thought she might have caught Aids or some other disease from those filthy creatures. I probably said some terrible things to her.'

'Such as?'

'I can't remember.'

His blistered gaze returned to the television screen. A red toy car seemed to be chasing a blue toy car.

'Schumacher's in a class of his own when it rains,' he said.

'What might you have said to Jenny?'

'If you must know, Miss Johnson, I told her to go for a sauna to sweat those stinking youths out of her. I also locked her out of our bedroom and made her sleep on the sofa. Does that satisfy you?'

Auriol thought fast. 'How terrible,' she said. 'Terrible for you both. How long was it before you could no longer share the same roof?'

'I can't remember the date. We'd had a violent row. She said her parents had been right – she should never have married me. They always regarded themselves as genteel, the Powells.'

'Her maiden name?'

He nodded. 'They pronounce their name "Pole" –

full of airs and graces. Anyway, after that row she packed her bags and fled. I yelled after her, "Why don't you go back to London and have some more fun?" She slammed the door like Nora in *A Doll's House*.'

'Ibsen?'

'She'd taken me to see the play at the Yeominster Playhouse. She was always trying to educate me, you see.'

'Did she share your political views?'

'Never. When I stood for the city council she wasn't interested – wouldn't even deliver leaflets through doors. I was an activist of the NUT and she hated that. When we went on strike over pay and working conditions, she walked through the picket lines.'

'After you parted, who had the children?'

'I sent them to my mother – here. Neither of us could cope. She didn't want to tell her own parents. The children were tearful and couldn't sleep. Alan, the boy, began refusing to go to school. He said he suffered nightmares at night.'

'You mean he understood what had happened to his mother?'

'No, never. She had told the kids that she had been attacked. I suppose she had to, she looked so obviously battered.'

'Did you and Jenny ever make an attempt at reconciliation?'

'I began to miss her and to feel guilty. She was staying with a friend in her spare room. I sent her a CD of her favourite Mozart piano concerto. It was our sixth wedding anniversary. I tried to visit her. She wouldn't let me in. I told her that I had taken the train to London to inspect the rape scene.'

'Why did you do that?'

'I don't know. I felt I was too removed and remote from what she had suffered. The police were helpful and took me in a car to the canal. I stood there, on a very peaceful, sunny day, forcing myself to imagine what she had been through that awful night. The police showed me where she had been thrown in the canal, and how she had managed to swim to the other side.'

'What did Jenny say when you told her about your trip to London?'

'She was standing in the doorway with her woman friend hovering protectively behind her, as if they expected me to push my way in by physical force. Jenny went berserk. She said I had invaded her intimate space – or some such expression. She said I'd only gone to "gloat".'

'Did she ever come home?'

'Yes, once. At Christmas we slept in the same bed, had a tree, a turkey, and put on a brave face for the kids.'

'How long did that last?'

'A few weeks, perhaps less. My son Alan said to me, "Daddy, I don't want two homes, I want one home, why can't you and Mummy be together again?"'

'Now you have had to sell your home?'

'I was falling behind on the mortgage payments and Jenny was refusing to contribute.'

'Please tell me, Mr Glendower, and forgive me for

asking, but had you and Jenny enjoyed a good, normal sex life before catastrophe struck you both?'

'That's my business.'

Auriol dipped her eyelashes in contrition. 'Yes. I'm only trying to understand.'

'There were times when she would not make love to me because of something or other I'd done.'

'Like what?'

'I'm not perfect. I like a drink. Sometimes, after a big row in the District party, I like more than one. Jenny thinks she's very upper-class, married beneath her, teaches in a private school.'

'Your wife was often sexually frigid?'

'She can be quite hot when the mood takes her.'

'Might she have been having an affair with someone else?'

'Ask her. I often wonder. It didn't occur to me then, but now I'm not so sure.'

'Why?'

'She'd been writing letters to some bloke in London, an old flame, I gather.'

'Really! How did you find out?'

'She told me.'

'Why? To make you jealous?'

'To make me feel inadequate.'

'Do you know who the man is?'

'Yes, she enjoyed telling me.'

Auriol waited.

'I don't intend to land him in it,' Phil Glendower said. 'He's a lawyer and married, or whatever passes for "married" in London. No doubt he has a reputation to protect.'

Auriol's tongue ran delicately over her full red lips. 'Why should you protect him?'

'It's clear to me now that Jenny went up to London to see this man. The teachers' conference was just her alibi.'

'He's an old flame, you say?'

'From student days.'

'Ah. Nothing since?'

'Who knows.' It wasn't a question.

'I'd like to talk to this man.'

'No, I can't do that.'

Auriol re-crossed her legs. 'It's odd, Phil, you're talking freely about your wife, the mother of your children, yet you won't mention her lover's name. I must say, you men stick together.'

'He'd probably sue me for slander. I told you, he's a lawyer.'

'For slander! Are you joking? You haven't said a word against him.'

'That's the problem with you people. How do I know what's in your notebook?'

'I'll tell you what's in my head – Oliver Rawl.'

He stared at her, flabbergasted, all thoughts of Schumacher's genius in the rain relegated.

'I know Oliver Rawl,' she added. 'He's not as reticent as you are. In fact he happens to be defending one of the boys who raped Jenny.'

Phil Glendower was shaken, all defences down.

'The bastard! Those London bastards! Does Jenny know this?' He had uttered his wife's name for the first time.

'I haven't spoken to her. It's your story we want.'

The other thing Auriol wanted wasn't much: just one or two family photos of a loving couple with their two happy children, perhaps with the little boy sitting on Dad's knee, the little girl on Mum's. Auriol had noticed that the only framed photos in the sitting room were posed studio portraits of Phil's parents and their offspring.

'We'd be obliged to blank all the faces,' she promised. 'And we would pay handsomely.'

His sad eyes were drawn again to the television screen. He couldn't resist turning up the sound for a moment.

'Schumacher again,' he said.

'Is he the red car?'

'The Ferrari.'

'But aren't the other cars in front of him?'

'He's lapping them.'

'Oh. How clever of you to know.'

Braithwaite had once again brought Marcus before the Commons Legal Affairs Select Committee.

The press benches were packed. Freemasonry was hot news. Summoned before the Committee, the President of the Grand Lodge's board of purposes had provided some statistics but declined to name names.

None of the Law Lords was a Mason, he testified, and only two out of thirty-nine Appeal judges, and only one of ninety-six High Court judges.

'Not very many,' he had told Braithwaite, 'and no cause for public concern.'

'This Committee will be the judge of that,' snapped Braithwaite, who was known to be disgruntled since being omitted from the Boy's post-election list of ministers, and who was said to be at work on a thriller novel in which the seizure of power by the Grand Lodge was averted only on the last page.

'Now let's separate fact from myth, sir,' he had pressed his reluctant witness. 'To become a Mason a man must present himself outside the closed door of the lodge wearing a shoe on one foot, a slipper on the other, one trouser leg rolled up, one breast bared – and wearing a blindfold and a hangman's noose? Is that correct?'

'It is not our policy to discuss our code,' the President of the Grand Lodge had answered quietly. 'I don't imagine you would summon a Catholic bishop and force him to describe the rituals of his church.'

The press gallery understood the thrust. Braithwaite was a devoted Catholic who had often warned of a tie-in between Masonic lodges and Orange Order lodges in Ulster. Lodges, lodges – conspiracy.

Braithwaite had persisted with questions he knew would not be answered – silence, after all, could be construed as conspiratorial.

'Am I right that, after being allowed through the

lodge door, the blindfolded initiate, still wearing the hangman's noose, feels a rapier pressed to his heart? He is then warned that if he breaks the vows of secrecy he will have his throat cut and his tongue pulled out by the root? Yes? Did that happen to you, sir?'

'I can only give the same answer.'

Now it was Marcus Byron and his fob watch before the Committee. Braithwaite opened the questioning in his most respectful tone.

'Judge Byron, are you opposed to a Masonic register for judges, magistrates and police officers?'

'You'd have to go the whole hog through the criminal justice system and apply it to all policemen, prison officers, probation staff – the lot.'

Braithwaite was not impressed. 'That's as maybe. I repeat my question, Judge: are you opposed to a register as proposed?'

'It would be contrary to freedom of association and rights of privacy. And I see no evidence that membership of Masonic lodges has any effect at all on the conduct of judges and magistrates.'

'And policemen?' Braithwaite challenged him. 'Can you deny that fourteen out of ninety-six members of the West Midlands crime squad were Masons between 1974 and 1989, when the squad was at the centre of a succession of scandals and miscarriages of justice?'

'If Masons tickle each other's palms, I can live with it. It's not my business which church, synagogue, temple or club a person chooses to belong to. I might be a Friend of the Earth. I might be hostile to motorway constructors. I might be a member of Freedom. If you start introducing registers, where do you stop?'

'Are you a Freemason yourself?' Braithwaite pressed him.

'I am simply against a demagogic witch hunt.'

'I'm asking you again: are you a Freemason?'

'I decline to answer such a question to an arm of government. We should have learned these lessons from what happened in America during the McCarthy era.'

'I find that downright insulting,' Braithwaite fumed. 'Insulting to me, insulting to this distinguished Committee.'

'You do? At that time, back in the 'fifties, people were asked, "Are you now or have you ever been a member of the Communist Party?" The Communist Party was held to be a secret conspiracy – like the Freemasons.'

'I believe you are in effect telling this Committee, indirectly, that you are a Freemason.'

'No, I'm not hinting or winking. Show me the instruments of torture.'

The press gallery laughed but Braithwaite was not amused.

'Judge Byron, this Committee may decide to report your apparent contempt to the Speaker of the Commons. The matter would then be referred to the Commons Standards and Privileges Committee.'

'That will be my privilege, Mr Chairman. May I leave now?'

*　　*　　*

Auriol waylaid Jenny Glendower outside the staff entrance of the girls' school, pursuing her down Plymouth Street and past the Abbey close.

'Mrs Glendower, your husband Phil has been talking to me. For two hours, actually. He seems to think you deliberately got yourself into trouble in London. As a woman, I don't believe him but I must have your version.'

Jenny stopped dead on the crowded pavement, her face set but her gaze (Auriol noted) quite tranquil.

'My version is for the court. You say you're a journalist. Have you never heard of *sub judice*?'

'Well, of course. We couldn't publish a word until after the trial. Mrs Glendower, I'm asking you about what happened to your marriage. Believe me, that cannot prejudice the case against the accused boys.'

'Please leave me alone. That's my last word.'

Jenny began to walk fast, a satchel of homework on her shoulder, Auriol following, turned into a shopping mall, then dived into Safeways and grabbed a wire basket.

'I don't suppose you need a trolley without the children to feed,' Auriol said.

Jenny ignored her but Auriol saw she was trembling. Reaching the fruit and vegetables, she snatched at onions, peppers, mushrooms. To Auriol's surprise, she ignored the organic produce – probably too expensive. Her satchel kept slipping from her shoulder.

'Have you already sold your story to some other newspaper?' Auriol pursued her to the fresh bread counter.

'My story is not for sale.'

'Phil says you went to London to meet your lover.'

'He—'

'He thinks the teachers' conference was simply your alibi. Why did you decide to stay on in London after the conference?'

Jenny had a large, wholemeal loaf, unsliced, in her hand. For a moment Auriol expected it to be thrown in her face. The woman simply couldn't cope with her own anger.

'You mean I was asking for it. Is that what you mean?'

'It may be what Phil means.'

'Will you leave me alone!'

'He's a lawyer, isn't he – the man you went to see in London?'

Jenny Glendower turned away and headed for the frozen foods. It wasn't clear what she was looking for. She no sooner picked up a bag of beans than she dropped it and grabbed peas instead. Auriol followed, a pace behind.

'You met this lawyer at Warwick University, right? You were both studying English. Later he must have gone on to law college. Now he lives with his wife or partner and practises in London? You have been writing to him? You even told Phil. Is that correct?'

Jenny seized a bottle of something – a heavy glass bottle.

'If you don't go away, I shall throw this in your face.'

Auriol stepped back a pace, as she had stepped back on Phil Glendower's mother's doorstep.

'That would make a fine story in the local paper, Mrs Glendower. I'm sure your Headmistress would love it. You haven't told her what happened to you in London, have you? The girls don't know and their parents don't know.'

Auriol followed her to the check-out counters. There was a queue at each – no escape. Auriol dropped her voice.

'Look, I can imagine what you've suffered. Not just the attack but the break-up of your family. It so happens that there's something about Oliver Rawl that you ought to know.'

Jenny stared at her. 'So why did you ask me his name?'

'I didn't. I wanted to find out whether you still love the man.'

'Of course I don't love him. Why should I?'

'Did you know that Oliver is still representing one of the boys who raped you? Have you any comment on that?'

Jenny Glendower could have been fashioned out of stone. The conveyor belt was moving her shopping towards the till but for the moment it was as if the mushrooms, peppers, cheese, wholemeal loaf and frozen peas had nothing to do with her.

'The *World* is extremely anxious to know how you feel about it,' Auriol added.

'I don't believe you,' Jenny whispered.

'Then ask Oliver. It was two boys to begin with but Oliver had to let one go – conflict of interest. He's still representing the leader of the gang, Charco Rios.'

'No, I—'

'By the way, Mrs Glendower, Oliver's lady friend, Sarah Woods, is representing the big black boy who raped you three times, Luke Grant. Remember him?'

Fumbling, and obviously close to tears, Jenny began to load her shopping into plastic bags which resisted her frantic efforts to open them up with fumbling fingers. Auriol gallantly lent a hand.

By the time they walked to the bus stop, Auriol was carrying two of Jenny's plastic bags.

'Cup of tea?' Auriol suggested. 'Gosh, I admire you. I think you've got miles of pluck. It seems to me you have been betrayed by everyone – your husband, your lover, his partner – everyone. Do you agree?'

And then they were seated in a nice, West Country tea room, the sort of thing you couldn't find in London, alongside other ladies of the cathedral town.

Auriol smiled. 'I have to admit I rather fancy one of your local cream teas. Fatal to the figure, of course.' She fished a clean handkerchief from her bag. 'Here,' she offered it. 'I always think there's nothing like a few tears to clear the head.'

The names of Paul and David Glass had begun to appear abroad, in the foreign press and in the Irish Republic. *France-Soir* criticised 'typical British hypocrisy',

adding: 'Outre-Manche, no one must know what everyone knows.' Then the story surfaced in the Scottish papers,
too, on the ground that Judge Sawyer's injunction did not
extend to Scotland, a separate legal jurisdiction. One Scottish paper pointed out that six million users of the Internet
could gain access to the naming and shaming in seconds.

The Boy and Ben Diamond decided that it was all
over. They would have come clean long ago had not
Judge Sawyer's injunction – the stern inhibition of the
law – prevented it. The Attorney General now went in
front of the judge. 'Common sense and the public interest
must prevail,' he argued.

Judge Sawyer nodded.

Shuffling along behind the Home Office's press person, some twenty journalists filed through august corridors and up a grand flight of stairs to the level coded Grey
Area, passing posters advising the public on how to fight
fires. Brigid Kyle later called it 'perhaps the smoothest
political firefighting exercise in modern times'.

The journalists found an ashen Paul Glass already
seated on the platform. Moments later Ben Diamond
strode on stage.

To the astonishment of their fellow-journalists, Brigid
Kyle and Auriol Johnson were discovered seated together.
Auriol had sent Marcus a written report from Voice
Identification Services, revealing the identity of the man
who had guided her, on a particular evening, to the
Golden Dragon. But what sealed Brigid's willingness to
trust Auriol as a friend to Lucy, if not to herself, was
the fact that never once had Auriol mentioned in the

World that 'the well-connected youth' who had sold her cannabis had been in the company of his well-connected girlfriend.

The Home Secretary was speaking. Big Ben wanted to make 'very clear' a number of things. The Government regretted what had happened. There had been no attempt at a cover-up, 'quite the contrary'. The fact that Dr Glass's son David had done something 'impetuous and foolish' was regrettable. The Home Secretary and Dr Glass remained adamantly opposed to legalising cannabis. The price would fall sharply if the substance was de-criminalised. In Alaska consumption had doubled during a period of legalisation.

The first questions from the floor were all directed at Paul Glass's current position. Ben Diamond staunchly stood by him.

'No, I have not asked for Paul Glass's resignation. I have full confidence in him. This could happen to any of us. But I can tell you that words have been definitely exchanged within his family, and certain relevant punishments agreed to.'

Paul Glass nodded in confirmation. 'My son is an intelligent young man who deeply regrets what he did.'

Ben picked this up with a grin. 'I think we can assume that the best tag David can wear for the immediate future is the knowledge of the pain he has caused his parents.'

A journalist asked why David Glass had, finally, received a mere caution from the police.

'Wouldn't any ordinary boy have been charged for

supplying? Isn't supplying much more serious under the law than mere possession? Is this a special favour?'

Ben Diamond's jaw was set rigid. 'The street value of the cannabis, you well know, was only thirty pounds. It's a Class B drug. David has no previous convictions. And I am not responsible for the Crown Prosecution Service's decisions.'

The foreign reporters, in particular the French and Irish correspondents, were not satisfied, as the man from *Le Monde* made clear.

'But is it not true that immediately after the incident a young lady living in Ruskin House had her parole conditions revised? Was she not once again tagged round the wrist to prevent her leaving the building?'

The Home Secretary refused to talk about a juvenile legally protected by anonymity. The press corps laughed openly.

'You are not entitled to print her name!' Ben Diamond shouted from the platform.

But the reporters had had enough of injunctions and artificial silences protecting the offspring of Ben Diamond's favourite lawyers.

'We hear that Lucy Byron's rehabilitation on parole was to be held up as a model to the young,' said a woman from *The Times*. 'Did something go wrong?'

'If Judge Byron cannot control his own daughter,' asked the man from the *Telegraph*, 'how can he control the nation's juvenile delinquents?'

Gathering his papers, Ben Diamond strode from the room – but the damage was done. That same afternoon he went before the Commons to announce tersely that the Chairman of the new Criminal Law Commission was to be Judge Worple.

The Rt Hon Jeremy Darling rose on the Opposition front bench, ecstatic.

'May we know, Madam Speaker, whether the Home Secretary has informed Judge Marcus Byron?'

'I have informed the House,' Ben snapped. Ribald laughter, barracking and mocking jibes enveloped him as he fought to be heard. The press gallery concluded that the game was finally up.

But how finally? News reached Marcus from Commissioner Price that Keith Mariner had vanished from Ruskin House after being challenged in the act of a serious crime by an undercover police officer, Helen Winter, otherwise Fiona Sheehy. Mariner had attempted to enlist Fiona's co-operation in substituting heroin-contaminated urine for Lucy Byron's before it was sent to the lab.

The police, who were now looking for Keith Mariner, were convinced that he would sing the loudest of songs when they caught up with him. David Glass had finally confessed that Mariner had regularly been supplying him with drugs – as had Edmund Joiner, junior political adviser to the Home Secretary, whose sudden and unscheduled 'vacation' was as yet unknown, mercifully, to Jeremy Darling and the Opposition.

This time Joiner had gone further than Amsterdam,

despite his 'fear and loathing' of flying. The *Sentinel*'s rogue reporter, Amos Lewin, tracked his occasional lover to Los Angeles, via 'disappearances' in Toronto, Mexico City, and San Francisco – all power-centres of the clandestine Progressive Coalition and its proliferating Internet websites.

Amos finally caught up with Edmund in a gay bar on the Malibu beach.

'Ah, Amos! What a surprise! Lovely to have you with us. I hear you took a bandit taxi in Mexico City and were relieved of your wallet – but happily not your life. Not this time, Amos.'

'You have eyes in the back of your head?'

'Let's just say many pairs of eyes. Frankly, travelling without you has been tedious. I keep finding myself sat next to some Internet freak or one of those Americans who always tell you what they do, and how much they earn.'

'And what's your story, Edmund?'

'Story, dear? I always find my own lies terribly hard to remember.'

'It was you and Keith Mariner who set the trap for David and Lucy?'

Edmund sighed. 'Nothing is more tedious than an investigative journalist investigating. What will you drink? I must say, the daiquiris here are *delicious*. Like you, Amos.'

'It was Keith who knew in advance the date of Lucy's first release from her Ruskin House curfew. But who is Keith Mariner? Who is your little Hubert Hare? Minor figures to be conspiring at so high a level, surely. But Edmund Joiner—'

'Ah. Do I know him?'

Less minor by far, as, later that evening, he happily confided to Amos, cruising along the prettiest stretch of Sunset Boulevard, winding west from Beverly Hills towards Malibu, where almost every house, whether palatial, grand or merely unaffordable, carries a security sign on its gate warning intruders to expect an Armed Response. 'WARNING. This area is patrolled 24 hours a day. Deadly force policy operates.'

'I suppose the Great Marcus would call it Zero Tolerance,' Edmund sighed.

Happy on heroin, Edmund was in no mood to conceal his continuing links with the Bar's favourite criminologist, Siegfried 'Pavlov' Alexander. Edmund was always happy in Amos's company, whether 'crucifixion' or 'cross-bow', and afterwards they sat sipping martinis in a hotel lobby where signs warned against pickpockets, hookers and loiterers. When Amos paid the bill, the waiter held his two $20 notes up to the light.

But why was Edmund so helpful? 'You're telling me these things because I'm already dead, is that it?' Amos asked.

'Don't be ridiculous, darling. I know perfectly well that you're chattering nonstop to the awful Brigid Kyle between every sip of that daiquiri.' Edmund yawned and stretched himself languidly. 'Anyway . . . I'm in retirement now. I shall die here. Of love. I've always wanted a Californian funeral à la Evelyn Waugh.'

'Never read him.'

'Oh you must. It's called *The Loved One*.'

'Tell me why you care so much, Edmund?'

'Care? I haven't a care in the world. Dear Siegfried Alexander is very generous you know, I'm never short of a snort. Ben Diamond and Marcus Byron can bang up the entire British population for all I care.'

'But you did care. Just as little Hubert and Keith Mariner passionately detest Marcus Byron as an Uncle Tom, so you with Ben Diamond. But why?'

To this Amos never got a straight answer. Edmund's father had cleared out and off when the boy was eight. After his mother re-married, Edmund suffered sexual abuse from his stepfather, an upstanding Crown Court judge. Edmund had read Dostoyevsky – crime for crime's sake – and Jean Genet, falling in love with the vagabond and homosexual prostitute who flowered as a literary genius. Edmund described Ben Diamond and Marcus Byron as 'the enemies of art and liberty', but these things were always said in a tone of self-mockery: you never quite knew where you were with Edmund Joiner and he didn't intend you to know.

By the time Amos booked his return flight to London, he was in no doubt that the Progressive Coalition was indeed the old Congress for Justice 'dead and well' – Brigid's hunch confirmed. A close study of the Coalition's disguised websites, 'Friends of Penal Reform', 'Justice Seekers', 'Rehabilitation not Vengeance', 'End Prison Cell Abomination', revealed always the same underlying message:

Every offender is also a victim.

All across the Western world, from Britain to America, from Canada to Italy, the Justice Seekers were exposing the 'insane cruelties' of criminal justice systems addicted to the Prison Cell Abomination. But who were they, the Justice Seekers? Many of them sincere liberals and progressives like Hubert Hare, no doubt. Others with a deep and abiding grudge against 'authority' – what Edmund called 'the Abusers' and Keith Mariner 'the motherfuckers'. And Siegfried Alexander? For him a criminal was fodder for science, for the laboratory, another guinea pig ready for reconditioning. Men like Marcus Byron and Ben Diamond got in the way of that and had to be destroyed. But who supplied the funds that Edmund boasted now cushioned his idleness, the money that floated the websites?

Amos spoke frequently with Brigid across the Atlantic, and once with Marcus himself.

'The money, Amos, you want to know where it comes from? How can a defeated Communist empire, a shattered Communist dream, rise again out of the ashes?'

'It can't,' Amos replied coolly. 'Period.'

'"Can't" is not a big word among dedicated Marxists like Siegfried Alexander,' Marcus said. 'The democratic, pluralistic societies of the West can no longer be destroyed by external attack or by violent mass revolution – but they could decay internally. Modern crime is closely linked to prosperity as well as relative poverty, Amos. Some of the most high-income cities of the West are the ones where no one dare walk abroad after dark.' He chuckled. 'Or before dark.'

'Do I understand what you're saying?' Amos was scribbling in a notebook, the receiver tucked between chin and shoulder. 'Alexander is well aware that the "progressive" penal policies he recommends simply don't work. Is that it?'

'Yeah, Amos, he wants to emasculate the British Criminal Justice System as a step towards the collapse of society. Look further and you'll find threads of cotton leading from our Siegfried to the old East German Stasi.'

'How do you know, Judge?'

'I don't. I said, "Look".'

Amos, who loved parties, planned to float down over the Thames just as Marcus and Brigid were holding their big party in the Temple gardens, beside the Embankment, to celebrate Lucy's release from Ruskin House. But Amos never made the party. He never boarded his plane at LA. He had misread the insouciant Edmund, mistaken his cynicism for indifference, his easy banter for easy come, easy go. When Edmund's friends in LA invited Amos to an all-night gay beach festival on the eve of his departure for England, Amos not only accepted, which was wise, but actually went, which wasn't.

Only Amos's surfboard was recovered from his favourite stretch of beach at Malibu.

At long last Judge Byron's daughter was free. Marcus

had spared no expense: waiters and waitresses circulated among the guests, dispensing champagne, vol-au-vents, truffles and smoked salmon sandwiches.

Brigid was sporting a bold, low-cut dress in lime green – to celebrate, as she told everyone, 'Lucy's liberty and Marcus's non-appointment as Chairman of the non-existent Criminal Law Commission.'

Lucy herself was shyly sheltering near the food tables, wolfing vol-au-vents as an alternative to talking to any of these loud, smart, braying people, few of whom she knew.

Oliver and Sarah arrived as late as they decently could. Sarah hadn't wanted to come at all.

'We'll go disguised as two humble young solicitors,' Oliver had consoled her.

'Supposing Lucy doesn't want to talk to me.'

'You'll be the only person she wants to talk to.'

'My God, everyone's here,' Sarah exclaimed on arrival in the Temple garden, nervously sipping the champagne that had instantly landed in her hand.

'I smell a lot of policemen under these civvy suits,' Oliver murmured. 'Half of them must be looking for me.'

A woman came up to him.

'I'm Trish Callaway from *The Times*. Who are you?' she asked.

'Oliver Rawl.'

'Don't know you.'

'My work is to impede justice wherever possible.'

'That shouldn't be difficult.'

Auriol Johnson slid between Oliver and the woman from *The Times*.

'Hi, Trish. Hi, Oliver. Don't say a word to Trish about anything – promise?'

'Now I'm interested!' declared Trish Callaway.

'Oliver and his partner Sarah Woods are representing half of the lads accused of raping a lady who cannot be named.'

'Really? And do you intend to thwart justice in that case, too?' Callaway asked Oliver.

Auriol moved in on Brigid.

'Tell me, darling, where are the Boy, Ben Diamond, the Lord Chancellor and all that mob? Aren't they the true celebrants of this occasion?'

Brigid smiled. 'We didn't invite Hitler either.'

A moment later Auriol was beside Sarah, eyes wide in innocent friendship, as if she had not long been planning a devastating story linking Sarah, Oliver and the unnamed rape victim in a 'deadly triangle'.

'Isn't Lucy looking lovely, and finally at peace with the world?'

'Yes.'

Lucy had now been rescued from her isolation by her father's charming divorce lawyer, Simon Hoare. Fortunately it wasn't Lucy's mother that Marcus was divorcing, this time round.

'Dad is bitterly disappointed about the job – but he won't admit it,' she told Hoare.

'Believe me, Lucy, your father is well out of that snake pit.'

'He can always become an archbishop. He loves fancy dress.'

'The church is nowadays much more liberal than the law,' Hoare quipped.

'Yeah, why not the church?' Marcus guffawed, over-hearing the exchange and moving in on them, beaming, giving his daughter a bear-like hug. 'We black judges always feel close to God, perhaps because there are so few of us. I cannot commend enough the judgment declared in court by the Chief Justice of the British Crown Colony of the Solomon Islands, Sir Horatio Pincus. He had just given a conditional discharge to a man who had murdered his wife: an unusual sentence. "You realise", he told the offender, "that this is not a let-off. If you do it again within the next twelve months, you will be punished by Almighty God – for both mur-ders."'

Lucy had drifted away. She found Sarah and kissed her.

'Hello, Lucy, still speaking to me?'

'They let me out.'

'And you're living with your dad and Brigid, I hear?'

'Hm.'

'I hope you like your new solicitor. Gerry Raksin, isn't it?'

'Yeah. He's not as bad as he looks.' Lucy giggled. 'Like your Oliver.'

'I'm working on it,' Oliver cut in.

Simon Hoare, a fashionable media figure as well as lawyer to most of the ex-monarchs of Europe, was entertaining two judges and their wives.

'The plaintiff brings civil proceedings against Satan for

causing him boundless misfortune and misery. Why is the case thrown out?'

Overhearing this, Marcus chortled and roared out the answer: 'No fixed abode within the jurisdiction of the court.'

'Oh, Marcus! You always spoil my stories.'

Brigid was clapping her hands for attention. 'Now I want everyone to meet Lucy,' she called out. 'Lucy Byron is our guest of honour.'

'The alleged guest of honour,' Oliver remarked to Lucy.

'Yeah, well,' Marcus cut in on the word 'alleged', aggrieved at being ignored, 'experience of the courts soon teaches us, Oliver, that nine out of ten alleged facts are facts. I'm touched that Police Commissioner Mike Price has found time to be among us today. I admire him for what he was bold enough to say about ethnic minority crime. People claim that he was appeasing his mainly white police force, but to my mind the men and women who serve in the police are human beings mainly fearful of violence rather than "mainly white".'

Glances were exchanged among the guests. Lucy had curled up like a knot of string that wants to conceal its ends. Even Brigid could not disguise her discomfort.

'Today,' Marcus continued, 'ethnic minorities constitute some twenty per cent, or 1,378,000 people, in London. That's 362,000 Indians, 304,000 black, and 170,000 black Africans. I'm not including growing numbers of so-called refugees. By the year 2010 the demographers calculate that ethnic minorities will constitute twenty-eight per cent of London's population. If we don't do something drastic to reverse present trends of behaviour, our capital city will no longer be habitable.'

'This must be a speech party,' Oliver murmured to Sarah.

Seeing Lucy drifting away, Brigid pursued her.

'Just live through it, darling,' she whispered.

'We black criminals are not wanted here.'

'Lucy, please.'

Marcus was in his stride, oblivious to his guests' embarrassment – or was he?

'I am myself born of immigrant stock. Proud of it? Yeah. But I do not feel proud when I observe many young black males picking up the worst habits and attitudes of inner-city civilisation – if that's the word. Let's not be too politically correct to face facts. I know I'm frequently called Uncle Tom by young blacks, and by some black probation officers I know who are not so young.'

'He doesn't mind being unpopular so long as he gets elected Mayor of London,' Oliver remarked to Simon Hoare.

'What a splendid idea! And he'll need a lawyer.'

'When the champagne runs out, I'm off to Islington to be tough on the causes of crime.'

Simon Hoare smiled. 'Would you like a job writing my jokes for me? Three hundred an hour?'

'Jokes or pounds? I'll offer you one now – free.'

'Go on, go on, go on.'

'How many lawyers does it take to mend a light bulb?'

'How many?'

'As many as you can afford.'

'I love it!'

Marcus was still orating, eyes glazed, to everyone and no one while draining glass after glass of champagne.

'The walkout culture of the Afro-Caribbean male repeats itself, recycles itself, generation after generation, with fatal results. Within young black society crime is increasingly glorified. Consider the exploits glamorised in Yardie-style books, or listen to the gun-totin' lyrics of reggae records. Even job opportunities will not dissolve an entrenched culture that revolves around drugs, idleness, hedonism and easy money.'

'That bit about hedonism and easy money sounds rather attractive, Marcus,' Simon Hoare called out. 'Where do we go for it?'

Kernan O'Sullivan, proprietor of the *Sentinel*, and by now well oiled, suddenly shouted at Marcus.

'When do we Irish villains get into your speech?'

'That will be the racing scandals section,' Brigid told him.

'And I thought I was your boss,' O'Sullivan complained, seizing her by the waist.

'Marcus is plastered.' Auriol slid her arm through Oliver's. 'If he's not careful, Lucy will do a bunk. She's drunk, too.'

'Yes, she does look miserable – and I'm not talking to you.'

'Why?'

'I can't remember.'

'Come home with me afterwards. No talking needed.'

Sarah was back with Lucy, whose rising stress was obvious to everybody.

'Fuck off, Sarah,' Lucy hissed. 'I know what you're up to. Got a spliff? I need a spliff. Yeah? Shocked? And now,' she said loudly, 'his Honour will tell us about Operation Eagle Eye.'

Marcus heard this – everyone did. He looked around, with hurt, bewildered eyes, in search of his daughter. Sarah was trying to restrain Lucy from leaving.

'Don't go. Please don't hurt him.'

'I'd forgotten why I hate him.'

'No, you don't.'

Commissioner Price had slipped away. Simon Hoare leaned towards Oliver, his eyebrows raised in dismay.

'What shall we talk about? Identification parades? Presumably you attend a lot of them?'

'I've been lucky, no one has picked me out.'

Marcus was wandering like a wounded bear among his guests, recognising some and staring blankly at others, while Brigid fought to hold him steady. A long spill of champagne ran down the bodice of her beautiful green dress.

'Yeah, the clever people can sneer,' he grumbled. 'They can disparage, yeah, it may not be a dog's fault he's rabid, you still have to put him down.'

Brigid was hauling Marcus away from his own party, towards the gate.

Lucy was in Sarah's arms, sobbing.

'Tell me,' Trish Callaway of *The Times* loudly asked

Oliver, 'would you make our host Chairman of the Criminal Law Commission?'

'Mike Tyson would probably fill the bill.'

'Who's he?'

'If *The Times* doesn't know who Mike Tyson is, you'd better slash the cover price to 5p.'

Simon Hoare smiled. 'Still, Marcus *might* be the ideal Mayor of London,' he remarked to Oliver. 'Time to go, I suspect. Lovely to have met you. Bye.'

'Yes, Oliver,' Auriol said, again sliding her arm through his, 'time to go. Oh come on, you know it's all over between you and Sarah.'

Thirteen

A week before the Old Bailey hearing, the huge Luke Grant, who had grown a further inch since raping Jenny Glendower, was still determined to plead not guilty and go to trial. At fourteen, Luke had the intelligence of a ten-year-old. The fact that the Crown had dropped the attempted murder charge against all eight of the boys convinced Luke that they were 'running scared'. By 'they' he meant the police – to him the CPS was merely an extension of the police.

'The fuckers can't prove nothin' against me.'

Visiting him in Downton, Sarah informed Luke that the victim herself was, as predicted, set to give evidence.

'She is adamant that you were the first to rape her while others held her down. She will say you raped her three times. She will also identify you as one of those who threw her into the canal.'

Luke was picking his nose in the interview room. 'She may not show up . . . when it comes to it.'

'She will. She is very determined.' Sarah stared hard at Luke. 'In my view, only a plea of guilty before the proceedings begin can get a year or so off your sentence.'

His sad gaze fell. 'How long?'

She almost felt pity for him. 'I'm not the judge – but don't expect less than ten years, Luke.'

Jenny Glendower turned up at their flat on a Saturday morning, unheralded. Sarah answered the door, still in her dressing gown.

'You're Sarah,' the woman said.

Sarah nodded cautiously.

'You're just as I imagined,' the woman said. 'You look very businesslike. Quite unemotional.'

The woman made no attempt to introduce herself.

'Are you Jenny?'

'Yes, of course.'

And here she was, stylishly dressed, a new hairdo, an early riser, recognisably provincial – Oliver's old flame making a new claim.

'Come in.'

'I'm here to see Oliver.'

'He's in the bath. Please sit down.'

The woman glanced around her. 'I often wondered how Oliver lives now.' She stared at the Crimson No Painting on the Crimson No Wall. 'Obviously his taste has changed since I knew him – unless it's your taste.'

'The flat's always in a mess by Saturday, I'm afraid. Coffee? I was just brewing some.'

'No, thank you.'

'Tea?'

'No to everything, thank you.'

The woman observed Sarah talking urgently through the quarter-open bathroom door before making for the kitchen. Oliver emerged almost immediately, in a dressing gown which insisted on falling open to reveal a member shrivelled by a hot soak and thoughts of Delia.

'Ah. Hello, Jenny. How are you?'

'Good morning, Oliver.'

'This is a surprise.'

'Is it? I wrote to you. Several times. You never answered.'

Sarah brought the coffee for Oliver and herself, with a third cup, just in case. The woman sat rigid, all softness gone from her face. Naked and slug-white under his dressing gown, Oliver reminded Sarah of a broken-legged rabbit quivering in a trap.

'Hadn't you better get dressed, Oliver?'

'Don't bother,' Jenny said. 'I know what he looks like – though he's not quite so skinny as he used to be. And I can't stay long. I have a meeting with the prosecutor.'

'Yes, of course,' Oliver mumbled.

'"Of course", Oliver? You didn't regard it as an "of course" to tell me the truth – that you and your partner here are representing three of the boys who raped me.'

'We didn't think it would help . . . to tell you, I mean,' Oliver said.

'Help, Oliver?'

'We thought,' Sarah said, 'that you might not understand.'

'You were right. I don't.'

'It doesn't mean we don't feel sympathy for you. For what happened.'

'But making money out of my ordeal is more important? What a pity they have all pleaded guilty. You could have stood up in court and argued that it never happened! You could have called me a liar. Or a fantasist. A hysterical woman suffering from a failing marriage!'

Jenny Glendower reached in her bag for a handkerchief.

'We're not barristers,' Oliver murmured. 'We don't speak in the High Court.'

'But you'll be sitting behind your barristers, won't you, or is it in front, and you'll pass them notes, advising them about flaws in my evidence and what questions to ask me in cross-examination.'

'No one will cross-examine you, Jenny.'

'Oh for God's sake, Oliver,' Sarah snapped, 'don't be so utterly pathetic!' She scrutinised their visitor coolly. 'What do you want of us? You may find there's not much we can give.'

'"Us"? I came to see Oliver. I have nothing to say to you.'

Sarah looked hard at Oliver. 'Do you want me to leave the room?'

He hesitated. 'No. I mean, not unless you want to.'

His indecisiveness was infuriating both women. Jenny kept closing and unclosing the gilded snap catch of her handbag – click click click.

'I suppose business is business, Oliver. Just one question: if a "client" of yours was accused of raping this lady here – your "partner" – would you refuse to represent him? You would, wouldn't you?'

Sarah had folded her arms across her breast as if useful life could not resume until this woman went away.

'Oliver lives with me,' she said icily. 'When did he last live with you? What possible obligation can he have towards you?'

Silence.

'Well, I'll get some clothes on,' Oliver mumbled.

'That Auriol Johnson evidently knows all about you both,' Jenny said. 'It was she who told me you're both involved in my case – and in the case of the boys who murdered my old friend and colleague Edward Carr.'

Oliver and Sarah stared at her, aghast.

Jenny clicked her handbag catch twice. 'We provincials aren't completely naïve, you know. You imagine you can run rings round us, don't you? It so happens that Edward Carr used to teach at my school in Yeominster. Before his promotion as Head of St James's. I knew him and Emma Carr quite well – and their children.'

Silence.

'I just thought you ought to know,' Jenny went on, 'in case you think you can get away with anything. I was talking to Emma only yesterday. I rang her up. I told her I'd wanted to contact her months ago, to express my sympathy, but hadn't liked to intrude. Now I felt I had to let her know that the two of you are defending not only Edward's killers but the youths who raped me. She . . . She . . . Emma was quite shocked. She said she'd read a brief report of a ghastly gang-rape but couldn't have imagined I was the victim. I told her what a wonderful woman she is, all the speeches she has given since Edward died, her work for charities, and the way she teaches understanding and forgiveness whereas all I can think of is revenge.'

During the next five minutes Jenny Glendower must have uttered the word 'revenge' a dozen times. Then she was gone, departing as abruptly as she had arrived.

The hearing took place in the Old Bailey, the Recorder of London presiding. All eight boys were now pleading guilty to rape in the hope of mitigating their sentences.

Jenny Glendower was not in court when the prosecutor opened for the Crown but she was the first witness to be called and thereafter, as the victim, was allowed to sit in the same place throughout, a quietly resolute figure who seemed to be inviting eye contact with the defendants, the boys who had raped her. Even Charco Rios averted his Aztec eyes. Both Sarah and Oliver, seated in front of their respective barristers, felt the force of Jenny's gaze. Oliver nervously sipped water, excused himself, hurried out, began smoking again for the first time in years.

The victim's torn, soiled, bloodstained clothes, her two-piece costume in pink and her white underwear, were shown to the court exactly in the condition in which they had been found by the police, strewn about beside the canal. The court was also shown photographs of the victim's injuries: an inch-long cut to her eyebrow as well as cuts inside her lower lip. A medical examination had also revealed bruising and tender areas over much of her body along with dried blood from her nose.

Almost every evening Sarah and Oliver found themselves fighting at home. More than once he accused her of having no pity for Jenny, of 'positively enjoying' her role as solicitor to Luke Grant and Ally Leagum.

'Sorry, Oliver, I cannot share your personal feelings for that woman.'

'Why don't you go the whole hog and say she was asking for it?'

'It's no use scapegoating me simply because you have a bad conscience.'

The silences that lay between them were worse than the words. On the second morning of the hearing they could not bring themselves to travel to the Old Bailey on the same tube. Sarah set out ten minutes before him, but the train was delayed and there she was, on the platform. He took a different carriage.

Only Sarah's client Ally Leagum maintained his cocky demeanour. He revelled in the limelight. Brought into court under guard, Ally lifted two fingers to the press benches: up yours. The *World* would carry Ally's cocky smile on the front page to rouse the fury of four million readers, alongside a report from the Old Bailey by Auriol Johnson. Embedded in her article was a blurred black-and-white of a video camera still showing a pavement and parked cars:

Wharf Way LT. Time 00:53:21 17/08/97. NOT FOR COURT USE. U/5354/97 EM/6 NO. 2

> *'Security camera catches thugs leading woman*
> *tourist away. This unfortunate woman was a major*
> *headline waiting to get printed!'*

The Attempted Murder charge had been dropped largely because it could not be made to stick equally against all eight youths. Composed, indeed commanding, in the witness box after swearing on the Bible to tell nothing but the truth, Jenny Glendower was very clear that the three who threw her into the canal were Charco, Luke and Pete – with little Ally egging them on; it had been Charco who asked her, 'Can you swim?'

It was now time for separate pleas of mitigation on behalf of each defendant. As Oliver wryly commented, 'That means that none of them really did it, though they did.' And indeed, those gathered in Court 5 of the Old Bailey were now treated to a free hearing of some of the most expensive evasions obtainable from members of the Bar.

According to Antony Laughton QC, for example, Charco Rios had been 'under tremendous fear and stress because of another matter'. He had never committed rape before, 'Whereas at least three of the other boys had been found guilty of rape on previous occasions'. Charco had always been shy with girls.

'Indeed, extreme shyness is one of his problems, inability to express his emotions in the normal way. And, of course, he was uprooted from his native land at a tender age. His father is now in prison, an extremely violent man who often beat Charco. I ask the court whether this boy ever had a decent chance in life,' declared Laughton. 'How could he know better?'

Then it was Luke Grant's turn. Bob Jolly QC denied that Luke had been the ringleader, despite his size – he was, after all, the youngest of them all.

'Luke sincerely claims that the first act of intercourse with the victim, which Luke now sincerely regrets, only happened because he mistook the lady's words for consent.'

'He says so?' the Recorder of London asked Jolly dryly.

'He does.'

The Recorder leafed through his notes. 'No one else says so. Least of all the victim. Do they?'

'May I draw the court's attention to Luke's sincere remorse and his courageous plea of guilt?'

'Three days ago? Frankly, Mr Jolly, Luke Grant's last-minute plea of guilt strikes this court as having more to do with the victim's brave decision to give evidence – than with remorse.'

Bob Jolly would not give up. 'A boy of fourteen, gravely short of education, taken from his home and put in care, is unfortunately likely to pick up the worst habits of survival in the jungle of cities.'

The Recorder nodded. 'Quite so. Well, I am calling for reports on all eight, due four weeks from now, when the court reconvenes to pass sentence. I also advise that on the evidence no disposal other than custody is likely to be entertained.'

The Recorder then ruled that after he had passed

sentence, but only then, reporting restrictions be lifted and seven of the eight defendants could be named, because of the hideous nature of the offence.

'However, I have to make an exception in the case of the eighth, Charco Rios, even though he emerges as the gang leader, and carries particular responsibility for this heinous crime. He faces serious charges elsewhere and no jury should be prejudiced, as they might well be.'

Charco had remained deadpan passive throughout.

It was Luke who was blitzed across the front pages as the ultimate degenerate brute. Reporters and photographers camped on his mother's doorstep in Eden Manor. What had she to say? Didn't she feel some responsibility for what he'd done? 'Ask his father!' she yelled. 'He took off when the boy was five!' She became tearful, defensive. 'Luke would go out all night and I wouldn't see him until the next day. He got into the wrong crowd. Now I blame social services. They let him run wild.'

Still the press crowded in on her. Did she have any photos of Luke as a small boy, a sweet little chap, which they could print beside the great big scowling brute that the world now knew?

Even before sentences were handed down, the *World* published seven of the eight boys' faces, with the eyes blanked out. Only Charco was represented by an abstract silhouette.

The paper also ran a separate story, by Auriol Johnson, of a more personal nature. It featured three photo portraits, the middle one of the rape victim, with her face blanked out, but not her hair or her neat, attractive body dressed in good, fashionable clothes and wearing platform heels.

Flanking the victim's were recent photos of Oliver Rawl and Sarah Woods – plus their names.

THE OTHER COURT ROOM DRAMA –
NOW IT CAN BE TOLD
TRIANGLE OF LOVE IN DEADLY LEGAL TANGLE
by Auriol Johnson – Exclusive

Hurrying out of the Holborn hotel where she is accommodated by the Crown Prosecution Service, Jenny takes the tube to Great North station, comes up the escalator, turns and turns again to get her bearings amid the roar of traffic, then starts to walk. She hears her own voice: 'Be as brave as Emma Carr, Jenny. Your marriage is finished.'

She stops to examine the window of a tatty shop calling itself VIDEOS BOOKS MAGAZINES. She sees *The Triumph of Vice*, a novel by G.W. Target; *A Baroque Novel*, by Brigid Brophy, and *Bring on the Virgins* by Porsche Lynn. She walks on, then pauses at the iron-grilled window of a shop called Call Saver, laden with images of mobile phones: cellnet vodafone oneZone. She remembers wondering why these brand names come without capitals; she examines the lonely Z. She still wonders.

Am I the same person who walked here alone? No, I had a marriage then.

Yes, there! Suddenly it dawns on her that the youths

must have emerged from that neon-lit, all-night corner place called Game Zone. She approaches it and sees 'Leisure Centre. Play Pool Here'. She steps inside, feels foolish, comes out.

Ever since it happened she has been thinking about the young night receptionist in the Winfield hotel. By his accent she had taken him to be French. Quite good-looking. Such a wistful gleam in his expression as he looked up from his newspaper to receive her room key. She could tell that he wanted to engage her in conversation. She wishes she had let him.

History is repeating itself: you come to London to see a man. She wants to see Oliver, alone, tell him about her marriage. But where, how? He's a man without a heart, a tape-recorded voice, concise and businesslike, on an answerphone.

Jenny stops to gaze, fascinated, at the prostitutes gathered round the big railway station, hurrying lonely travellers away to seedy rooms in ancient tenements owned by pimps, racketeers and drug pushers.

Am I a prostitute?

She resumes her fast walk, constantly glancing behind her, terrified by every reeling drunkard, every knot of idle youths, but forcing herself to continue. It's all coming back. Extending for hundreds of yards down one side of the long street is the vast, bleak, faceless all-brick flank of the Great North railway station. On the other side, her side, are shops fashioned out of other old warehouses, with numerous locked gates and doors plastered in posters, leading to inner courtyards she will never glimpse.

Duke of York pub.

Courtyard Theatre (August only).

Big silent gates without eyes, ears or human heart.

Caledonian Fish and Chips.

Yum Yum Chinese and Peking Cuisine.

Unknowingly, she again passes under the steady scrutiny of the video-camera sited high above a shuttered off-licence. Inscribed on it, beyond Jenny's gaze, is 'Delta Fire & Security' and an 01753 emergency number.

She recognises the Chinese takeaway called 'Peking, Cantonese and Vietnamese Cuisine' where she had made a feeble attempt to escape from the youths, to seek refuge. Between it and the off-licence is the dental surgery, with the bottom half of its window permanently screened out, advertising the services of N.Y.D. Chen, B.D.Sc (New South Wales).

Passing All Saints Church, it occurs to her that the boys are not walking with her now because they are locked up, behind bars. They are no longer at liberty. 'Jesus turns my darkness into light', the church says outside. 'Jesus said, "I have come that you may have life; and have it to the full." John 10:10.'

Gaston Dubois is half asleep behind the reception desk. Again (and again) he dreams of girls as a dog dreams of hares in the open, but he is always fearful lest the girls fleeing across the open countryside of Aquitaine be caught, trapped, destroyed by the pursuing hounds.

The dogs are black. They are not hounds, perhaps

Rottweilers. They do not bark, they sneer: Asking for it.

He wakes, lifts his head: the hotel main telephone is ringing. A light on the switchboard indicates an outside call. At the same moment he sees a woman in a dark trouser suit hesitating outside the hotel's reinforced glass door plastered in credit card stickers, Visa, Delta, American Express and the rest.

'I'm sorry, sir,' he says into the telephone, 'we have no vacancies tonight.'

She enters, finding the hotel lobby empty, and smiles at the handsome young receptionist as she approaches his desk.

'Do you remember me?'

He stares, lost for words. Yes, she still looks like Mrs Hillary Clinton.

'You never told me your name,' she says.

Gaston remembers the little black handbag with a gilt chain which had swung gaily from her wrist, beside a comfortably glinting Rolex ladies' watch. He had guessed her age at past thirty – an observable thickening of the waist and thighs which could suggest motherhood. Now, dressed in a dark trouser suit, she seems older.

'My name is Gaston, madam.'

'Gaston? That's a nice name. Are you French?'

'Yes, madam.'

'Where from, if I may ask?'

'From Bordeaux.'

'A beautiful city.'

'Thank you, madam.'

'You tried to warn me not to go walking alone at night, didn't you – Gaston?'

'Yes, madam.'

'I should have listened to you.'

'Yes, madam. And when the police came later that night to collect your clothes, my heart was full of fear and dread for you – madam.'

For a moment she turns away from him, examines the potted plant in the lobby.

'I was mugged. They stole my watch.'

Not a trace of incredulity creases his youthful features. A receptionist is a diplomat.

'Please accept my condolences, madam.'

'Jenny.'

'Ah. From Jennifer?'

'I must say, you do speak English beautifully.'

'Thank you. I try my hardest. "Best foot forward".'

She smiles appreciatively. 'When do you stop work, Gaston?'

'Ah,' he sighs (delightfully, she thinks), 'I must first complete my language diploma at the Holborn College.'

She nods politely, though it isn't what she means.

'And today? When are you free today?'

'Normally I am the night porter here, but today someone fall – sorry, fell – sick and the manager called me in at short notice. I am on for twenty-four hours.'

'Twenty-four hours!' He notices irritation as well as pity in her expression. 'Surely there are regulations, I mean . . .'

'I shall get a special bonus. The manager will stand in

for me between eight and midnight – or so he promises. His promises are sometimes having a tendency towards the problematical.' Gaston pauses proudly. 'Is that the right word, madam?'

She rolls her eyes as women do with men. 'Do you really want to know?'

'Yes, please.'

'You should say "His promises sometimes tend towards the problematical."'

'Are you a teacher, madam?'

Her mascara'd eyelashes dip coyly. 'I might be. And where will you rest between eight and midnight?'

'Here. A small room in the . . . *mansarde*.'

'The attic.'

'Madam speaks the French language?'

'Madam speaks French,' she corrects him. 'Supposing I come by taxi at eight and take you to my hotel? You will sleep better there.'

His gaze falls. Gaston is an attentive reader of newspapers. He has taken note of the reported arrest of eight youths charged with the gang-rape of an unnamed woman in Great North, beside the canal. He has 'put two and two together'; he has 'drawn conclusions'; he is 'no fool'. She was 'asking for it'. And now she may be carrying all manner of diseases.

His gaze remains lowered. 'Madam, I regret that my duties will not permit me to accept your kindness beyond the call of duty.'

When he dares to look up he sees a face flushed in anger, humiliation and self-contempt. A moment later she strides through the door, and then, beyond his sightline, Jenny Glendower sets out in search of the canal.

Charged with the murder of Edward Carr, Charco Rios was duly 'produced' by Downton Juvenile Offenders Institution for every scheduled court appearance, along with his co-defendants Miguel and Gregory. All three maintained pleas of innocence.

On an application from the prosecution, the court ruled that the lesser charge of attempted witness intimidation against Charco should be bracketed with the murder charge. In terms of the 'facts' it made no sense to separate them. Antony Laughton QC, representing Charco, did not dissent.

Oliver was in no doubt why. The morning before he and Dodgett were due to confer with Laughton in his Lincoln's Inn chambers, Oliver entered Dodgett's office with his head under his arm.

'You don't look well, Oliver. Short of sleep?'

'I lied to you.'

'Lied?'

'Yes. I did in fact mention to Sarah that both Charco and Miguel indicated that they knew where Tony Marquez was living – and that they intended to catch up with him. "He's dead – as good as."'

Dick Dodgett rarely displayed anger, but this confession propelled him out of his chair, his bushy eyebrows dancing.

'Of all the younger fellows working in this firm, I have

had the highest regard for you, Oliver. Perhaps you knew that? Perhaps you came to take my complete confidence in you for granted?'

'May I remind you,' Oliver answered in a tone that Dodgett had never heard from him before, 'that I took care to consult you about the dilemma that Charco's threats presented – and you gave me to understand that whatever I decided would have your full support.'

'True. *Nolo contendere*, Oliver – but you should have informed me that you had talked to Sarah – rather than lying about it. Tell me: did you yourself inform the police?'

'No, I told only you and Sarah. Tony Marquez is her client, that was the problem.'

'I don't want excuses. It wouldn't have been a "problem" for you if she'd been anyone else.'

'But she isn't.'

Dodgett's anger was now fighting a losing battle with Oliver's.

'Have you asked Sarah whether she informed the police?'

'She denies it. She also denies any contact with Tony Marquez.'

'I see.'

You may conclude that I should withdraw from this case.'

Dodgett had calmed down, resuming his chair and bringing his fingertips together.

'Look, Oliver, if you suddenly bow out, I will have to explain to Laughton. He may then very well insist that

Charco instructs an entirely new firm of solicitors. Quite apart from the loss of many thousands of pounds, do you understand the potential damage to the reputation of Hawthorne & Moss?'

Oliver nodded, mute. The world was suddenly flat and he, like an ancient mariner who had failed to master his astrolabe, was about to fall off it.

'In my head,' pondered Dodgett, 'it keeps coming back to this: why is Laughton so sure that the police received a tip, or tips, from a third party? After all, it's routine procedure to maintain a watch on the residence of an essential and vulnerable witness in a big case.'

'Perhaps it's because the CPS bundle mentions "independent corroboration" and "reason to believe".'

'Which they have no intention of producing – don't forget that. Frankly, I'd prefer to hold my breath on this one. As far as I'm concerned, this conversation between us never took place.'

Driving to Lincoln's Inn, Oliver ran through the ramifications again.

After Charco was securely behind bars, and only then, the Crown had finally produced a signed witness statement from a pupil of St James's School, claiming that he had been the victim of an assault outside the school gates by 'three boys I don't know'. Hazy as to their appearance ('white and maybe foreign'), he could not explain the motive for the attack. 'They just went for me.' No, he could not remember them saying anything. The Headmaster, Mr Carr, had attempted to intervene – then fell to his knees, moaning and bleeding. The witness had not seen the stabbing 'because I was up against the railing, covering my head with my arms at the time'.

At a recent witness parade he had failed to identify the 'three boys I don't know'.

The gaps in his evidence did not seem credible – and why had he failed to offer a witness statement for many months after the murder, despite two police interrogations, until Charco, Miguel and Gregory were safely behind bars? Clearly he remained afraid. A Triad-style gang like Charco's does not leave a 'gasser' unpunished.

Could the prosecution hope for a conviction on such slender evidence?

All they had was the dubious word of Tony Marquez, whose testimony Laughton regarded as 'inadmissible hearsay' – though 'hearsay', he had conceded, 'is always a fragile notion. Many a thick tome has grappled with it.'

Reaching Lincoln's Inn, Dick Dodgett and Oliver Rawl were shown into the oak-panelled room reserved for Antony Laughton QC, head of chambers. Laughton's junior was also present at the conference. The style and comfort of this beautiful room reminded Oliver that Laughton had made himself the most outspoken champion of barristers' legal aid fees.

'Let's not forget,' Laughton began, 'that the public pressure on the CPS to produce a conviction in the Edward Carr case is by now ferocious. Ben Diamond himself badly needs a conviction – though he can't say so in public. In my view, the Crown has not come clean regarding the circumstances of that vile rat Charco Rios's arrest. My apologies. I interviewed him in Downton only yesterday – a rodent if not a reptile. The Crown is supposed to disclose any information that might be helpful to the defence. But why should they? That's why the Criminal Procedure and Investigations Act, foisted on us by the "late" Jeremy Darling, is hostile to justice.'

Dodgett nodded. 'But the Act does allow us to insist on disclosure of all the witness statements. Oliver has twice written asking for all telephone and other conversations logged by the Edward Carr hotline.'

'But no joy?'

'None,' Oliver said.

Why did Laughton address himself exclusively to Dodgett, with scarcely a glance at the acting solicitor on the case?

Laughton began pacing his very nice Persian carpet.

'I believe that the apparently minor charge against Charco of attempting to intimidate the witness Tony Marquez is crucial. The inference would be clear to any jury. You don't threaten a witness unless he's got something on you – particularly if you breached your bail and went into hiding, as Charco did. Therefore you're guilty on the main charge – murder. But Charco was merely found by the police loitering suspiciously near Marquez's place of residence. The prosecution tell us that they have "independent corroboration" and "reason to believe" that Charco had tracked Marquez down and meant to threaten or harm him. But what "reason to believe"?'

Dodgett and Oliver listened in silence, both painfully conscious that they had not disclosed to Laughton what

Oliver had confessed to Dodgett the previous day: the Sarah factor. In Oliver's mind Laughton's tactic could backfire; if the police were forced to produce their hotline tapes, could Sarah and Oliver shelter behind 'professional silence'?

Unknown to the two solicitors in Laughton's chambers, it was the QC who was keeping a vital disclosure from them.

'If it can be shown,' Laughton continued, 'that someone planted in the minds of the police the idea that Charco was attempting to intimidate Tony Marquez, we would take a big step towards having a defence. That's why I want transcripts of any calls or other conversations the police may have received warning them of a danger to Tony Marquez. Plus all police comments in the log book. And I'm insisting on copies of the voice tapes as well.'

Oliver left Lincoln's Inn in a mood of deep gloom.

After further delay, the Crown Prosecution Service replied to Mr Oliver Rawl, of Hawthorne & Moss, resisting the demand that they disclose confidential hotline information – but for the first time admitting the existence of taped conversations. The police had promised absolute confidentiality to members of the public who could assist them in their inquiries. The Act permitted non-disclosure where it was 'in the public interest' – and it was.

Laughton's clerk fixed a date for a pre-trial hearing on this single issue.

The papers were sent to his Honour Judge Marcus Byron – whose attack on exorbitant legal aid fees had been publicly rebutted by Laughton in *The Times*. The purr from Laughton's chambers could be heard across the city.

Oliver could no longer confide in Sarah. He knew he would soon have to part company with Hawthorne & Moss. Even if he wasn't actually struck off the register by the Law Society, his future in criminal legal aid work was nil. He might find, after a decent interval, a job in probate or conveyancing houses in the provinces.

If he survived the vengeance of Charco's pals.

Oliver sat in front of Laughton in the Crown Court, holding his breath against the odour of eau de cologne. The word was out that the prosecution intended to call the Metropolitan Commissioner of Police himself to testify.

The usher commanded the court to stand. Judge Byron came in, bowed, said 'Good morning', sat down, looked to Laughton.

'You have an application, Mr Laughton.'

'Yes, your Honour, but I request a word with you and my learned friend in chambers.'

Oliver understood the strategy.

Marcus led Laughton and the counsel for the CPS, Michael Rorty QC, to his office. He didn't take a seat or offer them one. He could guess what was coming.

'Yes, Mr Laughton?'

'I'm inviting your Honour not to hear this case.'

'Yeah? Why?'

'Because of your personal friendship with the main prosecution witness today, the Commissioner. You have repeatedly praised his stewardship in public statements.'

Marcus had been expecting this ever since the papers had been sent to him – Brigid had been certain that Laughton would invite him to stand down.

'He loves to humiliate a judge – particularly you. But don't yield, Marcus.'

Marcus turned to the Crown prosecutor. 'Mr Rorty?'

'I have no comment to make, your Honour.'

This shook Marcus, though he gave no outward sign of it. Did Rorty agree with Laughton that Marcus was unacceptably biased? Was every QC in the land against him?

Marcus said, 'Mr Laughton, I am here to interpret the law as laid down by Parliament and the public interest under the law.'

He wanted to say more but knew that many of his colleagues despised his inability to keep his mouth shut. Despite an entire lifetime in England, and the privileges of Oxford, he had never assimilated the English cult of the urbane silence. Much is understood, little is said.

Marcus declined to stand down. Back in court, he heard the evidence for and against the production of the hotline tapes.

Called by the prosecution, Commissioner Price took the oath, bristling with silver braid.

'The whole fabric of our relationship of trust with the public is at risk,' he told Michael Rorty.

Cross-examining Price, Laughton was derisively unimpressed.

'You would say that, Commissioner, wouldn't you?

And why? Is it because you have kept faith with the public or because you have deceived the public?'

'There has been no deception at all.'

'Commissioner, you now admit what was not previously admitted – that the team investigating the murder of Edward Carr secretly recorded phone calls from the public, without warning the caller. You even conducted spectrogram voice checks?'

'Given the public interest—'

'Yes or no?'

'Yes. And I entirely endorse the view of officers on this case that disclosure would put individual members of the public at risk.'

'Are we talking, in this case, of one individual or more than one?' Laughton asked casually.

The Commissioner looked to Marcus. 'Your Honour, that is part of the information we do not wish to disclose.'

Summing up, Laughton again reminded Judge Byron that the new Criminal Procedure and Investigations Act had been vigorously resisted by both the Bar Council and the Law Society 'precisely because in cases such as this it palpably hinders the defence and therefore a fair trial'. The Act gave the police and prosecution 'the invidious – and arguably ludicrous – role of deciding what the defence needs to know in order to thwart the prosecution'.

Marcus nodded. 'Mr Rorty?'

'I have to inform your Honour that if you have in mind to order disclosure of the hotline tapes, the charge of witness intimidation against Charco Rios will be withdrawn – thus rendering their production unnecessary.'

'I do so order disclosure.'

'In that case the charge of witness intimidation will be withdrawn in the proper place.'

Afterwards, heading for the reserved car park, Laughton dryly remarked to Oliver: 'That must be a personal relief to you.' The great barrister's mouth had curled into an arabesque. His gamble had paid off.

It was the most wounding remark that Oliver had suffered since leaving law college. Laughton was openly conveying his conviction that Oliver himself had passed information about Charco to the police – while concealing the truth from Dodgett, from Laughton, and, most grievous sin, from his own client, Charco Rios.

Returning home that evening, Oliver did not say a word about the hearing, and Sarah did not ask.

Again they brought Charco Rios back to the Old Bailey from Downton, where he had now begun a twelve-year sentence for the rape of (the unnamed) Jenny Glendower. Luke Grant had got the same, and none of the eight youths fewer than ten years.

Edward Carr's widow sat in the same chair at the back of Court 5 every day. By posture and appearance Emma Carr reminded Oliver of the kind of woman who was awarded the CBE, or was it the OBE, for public service. He was monitoring her reactions when he noticed her glance up at the visitors' gallery, receiving in return a small, sympathetic wave of the hand from a woman seated in the front row. Oliver almost jumped out of his skin: it was Jenny Glendower.

He knew at once: both women were convinced that Charco Rios, the leader of the gang that had raped Jenny, was the killer of Edward Carr. It was this knowledge, this certainty, this thirst for justice, that passed like an electric charge every time Emma Carr glanced up to the gallery. And Jenny was up there, watching Oliver, looking down on him – despising him, hating him – as he sat in front of Antony Laughton, servicing the illustrious QC's serpentine frustration of justice.

The prosecution went into the trial without even a murmur about attempted intimidation of a witness. Laughton had won that one. The CPS's strategy was to charge all three – Charco, Miguel and Gregory – with murder (joint enterprise) in the hope that at the last minute each would blame the other. Miguel, therefore, was no longer represented by Oliver Rawl, of Hawthorne & Moss.

The first scheduled prosecution witness was the boy who had been attacked outside the school gates and who had seen the Headmaster fall to the ground, groaning and bleeding. By mutual agreement he was to be presented in court as Witness A, though his name was known to the trial judge.

Very tall, stick-thin and carrying the miniature head of the Upper Nile, he was immediately identifiable as Sudanese. Large, melancholic eyes focused reluctantly on the card held by the usher as she placed a Koran in his hand: 'I promise before Allah,' he mumbled, 'that I will truthfully answer any question that I am asked.'

Judge Moses Findlay, the Common Serjeant of London (an ancient judicial title), immediately invited him to speak up.

Clearly Witness A would have rather been in hell than here. Indeed he was now trapped in his own hell – only a few yards away Charco, Miguel and Gregory sat under heavy guard, their stares steady and relentless. Visibly recoiling from the gentlest questioning by the prosecutor, Rorty, the Sudanese boy rapidly lapsed into total amnesia – he couldn't even remember being attacked outside the school gates. When in desperation Rorty began to ask leading questions, Laughton regularly leapt up, the judge sustaining every objection.

Finally Rorty asked Judge Findlay for permission to treat the boy as a hostile witness, allowing free rein to aggressively challenging questions in cross-examination: Why can you not now remember what you told the police in your witness statement only a few weeks ago?

Laughton objected eloquently.

Judge Findlay turned to the prosecutor. 'The issue, Mr Rorty, is not what the witness may have said in his statement, but what he says here in this court under oath. You can lead a horse to water, but you can't make him drink. It's just bad luck, Mr Rorty.'

Lacking flesh when he first appeared, the witness by now resembled a skeletal victim of famine.

It was Laughton's turn to chew the cadaver in cross-examination.

'Have you ever met or seen a youth called Charco Rios?'

The Sudanese offered an almost imperceptible motion of his head.

'Please answer clearly,' Laughton said.

'No.'

'No never?'

'Never.'

'Did you attend an identity parade?'

'Yes.'

'Did you identify Charco Rios as one of the youths involved in an incident outside St James's School?'

'No,' the Sudanese whispered.

'You did not recognise him?'

'No.'

'Thank you.'

The counsel representing Miguel and Gregory went through the same routine. The judge then instructed the young witness to leave the court and go straight home or back to school or whatever a terrified Sudanese boy should do. Let the earth swallow him up.

Oliver glanced towards Edward Carr's widow, sitting rigid at the back of the court. He dared not turn his head to the visitors' gallery, so sure was he of Jenny's obsessive scrutiny.

The prosecution now produced Tony Marquez, who took the oath on the second day, nervous, tremulous, sometimes incoherent under the relentless stares of Charco, Miguel and Gregory. Questioned by Rorty, he repeated the story of having heard Miguel and Gregory boasting about their involvement, and Charco's, in the murder of Edward Carr – the pool hall story.

'These boys, Charco, Miguel and Gregory – did you know them well?' Rorty asked.

'Yeah.'

'Had you previously been involved in any alleged crime in which some or all of them were co-defendants?'

At this all three defence counsel leapt up to object in the most vehement terms, Laughton swishing his gown and outstripping his colleagues in indignation.

'Is my learned friend actually implying that Charco Rios has been convicted of any crime?'

'I said "alleged crime" and I said "co-defendants",' Rorty parried. 'I implied nothing about previous convictions.'

Judge Findlay instructed Rorty to withdraw the question and the jury to forget that they had ever heard it.

Rorty resumed his almost desperate questioning of Tony Marquez, his last hope. 'Did you later pick out all three, Charco, Miguel and Gregory, at a police identity parade?'

Tony Marquez looked as if he wished he hadn't. 'Yeah.'

'Did you go to the police on your own initiative?' Rorty asked.

'Nah. They came looking for me.'

'Any idea why?'

'I think it was my mum . . .'

'Was she the only person you had told about the pool hall conversation?'

'Yeah.'

After half an hour Tony Marquez was offered to Laughton for cross-examination. The crowded court-room might have been observing an infant crawl into a lion's cage. Glancing sideways at the prosecution team, Oliver observed fear and loathing of imminent defeat.

'Do you have a criminal record, Mr Marquez?'

'I, like—'

'Yes or no?'

'Yeah.'

'Handling stolen goods twice?'

'Yeah.'

'Theft – twice?'

'Yeah.'

But here Laughton could not ask how often Tony Marquez's crimes had been associated with those of the three defendants. The jury must not be informed of their 'previous', and remained unaware that Charco was serving twelve years for the rape of Jenny Glendower.

Oliver often wondered what his senior counsel's reaction would be if Oliver informed him that Mrs Glendower herself was in court, watching, listening, always in the front row of the visitors' gallery, poised to shout out, 'I know that devil Charco Rios, he raped me and he tried to murder me!' Laughton, of course, wouldn't turn a hair. The Recorder would immediately discharge the jury and declare a mis-trial, whereupon Laughton's fee would grow fatter. And yet . . .

And yet a shriek from Jenny, loud and clear, might none the less seal Charco's fate, because such a sensational incident could not go unreported, no way, not with Auriol Johnson or Brigid Kyle alive and well, and the whole criminal justice system would then choke on an impossible double-silence: Jenny's identity and Charco's.

'How much money were you earning in that pool hall?' Laughton was asking Tony Marquez.

'Maybe a hundred a week, depending on—'

'Not a lot?'

'Nah.'

'Not enough for a young man with expensive tastes?'

'Well, nah, like, I mean—'

'Where did you learn about the reward of one hundred thousand pounds for—'

Michael Rorty QC was up in protest. Laughton rephrased his question as effortlessly as daubing himself in after-shave.

'Did you hear about a reward of one hundred thousand pounds for information leading to a conviction in the case of Edward Carr?'

'Nah.'

'Never to this day?'

'Nah.'

Laughton studied the heavens. 'This is the first time you've heard about it? You really ask the ladies and gentlemen of the jury to believe that?'

'Yeah.'

'You never discussed it with anyone?'

Tony Marquez looked at Rorty as if appealing for help. Indeed Oliver could guess that Tony's stranded

404

gaze was in search of Sarah – but Sarah Woods was not in court. A witness is on his own, unrepresented.

Laughton wore the faintest of smiles – anything broader might offend the twelve men and women of the jury.

'Tell me, Mr Marquez, did you go, on a particular day, to anyone you trusted, an entirely respectable person, a lady perhaps, to discuss your chances of obtaining the reward?'

Silence. Oliver was stunned by Laughton's question; the bastard *must know*!

'Well, Mr Marquez?'

The jury watched, fascinated.

'I don't rightly remember, like, I mean—'

'You mean you might have done but you're not sure?'

'Yeah. Nah.'

'Yes or no, Mr Marquez? Or is it both?'

'I dunno.'

'But, Mr Marquez, if, as you have told this court, under oath, you knew nothing of a financial reward until this morning, you could not possibly have discussed it with anyone, could you?'

'Nah, see, I might have asked, like . . .'

Laughton played with the tail of his gown.

'"Asked?" Asked someone for their expert opinion . . . Your solicitor, for example?'

Rorty leapt up, furious. 'Privileged,' he snapped. The Recorder upheld the objection, of course, yes indeed, but the damage was done – when you tell a jury to forget something, to wipe it from their minds, it's always the one thing they remember for ever.

Laughton apologised. He swished the tails of his gown as if cleaning away the world's sins and confusions.

'Mr Marquez, when you were charged – in an entirely different matter – with handling stolen goods, did you first refuse to make a statement to the police, then plead not guilty, then plead guilty at the eleventh hour when you saw the prosecution witnesses were in place?'

Rorty objected but the damage was again done and Laughton sat down a few minutes later like a cat awarded a bowl of cream.

Oliver glanced back down the court at the rigid figure of Emma Carr. She was wearing a green suit today, old fashioned and comfortable – she never wore black. He saw her eyes lift, momentarily, to the gallery, as if sharing a horror. She seemed to have aged ten years during the ten minutes that Laughton had Tony Marquez between his paws.

Laughton and the two other defence QCs were no longer in a dilemma whether to put Charco, Miguel and Gregory into the witness box, navigating the reef of cross-examination by Rorty. There was no need because no defence is required unless the prosecution has made a case to answer. One after the other the defence counsel made the same application to the trial judge:

'There is no case to answer.'

And so it was granted: no case to answer. Judge Moses Findlay explained the situation to the bemused members of the jury before standing them down. He had one further announcement to make.

'The Recorder of London advises me that Charco Rios should now be named as recently sentenced by the Recorder in this court to twelve years for rape. Reporting restrictions were not lifted by the Recorder in view of the pending proceedings now concluded.'

Miguel and Gregory walked free while the Securicor van shipped a snarling Charco back to his twelve years.

'It would take a Hogarth or a Daumier to do justice to the faces of that jury,' Laughton murmured to Oliver on his way out. 'By the way, do thank Sarah on my behalf – without her timely help I might have had to forgo my weekly round of golf at Wentworth tomorrow.'

Oliver stopped in his tracks. 'Her help?'

'Yes, Sarah came to see me a few weeks ago – shortly before we went before Judge Byron – to explain what she had done. She told me about her conversations with Tony Marquez and with the police.' Laughton's eyebrows arched. 'Didn't she tell you, Oliver?'

It was then that Laughton became aware, among the lawyers, journalists and other 'square mile' people, of Edward Carr's widow standing rigid on the pavement in her green suit, looking at him.

'Oh dear,' he murmured, 'she's upset. Should one commiserate with her? I always try to avoid it.'

Laughton did not notice, because he did not know, the other woman standing with her arm threaded through Emma Carr's.

Oliver turned and fled.

*   *   *

Perhaps it had all been over between Oliver and Sarah since Auriol Johnson ran her friendly little story in the *World* about the 'deadly triangle' involving the woman who was gang-raped. Sarah had come to believe that Auriol was her friend, and the impact of this betrayal on her was traumatic. Wherever she went, everyone was looking at her, whispering, mocking – or so she kept telling Oliver, unforgivingly, as if he had been a party to Auriol's 'vicious attack', as if there was something between Auriol and himself – as if Auriol was using the Jenny Glendower story to prise him from Sarah.

Oliver finally announced his intention of moving out of the flat. Sarah, of course, was the last person to try to hang on to a man who had virtually been calling her a liar for weeks. Sadly, they failed in the end to avoid humiliating arguments about the rent, council tax, utility bills and which items of furniture belonged to which.

He turned at the door. 'There's one thing you can keep – Ivan's No Painting and your No Wall.'

Sometimes in her sleep Sarah reaches across the bed and touches the pillow on which his head used to lie. Often she wonders whether their relationship would have prospered but for the fatal intervention of Tony Marquez and Charco Rios. Her colleague Patty assures her that she never loved Oliver, who is a 'bully' and a 'bore'.

'He'd represent Hitler without a qualm.'

Oliver's period of residence in Auriol's comfortable

flat lasted five weeks. They parted amicably after Dodgett accepted Oliver's resignation – to Oliver's surprise and fury – and no comparable firm of London solicitors even answered his letters of inquiry. He is currently employed on a temporary basis by a firm in Yeominster, mostly in probate and conveyancing, which he finds excruciatingly dull.

He now lodges with Jenny and her children. An award of ten thousand pounds from the Criminal Injuries Compensation Board helped her with the down-payment on a small, terraced house not far from the one where Phil Glendower co-habits with his mother. The children spend the weekends with Phil (and Schumacher).

The first time (in many years) that Oliver and Jenny slept together he could not help thinking, at the moment of penetration, of all the young clients of his who'd been there before.

She had anticipated his thoughts. 'Wear a condom if you prefer, Oliver.'

Jenny believes he still loves Sarah. He has never given her a plausible account of why they split up or (but she does not complain, not yet) of anything.

Judge Marcus Byron is no longer a man in the news. He has deserted Baby's Bottom tobacco in favour of Alfred Dunhill's Bowled Out – more appropriate, per- haps. He makes few speeches and when he does, few listen. Reports of his heavy drinking are not reassuring. Auriol Johnson believes that it's only a matter of time before he is arrested for driving MB1 two or three times over the limit.

She has already written the story – only the details remain to be filled in.